AF620965

BELINDA BENNA

ALL I Need

VINCI BOOKS

Vinci Books

vinci-books.com

Published by Vinci Books Ltd in 2026

1

Copyright © Belinda Benna 2026

The author has asserted their moral right to be identified as the author of this work in accordance with the Copyright, Designs and Patents Act 1988.
This work is a work of fiction. Names, characters, places and incidents are the product of the author's imagination or are used fictitiously. Any resemblance to actual persons, living or dead, places and incidents is entirely coincidental.
All rights reserved. No part of this publication may be copied, reproduced, distributed, stored in any retrieval system, or transmitted in any form or by any means, including photocopying, recording, or other electronic or mechanical methods, nor used as a source for any form of machine learning including AI datasets, without the prior written permission of the publisher.
The publisher and the author have made every effort to obtain permissions for any third party material used in this book and to comply with copyright law. Any queries in this respect should be brought to the attention of the publisher and any omissions will be corrected in future editions.
A CIP catalogue record for this book is available from the British Library.
Paperback ISBN: 9781036734114
The EU GPSR authorised representative is Logos Europe, 9 rue Nicolas Poussion, 17000 La Rochelle, France contact@logoseurope.eu

By Belinda Benna

By Belinda Benna

All I Need

Every Step I Take

Love and Other Dreams

The Dreams We Share

The Sky We Seek

The Colors We Desire

The Dance We Remember

The Stars We Chase

Marie & Lukas

Promise Me

Show Me the Stars

Halifax Harbor Hospital

A Glimmer of Hope

A Twist of Fate

Miracle Glow

A Longing for Light

Dear Reader

All I Need contains potentially triggering content, including infanticide and depictions of self-harm. Please be aware that these—and some other—sensitive issues are explored within the text and some readers may want to proceed with caution in this respect.

Lots of love,

Belinda.

Learn to let go.
That's the key to happiness

–Buddhist wisdom

Prologue

The world around me stands still; not even the air is moving. My friend Eva is sitting close beside me, upright and rigid like a mannequin fixed in a shop-window. I grab hold of her hand and let out a shaky breath. It's hard to believe, but I feel as if I were the one sitting up there, awaiting my verdict. The fabric of my blouse clings damp and cold to my back, but that doesn't matter. All my attention is directed toward the judge, who is now sitting behind the massive wooden desk and turning his gaze toward the dock. With his black robe and stern expression, he looks like he could be a gravedigger. On any other day, my friend and I would have made a joke about that, whispering behind our hands, but today we don't feel like laughing.

Not today, and maybe never again.

Now the moment has come; the judge is about to pronounce the verdict. The sound of his voice reaches my ears as if travelling through cotton wool.

'In the name of the Republic of Austria, we find the defendant… '

Every single muscle in my body tenses. I want to hear what he has to say. And at the same time, I don't.

'Guilty.'

No hammer blow, only a murmur runs through the courtroom.

Guilty, guilty, guilty, it echoes in my head as I try to grasp what that word means.

My gaze wanders across the room, desperately searching for any sign of help. Over to the other side, to where Kathi is sitting.

We look at each other.

Her features are hard as stone; her moss-green eyes convey nothing, concealed by a thin, watery veil. And yet, I can see through it all the way into her soul.

She despises me. That's all that's left of our friendship.

With a creak, the chairs of the defendants' bench scrape back, Heinrich gets to his feet. Now he turns to me. Deep worry lines furrow his forehead. He looks tired. And spent. As if his strength had finally left him too.

'You know I didn't do it. Mira, please, believe me!' It's no more than a whisper that leaves his mouth. He sounds as if he were ready to give even his life if it could convince me.

Still, his words roll off me like raindrops on a window-pane. I can't let him get close to me anymore. Not after what has happened.

Guilty.

That's what he is, the judge doesn't doubt it either. With all my strength, I clench my fists and press my fingernails hard into my palms. Because I still can't grasp it. I shared my life with this man.

How could I not see for all those years who he really was?

A police officer snaps handcuffs around Heinrich's slender wrists and lets them click shut loudly.

For one last time we look at each other. One very last time.

Then he is led away. I stay behind, sitting amongst the wreckage of the war he started and ultimately lost. He disappears through the side exit, the door falls shut slowly behind him. And I do what I should have done months ago.

With a sharp inhalation of breath, I pull the wedding ring from my finger. Dull and heavy, it now lies in my hand. A relic from the past, with no future ahead.

Around me, a flurry of activity commences. The lawyers pack documents into their bags, onlookers leave the courtroom, talking animatedly. Only the two of us, Eva and I, are still sitting here. We don't move, we just silently watch as the world keeps turning without us. It's as if the clocks tick more slowly in this newfound reality.

Right now there's only one thing I still know with absolute certainty: this is the end. For Heinrich. And for me.

Chapter One

The crowd laughs, roars, and sings. The sound of the bass makes my muscles vibrate; for a moment I close my eyes and move my head to the beat. Red, violet, and white disco lights flicker across my eyelids while I take a deep drag on my cigarette. As I exhale, I imagine the nasty thoughts leaving me along with the cloud of smoke, vanishing into the abyss of the stuffy air in this room.

It works; satisfied, I open my eyes. In and amongst the constantly shifting light of the club I see the cheerful faces of my friends. Pressed close together, they laugh, joke, and drink with me. Tonight of all nights; for that I'm more than grateful.

Smiling, I reach for my shot glass and fling it into the air. Some of the clear liquid spills over my hand, but so what.

'Cheers!' I shout, exaggeratedly cheerful, and knock back the shot in one go.

'To this awesome party,' I hear my best mate Paul roar.

'And my trip!' I add. The rest of the guys immediately join in, laughing.

I've barely set my glass down on the sticky tabletop when Paul refills it with a jittery flourish. That's just fine by me. After all, I didn't order a whole bottle for our table for nothing.

I tap my phone screen. It's two in the morning now, a large part of the night is already behind us. I have to hold out for another 22 hours, then the worst will be over. And in 93 days everything will be fine anyway.

Once more I clink glasses with the group, empty mine and then another one right after. The feeling in my head grows more numb with every minute that passes. The infectious party spirit spreads through me until there's no room left for anything else.

I lose control. And that's a good thing.

'Hey, handsome.' A husky female voice is suddenly right by my ear, a warm body pressed against my arm.

Just from the glint in Paul's light eyes I know it must be a real beauty standing next to me. Automatically, I slip my arm around her hips and pull her closer.

'Hello, stranger,' I say, look up at her and put on my coolest smile.

Oh yes. This woman is fucking hot. With her long dark curls, the tight bright red dress, and her firm body, she looks like a flamenco dancer. And from the way she's looking at me, I begin to sense, despite my now considerable blood alcohol level, how this evening could end.

Without taking my eyes off her, I get up from my stool. I'm instantly dizzy. I stumble into the dark-haired beauty, but that doesn't seem to bother her at all.

'Wanna dance?'

To the cheers of my friends, she pulls me onto the dance floor, and what proceeds to happen there is exactly what I need. Together we get carried away by the beat and feel as if we've left the real world behind. There's only the two of us, rubbing up against each other, wrapped tightly in each other's arms, and her looks that tell me I've been naked in her thoughts for a long time already.

'I want you,' she finally whispers in my ear while her fake fingernails scratch the back of my neck. 'Right now.'

As if on their own, my hands wander down to her ass. Her leg presses in slow circles against my crotch while she works my neck over with her lips.

This woman is robbing me of every last bit of my sanity.

Still, I put some distance between us and look deep into her eyes. Because I need to see how she reacts to what I'm about to say.

'One night. No strings,' I make clear so there can't be any misunderstandings. In 93 days I'll be out of here, and I'm not made for committed relationships anyway.

A not-at-all disappointed grin appears on her face.

'That's exactly what I had in mind.'

Chapter Two

With her eyes, as big and dark brown as a doe's, she follows my every move. In the harsh light of the morning sun she looks far too expectant.

She'll remember our deal, won't she?

As fast as my hungover body allows, I roll off the sofa bed, pull on a T-shirt, and trudge to the kitchenette. On the way I stop at the kitchen table and, like every morning, tear off the top sheet of my homemade calendar. Underneath, the number 93 appears, together with the date.

I wish it weren't, but of course it's still the fourth of May. I don't want to see that date.

It has to go. Out of my sight and out of my head.

I turn away so hastily that my studio apartment starts spinning with me. The rumpled sofa bed in front of the dirty window blurs together with the small round kitchen table and the sad plant in the corner.

Instinctively, I touch my forehead, which feels as if someone is sitting up there and doing some construction work on my skullcap with a jackhammer. I really need to take care of that, but something else is more pressing.

The woman in my bed is staring at me, I know that for sure.

I don't want to explain it to her again. Besides, I'm running out of time, as the pale blue blinking display on the microwave tells me. In thirty minutes, at the latest, I have to head out, and I haven't even showered yet.

'Coffee?' I switch on the espresso machine, grab a cup, and let it fill. With the strong scent of the thick, dark liquid in my nose, I turn to her and set the cup down on the nightstand.

In the meantime, thank God, she has at least wrapped the sheet around her slender upper body. She sits up and beams at me.

'That's really sweet, thanks.'

I clear my throat and pointedly look at my wristwatch.

'Wow, that late already? I really have to hurry now.'

Instead of drinking the coffee and finally gathering her things, she leaves the sofa bed and comes toward me in one sweeping motion. Her hot curves are covered only by the sheet, her hair is piled up into a loose, dark brown bird's nest. Nevertheless, she moves as if she were a model at some fashion week show.

This can't mean anything good. Damn, I should've known.

'Hmmm,' she says in a seductive tone. 'So you can make coffee too.' Now she traces the hollows of my pecs under my T-shirt with her fingers.

This has to stop, right now. As if her hand were doing something forbidden, I push it away from my torso.

'Listen…' I try to sound serious.

'Yeah?' She wets her full lips and presses herself against me.

Just to be safe, I take a step back. My thighs bump into the kitchen counter; I can't retreat any farther.

'I really have to go now, so if you could get dressed...'

She lowers her gaze and draws a half circle with her bare toes over the worn plastic mat in my kitchenette. The shade of her nail polish reminds me of a traffic light's stop signal.

'Already?'

Apologetically, I hunch my shoulders. 'Duty calls.'

'So what do you do for a living?' There it is again, that doe-eyed look. Please no.

'Cliff diver,' I answer out of sheer desperation; after all, we're not actually trying to get to know each other. No strings attached, that was the deal. So I start picking up her clothes. Luckily, there isn't much, and the living space itself, at twenty square meters, is more than manageable.

'Really?' Her voice almost cracks with excitement.

She believes that? Are there any cliffs here in Vienna I could jump from?

I push the dress and the underwear into her hand.

'Come on, I can't be late. The boss already has it in for me.' That's no lie. I just can't afford to put another foot wrong, because I depend on this job.

Disappointed, she presses the little scrap of fabric to her chest. 'Don't you even want to know what I do?'

'Sorry, I really don't have any time left.' My apologetic gaze probably isn't enough; what else am I supposed to do?

I can't stand around out here any longer, so I disappear into the bathroom. At least here, in this long, completely light-blue-tiled room, I'm by myself. And the fact that there's no window suits me just fine. The sun is much too bright anyway.

With my hands gripping the sink, I hold still for a moment and listen to what's happening in the other room. I hear the rustle of the dress's fabric. Then there's a clinking sound, as if she were loading herself up with jewelry.

Thank God. She still remembers what we agreed and she's going to stick to it. Everything is fine.

In the mirror I can clearly see the relief in my face. I ignore the rest. I know what I look like anyway. Short brown hair, three-day stubble, angular chin. There's a scar running above my left eyebrow, but hardly anyone notices it because my eyes, with their intense blue-green color, draw all the attention.

That's me. Irresistible—or at least that's what women claim. Because they don't know that in reality I'm anything but.

As if to prove it, I suddenly hear shuffling footsteps in front of the bathroom door. A second later, the beautiful lady is standing in the old-fashioned, brown-painted doorframe.

'I'm gonna go then,' she says, to my surprise. Still, she looks at me as if she wished I would stop her. Tell her she should stay, preferably forever. But this isn't Hollywood, and I'm not Richard Gere.

'It was nice meeting you,' I say in a conciliatory tone; after all, I don't want to hurt her. I only want what we agreed on. To be safe, I bury my hands in my pockets and give a brief nod. 'Take care.'

'My number's on the coffee table. Call me, sweetie.' Without warning she throws her arms around my neck and presses her lips to mine. Then she turns to the apartment door, which clicks shut behind her a few seconds later.

It's impossible to say whether the nasty feeling in my stomach comes from the night of heavy drinking. Or from the guilt that's eating away at me from the inside out, even though I know I don't have any reason to feel guilty. Maybe it's also because, now that I'm alone again, my thoughts immediately go where I don't want them. To today.

The fourth of May hasn't been a good day for me for a long time, and the night before it even less so. At least this year will be the last time, because in 93 days that will be over too. That's what I cling to. With that one number in my head, I run through my morning routine, swallow some painkillers, and even leave the apartment on time twenty minutes later.

On the way to the tram stop, I imagine day zero has already come. Vienna is behind me; there's only me and my motorcycle. I'm wherever life takes me. The past no longer exists. I'm as free as I can possibly be. I'll finally have everything I need.

In my mind, I'm already standing on the cliffs of Ireland. I breathe in the salty sea air and hear the rumble of the waves crashing against the rocks below. Meanwhile, I barely notice how my body, here and now, boards the tram and sinks into a seat in the back row. The carriage jolts into motion. I close my eyes to sink even deeper into my daydream. Just as I'm crossing the Scottish Highlands on my bike, the ringing of my phone yanks me abruptly back to reality. I pull it out of my pocket.

It's Sandy. And I know why she's calling me.

On cue, my pulse speeds up. Scotland is gone; outside the window, Vienna's prefab housing blocks slide past. Gray, brown, their facades crumbling and decorated with more or less artful graffiti.

I'm back again. And even though this is reality, I feel completely paralyzed, as if it were a nightmare.

Hurriedly, I switch the ringer off. I can't answer this call, but I can't decline it either. Unable to decide, I stare at Sandy's picture on the display.

We have the same blue-green eyes. And her features around the cheeks also remind me of my own. Otherwise, we hardly look alike. She's built like an elf; she inherited the long blond mane and the small mouth from our mother. Just where she got that radiance from, nobody knows.

Nervously, I gnaw on my lower lip. I don't want to turn her away, and still I can't help it. I can't take her call. Not today. Because if I hear now what Sandy wants to tell me, then I might…

Stop. Imagining that doesn't help me. On the contrary, my head grows so heavy it feels like it's made of lead. Pull yourself together and keep going. That's the only thing that matters now, nothing else.

So I do what I always do. I swallow, breathe, and bite my lips. I repeat this until the load on my forehead eases at least a little whilst I look for something on the other side of the window that can distract me.

Outside everything is still gray-brown. Towering buildings with rows and rows of windows in military formation, packed tightly together. People hurry through the streets with their heads down.

This is Vienna's tenth district: Favoriten. I live here, and where I'm going doesn't look much better. Even though I rarely get to see it, I know this city does have its beautiful parts also. But they're out of reach for me, and always will be.

At last the vibrating has stopped. Now I should text my sister; I owe her at least that much.

'At work. Couldn't pick up. All good, don't worry. Normal day.' I type up the message and send it to Sandy while the tram slows down with a piercing screech. It jolts violently, but I still spring up from my seat at once.

I have to get away from here. Because I have no idea how much longer I can keep lying to myself so brazenly. So I rush outside, light a cigarette, and start walking.

Then I start the ritual again. I go through it once more, and a third time. Because I simply have to eliminate these heavy thoughts from my head. I have to.

I don't have any other choice, because it's all about to start again. Just a few more meters, then I'll show the world the side of me it's allowed to see. The smiling, cheerful Simon. A joker at heart who has absolutely no reason to feel bad.

I can do that. I just have to want it. From now on, I won't think any longer about what happened on this day, eleven years ago. I take one last deep breath, then force the corners of my mouth up and lift my head. A stone-gray wall materializes in my field of vision.

The long building looks like some mythical creature. With hair made of barbed wire and pale blue roller doors serving as its eyes. I'm walking toward this building now knowing I'll be spending the next nine hours right inside. In prison. I'm on duty at Simmering Correctional Facility.

Not less than half an hour later I've got myself firmly under control. Getting on with today's duties allocated on the roster, I'm a good deal more tired than usual; my short night of sleep is really starting to make itself felt. Behind the curtainless windows someone has also closed the blinds just enough so that it looks as if there are bars standing in front of the panes of glass. Dimmed like this, the room feels like a cave. A total of fifteen female and male guards are on duty in my wing today; all of us, like a dark-blue-clad army, are receiving our instructions.

All of us except my colleague Petra.

She fusses with her short boyish haircut and glances over at me with a more than obvious grin. She'd better not. Even if I were up for some fun with her, the boss would fire us both on the spot, and I absolutely can't afford to lose this job. It was hard enough to find any work at all, and the extra pay is like lottery money for my travel fund. So I pretend not to notice Petra's advances, pull my shoulders back, and fix my gaze straight ahead.

Like a rearing Canadian brown bear, the boss stands there at the board and rattles off names and assignments.

'Weininger. Yard duty. Keep an eye on the one from cell H-25, understood? Kaufmann.' His gaze wanders along the rows as his bushy eyebrows draw closer and closer together. 'Where is Kaufmann?'

The digital clock above the door displays eight thirty; Horst should have been here a while ago. He hasn't overslept again, has he? I clear my throat quickly.

'Kaufmann's coming in later today, boss. He has a doctor's appointment.' That's a lie, but Horst already has enough problems. He doesn't need the boss's wrath on top of all that.

'I see.' He doesn't bat an eye and makes a note. Then he runs his hand over his neatly cut brown hair to the broad nape of his neck and turns back to the board. 'Hermann. Kitchen.'

Silently, I breathed a sigh of relief. The boss could be unpredictable, but today he seemed to be in a good mood. Still, I had to remain careful.

Just as I was using all my strength to stifle a yawn, the door of the meeting room was flung open. Horst burst in, his face flushed. At this particular moment, he looked like an overweight, battered dog. At just under thirty he was only five years older than me, yet he seemed as though his life was already largely behind him.

'Sorry,' he gasped breathlessly.

At once the boss zeroed in on him. 'Mr Kaufmann, how nice of you to join us this morning.'

Horst visibly flinched. 'An urgent family matter,' he muttered, with an expression that made any further explanation unnecessary.

In a flash, the boss turned to me. Of course, I immediately started to sweat. 'A doctor's appointment, you said?' His words were sharper than a blade.

Damn. 'Sorry, sir. I really thought that—'

I didn't get any further. In one sweeping motion he was in front of me; at six foot six, he towered over me. 'You can spare me your excuses, Herbst. Need I remind you that you're already on a warning.'

A murmur rushed through the room, followed by a flurry of excited whispering. Great, now everyone knew. Yes, I had screwed up. Several times. But only because I'd wanted to help.

'For the rest of the month you'll be taking all the weekend shifts.' His eyes narrowed to slits. 'First shift: the day after tomorrow.'

As I see the relief set in across my colleagues' faces, the corners of my mouth grow heavy. No parties on the weekends. All through May.

'Is there a problem, Herbst?' the boss snaps at me.

'Of course not,' I answer quickly and hold his gaze. Thinking of the weekend bonus, I even try to force a smile.

At least he turns away from me. 'I should hope so. Where was I? Brandstätter carpentry, Zauner mail inspection, and our unshaven Mr. Herbst here will take care of the new intake. Kaufmann, you'll help him. Well then, off to work, ladies and gentlemen.'

With a purposeful stride, the boss heads for the door, and a few seconds later, all that's left of him is the faint odour of his old-fashioned aftershave.

Horst comes straight over to me. 'Thanks, Simon,' he says as we leave the conference room together and step into the long corridor leading to the admissions office. 'That could've ended badly for you.'

'At least it wasn't all for nothing.' We both know there's bound to be a note in my file because this incident. It's my fourth, and at five it's game over. From now on I can't afford a single misstep.

'You've got one coming from me,' Horst says with a yawn and shuffles on toward the office wing.

For a moment I stop and watch him go. Maybe it's the white neon light in the corridor, but he looks as if he was well passed his hundredth birthday. I'd love to cheer him up somehow; I can see how poorly he's doing. He doesn't know how he's going to pay his bills, and on top of that he has no time for any hobbies. If I'd married his wife and had a baby with her, whose screaming didn't let me sleep through a singly night, I'd probably have forgotten how to smile too.

I notice a distant memory starting to rise up in me and immediately push it back down where it belongs. Behind the locked door that holds in everything that mustn't get out.

As if everything were perfectly fine, I put on a smile and march off to catch up with Horst. Not a minute later we enter the plainly furnished room where we deal with the paperwork. A collection of gray desks stand pushed together in pairs. Red and black binders are stacked on the metal cabinets behind them, all uniformly labeled. Dust hangs in the air. And the smell of stale coffee.

I drop into one of the swivel chairs and push the pot with the half-withered green plant on the table to the side. 'Are you excited to see who's checking in with us today?'

Horst takes the registration forms for the new guy out of the hanging file with a sigh. 'Not really,' he mumbles, but proceeds to open the documents nonetheless.

Me neither. Most criminals are the same. Loud, restless, and damn rough. The fact that Horst is now tilting his head thoughtfully to the side does make me curious, though.

'Heinrich Peters. Life sentence,' he reads out and throws me an inquistive glance.

An interesting combination of information. 'Maybe he went on a rampage because his parents named him Heinrich?'

Horst comes closer and leans against the desk next to me. 'He might also have kept a woman locked up in his basement at home because no one wanted to stay with him voluntarily,' he says with a mischievous smirk. 'Care for a little wager?'

'But of course.' Without even knowing exactly what it entailed, I already come up with the perfect reward. 'Whoever wins gets to take a nap while the other one handles intake.' If you ask me, we could both really use that.

Horst's smile now stretches all the way to his ears; he leans over toward me. 'I'm in. And I'll definitely throw in an extra-strong piece of gum for you on top of that.' He wrinkles his nose in disgust. 'So much for the stakes, now for the bet itself,' he then whispers to me conspiratorially.

A wonderfully excited tingling sensation shoots down my back. I finally have a worthwhile distraction.

'The question is: What does this Heinrich Peters look

like?' Horst presents the bet to me as if he were a tabloid reporter. 'Whoever comes closest wins.'

I nod. 'You first.'

After a brief moment of consideration, Horst spits out the facts, fluently strung together without a pause. 'Old. Bald. Chubby. Horn-rimmed glasses. Crazy eyes,' he sums up. 'Now you.'

I take a few seconds; after all, the stakes of this bet are pretty high. 'No, I don't think so,' I say thoughtfully, 'you're letting the name fool you. I'm sure he's not even twenty yet. A rich brat from a good family, no manners, but a slick, gelled hairstyle. Arrogant expression.' I can already see the guy in my mind's eye, walking into intake as if he owned the prison. With a triumphant grin on my face, I hold out my hand to Horst. 'May the better man get his slumber,' I say, and squeeze his fleshy fingers.

We don't have to wait long to discover the outcome of our bet, because less than a minute later the police car pulls up. Neither Horst nor I can keep our cool; we both jump up from our chairs and press ourselves against the only window through which we can see the forecourt.

'Nervous?' I ask in an exaggeratedly deep voice, raising my eyebrows.

'No more than you.' Without looking at me, he cranes his neck desperately in every possible direction. The tip of his nose draws greasy lines on the glass. 'Ha!' he finally bellows, far too pleased with himself.

That's not good.

I immediately push past him, then I see the disaster.

Heinrich Peters is old. And he's even wearing horn-rimmed glasses.

Horst was wrong about everything else. Except maybe the crazy eyes; I can't make that out from here. The new guy is slim, you could almost say gaunt. With his thinning dark-blond hair and full beard, he looks like a scatter-brained professor.

'Damn,' I quietly concede.

'I'm really sorry for you.' What Horst says isn't what he means, I can hear that clearly enough alright. Reassuringly, he pats me on the shoulder. 'Right, I have to go now. Enjoy the intake.'

I'm not letting him get away that easily. 'Hey, didn't I just save you from the boss?' As soon as I utter these words, I see an expansive yawn descend over Horst's face, and one thing is very clear. He needs this nap more than I do. 'Got it. Sweet dreams.'

While Horst shuffles out of the office, I hear the squeak of the sliding doors at the entrance and right after that, the dull sound the heavy steps of the police boots make on the worn gray plastic floor. I usher the two officers and the new guy through to the intake room and head there myself.

Once I'm in the bare room with the white-barred skylight windows, I can see the inmate much better than before. He's sitting hunched on the wooden chair, his head bowed humbly toward the tabletop. He seems less disheveled than I thought earlier, and more well-groomed. Although he's wearing the plain olive-green remand clothes, there's somehow an air of sophistication about him, like a civilized night at the theatre. Only upon second glance do I realize why. The skin on his hands looks velvety, his finger-nails appeared as if he'd had one of those treatments that only women get usually. His beard, just like his eyebrows, is perfectly trimmed.

'Heinrich Peters?' I noisily pull the chair on the opposite side of the table back.

He nods without a word, without looking at me.

I sit down, open the folder with the intake papers, and pull a pen from the breast pocket of my dark blue uniform shirt. 'Alright, let's go through a few points.'

There's no reaction from the man opposite me. Does he understand what I'm saying?

My questioning gaze wanders to the police officer who has stationed himself in the corner of the room. But all he has for me is a dismissive wave of his hand, as if to suggest you can't expect much from this guy.

I can't make sense of that either, so I turn back to the prisoner. 'Is everything okay with you?'

At last he lifts his head, our eyes meet. In his light blue eyes I see a kind of sorrow that overwhelms me instantly.

No. Please don't.

Every fourth of May, this is exactly what happens. My eyes play tricks on me, show me people who aren't really there and make me feel things that don't exist at all. I hate it, but there's nothing I can do about it. *This is Heinrich Peters and no one else,* I remind myself with full force.

Only one thing can help me now. Swallow, breathe, bite my lip. Clearly, I should say something, yet I just stare at him as if he were the victim of a car accident.

While I'm trying to get myself under control, the new guy breaks the strange silence between us. 'Please excuse my brief absence.' His voice, warm in tone, fills the whole room. 'Do go on,' for a moment his gaze flicks to my name tag, 'Mr. Herbst.' With a smooth hand movement he gestures toward my documents.

Weird. How can someone speak so nobly and at the same time commit a crime that lands him behind bars for life?

'Um... yeah...' I stammer awkwardly. 'First, the basic facts.' Oh my God, if only I hadn't lost that stupid bet.

Then I wouldn't be sitting here now, shifting back and forth on this hard chair and coming across as if I couldn't form a single proper sentence.

Heinrich Peters stares at me without blinking. 'Do you need another moment to yourself?' All at once the expression in his eyes changes, becoming understanding and warm.

That is the last thing I need right now. 'No,' I say far too harshly, thankfully without stuttering. Feverishly, I drop my gaze to the form lying on the table in front of me. The writing is blurred, but at the very bottom I can make out a single word and quickly say it out loud. 'Allergies?'

'I do suffer from a genetically caused intolerance to house dust and lactose. I also have a reasonably well-founded suspicion of fructose malabsorption,' I hear him say.

I find the boxes for the first two allergies and tick them with unerring precision. Fructose is there too, but what the hell is malabsorption? And how do you even spell that?

Without a single movement, the new guy waits while, every passing second, more beads of sweat seem to appear on my forehead. Then he leans over the desk toward me. 'The first box in the left-hand column.' He whispers it like he's trying to help me cheat on a test. 'Don't worry, we've got this,' he even adds on top of everything, while I eventually tick the appropriate box.

He smiles at me again. And this time I smile back. Because I can hardly think of anything else I could do in this absurd situation.

Nothing here is the way it should be. Absolutely nothing.

All through the admission procedure I maneuver my way through the conversation with brief replies and want only one thing: not to let myself get rattled. Not by his elegant gestures, or that peculiar way of speaking. And least of all by his eyes, which show me emotions I absolutely do not want to see today.

Relieved, I close the file with the completed forms twenty minutes later. 'You've been assigned to cell H-33, second floor, south wing.' I sound as if this were a hotel and I were the receptionist telling him his room number.

He nods hesitantly, as if only now realizing that it's true. Here, in this prison, he will stay. For life.

He doesn't understand it, and neither do I. Because there are too many questions I don't have answers to. Who the hell is this Heinrich Peters? How did he end up here? And why did he look at me so strangely earlier?

Chapter Three

I'd only gotten one of four weekend shifts in May over with, and already the boss wanted to saddle me with another punishment. I followed him into his office after the duty roster was posted so I could try do away with the worst of it.

'Mail inspection? Seriously, boss?' Leaning against the doorframe, I tried to look relaxed. The intense floral scent of his little makeshift greenhouse in here drifted into my nose. Maybe I should say something about his plants, but I didn't really know anything about them. 'Can't I do some other shift? Yard duty, carpentry?' I asked hopefully.

He didn't sit down but watched me closely. Then he took a step toward me. 'Everyone has to do their turn, Herbst. You'll manage.' His paw slammed down on my upper arm, which next to his hand looked like a dented drinking straw.

I could handle the pain, but when it came to work assignments, I didn't give up that easily. 'What if someone swapped with me?' I suggested. 'Maybe—'

'Take a good hard look.' His index finger pointed

straight at his stern expression. 'Do you notice any feminine features on this face?' Silently, I shook my head. 'Exactly. So stop trying to charm me. You're doing the mail. Period.' The tone of his voice was more than clear.

If I wanted to keep my job, I had to keep quiet now. I was at the very top of his hit list anyway. He was probably even trying to drive me out by giving me nothing but the crappy jobs. But that wasn't going to work; I would stick it out, because it was more than worth it. Exactly 89 days left —I could do that.

With my shoes snapped together and my back straight, I gave a mock military salute. 'Yes, boss,' I said, turned around, and marched off with stiff, angular movements. Behind me I heard the boss giggle. He had the bulk of a Canadian brown bear, but he laughed like a little girl. That, in turn, lifted my mood as I headed for the mailroom.

On the way I ran into Horst, who had just bitten off a piece of his chocolate bar. 'Mail inspection, huh?' he asked with his mouth full.

I shrugged. 'What the hell.'

He came closer, and on his earlobe I spotted something that looked like baby puke. 'What are you staring at me like that for?'

Horst's angry glare doesn't hit me; I even grin at him. 'Just wondered if that mush on your ear is fresh or if it's already been through your kid's stomach once.'

'Shit.' His hand immediately flies to the spot in question and he starts rubbing the gunk off.

'Honestly, Horst, that's not how you talk,' I say with a wink and fish a tissue out of my pants for him. 'Come on, let's have another smoke. To relax.'

Smoothly, I steer him out of the tunnel-like corridor into the paved courtyard. Surrounded by gray surfaces adorned with barred windows, I light a cigarette. As I blow the smoke with relish into the sky, I notice how dejected Horst looks again today. He looks as if he's forgotten all the beautiful things in life.

Since I don't have anything else to offer, I hold the pack of cigarettes out to him. 'Want one too?'

'I was going to quit.' His shake of the head looks despondent. Then suddenly a grin spreads across his face, so brief I barely catch it. 'But tomorrow would as good of a time as any, right?'

I'm definitely not getting involved in this. I've never tried to quit smoking, but supposedly it's pretty hard. 'Your call.'

He looks like a toddler about to sneak a bite before dinner. He hesitates once more, then pulls a cigarette from the pack. I give him a light and watch as he takes the first drag with his eyes closed.

'Oh man,' he says, releasing a cloud of smoke from his mouth.

Now he looks better, and that helps me relax too. Comfortably, I lean against the stone wall next to the entrance door. 'Alright then, fire away.'

As Horst relaxes more with every drag, he tells me how much his life had changed since his baby was born a few months ago.

With every new piece of information another shiver runs down my spine. Disturbing images flash through my mind and put an all too familiar pressure on my forehead. From the outside, his days were not much different from those of the inmates. Scheduled down to the minute and controlled by others.

'It's the best goddamn thing you can imagine,' he said suddenly as he crushed the last bit of his cigarette in the ashtray. 'But sometimes it's hell. In some countries, they don't let suspects sleep during interrogations. That's torture, and I experience it every fucking night.'

I empathized with him more than I would have liked. I couldn't allow that, so to distract myself I pulled the energy drink out of my pants pocket. It was actually supposed to get me through the day, but now I handed him the can. 'I think you need this more than I do today.'

He immediately took the drink from me and downed several big gulps at once. 'Thanks.'

I held out my fist to him and he bumped it with his. Suddenly I felt strangely content. 'No problem. When we say goodbye, I'm going to give you a jumbo pack of these drinks. And then—'

Horst cut me off at once with a defensive wave of his hand. 'Oh please, not another travel story. Sorry, Simon, but I've had more than enough of those over the last few months. Besides, we really have to go now.'

'It's possible I might have mentioned it once or twice,' I admitted with a grin. Still, in my imagination I was revving the engine of my bike ready to fly off, while in real life I said goodbye to Horst and walked over to the mailroom to pick up the letters.

A little later I entered the admissions office with the mail crate under my arm, dropped into a swivel chair, and pulled on the latex gloves. The smell of rubber filled my nose and the skin of my palms immediately started to sweat.

These were just two of the many reasons I hated this job. As always, I also felt like a burglar as I carefully slit open the first envelope. Of course the inmates knew their mail was checked. Still, the contents were often more private than what usually happens behind closed bedroom doors.

Private and disgusting.

Unsurprisingly, the first letter is exactly so. Down to the smallest detail, the scruffy inmate from cell G-05 describes everything he's going to do to his beloved the next time she comes for a family visit. I gag. I skim the text only as much as I have to, but I don't find anything that would violate the guidelines. Then I slip the stained sheet of paper back into the envelope and turn to the next letter.

For hours I force my way through the envelopes, which are hardly distinguishable from one another, not just on the outside but on the inside as well.

The last letter is bright white and, for a change, doesn't smell of anything at all. My intuition tells me it can only be from the new guy. The mysterious man from cell H-33. Heinrich Peters. I pull it out and turn it over.

'Mira Peters' is written on the front in flowing script.

Mira, an unusual name. Could be one of those old-fashioned women's names that nobody uses anymore these days.

Is she his daughter? Or his wife? Maybe even his mother, the one he still lives with?

Under her name I find an address in Vienna's nineteenth district. That's where only the people who can afford a certain lifestyle live. Apparently this Peters isn't just polite and smart, but rich as well.

At the very least he has relatives who are rolling in cash.

Maybe he really is a professor?

But what on earth did he do to end up here?

Thoughtfully, I open the envelope, pull out the sheet of paper, and begin to read.

My dearest Mira,

I hardly dare to hope that you might be doing well. The image of you in that courtroom is still far too vivid in my mind's eye.

You, the love of my life, deflated like an old balloon, your face frozen and your gaze empty.

The memory of it hurts me more than anything I've had to endure since my arrest. I don't want to think of you like that. I'd much rather go back to another time. Back when we were still happy.

That alone is enough, because the memories paint pictures in my mind all by themselves. I look upon your beautiful complexion. The expression in your magically dark eyes says more than all the words in this world ever could.

Do you still remember, Mira? How we looked at each other before that terrible tragedy stole our love and our proximity? And do you remember how it felt when we kissed for the very first time back then in the park?

Flee there with me; let's relive it together, one more time, how I lost my heart to you.

The birch leaves, bright with autumn colors, glow in the golden light of fall. You brush your hair back from your face and smile in that special way that makes everything inside me light up. I'm helplessly at your mercy; I don't want anything except to be with you. All that matters to me is your kiss, as gentle as the flutter of a butterfly's wings. I feel my heart pounding up to my ears, so forcefully that I'm absolutely certain of one thing.

As long as you're by my side, I'll be happy. I love you, more than anything else in this world. Because there are so many things that make you special. Not least of all the incredible passion that burns inside you like a beacon.

Our fire is still there, too. Even if it's only a tired glimmer now, we still have it! Let's rekindle it together, so we can become who we used to be. We have to. Because being here, in this terrible place and without you, is wearing me down. It makes me forget how to smile, what joy is, and what my heart beats for.

I'm begging you, Mira, come visit me. Give me something I can hold on to while all my days here turn into nights.

I will never stop protesting my innocence. Because that's what I am, Mira. Innocent. I didn't do it, believe me!

With love,

Yours, Heinrich

With a wrinkled nose, I let the letter sink onto the table.

What the hell is this?

The text sounds like it came straight out of dreamland from one of those old poets I had to endure back in school. Man, did he lay it on thick.

I wonder if this Mira likes it.

I read the lines once more and try to picture the woman's face. Attractive, with dark eyes and about his age. She could be fifty or even already sixty. She lives in an upscale neighborhood and is definitely dressed like a lady. She probably also wears that terribly old-fashioned gold jewelry. I can clearly see her in front of me, with her hair pinned up in a bun, gray streaks at her temples, and those brown spots on the backs of her hands that only old people have. Strangely enough, she looks a bit like my own grandma.

I really don't want to think about her right now, so I quickly slip the sheet back into the envelope and seal it carefully. Still, it won't release me from its grasp.

Peter's words are so different from what I usually get to read here. As if a classical piano concerto had strayed onto a Rammstein CD. I'm already curious about Mira's reply. Will she believe in his innocence? And if so, why?

Since I took Peter's in last week, a miserable wreck in prison, the list of unanswered questions has just kept getting longer. I can't escape them. And at the thought of his sad eyes, the pity starts flowing out of me. I shouldn't allow that, because that's exactly what has already caused me trouble in here several times. I shake my head hastily. He must be guilty.

But what if he's locked up for nothing?

I leave the still unread letters where they are, spring up from my chair, and pull open the big, heavy drawer of the cabinet with the inmates' files on the opposite wall.

At that very moment Horst enters the room. 'What are you looking for?' He yawns, again.

My fingers riffle through the folders in the hanging file and immediately find what I'm looking for. 'That Peter from cell H-33,' I say thoughtfully as I walk back to the desk with the file in my hand. 'There's something off about him.'

Horst is at my side in an instant and leans over the table next to me. It would've been nice if he'd skipped the onions in his döner at lunch. 'Ah, our scholar.'

His ironic tone makes my ears prick up; so he's already made the acquaintance of that odd bird too. 'That's the one. Why is he here?'

'How am I supposed to know that?' Horst shrugs. 'You're not going to find any answers in there either. Data protection, you know.' With a dismissive wave of his hand, he turns around and heaves his massive body onto one of the office chairs. 'Don't tell me he's already done something wrong. Or else why are you so interested in him?'

'No, he hasn't.' I hurriedly scan the file with my eyes. No new clues, of course not. 'He acts like he's a guest in some five-star hotel. Just the way he holds his teacup at breakfast with that posh little finger stuck out. And how he wears his old-fashioned glasses right on the tip of his nose when he reads one of the dusty books from the library.' I sound more invested than I'd like. 'Life sentence,' I read from the file. 'What does someone like him get a life sentence for?'

Horst answers my question with a snort. 'Do I look like a lawyer to you?'

'Oh, come on, this really isn't about your looks.'

I turn to the computer on the desk and put the question to the otherwise all-knowing internet. 'Murder, kidnapping and extortion, manufacturing and distribution of weapons of mass destruction.' Shaking my head, I go through the various possibilities the search engine shows me. 'There's also crimes against humanity. What would that be?'

'Come on, leave it. You're not going to find out anyway.' With a deep sigh, he turns back to his desk.

'Oh please, you want to know too.' There has to be something I can use to bait him. 'We could make a bet.'

A mischievous glint in Horst's eyes. 'We absolutely should.'

We quickly settle on the stakes; there are just too many things we both want. The loser takes over the other's next night shift. This time I have to be right; after all, I still want to celebrate properly with Paul before we say goodbye to each other.

Leaning far over the desk, I go through the options one more time. 'Murder,' I say at last.

'Arson, resulting in death.' Suddenly Horst is standing next to me, grinning. He quickly grabs my hand and squeezes it to seal the bet. He looks as convinces as a politician who has is certain they have just won the election. '

'You seem pretty sure of yourself. Care to tell me why?'

An emphatic nod, his whole body vibrating with glee. 'With pleasure, my young, inexperienced friend. I reckon the old man is a chemistry professor who blew up half the university during some weird experiment.'

Damn, not again.

While I thought it would be smart to bet on the most

common reason for life sentences, Horst even came up with a logical explanation. Feverishly I search for a clue that he's wrong. Luckily it doesn't take long to find one.

'Half the university? That would've been on the news.'

While my grin grows wider and wider, his slowly fades. 'Damn,' he mutters, and I can see his brain searching for an explanation for the missing headlines. 'Who says it happened here in Vienna? Maybe he was somewhere else, at a small university. It would've just been a short item on the news, a footnote. Easy to miss.'

'Nice try.' Smiling, I snap the file shut in my hands and put it back where it belongs.

Horst rubs his belly as if he were hungry. 'We're never going to find out anyway,' he says, and lets out a long yawn. Then his gaze wanders to his wristwatch. 'But for now, it's home time.'

What, the day's already over? Not bad, that's how I like it. 'Well then, what are we waiting for?'

When I enter my regular bar, Flenn, half an hour later, the professor is still in my head. Along with his look of desperation and his elegant words. I can't quite put my finger on why, but he won't let me go.

Absentmindedly, I let my eyes wander across the Irish pub, with its rustic wooden furniture and green-and-white checkered cushions. Today there are barely more than ten customers here. It smells like freedom, coziness, and good times. Spilled beer, stale cigarette smoke, and frying fat is what Horst would highlight. But for me, the Flenn is a refuge. Here I have everything I need: pleasant company, distance from everyday life, and Irish music in the background.

Paul is already squatting in our usual spot all the way at the back of the wood-paneled bar. With his rounded back, he reminds me a bit of a turtle. He swirls the dark beer in his half-full pint glass and chats with the hot waitress, Jessy, who is polishing glasses at a snail's pace.

Unerringly, I make my way through the room crammed with tables and chairs and raise my hand to greet the two of them.

'Siiiiiimon!' Jessy, who a moment ago was still leaning back totally relaxed against the bar, straightens up and tugs at her tight black top. 'Good to see you,' she says, smiling at me. Today she's wearing her straight hair pulled back into a severe ponytail. Silver rings as big as saucers dangle from her ears.

I smile back, then Paul is already holding out his fist to me. Today he's wearing a sweatshirt from the TV series *Californication*. A welcome change from his hundreds of shirts with comic-book heroes on the front. Even as I'm getting comfortable on the wooden stool with the low backrest, Jessy, reliable as ever, is already setting a large Guinness down in front of me.

'What's new behind bars?' Paul runs a hand over his light brown hair that reaches down the length of his chin, even though it's already plastered to the top of his head with tons of gel.

I actually don't want to think about work right now, but Paul can't get enough of the stories from the slammer. As if he were a junkie, he needs his daily dose. 'I already clashed with that one inmate again. You know, the one who swore to me in tears last week that he'd never cause trouble again,' I admit with a sigh.

'The drug lord with the tattooed bald head?' His eyes sparkle with excitement.

'That's the one. I really believed the coke didn't belong to him. He looked at me like he couldn't even kill the most irritating mosquito. Serving his sentence had made him think about his life, that's what he claimed. He was clean and would stay that way. Because when he gets out, he wants to start over.'

With his unshaven chin propped on his hand, Paul pulls a face. 'Don't they all say that?'

'Yeah,' I admit, chastened. 'But with him, I really thought he meant it. There was something in his eyes, something sincere. Like an idiot I believed him, quietly took the drugs and logged them as unassigned lost property.' I smack myself on the head with the flat of my hand. What a fool I'd been! Horst had warned me so many times. You can't let the inmates get close to you; that kind of thing can cost you your job in no time.

With a snort, Paul spins his beer around in his hand on the wooden bar. 'You're just a softie deep down,' he says, then points his index finger at my chest.

Yeah, I am, but I'd never admit that. So all I can do is smoothly steer the focus away from me. 'I'm probably wrong about the new guy too,' I say thoughtfully.

'The new guy?' Paul's eyes widen.

'He acts like he's some kind of scholar and the prison is his lecture hall.' Should I tell him more? No, the work day is over now. 'But whatever, let's not keep talking about work. Otherwise I might as well just have stayed there.'

I look around for Jessy and spot her at the other end of the bar by the coffee machine. It doesn't take her a second to notice I want another beer. That woman really is the best.

Paul gives a crooked grin. 'I really don't envy you with that job of yours.'

'It's still good for something, though,' I remind us both. As if someone flipped a switch, my mood lifts and the room seems brighter. Even Jessy seems to be smiling more warmly as she sets the beer I just ordered down in front of me.

'Here you go, my dear,' she sings, turning the handle of the glass into the right position. Then she studies me for a moment, her eyebrows drawn together. 'What's got you grinning over here?'

Before I can say anything myself, the answer erupts out of Paul. 'In a few months you'll have one less regular.' With a sweeping jerk of his head, he points at me.

Curiously, Jessy leans over the bar toward us so that we both have an unobstructed view of the hilly landscape framed by her cleavage.

'Tell me everything!' she compels me conspiratorially.

I move my stool closer, but then I hesitate. There's a reason why the whole world already knows about my trip, except for her. Just the way she's staring at me now, all tense and seemingly breathless, makes it hard for me to say it out loud. For a few seconds the Irish folk song in the background is the only thing to be heard while I force myself to finally do it.

'Of course it breaks my heart to have to part ways with you,' I say, pressing my hand firmly to my chest, 'but the world out there is calling my name.'

With a sweeping motion Jessy pulls the green-striped dish towel from her apron, as if she wants to arm herself against whatever comes next. 'Could you please be a bit more specific?'

'You really can't stand it if you don't know everything about your customers, can you?' Paul grins at her openly.

We all know that he's right, but that doesn't bother Jessy in the slightest. On the contrary, she uses every trick in the book to get information. Now she twists her mouth and lowers her chin. Her fake lashes flutter for all they're worth and her eyes shine so dangerously it's like she's trying to put a spell on me.

'Only about this hot piece of ass here.' Her voice suddenly has a smoky undertone that sends a tingle down my spine. She's really got this act down, you have to hand it to her. 'Come on, you want to tell me just as much as I want to hear it. Go on. Tell me.'

I can hardly stand it. 'Alright, you asked for it. But I don't want to see any tears now, got it?'

Jessy rolls her eyes toward the ceiling and lets out an exaggerated groan.

'Eighty-nine days from now, I'm gone. Just me, a backpack, and a motorbike. No obligations, no job, no bills. Just enjoying life.' Oh yes, just saying it out loud feels absolutely amazing. I'm going to leave Vienna and nothing will drag me down. I can finally stop fighting. And I won't have to keep pushing thoughts behind that inner door that keeps slamming back against them. Everything will be fine. Absolutely everything. The prospect is absolutely fantastic.

'You're fucking with me.' Jessy pulls her eyebrows together sceptically.

'Not at all.' I take a sip of my beer and watch as the information slowly sinks in. There it is, her fingers are playing with her right earlobe. She's thinking, and I can clearly see she's having trouble keeping her expression under control.

'Looks like someone's at a loss for words.' Laughing, Paul lights a cigarette and hands it to her. 'To calm your nerves,' he says in a friendly tone.

My confession must have hit her hard. Because our otherwise militant non-smoker Jessy takes a drag and coughs it back out not a second later. 'Shit,' she comments, shaking her head, and turns to me.

Am I imagining it, or does she have tears in the corners of her eyes? Hopefully from the smoke and not because she's imagining her own wet dreams slowly fading, the ones where, up to now, I've played the leading role. Shit. This was exactly the reaction I'd been afraid of.

'Are you coming back?' She sounds shaken.

I bite my lip and shrug. Seeing her like this is not fun. On the contrary, answering this question feels like I'm stabbing her in the gut. Because in truth I'd rather never set foot in Vienna again. 'Who really knows what's going to happen,' I say vaguely, while I force myself with all my might to focus on what's ahead. So that what has already happened doesn't ruin my mood now, like it's done so many times before.

Our eyes meet; she looks disappointed.

'Well, I think it's awesome!' Paul cuts in and, with his impetuous manner, saves the situation. 'And you know what? Someday I'll do the same thing. When I'm done with my degree.'

Right on cue, Jessy and I burst out laughing at the same time. 'Yeah, as if that's ever going to happen.' I can barely breathe and my abs hurt, but I can't stop. Our eternal student, who maybe shows his face at a lecture twice a year, still honestly believes he's going to graduate?

I clap him on the shoulder. 'I'm really going to miss you,' slips out of me, a bit too sentimental. And in the same moment I feel how true my words are.

'Same here.' Paul lowers his gaze, then quickly pushes

himself away from me. 'But get your paws off me, or people will start thinking we're a couple.'

Once again, he's the one who makes Jessy and me laugh. I nod gratefully. That has to be enough; after all, the last thing I should do here is get emotional. Jessy's disappointment has faded too. I breathe a sigh of relief. That was harmless, no more than a few fair-weather clouds in an otherwise clear, blue sky.

For me, it's further confirmation. What I'm doing is right. My thoughts drift to the trip all on their own. Exactly eight thousand one hundred euros and twenty cents were in the travel fund this morning. The motorbike is as good as ready to go. And on the fifth of August, I'll be off. There's no route and no destination. Just pure freedom. The wind blowing over my skin and the power of one hundred and thirty horses beneath me. The whole world is waiting for me. I could breathe in the dirty air in Delhi, gaze out over the vast Siberian steppe, or eavesdrop on the conversations of rare bird species in the Thai jungle. But the detail doesn't really matter. The only important thing is that Vienna will be behind me, along with everything that has happened here.

At last I'll be free.

Chapter Four

As I maneuver the car into the garage, I feel as if I've travelled half the world in the last few hours. And although the place I'm arriving at right now is supposed to be my home, it most certainly isn't anymore.

Exhausted, I switch off the engine. Relaxing piano music is playing on the radio. The melody sounds as if it wants to envelope me, to give me support and reassurance. I loosen the tightly bound knot in my dark hair, lean my head against the headrest, and close my eyes. I wish I could breathe freely, but the memory lies heavy on my chest; the same scene playing over and over again in my mind.

Once again I see myself standing in front of the locked wooden door; I know the pattern of the grains by heart by now. In my dark blue slacks and white blouse I look small and worn out. I press the doorbell, knock as well, and beg for someone to let me in.

But I remain shut out.

No one is here anymore, in truth not even I myself.

If I could, I would give in to the tears welling in my eyes

that this memory stirs. Here in the car, and all alone, I could do that. Still, I hold them back, together with the boulder in my stomach. My fists clench of their own accord until my fingernails press so deep into my palms that I can hardly bear the pain. The veins stand out clearly on the backs of my hands, the skin looks wrinkled. Everything about me feels used up. My thoughts, my body, and my life as well.

Still, that doesn't matter; it just has to go on. I tuck my hair behind my ears, flip down the sun visor, and check my eyes in the mirror.

Everything around the dark brown iris is white, just as it should be. Automatically I smooth the thin skin at my temples, then push myself up from the car seat, leave the garage, and step into the neatly landscaped front garden of our stately-looking townhouse.

The white-painted building with the green shutters and the perfectly trimmed lawn look as flawless as ever. Even the daisy heads all stretch in the same direction, as if there was a sun here that could still reach their faces with its rays.

Involuntarily I shake my head. How many people have time and again envied me for living like this?

Until that day, when it all came to an end. I wish I could erase from my mind every moment since Heinrich was led away from here in handcuffs. And the long years we spent together too for that matter. But as I walk along the paved path to the house, the memories stay with me. Will this eternal plight never end?

I should stop asking myself that. Because the truth is that I already know the answer. The feeling of helplessness, so familiar by now, settles on my shoulders, presses me down, and makes each step heavier than lead.

Minutes later I reach the front door, unlock it, and empty the mailbox. A thick stack of advertising leaflets spills out. That reminds me that it's time to get one of those stickers so that this will stop too. It was always Heinrich who used to comb through each and every flyer in search of bargains. In fact, the colorful sheets are a sign. A sign that he's no longer here. A reminder of the hell from which I will never escape.

Mechanically I enter the house. So here I am again, in the middle of a life that no longer feels like one. The fine parquet floor gleams in the daylight. It has remained free of scratches and dents all these years. It's grotesque just how perfect everything is here, or how it seems.

I need to distract myself, so I reach for the mail and sort bills and flyers into separate piles. In between I find an envelope. It's small and square. I take a closer look.

I know this handwriting. All too well, in fact.

I freeze, morphing into a statue that had been accidentally placed in the middle of the hallway.

Only my fingers trace the letters that pressed themselves into the paper with their unmistakable flourish. 'Mira Peters' is written there, by the man I once thought would be the rest of my life.

Am I still her? Am I Mira Peters, or was I her a long time ago?

The images from the courtroom materialise before my eyes. I see Heinrich, with all his pain. And I hear him talking to me.

'You know I didn't do it. Mira, please, I love you,' he whispers hoarsely.

Hesitantly, I turn the envelope in my hands, looking at it from all sides. Do I want to see what's inside?

No.

Nothing Heinrich writes could change anything. He did something terrible and dragged not only himself into the abyss. How could he? And how could I ignore for so long what I kept seeing flash out from behind his mask? I let myself be dazzled. By his gallant gestures and his grand words.

Reflecting, I let the letter fall. I shouldn't open it. It's soaked with Heinrich's poison. Now it's lying on the floor. A gleaming white envelope next to the dark blue fabric of my trousers. The matte gold ring on my shoe looks far too much like the wedding ring I no longer wear. It's as if it were a sign of the stalled remains of our love. Powerlessly, it glitters up at me. It's tired, just like I am.

My gaze darts back to the envelope. Could I maybe bear to read Heinrich's words after all? And if so, where would that lead me?

Chapter Five

For an afternoon in mid-May it's pretty cold, even though the sun is shining. It might as well be March. Only the greenery along the edge of the otherwise completely asphalted prison yard is a sign that the clock isn't actually turning backwards.

Unfortunately, everything else feels exactly like that. With my hands buried deep in my jacket pockets, I shift from one foot to the other. I'd love nothing more than to smoke a cigarette right now, but I still have to hold out for another two hours until my break. It's a good thing I can at least distract myself with my travel plans.

My budget shrank last week to eight thousand seventy euros and thirty cents because I had to fill up my bike for a ride with Paul. But I'll make that up with the weekend shifts. I'd better, too, because working along the way could be tricky. Who wants to hire someone who has neither a vocational qualification nor a high school diploma? If they knew the reason, it would surely be different. They would understand that I couldn't finish my training because…

No, I don't want to think about that now. So I shake my head and focus on my work.

The same inmates pace the same laps in the yard in front of me. From now on I keep a close eye on them again, not just because of the illegal bartering that goes on here. There are often altercations among the men who don't know what to do with themselves between their cells, fresh air, and workshop.

While a group of inmates in front of Cell Block I listlessly toss a ball between one another, the professor is sitting all alone on the metal bench right by the wall in front of Cell Block G. He has his legs crossed like a lady, his head drawn in. Unlike the others, he isn't doing anything. Nothing at all.

It was only last Thursday I had another one of his letters on my desk. I'd never admit it, but I read it so many times that I knew every word by heart. Because these letters are new puzzle pieces; I just have to find the remaining ones and put the picture together.

The search for the truth has long since refused to let me go. Not least because it's exactly the kind of distraction I need to survive these last few weeks here in Vienna. So I go through the message to his wife in my mind once more and look for what I haven't yet found between the lines.

My dearest Mira,

Where are you when I can't sleep at night? Do you think of me, do you feel my longing? If we don't see each other again soon, it will devour me, and I'm afraid of what that will be set off inside me.

With every passing day, with every passing hour that I wait for you in vain, I lose a little more of my confidence. Don't let it die, Mira. Because who am I if I can't hope anymore?

Deep in your heart you know it. I'm innocent, I was just in the wrong place at the wrong time. Finding him like that, so lifeless and cold, was the most terrible thing I ever had to experience. I wanted to save him, but his life had already slipped away. And when the moment came, when I knew there was nothing more I could do for him, time suddenly stood still for me. Like a river, the tears were waiting to stream down my cheeks and yet, nothing of the sort happened. I only brushed a damp strand of his black hair from his forehead. Then I helped him to close his eyes one last time.

As I write these lines, a dark shadow looms over me. Because today I know that it wasn't only the boy who died back then. Our love, our mutual trust, and the respect we had for each other were damaged too. Like an ornate vase destroyed by a stranger's carelessness. At first it was just a tiny crack, barely visible and hardly worth mentioning. But just a little pressure was enough to turn it into a fissure and finally to make it break.

How big are the shards of our vase, Mira? Can we put them back together, carefully glue the edges to each other and make it shine again? Even if it would never be as perfect as it once was, it would still be the most beautiful thing I can imagine.

Let's try, that's all I'm asking you for. I've lost everything; I don't want to lose you as well. Until the end of my days I'll fight for our love, because it's the only beautiful thing I have left.

With love,

Yours, Heinrich

I shake my head. This sentimental revelation is confusing to me. But at least I've got a new piece of information. Apparently he murdered a boy. He knew him. And so did his Mira.

Across the prison yard I fix my eyes on Peters' face. He didn't kill his own grandchild, did he? An icy shiver trickles relentlessly down my back and spreads along my arms all the way to my fingertips. I personally keep my distance from those little brats, and with good reason. Still, the thought that he might be responsible for a child's death fills me with a ferocious rage.

Searching for clues, I scan Peters' eyes. As always, he keeps his gaze lowered to the ground, the wrinkles in the almost translucent skin around his eyes pointing upward. Even now, although the corners of his mouth are clearly dragged down by gravity. He looks like someone who laughed a lot all his life. On top of that, he looks like he couldn't hurt a fly.

Could this man be a child killer?

Even if it's hard to believe, there could be something to it. If only because this Mira doesn't heed his pleas. She doesn't show her face and doesn't answer any of his letters.

Before I can sink any deeper into brooding, I suddenly register jerky movements at the edge of my vision.

Something's wrong here.

I glance at my wristwatch. Yard time is almost over; do there really have to be problems now, right at the end? When I look up again, I immediately see what's going on. The drug gang is heading straight for Peters. Just what I need.

The professor doesn't even seem to notice the men. Not until Joe, the head of the gang, plants himself in front of him like a predator before its prey. Slightly off to the side, behind him, his henchmen lurk, both with their arms folded and serious expressions. I get ready to step in, even though nothing has happened yet, and stride off at a brisk pace.

On the way I can already see the gang leader's threatening gestures. Now and then his underlings grin stupidly and edge closer and closer to Peters, step by step. I haven't even reached them when one of the two starts stroking his face as if he were his lover.

I feel sick. I don't even notice the cold anymore.

'Time's up, Joe,' I call out to the stocky man and, just to be safe, grab my belt. I don't want to use the baton, but I will if I have to.

Joe raises his hands defensively. 'We're just talking.' With an exaggeratedly innocent look, he stares straight into my eyes.

'Oh yeah, I'm sure you are.' I push myself between Peters and the gang. 'Yard time's over for today,' I say sternly and jerk my head toward the cell block.

'Sure thing, boss.' Joe signals for his two helpers to follow him, and they trail after him like trained little monkeys.

I breathe a sigh of relief; this could have become a lot more difficult.

Now the gang boss turns around once more. 'The two of us'—Joe's index finger moves back and forth between himself and Peters—'we'll talk again tomorrow.' There's a filthy grin on his face.

'Watch yourself, Joe, or there won't be a 'tomorrow' in the yard for you. Now get out of here.' I leave no room for doubt, and that has exactly the desired effect.

Joe immediately turns around and signals to his followers to come with him. I use the moment to take care of Peters, who is crouched on the bench, staring after the men.

'Thank you,' he mumbles, his mouth buried in his shirt. Only now do I see how violently his hands are shaking. The trembling spreads and takes over his whole body, as if it were disrupting some kind of paralysis. Seeing a grown man like this doesn't leave anyone cold. Least of all me. I don't know why, but he of all people has something about him that makes it even harder for me to stay cool.

'It's fine.' I can't let myself go soft. 'It's my job, after all.'

He looks up at me with an air of desperation. He blinks suspiciously often, and I can only hope it's because the sunlight is blinding him. 'I'd already looked into life in prison beforehand. But I didn't think it would be this hard.'

I sit down on the bench next to him, leaving a substantial distance between us. I feel the urge to help him, but I'm not allowed to. I'm one warning away from getting kicked out, I can't risk that, no matter how sorry I feel for him. I can still give him some good advice, though; nobody has to know about that. 'Don't trust anyone. Least of all the guards here, okay?'

He looks at me questioningly, his brows furrowed. 'Not even you?'

I nod. His gaze tells me how much that confuses him. 'The only reason we're sitting here talking is because the others are already in their cells and can't see us.'

The professor catches on quickly. 'They'd think I was a traitor and would worry I'd spill their secrets.'

'Honestly, just the way you talk and move is already like you're walking around with a neon-yellow blinking arrow over your head, pointing straight at you. Everything about you practically screams 'snitch.' If they think you're in cahoots with us guards, you won't survive in this place.'

His gaze drifts up to the sky, which, ironically enough, is clear and cloudless above us. Hopefully he doesn't start crying now, because then I really wouldn't know what to do.

'What can I do?'

I hesitate, because I know full well that he hardly has a chance either way. 'Grow a thick skin and give them what they want. Whether it's dessert or you having to clear your spot in the cafeteria for them. The less of a target you present, the more likely they are to leave you alone.'

The despair at my answer seems to overwhelm him; he

buries his face in his hands. 'How could this happen?' I hear him ask in a choked voice.

All at once I feel like I can't breathe either. I'm small. And helpless. Why? This has nothing to do with …

No, that has no place here. I quickly run through my routine. I breathe, swallow, and bite my lip.

By now the situation is more than uncomfortable; we've been sitting out here for too long. Apart from the cold that's eating its way through my jacket, I'm not allowed to extend yard time for individual inmates. The poor man has to go back to his cell before someone notices he's missing.

I quickly jump up from the bench and clear my throat to get rid of the last bit of pressure in my throat. 'We have to go.'

Peters gets up too, but when I'm about to set off, he holds me back. 'I'm innocent,' he says with great fervor.

Again I see the desperation in those pale blue eyes; again I can't get past his grief.

Outwardly, I act unimpressed. 'That's what they all say.'

Peters shakes his head, his feather-light hair floating through the air. Then he fixes his gaze on me. 'You should form your own opinion, don't you think?'

The way he looks at me makes me shudder. I have to keep my distance from him, mustn't talk to him and certainly mustn't feel sorry for him. And yet, I can't switch it off; this man does something to me that I can't control.

I nod as if on my own. 'Well then, go ahead.'

Chapter Six

Peters cleared his throat. 'It happened on a day that was much frostier than today. Thick clouds were tumbling across the sky, and I could sense that it was going to snow soon. I was on my way home from work on foot, so I hurried.'

We strolled along slowly side by side, but if he kept telling his story at this pace, he definitely would not be able to finish it before we reached his cell. 'And then?'

With a placating wave of his hand, Peters continued. 'Mira called me. She sounded upset. Practically frantic. In the background I could make out voices. Some I could place, and some I had never heard before.'

'Mira is your wife?' The way we were walking so close together and having this conversation, it felt as if we were friends. So much so that it seemed absolutely logical to me to address him informally.

He nodded, his eyes filling with tears. He quickly wiped them away before he went on. 'And so much more. She is the love of my life, my best friend, my soulmate.'

What on earth was I supposed to say to that? 'I see,' was

the only thing that came to mind. 'What was going on with her?'

'She did not mention that.' He brushed his dark-blond hair back from his worry-lined forehead. 'She should have. Then maybe everything would have turned out differently'

There it was again, that deep despair in his eyes and in his voice. Just seeing him like this really got to me.

Carefully, I opened the door to Cell Block H and let him step inside. 'From now on we have to be quieter, okay?'

'Of course.'

We start moving again, as slowly as we can. For a moment, the only sound is our footsteps on the plastic floor.

'So, you went straight home?'

He shakes his head. 'Back then I must have misread the situation. I assumed Mira had unexpected visitors and was overwhelmed. After all, she only asked when I'd finally be home. Since I was already running late anyway, my biggest fear at that point was that I'd made her angry. So I decided to buy her flowers. A bouquet of colorful gerberas was supposed to cheer her up again, like it always did.'

That sounded anything but logical. The woman was already pissed off, so why waste even more time? By now I can already see his cell; we have to hurry.

'Fine, you bought flowers,' I say, deciding not to press further. 'And then?'

'No. It never came to that.' His breath hitches now; I can see it clearly. 'The way to the florist took me through a park, not very big, and deserted on that cold day. There were no joggers, no dog walkers. It was unusually quiet.'

In my head an image of that park appears, with leafless trees, winter-brown lawns, and weather-beaten park benches. I see Peters walking along the path under a sky full of clouds. Wrapped in a thick coat, one of those old-fashioned leather briefcases tucked under his right arm.

'To this day I don't know why, but in the middle of the park I stopped. The atmosphere was suffocating. I could feel that something was wrong. Of course, I thought it was a trick of the mind. Instinctively, I looked around.'

His hands are trembling. Even so, I can hear the first alarm bells ringing inside me. A strange feeling? Like in *Supernatural*? I don't know. In silence I unlock his cell door and open it. Peters walks in with slumped shoulders, then turns around and looks me straight in the eye.

'Under a bush, a rainbow-colored striped pattern caught my eye. I knew right away it was the hand-knitted hat Chris had made. I thought the child had lost it while playing…'

He exhales noisily while I stop breathing altogether.

'All I wanted was to bring it back to him!'

Oh man, I can already sense where this is going. The memory makes Peters' body sway dangerously. I have to support him, help him sit down on his bed, and sit beside him.

'Oh my God, I…' His gaze goes blank, his already sunken cheeks hollowing even more. '…I bent down. I wanted to pick up the hat. And when I pulled it up from the ground…'

Restlessly I search for words, but I can't find any. Like a freeze-frame, I see the moment before me. That single second when Peter touches the colorful child's hat.

'Right where the hat had just been lying…' His voice has lost all resonance, it's nothing but a hoarse whisper. '… right there I suddenly saw the boy's dark head of hair.'

His pain shoots through my whole body like ice. It's one thing to sense what's coming next, but hearing it is something else. I'm helpless, I don't know what to say. What else can I do but pat his arm soothingly?

'I have no memory of what happened after that. It's like a nightmare that fades over time. The images are distorted, the faces nothing but grimaces, the colors pale.'

He hesitates.

I wait.

'The small body was completely rigid. His eyes were wide open and staring. His skin unnaturally white.' The words leave his mouth in choppy bursts; over and over again, he pulls himself together only to force more information out of himself.

I don't interrupt him; I'm afraid of doing the wrong thing.

'He was dead,' he says in a feeble voice.

The words echo through the room, as if they were bouncing against the narrow walls of the cell only to return to us again. Whether I want to or not, I feel close to him. Far too intensely.

'He was still so young. Far too young to die.' As if he himself couldn't believe any of it, Peters shakes his head. 'But he was dead, and I was the one who was bending over him when…' His voice breaks. All of a sudden he slams his fist down on the bed so hard it's as if he has no choice but to expel his pent-up rage. His gaze turns to ice, the muscles in his face harden.

Cold and embittered is how he looks, and there's something in his eyes. I can't put a name to it, and I can't really feel it either. Even so, I can't shake the feeling that I have to stand by him.

'There was a scream, as shrill and piercing as that of a wild animal. Then footsteps. Thundering. And loud. They came closer. You understand, I registered everything, and still I couldn't tear my eyes away from Chris. The compulsion to keep stroking his hair was overpowering. The two of us were trapped in our own world. Until the footsteps made the ground beneath me begin to tremble. Someone shouted my name. Then Chris's. When I finally managed to look up, I recognized my wonderful wife. Rigid like an ice sculpture, with a desperate look in her eyes. She studied me as if I were a stranger, and that's when I knew. From that moment on, nothing would ever be the way it used to be.'

I can hardly bear to look at him. Hearing his story is too much for me. Too much grief, too much misfortune. And too much desolation, which I can suddenly see all over his face again.

A thousand thoughts are firing around my head, and even more questions. What happened then? Who is Chris? Where was Mira until that point? But there's one single question that pushes its way to the front.

Why did everyone think he had killed the child?

It would have been easy enough to explain that he was only responsible for the gruesome discovery. Is he even telling me the truth? What if he's just a damn good actor?

'Please, no. Don't look at me like that.' Peters shrinks beside me on the spot. 'I could never take a person's life, that's not who I am!'

Can such intense despair be an act? I need to think, but I can't do that here. The air in the cell is scarce, the walls seem to close in a little more with every second.

Tears gather in his eyes and I want only one thing. For it to stop. 'I believe you,' I hear myself say.

Have I lost my mind? Damn it, I shouldn't have done that.

The lines on his forehead smooth out, the hopelessness eases. 'Thank you,' he whispers shakily. 'You're the only person who has stood by me. No one else has. Not even Mira.'

I can't help thinking of the letters and of his wife's silence. Because that means something too. 'Why not?' I ask, even though I really ought to leave right away.

'I tried everything, absolutely everything. But she turned away from me. Being locked up in here for life is bad enough. But the fact that she can't love me anymore because of something I didn't even do, that breaks my heart.' He puts his hand to his chest, and I can clearly see his upper body curl in on itself.

Can a man love a woman so much that he still wants her even when she leaves him out in the cold during the worst time of his life?

'I write to her. Again and again I beg her to stand by me. She doesn't answer. Why?' Out of nowhere he grabs me tightly by both arms.

I tear myself free at once. 'I don't know.'

'What if I chose the wrong words?' he asks, and I watch the freshly ignited energy leave erupt from his body once more.

I'd rather see him angry than this small and helpless, like a baby bird that's been thrown out of the nest by its mother. 'You didn't. Women are into that cheesy stuff. Straight out of Hollywood and all that,' slips out of me. For God's sake, I really need to get a better grip on myself.

He looks anything but surprised. 'You've read them,' he confirms.

'It's part of the job.' I shrug.

'Do you think Mira will ever respond to the letters?' There's a plea in his words. It's far too intense for me to disappoint him.

Something in me doesn't want him to lose heart. And no

matter how much I'd like to switch it off, it doesn't work. 'Maybe she just needs more time.'

A wistful smile flits across his lips. He's probably already holding her answer in his hands in his mind. 'Then I can carry on hoping.'

His back is straighter now and his eyes clearer. Even if I'd never admit it, it feels good to see him like this. This way I can leave him on his own. 'Listen, I really have to get going now.'

He clears his throat. 'Of course. Goodbye,' he then says in full professor mode. Matter-of-fact and reserved, as if I were a student and this were his office hour. As if at the push of a button, he turns back into the person I took in just under two weeks ago.

Thoughtfully, I leave the cell, lock the heavy door behind me, and lean against the wall opposite, exhausted.

I can't make sense of this man. From one second to the next he can be obliging, desperate, or full of hate. Would I not react the same way if I'd been wrongly convicted and cut off from everything I hold dear?

But what if there's more than one Heinrich Peters inside this shell of an old man? What if he really did it and he is just pretending to be the poor professor with me?

It quickly becomes clear to me that there's only one way to learn the whole truth. I have to find this Mira. If Peters' story is true, I'll try to help him.

And if it isn't?

No. I don't even want to imagine that possibility. He has to be innocent.

Chapter Seven

Pressing his cuddly toy rabbit tight against his cheek, Michael looks at me with his big eyes, full of light. 'When is he coming back?'

We've stopped saying Heinrich's name, and yet we keep having the same conversation over and over. I hold back my tears, bury my anger and disappointment deep inside me. Today, too, I carefully tuck the blue checkered blanket around Michael's small body and pretend that this task requires all my attention. 'You already know the answer.'

'But I want him to be here again!' he says with the demanding conviction of a grown boy, even though he'll only just be turning five in a few months.

I take a deep breath before I answer him. 'We all want that. But he can't be with us.' Quickly I press a kiss on his forehead. 'Sweet dreams,' I say and bury my nose in his hair. For a moment I don't want anything except to smell his scent and forget everything else.

'Why isn't he coming? Where is he?'

He'll never stop asking, I can feel it. But how do I tell

him that Heinrich isn't on a reading tour with his new volume of poetry? And that he's not coming back. Never again.

I gather all my strength, brush a strand of hair from his face, and look at him intently. 'He's in prison.'

Tense, I watch his reaction. Michael's eyes grow wide. 'Where all the bad people are?' he wants to know. Quickly he stretches his arms out from under the blanket. 'We have to go get him!'

Seeing him like this breaks my heart. 'Don't worry, he's fine. We will go get him, just not yet. You understand?'

What kind of person am I, lying to a child like this. Heinrich is serving life; even with parole, decades will pass before he's released. We'll both be old. And Michael will have long since grown up, just like his little brother Moritz.

He shrugs. 'Fine, then we'll go next week,' he says as if it were the most ordinary thing in the world.

Gently I stroke his cheek. 'Not next week. But soon.' I try to smile, but I still can't manage it. 'Now sleep well.'

I manage to give him one last kiss on his sweet-smelling cheek, before I flee the bedroom. The pressure behind my eyes is too great to endure for even a second longer.

Barely have I closed the door when the floodgates inside me burst. In the middle of the elegantly decorated hallway, I sink to the floor, my legs buckling under the weight, no longer able to hold me up. My heart contracts painfully. It feels as if it will never beat normally again.

I want to let go, to break down sobbing and screaming and refuse to ever get up again. I want to slam my fist into the parquet floor, over and over, so hard that with each blow it grows a little more numb. And yet, I mustn't let myself go, I have to keep marching on. For the children's sake, who are hopefully dreaming of better things than I am right now on the floor of the hallway.

So I do the only thing that helps me. I dig my fingernails into the area of sensitive skin on my left forearm, so that one pain will drown out the other. Without making a sound, I finally push myself up and drag myself downstairs.

When I reach the bottom of the stairs, I look around. There is so much that needs to be done, but I don't have the strength. While I stare ahead indecisively, I hear my phone ringing. It's Eva's ringtone, so I head for the kitchen, where the phone is lying on the large table.

Dirty pots from dinner are stacked beside the sink; everything else is as perfect as always. The high-gloss cabinet fronts gleam in the light of the hanging lamp. Still, I know they only shine because the maid forces them to every day.

With a sigh I reach for the phone. Eva smiles up at me from the display, her round face beaming. Her light eyes shine cheerfully.

For a moment I wish I could laugh the way she does.

'Hey,' I say, exhausted, after picking up the call. I don't ever have to pretend with Eva.

'Michael?' comes from the other end of the line.

If it weren't so sad, I'd smile. Because we know each other so well that we don't need to say more than a single word to know everything about each other. 'He won't stop asking.' I sink down onto one of the softly padded chairs and prop my head up on my hand.

'He just needs a bit more time, that's all.' Eva tries to sound encouraging, but we both know that with every day that passes, our hope grows a little smaller.

So what am I supposed to say to that? I don't know.

Eva falls silent too. She's probably tugging on the dark

curls above her forehead and letting them snap back while she thinks hard. 'Time heals all wounds,' she finally declares awkwardly. That's how Eva is. Whenever she doesn't know what else to do, she digs out one of those worn-out clichés.

And yet today, she's wrong about that. Time can't heal anything. Not when the past is sitting there in my living room drawer. I should finally tell her about it.

'He wrote to me,' I say hesitantly, letting my fingertips glide over the grain of the wooden table. Toward the narrow grooves Michael left years ago with his fork. Heinrich was beside himself with rage. Should I have already seen back then what kind of person was hiding deep inside him?

'Really?' Eva's skeptical voice disrupts my daydreaming. 'What does he want from you?'

Inevitably, my gaze wanders through the open door into the living room. Over there, in the chest-high cabinet with the antique handles, the envelopes lie safely hidden. And yet I can't forget them completely. 'I don't know. How could I read them? After everything that has happened.'

'Throw them away. Or better yet, burn them.' She sounds serious. If she were with me right now, she'd definitely take my hands and look deep into my eyes.

Throwing the letters away would certainly be the best thing to do. And yet I haven't been able to do it. Just imagining myself dropping the envelopes, unopened, into the trash can between cardboard boxes and newspapers feels wrong. Even though it's probably the right thing to do.

'Do it,' I hear Eva say now, even more insistently. 'Don't think about it, just do it.'

'Have I ever told you about how Heinrich and I met?' I ask gloomily instead of answering her. Because that exact scene is surfacing in my memory now. 'How he stood on the stage at that literary conference and read from one of his works? With a voice as warm and deep as a single cello playing, without an orchestra?'

'What does that matter now?' Eva sounds skeptical, and I can understand why.

'It doesn't,' I admit with a sigh, and I shake the image of Heinrich from my head, the way he looked straight into my eyes back then with that stunning aura of self-confidence. He's no longer the man I met all those years ago. He hasn't been for a long time. That's the truth, the only one. 'Alright, the letters are going to disappear,' I force myself to say, so that I'll finally grasp the reality myself.

My friend lets out a breath of relief; I can hear it clearly. 'Very good. And right after that you're going to do something nice for yourself. Promise?'

Her concern feels as if she were laying a warm blanket over my shoulders. 'Promise.' With tears in my eyes, I nod. 'Thank you, Eva. For everything.'

I want to do it; I resolve to with all the determination of someone whose life depends on it. And yet, as soon as we say goodbye to each other, a feeling of paralysis comes over me. My gaze fixed on the tabletop, I want only one thing. To understand how it could ever come to this.

Heinrich and I had been happy once. Not even in my worst nightmares could I have imagined that one day I'd be sitting here. With nothing but a gaping wound, right where my heart used to beat.

My life is nothing but rubble now, and I'm lying right in the middle of it. All around me floats a cloud of dust and dirt. So thick that I dare not hope to ever see the sun again.

Chapter Eight

Jessengasse 35, it has to be up ahead. I quicken my pace, but my speed is limited by the flip-flops I'm wearing. They weren't the best choice, just like the ripped jeans and the faded T-shirt. In these clothes I look completely out of place in the fancy surroundings of the nineteenth district. Unlike me, the outward appearance of the houses are spruced up; the front gardens look like they came out of a catalog.

A house painted cream white with green window frames and a wrought-iron garden fence appears before my eyes. Next to the gate I spot a plaque with the house number.

35. This is it.

Directly beneath the house number hangs a sign. 'Peters Family' is written on it. The golden lettering gleams in the light of the evening sun and looks just as old-fashioned as the professor himself. The whole place suits him anyway. Aged, impeccably maintained, and meticulously cultivated. I'm certain there's a silver-gray Mercedes in the garage.

Now that I'm here, I start to feel unsure. I can't just ring the bell and bombard Peters' wife with my questions.

Why would she even talk to a stranger who just shows up at her door?

Damn, I really should've thought this through. Why did I come here without any kind of plan?

With no other choice, I stroll over to the other side of the street and light a cigarette. I need to think, but my mind is blocked.

Of all times, my phone has to start beeping and distract me now. A message from Sandy pops up.

'I want to see you. Let's go out to eat this weekend,' she writes. Before I can reply, another message comes in. 'And, of course, it's my treat.'

Smirking, I read the last sentence a second time. She knows I'm saving for my trip and that this way she's more likely to get me to meet up with her. I'd love to, but just imagining her bombarding me with the same old questions makes me feel uneasy.

'No time, sis. Sorry,' I type quickly and hit send. That's not even a lie; May is far from over and I'm still doing one punishment weekend shift after another. Of course, I could collect on Horst's bet. After all, he was wrong with his guess about the reason for Peters' prison sentence. Yeah, I could do that. For Sandy's sake.

While I'm thinking, my phone screen lights up. 'For all of us, every day has 24 hours and every week 7 days. You alone decide what you do with them.'

That's her answer? I bite my lip. Of course she comes at me with this esoteric crap now. Whenever she starts on that, it doesn't take long before… 'No, I don't. I have to work,' I quickly type back. I don't even want to give my thoughts the chance to head off in the wrong direction.

'Then give me a day. And I'll be there. Because I always make time for the truly important things in life.' There's no winking emoji and no other indication that she isn't dead serious. That sort of humor wouldn't suit her anyway.

I nibble on my lower lip. Of course I'd like to see my big sister; after all, it's absolutely not her fault that… 'Will you promise me something?' I type on impulse.

'Anything,' comes back immediately.

'We're not talking about it.' Just writing the message triggers the pounding in my head. It's as if my head were swelling up to fend off the fear I don't want to feel anymore.

'Promise.'

It's only one word, but I feel the relief immediately. I swallow, breathe, and bite my lip. That helps as well, and while we settle on a place and time, I'm already able to smile again, relaxed. Suddenly something happens on the opposite side of the street. The green-painted front door of Peter' house opens, someone comes out.

I shove my phone back into my pocket and stretch to see something. A woman's head appears in my field of vision. I see straight, jet-black hair that reaches at least as far as her shoulder blades. Thick strands cover her face like a curtain. She waves to someone inside the house. Very faintly I hear the countless golden bangles on her wrist clinking together. Then she turns toward me.

She's young. And stunningly beautiful. With her almost black eyes and the bronze color of her flawless skin, she looks as if she had Indian ancestors. I watch her glide down the steps at the entrance and float toward the garden gate.

Oh man, if she were wearing beaded lingerie and fake wings, it would be like sitting in the front row at one of those hot fashion shows.

She leaves the property, and now I can see even more of her. Her hair reaches down to her rounded hips, which I can make out despite the baggy jeans. The bright white straps of her sandals glow against her skin.

Surely she can only be the maid. She would definitely have picked up quite a bit of what went on around the child's murder. Maybe I should get to know her first. She could then introduce me to this Mira. Not a bad idea.

Without thinking about it any longer, I follow the housekeeper down the street as inconspicuously as possible. Luckily for me, right after she turns into the next alley, she pulls out her smartphone. I don't dare get close enough to hear what she's saying. But I catch the sound of her voice, as velvety soft as chocolate that melts very slowly on your tongue.

I feel a bit like some perverted stalker as I run after her into a green space. I have to be careful not to lose her among the bushes and trees. The evening is pleasantly warm, the park is crowded. The beautiful woman glides through the throng and seems to know exactly where she's going. She heads toward a lake, passes groups of teenagers smoking suspiciously large cigarettes and old ladies parading through the park with their groomed poodles.

Hard to believe, but suddenly we're alone. I stop while she strolls along the shore and then settles down in a secluded spot right by the lake.

Sitting cross-legged in the knee-high meadow of flowers, she has something sad about her. One by one, she throws tiny pebbles into the water. She keeps her eyes fixed on the little ripples that form right in front of her. She looks a bit as if her thoughts were trapped in another world.

My mission on behalf of the professor can begin, so I get moving. A few seconds later, I'm standing right behind her. A hint of vanilla reaches my nose.

'Hi.' Hoping she'll like it, I make my voice sound deep and masculine.

She whirls around and studies me with her dark eyes. It would be helpful to see something in them, but they're just as closed off as her expression. 'Yes?'

Oh man, she's in a foul mood. I raise my hands defensively. 'Sorry, I didn't mean to bother you.'

She seems unimpressed. 'But?' she asks, raising her eyebrows.

I feel like a complete idiot. 'No offense, well, actually this is my spot.' Not exactly a stroke of genius, but whatever.

Her features relax. 'Oh, I see.' She immediately grabs her handbag and starts to push herself up from the ground.

She can't be serious. 'No, please stay. There's plenty of room for both of us, right?' With a winning smile, I drop down beside her and hold out my hand. 'I'm Simon.'

She hesitates, but I stick with it; after all, this is supposed to turn into a conversation that will help me support the professor.

Seconds stretch into what feel like minutes. Then she hesitantly raises her arm and, her bangles clinking, offers me her hand. 'Hi.' She smiles, finally. 'I'm Mira.'

What?

No, that can't be. Impossible. No way.

'Cat got your tongue?' She eyes me suspiciously. Then she immediately pulls her hand back, wraps both arms around her legs, and hugs them to her chest.

'Um...'

This is supposed to be Mira? Peters' wife? Slumped like an old balloon? Man, the professor really desperately needs new glasses.

I'm afraid the surprise is written all over my face. It's time I finally said something sensible. 'Nice to meet you.' I try a broad smile, tap a cigarette out of the pack, and light it. 'You've got a really intriguing name.'

She immediately turns serious again. 'It's Indian,' she says, fixing her gaze on a branch drifting on the surface of the water. There are still pebbles left in her fist, which she now grinds back and forth. On her left forearm I spot a collection of small, crescent-shaped injuries. What kind of pet does something like that?

'I see,' I say absentmindedly.

I take a deep drag on my cigarette; that way I can recover from the shock. Barely has the cloud of smoke left my mouth when Mira wrinkles her nose, reserved.

Helplessly, I turn the cigarette between my fingers. Normally, women show interest in me. They want to keep the conversation going, they're funny and approachable. But this Mira is different. She seems immune to my smile. It's even as if my presence makes her uncomfortable. If I bring up her husband now, she'll definitely run off faster than the Road Runner. No, first we need to be able to chat casually. Only then will I tell her why I came.

'Fish don't like pebbles,' I say out of sheer desperation. Yeah, that's nonsense, but maybe she'll react to it.

It doesn't take long before she turns her head in my direction. 'People don't either,' she replies dryly. Then she smiles faintly and rests her cheek on her knees.

That little amused curl of her lips gives me hope. 'Do you come here often?' I ask as casually as possible.

'Whenever I want to think.' She sounds sad. And that's exactly how she looks.

To distract myself, I pluck at the blades of grass on the patch of meadow where we're sitting. I have to stay cool; she mustn't notice that my curse is catching up with me, now of all times. Sandy says I'm a mirror person, because I feel other people's emotions way to such an intense degree, as if they were my own. I clear my throat; I really can't use the mirror thing right now. 'What are you thinking about today?'

Lost in thought, she twists her lips. 'About you, of course.'

So she's quick-witted. That's perfect, because at least I can keep up in that area. 'Don't worry, lots of people feel that way.' I give her a cheeky grin.

The corners of her mouth twitch suspiciously. 'Well then I can relax.'

'You can. And you know what?' Now I'm the one raising my eyebrows to make her even more curious.

It works, her gaze is reanimated, awakened from its sad slumber. 'What?'

'Studies show that this effect will still persist even long after we say goodbye to each other.' I stub out the cigarette and let the butt wander back into the now empty pack.

She smiles timidly, the features of her face, which had been so rigid just a moment ago, grow soft. Little by little she loosens her body, stretching out her arms and legs. Even though I wouldn't have thought it possible, the way she's looking at me now, she's even prettier than before. In the orange light of the evening sun, she looks like an Indian goddess. The professor has good taste, I'll give him that.

'You don't believe me, do you,' I press on.

Smiling, she turns her upper body toward me. 'Not one bit. Is there any proof of that?'

I let myself fall back into the grass and fold my arms behind my head. This is starting to get fun. 'More than enough. It's not at all uncommon for women to suffer from general dreaminess and sleepless nights,' I reply with a wink.

'I can't imagine that.' There's such a dry undertone in

her voice that I'm no longer sure whether this is still a joke for her.

'You don't have to, you'll experience it for yourself.' I quickly shrug my shoulders as if I couldn't care less what she thinks about it.

She laughs. Loud, free, and warm. 'Well then, I'm curious.'

I like seeing her like this. 'Just a warning, the symptoms can be so strong that you actually feel sick.' I look at her seriously and try to sound like a doctor. 'The only effective medication against it is another date with me.'

A sharp snort leaves her mouth. 'I see. So you're the trigger for the illness as well as the cure. A natural wonder, so to speak.'

'Exactly.' To confirm it, I nod vigorously.

Out of nowhere, she suddenly pushes herself up from the floor with an elegant movement. 'Let's see about that then.' She tucks a strand of hair behind her ear. Countless gold studs and small rings come into view. They adorn the entire outer line of her ear with their matte glow. 'Take care, Simon.'

What? She's not planning on leaving already, is she? Right now, when we're just starting to talk? No, I came here because of Peters and I still haven't done anything for him at all.

'Wait.' Even I can hear how frantic I sound. I quickly jump to my feet. 'I'll give you a prescription to take with you, just in the unlikely event that you do need the medicine.'

'That won't be necessary.' Now her features freeze again. It's as if she sees something in my eyes that scares her.

There's no way I can let her leave like this. 'That would

be extremely careless of you, negligent event,' I say as I walk beside her.

She's brooding, I can see it clearly. Something is holding her back, but part of her wants to give in. Hurriedly, I pull a pen from my pants pocket and reach for her arm. Then I gently force her to stop. She lets me pull her elbow toward me. I have to search, but among the countless small injuries I find a patch of skin where I can write down my phone number.

I've barely finished writing when I look up at her. She's staring at me in panic. As if I were a monster, a pretty terrifying one at that. Even my smile doesn't seem to change that. On the contrary, now she presses her lips together and abruptly tears herself away from me.

'Bye,' she says quickly, then turns around and races off, like a criminal on the run.

I watch her until she disappears behind a group of runners. Even though she's way too young for Peters, she still seems perfect for him. She's just as weird as he is.

Chapter Nine

With our empty plates in hand, Sandy and I have already been standing in line at the buffet for a few minutes. The small restaurant is full of people, and every single one of them is completely different from me. They fit in better with my sister, with their wide patterned skirts, jute bags, and Jesus sandals. And they also match the decor, which looks like a brightly jumbled antique shop.

'And you really want to go?' Thrown out casually, as if she didn't have any ulterior motives at all. Then she looks at me with that particular expression in her blue-green eyes. In moments like this she seems to have superpowers. An X-ray gaze that lets her see everything that's none of her business. She even gives me a knowing smile.

Deliberately casual, I motion for her to move along. 'Sure, I'll be gone in 78 days. It's my lifelong dream, and not even you can change that.'

'Mhm.' She doesn't say anything else, then she tosses her blond mane with her hand and instantly looks like one of those ponies from Iceland.

I can't help grinning while Sandy helps herself to the vegetables. I let her do her thing, seize the chance, and fish my phone out of my jeans pocket. No little light. Nothing. Still, I turn the phone on and unlock the screen. Nothing. I check my messages and my call history. Nothing.

Why isn't Mira getting in touch? Four days have passed; this is already taking too long.

'Should I recommend something?' Sandy, whose plate is now piled high with vegetables and something slimy, jolts me out of my thoughts.

I quickly glance over the pots and platters at the buffet. Everything looks the same. And it smells weird. 'Next time we're going out for burgers,' I mutter and scoop some of the rice onto my plate.

As if there weren't about a thousand people waiting behind us, Sandy suddenly grabs my hand. 'You know,' she says meaningfully, 'whoever always takes the same paths will always end up in the same place.' Without waiting for my answer, she spins around and puts one of those floppy brown lumps with the purple peel on her plate. 'Think about it.'

With these words, she disappears from my line of sight. Whatever she means by that, now is not the right moment to figure it out. My stomach growls, so I grab anything that even somewhat resembles food and plop it on my plate. Rice, potatoes, and that casserole with sheep's cheese. On my trip I'll be eating lots of unfamiliar things, so this is already good practice.

No less than a minute later I head for the small table Sandy picked out for us and sit down on the oddly shaped chair. Even though it only has a short backrest, it's surprisingly comfortable.

'It's a meditation stool,' my sister explains without being

asked. 'It makes sure your spine stays upright. That way the energies in your body can flow better.'

I gave up long ago on trying to talk her out of all that esoteric crap. So I just nod, pick up my fork, and push a small bite of the casserole into my mouth. It tastes like grass. And the white pieces are definitely not sheep's cheese.

Sandy can surely see how I'm wrinkling my nose now, but she chooses to ignore it. 'So, this trip. When are you leaving?'

'I saved up vacation time, so I can leave on August fifth and still get paid for the whole month. First I'm going to France and then maybe to Spain next. I'll probably drive along the coast and then on to Portugal. You can watch dolphins there, did you know that?'

'And you really think that's a good idea?' Her gaze is sincere, her voice caring.

We both know she doesn't mean my visit to the friendly sea creatures. In a split second, my defenses go up. 'We've been over this. Nothing has changed, Sandy, so drop it.' I turn to the potatoes, which could use some salt but at least don't taste like much of anything otherwise.

She tilts her head to the side and looks at me with her penetrative, X-ray gaze. She looks unwavering and far too determined. As if she were sure she could unlock that well-bolted door inside me. 'You can walk to the end of the world. It doesn't matter whether you go to Tierra del Fuego or the North Cape, which deserts you cross, or how tall the buildings are in the cities you visit.' She shakes her head, her hand moves to mine and forces me to give her my full attention. 'You can't run from the past. It'll be with you wherever you go.'

I have to swallow, even though right now I feel as if there isn't a single empty corner left in my stomach. I quickly shake off her hand and lean across the table toward her. Because what I'm about to say is really none of the business of the hippie couple at the next table. 'That's none of your business, and you know it.' I make my words sound very severe so there's no room for doubt. I regret it immediately. Sandy just feels it's her responsibility to help me.

Any normal person would back off now, but not my sister. She just looks at me, and instead of a silent reproach I see this enlightened expression cross her face. Without taking her eyes off me, she takes a bite of the yellow, curry-smelling mush on her plate. 'Do you really think you can go on like this forever?'

Instead of answering, I only shrug. I'm not about to sit here in this restaurant, in the middle of a crowd of people eating, and talk to her about something that in truth isn't supposed to be spoken about anywhere.

'Sometimes we cling to things we think will save us. We hold on to them, suppress what defines us, and believe we just have to try hard enough to finally be happy.'

She doesn't stop. Why? Why can't she just be quiet? Or tell me how to make jam?

'But in every one of our lives the day comes when we have to look at ourselves in the mirror. Then we're forced to ask ourselves where our actions will lead us in the end.' She looks at me as if she feels sorry for me.

She's not allowed to. 'There's nothing wrong with my reflection,' I say with a sharpness that makes even my sister, who usually seems so unshakable, flinch.

She knows. She knows she's forcing me to leave if she doesn't stop poking at wounds that only she believes still haven't healed.

Now she raises her hands defensively and silently turns her attention to the vegetables on her plate. I also turn to my food, but I only push individual grains of rice back and forth on the white porcelain, because all of a sudden I'm not hungry anymore. Instinctively, I feel for my phone in my pants pocket with my left hand.

It's still there.

And it remains quiet.

'What's with your phone all the time, anyway?' Sandy asks into the silent void that has now formed between us.

'I have no idea what you're talking about.' This topic is much more pleasant; I even give her a small smile.

Her eyes are alert. 'You're waiting for a call.' A mischievous grin spreads across her lips. 'Who is she?' she presses, as if we'd both suddenly turned into teenagers again.

'Not a woman, just something to do with work.' I try to sound as indifferent as I'd like to be. Still, my thoughts wander back to my dilemma. How can I help Peters if Mira doesn't get in touch with me?

'Liar.' She sets her fork aside and props her head on her hand. All her attention is on me. 'Come on, out with it.'

Why not, actually? I can tell her before she starts imagining God knows what. 'Fine, but this is top secret, okay?'

'Of course.' Her eyes sparkle like the gemstones on those expensive rings.

I glance around briefly, but the people at the neighboring tables seem absorbed in their own conversations anyway.

'It's about a strange inmate. We guards call him the Professor,' I say in a low voice.

A crease appears on her forehead, then she motions for me to tell her more.

'I want to find out what he did to end up with us. That's all.' With a shrug, I heap rice onto my fork. I'd rather not mention that, in truth, it's about helping Peters.

Otherwise she'll just tease me about that mirror thing again.

Sandy studies my face as if she were looking for a very specific reaction. 'And that makes you so nervous that you stare at your phone every few seconds? Who are you waiting to hear from?'

'His wife,' I say, hoping to bring this interrogation to a quick close.

There it is again, that knowing smirk. 'Aha, so there is a woman after all…' She looks very pleased with herself.

I just shake my head. 'Oh, come on. Why would I be interested in the wife of a fifty-year-old?'

For a moment that lasts far too long, she fixes her X-ray gaze upon me. 'Love chooses you, not the other way around.'

Of course that's nonsense, no matter how much she sounds like she knows exactly what she's talking about. I can see she'd love to say more, but for some reason she seems to hold herself back. Instead, she lowers her gaze and turns back to what she calls food. I quickly shake my head.

Everything is perfectly fine; I just have to make sure I don't let Sandy confuse me.

'Why don't you just call her? That can't be a problem if everything's cool,' I hear her ask now, a note of curiosity in her voice.

'I don't have her number.' This conversation is slowly starting to make me uncomfortable. Luckily, my wristwatch tells me that it's time to leave anyway. 'By the way, my shift starts at 2 PM, and I really shouldn't be late.'

'Because you really need the job. I know that.' Her lips curl. Even so, she lets me get up without protest and pulls me into her arms to say goodbye.

'See you very soon. And think about that whole

running-away thing,' she whispers in my ear. 'If not for you, then for me. And for Mom.'

Now she's bringing our mother into it as well. She has to stop that. She knows exactly what she's doing to me, and it's anything but fair. 'Bye,' I force out and tear myself away from her, because there's only one thing I want: to escape. Not from her, but from what she's doing to me.

Less than a minute later I leave the restaurant and step out into the sunlight. To calm myself, I light a cigarette as I walk and force my thoughts back to where they can't do any damage.

They land on Mira's sad eyes. And on the Peters family's secret. Will I ever find it out?

As if compelled, I pull my phone out of my pocket again.

There it is. A small white blinking light.

My breath stops for a moment as I turn the phone on. I have to shield the display from the sunlight, but then I see it. A message from an unknown number appears. I open it immediately.

'Is the prescription still valid?' it says, nothing else.

I read the words again, and then once more. A strangely pleasant feeling of relief spread through my body.

Quickly I type my reply: 'My practice opens tomorrow at 1 PM at the Wienerwald high ropes course.' I add a funny smiley emoji and send the text off.

Now things can move forward. And just thinking about that makes me smile. Because maybe I can still manage to help the professor feel a little better after all.

Chapter Ten

For minutes I've been standing rooted to the spot in front of my wardrobe, staring inside. But all I can see is a colorful jumble of fabrics in bright colors. Where are my dresses and where are my pants? I don't know. I don't know anything anymore. Least of all what got into me yesterday.

Why did I write to Simon? I must have been crazy, drunk, or pumped full of drugs.

I run my fingers over the neatly lined-up tops. I can't decide on any of them, even though it's not important at all. What I put on is as irrelevant as this meeting itself.

No matter how hard I try to drum that into my head. And no matter how determinedly I try to ignore how my pulse is skipping out of rhythm. I can't manage it.

Am I actually nervous?

Maybe, but not because of Simon. Definitely not. It's the first time in my life I'm visiting a climbing park, so it's perfectly normal to be excited.

If the Kathi from back then were here, she would wrap her arms around me. She would encourage me, smile at me, and be delighted that a little adventure was finally entering my dusty old life. Even as children we were inseparable, and even when I moved to Vienna for Heinrich, she never left my side. Hundreds of kilometers away from my Berlin, my parents, and my sister, she was like a piece of home to me.

I lost that home because of Heinrich, maybe now forever.

Deep in thought, I dig my fingernails into my forearm. The pain can't drive away how much I miss my friend, but for a moment it manages to overshadow it. With my teeth clenched, I exhale in short bursts. Then I turn back to my clothes. They shine in every color, from sky blue to cherry red, from rosé to sunflower yellow.

How can they still do that when my life consists only of gray and black?

I glance at the ankle-length turquoise dress. I take it out of the wardrobe, hold it in front of my body, and look at myself in the mirror. The fabric plays around my legs like the foaming waves of the sea. I can almost hear the water lapping against the shore and taste the salty air on my tongue.

In an instant I'm defenseless against the feeling that now wells up inside me. It's as if I were back there. On the Balinese coast, together with Heinrich.

It was our first vacation together, long before we dreamed of children. We strolled along the beach, the summery warm breeze in our hair, our hands tightly entwined. Far out on the horizon, the sun was setting, bathing the sky in orange-red light.

In my memory, Heinrich stops, gently turns me toward the sea, and wraps his arms around my body from behind. All at once he is very close. He smells like a Sunday morning, light and free. His lips touch my neck, so delicately, as if

I were as fragile as porcelain. Then they wander up to my ear.

'As long as I'm allowed to love you, the sun will shine for me,' he whispers.

A pleasant shiver runs down my back, I press myself against him, wanting to feel him everywhere. A single tear slips from the corner of my eye and runs silently down my cheek. I'm happy, happier than I've ever been before.

Today is different. Standing in the middle of the bedroom that only a few months ago still belonged to the two of us, I can barely hold back my tears of grief. There is nothing in this world I want more than for everything to be the way it was back then. I want to feel that happiness again, want to feel it flooding through me.

It left me, many years ago. And the last, pitiful remnant of it disappeared on that terribly gray November day. Without warning.

With a jerky movement, I hang the dress back in the wardrobe and shake my head, as if that could free me from all the memories. That belongs in the past; mourning it makes no sense. She is gone, she is never coming back.

I take one last deep breath, then pull a faded pair of jeans from the hanger. But as I unfold them, my movements falter again. Because in that moment it suddenly becomes clear to me why I wanted to meet Simon.

Back then in the park, it was there.

Only for a tiny moment. When his lightness suddenly rubbed off on me. When I had to smirk in secret. And could laugh without having to force myself.

In that moment my thoughts were free; there were no worries and no shadows. Instead, it was so warm and bright inside me that there was nothing I wanted more than to feel that kind of freedom for just a moment longer.

Chapter Eleven

The huge clock on the wall of the ticket booth ticks loudly. Over at the first station of the climbing park, a group of teenagers is getting ready. They laugh cheerfully while I pace around nervously because I simply can't stand still.

What if Mira doesn't come? She wouldn't just chicken out without getting in touch, would she? No, that's not who Mira Peters is. Definitely not.

I take a long breath, trying to calm myself down. The smell of mossy forest floor fills my nose. Somewhere in the far east of Europe there's a forest that no human has ever come into contact with. It's wild. And free. Does it smell the same there? I could go visit it and find out. At once I picture the moment when I swing onto my bike and say goodbye to Vienna. I'm wrapped in black leather from head to toe, even though I finally don't have to be sad anymore. This morning my tear-off calendar showed 77 days. Just two months to go.

'A climbing harness for your thoughts.'

I flinch. My daydream had me so completely enraptured

that I didn't even notice Mira arriving. Now she's suddenly standing in front of me again, and once more she has that sad look in her dark eyes. Today she's braided her hip-length hair into long plaits. Together with the sporty outfit it makes her look much younger than last week in the park. She's probably half Peters' age.

A strangely mismatched marriage. What could have brought those two together?

A trace of her scent reaches my nose. 'Hi, vanilla girl,' I say, leaning toward her to kiss her cheeks.

She immediately takes a step back and looks at me accusingly. Can anyone understand this woman? Just a moment ago she was totally relaxed, and less than a minute later she's as skittish as a wild hare.

For now I'd better pretend I don't notice her mood swings. With a broad grin I grab her hand. 'I've already got the helmets and harnesses, we can start right away. It starts over there.'

Even though Mira's hand feels stiff in mine, at least she doesn't pull away and walks with me to the starting point. We put on the safety harnesses and climb up the ladder.

Up there we have to wait a moment until the group ahead of us leaves the first station. I watch the fine hairs on Mira's forearms stand up in the cool wind. Just like in the park, I notice all the tiny wounds. What's going on there?

She shivers harder, so I quickly shrug out of my motorcycle jacket and drape it around her shoulders. 'Take this,' I say politely. 'You came here to get healthy, not even sicker. Right?'

My wink has an effect. She exhales slowly, the fine muscles around the corners of her mouth twitching suspiciously. 'Perhpas.'

'Don't worry, the suffering is about to end.' I put one of

the two helmets on her head and give her an encouraging nod.

She lowers her gaze, but at least she keeps still, even when I reach for the strap ends and fasten them together at her neck.

'Ready?' I guide her chin upward and risk a look into her dark eyes, even though my gut tells me not to. They could swallow me, like a black hole swallows matter. Sad people make me sad. And I already have more than enough of that feeling myself.

She nods. Then she exhales in short bursts and shakes out her body. 'I think so.'

It's clearly time for a distraction. For her and for me. So I turn to the first climbing station. In front of me is a simple walkway made of wooden slats, basically nothing more than a suspension bridge. It's harmless, more of a warm-up. 'You're not afraid of heights, are you?' I ask anyway. Then I clip her carabiner to the safety line and let her go first.

'No.' It sounds more like a question than an answer. As if she wants to prove her fearlessness to me, she impulsively puts one foot on the obstacle, which immediately starts to sway. 'Oops,' she says, and clutches the ropes so tightly that her knuckles turn white.

I catch her panicked look. 'Don't worry, I'm right behind you,' I say soothingly and lay my hand on her shoulder. 'Trust me, nothing's going to happen.'

It's impossible to miss that she dislikes the touch. She immediately pulls her shoulder away. Her usually untouchable beauty is gone; she looks vulnerable.

'Go on, give it a try,' I urge her, not least to escape the situation myself.

'On your head be it.' Hesitantly she sets off, taking such

tiny little steps it's as if she were a toddler. At least she's making progress.

When she has half the bridge behind her, she turns toward me in slow motion. The radiance on her face is as bright as a thousand stage spotlights. A thousand at the least.

'Fun, isn't it?' I call over to her and get a vigorous nod in return. I feel her joy spilling over to me, let her cross the last few yards of the obstacle, and only then run across myself. With the right technique, the bridge stays still as if it were made of concrete.

She punishes me with an accusing expression. 'You could've told me that beforehand,' she says when I reach her on the platform.

'I could have, but where would the fun have been in that?' I put on a gallant grin that has just the right effect. Now that her smile is back, I can be myself again too. And if the mood stays this way, I'll soon be able to bring up the Professor.

'Idiot.' All of a sudden she lifts her hand as if she wanted to hit me in the chest with it, but then lets it sink again with a startled look. She quickly glances around. 'Where do we go from here?'

I point out the direction with my hand. 'Right there, where the planks are dangling between the trees.'

She turns around. For a few seconds she turns into a life-size statue. Rigid and silent, she stands on the platform with her back to me. My eyes wander over the braided strands at the back of her head. A single hair hangs loose from one of the braids. On reflex I give it a gentle tug. That's when I notice how incredibly smooth the bundles of hair look, and at once I want to know how they feel. With my fingertips I trace the path of one of the intertwined strands. It's silky, yet my skin tingles as if it were gliding over a fine grater. Strange.

With a single jerk she whirls around. Her braids lift off like the seats of a chair swing ride at a fair. 'What do you think you're doing?' she snaps at me angrily.

This is not good. Not at all.

At least by now I knew how to handle these brief attacks. I raised my hands apologetically and presented the single hair. 'Just wanted to free you from this, sorry.'

'And I'm supposed to believe that?' She folded her arms across her chest.

I took a step back. 'Sure! It would've bothered you at the next climbing station.' I didn't suggest she trust me again; that had already gone wrong a few minutes ago. Instead, I put on my best smile. 'You're seeing ghosts. But don't worry, there's a remedy for that too.'

'Idiot.' Her arms relaxed, the crease on her forehead disappeared.

'Well, my actual name's Simon,' I said with a theatrically exaggerated sigh, 'but idiot is fine too, if you prefer.'

Her cheeks flushed slightly. 'Sorry,' she murmured meekly.

Someone really needed to figure her out one day. I was certainly confused. 'No worries.' I acted casual—what else could I do? We should've gone for a drink; that definitely would've gone better. But we were here, so I made the best of it. 'Let's keep going, that family over there is already hot on our heels.'

For a moment Mira looked wistfully over to where the father was just checking how his kids' helmets sat. Then she spun abruptly toward the next obstacle. Bravely, she headed for the planks hanging one behind the other on chains like individual children's swings and pulled the first plank toward herself.

This wasn't a good idea. I had to warn her.

Too late—she was already putting her foot on the slat and the swing shot off with her. A shrill scream escaped her mouth. She clung to the ropes as if her life depended on it, and it probably felt that way to her too.

The swaying of the plank grows smaller, but she still doesn't move. 'You okay?' I call to her. I sound worried, and I am.

'Mhm.' She doesn't say anything else. I can barely hear it over the children's laughter in the background, but I see how frantically her chest rises and falls. Still, she clutches the rope of the next plank and climbs on. This time the thing swings a lot less.

'Very good!' I clap my hands, and she turns her head in my direction. Her eyes sparkle the way I imagine the night sky over the Atacama Desert. Bright as hell. A wide smile materializes on her face.

Immediately I think of the words from Peters' letters.

Seeing you happy sends warm shivers through my body. Your radiance is so powerful it can light up all the shadows in this world. My shadows too, Mira, every single one of them. You are my sun; without you my life lies in darkness.

That's what he wrote, and in this very moment I feel what he meant by it so clearly. This woman is full of energy.

Fascinated, I watch as Mira bravely keeps climbing and grows more and more sure-footed. When she reaches the last board, she even turns all the way toward me. 'You coming?' she calls excitedly, making her board swing from side to side.

I board the first wooden plank. With quick movements, I make my way toward her until I'm dangling right in front of her. Her expression makes me light up too; I can't help but be happy. With her, or for her, I don't know.

I'd love to find words as beautiful as Peters' right now. 'Great, isn't it?' I say instead, with the eloquence of a two-year-old.

Nodding vigorously, she turns around and jumps onto the platform that leads to the next obstacle. Once there, she throws her arms up as if she's just won a marathon and starts dancing in place.

I catch up to her and slap her hand.

'Where do we go next?' she asks, breathlessly, spinning around as she looks. 'Ah, over there. That looks exciting!'

She has gotten a taste for it; there's no stopping her now. An exctied rush flows through my body. Am I actually proud that I coaxed her out of her shell?

So many things make you special. But the most beautiful of all is this passion that burns inside you like a beacon.

That's how Peters described what I can now see with my own eyes. Her enthusiasm is so genuine and so infectious that I can hardly imagine anything more beautiful. It has me in its grasp, and suddenly there's only one thing I want:

She should stay this happy so she can keep on shining all the time.

Stop! What am I thinking?

Hurriedly, I shake this trace of whatever it is out of my head. It disappears at once, just the way it should.

'Where are you?' I hear Mira call now.

I have to look several times to figure out where her voice is coming from. Up there, in the roll made of branches, she's sitting as if in a cradle and waving at me. 'Come on, the view is fantastic!'

Of course I head straight up. Once I reach the top, I sit

down next to her and take a breath. Only then do I really take in the spectacle of nature before us.

On one side lies the dense deciduous forest, on the other an apparently endless expanse. Lush meadows alternate with floodplain areas, interrupted only by the occasional farmhouse and field. The family from before looks from up here like nothing more than a cluster of colorful blotches.

'Fantastic, isn't it?' Mira's eyes were full of life.

'Absolutely.' I let my legs dangle next to hers; every now and then they brush against each other as if by chance. This is the moment, now I can try. 'Tell me something about yourself,' I say, looking at her expectantly.

Her features turn to stone, and I imagine I can see her roll her eyes for a second. 'What do you want to know?'

'Everything.' I sound just as serious as I am. 'So far I only know your name, but I want to know who you are.'

Her shoulders lift in a shrug. 'No, you don't.' The sparkle vanishes from her eyes at once.

Seeing her like feels like a stab in the chest. 'Let's start with something simple,' I suggest in an exaggeratedly cheerful tone. Then I begin lightly rocking the swing made of branches we're sitting in. She doesn't answer, so I pretend not to notice her hesitation and keep going. 'What do you do when you're not meeting strange men?'

Instead of saying anything, she inspects me. So intently that after only a few seconds it feels as if this is some kind of test.

'So that much, huh,' I say with a knowing nod. 'Wow, there's really a lot going on with you.' I give her a furtive grin; this just has to work.

'Very funny.' Her voice sounds as dry as the Sahara, but her expression tells me she'd love to grin.

'Got it, then forget it.' This woman is and remains a

mystery. And if she keeps this up, the whereabouts of Peters' letters will also stay in the dark forever. I definitely won't pressure her, that much is clear. So I have no choice but to end my mission for now. 'I'll wait for you downstairs, then.'

At a snail's pace, I turn around to give her the chance to stop me. But it's only when I'm almost out of earshot that she clears her throat louder than necessary.

My gaze shoots to her at once.

'I have children.' The information leaves her mouth at record speed. It seems to have taken an effort for her to tell me that. But why?

I give her an encouraging smile and close the gap between us. 'Girls or boys? Or a bit of both?' I ask, even though I'm not exactly dying to know. But at least she's finally talking, and that feels good.

A warm expression flits across her face. 'Two boys. Michael will turn five at the end of July, Moritz is two.'

'Great.' That's all I can come up with. I just don't have much to say on this topic. Should I ask about their father now?

'Those two are my life.' She studies me with her gaze as if she were searching for signs of a particular reaction.

Outwardly I stay cool, but in my head there's total chaos. What on earth am I supposed to say to that? I should probably have questions, or at least say something halfway sensible. 'I see,' I say instead, automatically feeling for the pack of cigarettes in my pocket and pulling it out.

With a curious spark in her eyes, Mira tilts her head to the side. 'Do you like kids?'

'Of course I like the little rascals.' That isn't entirely true. Still, it feels strangely easy to say it. Because I know it's exactly what she wants to hear. This answer makes her feel good, and it's nice to be able to do that for her. 'I've got two nieces. One is eight and one is four,' I add, to at least tell her something true. Then I tap a cigarette out of the pack.

Mira immediately wrinkles her nose, just like she did back in the park. She clearly doesn't care much for cigarette smoke. I should probably skip the smoking, so I stick the cigarette back into the pack.

A smile spreads across her face once more and suddenly it's hard for me to meet her gaze. There's something magical about that shine in her eyes. Or maybe it's the strands of hair that fall into her face and brush gently against her cheeks, where her skin looks as if it's glowing.

All at once she bumps me with her shoulder. 'And what do you do when you're not meeting strange women?'

Now is the perfect moment to tell her why we're here. That I looked for her because I want to help her husband be at least a little happier again. And that our first meeting went so badly that I was afraid to come out with the truth right away. 'I'm a cop,' I say, to take a step in the right direction.

She immediately furrows her brows and I can clearly see her muscles tense up.

Right on cue, I feel a heaviness too. Can't I, just once, shut myself off from other people's feelings? 'Don't look at me like that, I'm one of the nice ones. Honestly!'

'That remains to be seen,' she replies, her voice husky.

All at once it hits me that she must have had bad experiences with the police around the whole thing with Peters. To quickly lift her mood and mine again, I wink at her. 'I've got time.'

Mira furrows her brow. Then she glances at her delicate wristwatch. The thing looks expensive. 'But I don't. To be honest, I have to go.'

No, not yet! Not now, just when we're finally starting to have a conversation. 'Really?'

'Yeah, I'm sorry.' She shrugs her shoulders, and it even looks as if she means it.

'Don't leave me, you'll break my heart.' Theatrically, I press my hand to my chest and bend my upper body forward.

All at once her fingers search for mine. Her skin is damn soft. 'I would never do that.' Her gaze keeps flickering suspiciously often between my eyes and my mouth.

No, I'm imagining it. Or am I?

How can I suddenly not know, from one moment to the next, what's real and what's the result of some crazy fantasy? I'm not going to lose control of my mind now, just because she's looking at me like that.

My thoughts drift off all by themselves. They show me how I take her head in my hands and gently pull her closer to me. Then I kiss her.

Stop. What am I thinking?

This is nothing but nonsense. I spring to my feet and probably look just as confused as I feel right now. 'Let's go,' I say hastily.

'Love chooses you, not you the love,' I suddenly hear Sandy's voice in my head.

For God's sake, what is this? That crap has absolutely no place here.

While I climb down at breakneck speed, I run through my ritual mechanically. Swallow, breathe, bite my lip. And then again from the top.

Still, I feel something there, right in the middle of my chest. There's a throbbing that wants to make me believe it's going to stay with me. No matter whether I like it or not.

Chapter Twelve

A frightening wave of guilt eats its way through my stomach like a caterpillar, consuming me. How could I possibly have lost all sense of time like that?

An hour ago I should have picked the boys up from Eva's. I ran from the car up here to the second floor of her apartment building. Now I'm gasping for breath as I press the doorbell.

A moment later the door opens and Eva's round face appears behind it. The dark blue summer dress makes her eyes, already shining bright, glow even more.

'Hey.' She smiles at me kindly, but I can clearly hear the worried undertone in her voice.

Still breathing heavily, I raise my hands in apology and step into the airy hallway of the apartment. An oversized picture of the sea hangs on the wall, the turquoise curtains reach down to the floor, and a shell bowl stands on the whitewashed wardrobe. Water is my element, and coming here always feels a bit like going on vacation. At least it used to.

I wished I could relax now too, but out of the corner of my eye I noticed Eva studying me with a peculiar grin. Her gaze dropped to Simon's leather jacket, which I was still wearing.

'What is it?' I asked skeptically and set my bag down.

'Nice piece, but a little too big, don't you think?' She raised her eyebrows so high they disappeared beneath her curly bangs.

'Um…' I looked around, searching for help. 'Where are the kids?'

Eva gave me a knowing grin. 'Moritz is asleep, and Michael is next door drawing a picture for his best friend.' She pointed her index finger at herself with a proud expression. 'So we still have time. Which is good because there's a bottle of wine waiting for us in the kitchen, and I can't shake the feeling you might have the right story to go with it.'

Did I? Maybe.

I greeted my eldest and then followed Eva into the kitchen of her apartment. It was the vast, bright sofa and the cozy, wool-white faux-fur rug covering most of the floor that usually helped me relax here. I should have felt calm today as well, but I didn't. That was because of Eva. And the way she was looking at me. With that particular look, as if she knew what I was thinking.

Hesitantly, I slid onto the corner bench upholstered in dark blue woven fabric. On the table stood a bowl with heart-shaped floating candles. I watched them drift lazily on the water while Eva poured an especially dark red wine into the bulbous glasses.

She handed me a glass and raised hers to me. 'To you!?'

I couldn't help but smirk. Again. 'Is that a question?'

She doesn't answer but gives me a conspiratorial look. We take a sip. The wine is tart and dry, just the way I like it.

As soon as Eva has set her glass down in front of her, she props her head on her hand and studies me. 'All right, out with it. I can tell something special happened today.'

Part of me wishes I didn't know what she was talking about. 'Maybe…' I say meekly. I don't even understand myself what came over me earlier in the climbing park. So how could I begin to explain...

'Ha! You can't fool me, especially not when your cheeks look like you've just crawled out of an oven.' She leans across the table toward me and lowers her voice. 'Tell me everything,' she demands, sounding like a snake charmer.

I let my fingertips glide over the cold stem of the wineglass. It has to be said, and who knows, maybe it'll even lose a tiny bit of its magic once I do. 'His name is Simon, and we went to the climbing park together.'

Eva's broad grin says it all. 'The climbing park. Interesting.' She nods. Her short, dark brown corkscrew curls bounce in time and look like they're made of twisted wool.

'You know I've wanted to do that for ages, but with Heinrich…' I fall silent. What am I trying to say? That something like that was unthinkable with my husband? And that all of a sudden I have the feeling my life might have more to offer than cultural events?

'He wasn't exactly an action hero,' Eva remarks in her typically dry manner. 'But back to this Simon—what's going on with him?'

'Nothing at all.' The words shoot out of my mouth, unnaturally fast and full of tension. Eva doesn't react to them, though; she just smiles. 'I don't know,' I admit, dropping my gaze and pushing my wineglass back and forth in front of me. The burgundy liquid glows in the light of the low-hanging lamp and casts a colored shadow on the pale tabletop. Then I brace myself and say out loud what has so far only been drifting aimlessly through my head. 'He makes me forget. At least for a brief moment.'

Spending time with Simon is so easy; I feel free. I can even laugh again.

Eva's hand wanders across the table and squeezes mine in a friendly way. 'It's not a big deal if you like him,' she says, so understandingly it's as if she were my mother and Simon my very first crush.

As a reflect, I pull my hand back from under hers. 'He's just an acquaintance, that's all.' Even if it were different, it's not that simple. On the contrary, the truth is that something like that must never happen. A deep despair spreads inside me, overwhelms my heart and creeps down into the pit of my stomach. 'I can't do it, even if I wanted to.' I'm only whispering now; all at once I feel weak. 'Not after everything that's happened.'

With an intent expression, Eva shakes her head. 'Mira, you're only twenty-nine years old. Do you want to stay alone for the rest of your life just because you were disappointed once?'

The way she says it, it sounds as if Heinrich had left me for another woman. 'Disappointed?' I snap at her. Maybe a bit too harshly, but right now I can't help it. 'My life is nothing but a pile of broken pieces. The man I married with such blind trust is a murderer! Don't you understand? I let a criminal into my bed. Into my children's lives…' My throat tightens, I blink the rising tears from my eyes and dig my fingernails deep into my palms. 'And into my heart.'

In one swift movement, Eva is beside me and gently forces me to loosen my fingers. She knows what I do every time I clench my fists. It's wrong, she wants to tell me with that, and yet I can't stop. I need this pain; it drowns out the other one, at least for a moment of brief respite.

Exhausted, I let my head sink onto her shoulder; my nose swells shut, my temples throb. Eva's hand brushes comfortingly over my hair. 'I know,' she only whispers, over and over again.

'I trusted him, was so blinded by my feelings that I didn't want to see who he really is.'

Eva pulls out a tissue and hands it to me. 'I know,' she says again, as if she were a record stuck at exactly the right spot.

'I mustn't listen to my heart; it lies to me and betrays me. I did it once, and look what happened.' My whole body shakes, as if it wanted to free me from the memory. From everything that has happened.

I wish that were exactly what was possible. I'd sacrifice even the most beautiful moments if I could banish Heinrich from my life, and the memories along with him. Because only now do I see our shared past in the right light. As if I had just woken up, I finally recognize what I suppressed for years. I remember the anger in his eyes and the hatred in his expression. It was there, every time something didn't go according to his rules.

'Heinrich had two faces,' I murmur absentmindedly. 'And for far too long I could only see the one of the gallant poet. He carried me on his arm; he was the perfect gentleman.'

I pull myself together for a moment, then I speak the truth.

'But only as long as I was exactly the way he wanted me to be.'

Eva rocks me back and forth like a child who has just

woken from a nightmare. And, in fact, it feels exactly like that, with only one difference. My nightmare is still playing out when I open my eyes.

Chapter Thirteen

'So what time are we heading out tonight?' Paul's expectant gaze is burning into the back of my neck while I wipe the last bit of grime from my bike's rearview mirror.

I should answer his question, even though I know he won't like what I'm about to say. 'I can't come this time, sorry.' I try to sound casual, but I can't bring myself to look at him. Instead, I let my eyes wander, scanning over the allotment gardens. Here, on Paul's parents' plot, the two of us have parked our motorbikes between raspberry bushes and apple trees. Just 52 more days, then I won't need the space anymore.

'This time?' Paul lets out a snort of contempt. 'I can barely remember the last time we partied. Jessy says she's already forgotten what you look like.'

I grab the polishing cloth and move on to the bodywork, even though my motorbike is already gleaming in the sunlight as if it had never been ridden. 'I'm sorry, but something came up.'

'And what's that supposed to be, huh?' Suddenly he's standing right next to me, eyeing me up and down.

Should I tell him the truth? Better not.

'Got something to take care of. Something private,' I answer evasively, and immediately a nasty feeling begins growing inside me.

So many times over the past few weeks I've stood him up to meet Mira. We rode the motorbike along Lake Neusiedl, learned to water-ski on the Old Danube, and at night we secretly went swimming in the Donnerbrunnen on Neuer Markt. Clothes and all. Ever since then she hasn't just been Mira to me, but the water girl. I'll never forget the memory of the look on her face when she stood in front of me, soaked from head to toe, completely liberated. She was happy, and so was I.

'Since when do we keep secrets from each other?' Paul's voice tears me from my thoughts.

'We don't,' I answer, and keep inspecting my motorbike. There's still damp dirt from our joyride stuck under the front wheel's fender. I should clean that off right away.

'Then you can tell me what suddenly became so important today that you have to cancel our plans.' He raises his eyebrows, resulting in that that bulldog forehead that he gets.

A deep sigh leaves my mouth; like it or not, I have to give him something. Just a little morsel to keep him satisfied. 'You know I've got this project going.' Even as I say the words, it feels strange. It's probably my guilty conscience about Peters, whom I still haven't been able to help. And the fact that I've been avoiding him these past few weeks doesn't make it any better.

Paul's laugh sounds relieved. 'The murderous professor?

Well then, go on, tell me.' He leans against his bike and looks at me expectantly.

I hesitate, although I don't even know why. It's really not such a big deal. 'I'm meeting his wife today.'

'After nine in the evening? Aren't old folks long asleep by then?' he asks incredulously.

With instincts like his, he should've become a detective. Or a truffle pig.

To buy myself some time, I light a cigarette. My brain is running at full speed but not coming up with anything useful. Reluctantly, I decide once again to go with the truth. 'She's not quite as old as he is.'

'Aha,' he says, then a tense silence grows between us. 'And you're meeting up with her because...'

'To find out what was going on with the professor... O-obviously.' Damn it. Did I really have to start stuttering now of all times, when there's no real reason for it?

'Oh Simon,' is all he says. Then he turns away, pushes his motorbike off the stand, and rolls it back into the shelter made of roughly nailed-together boards.

I bite my lip. 'No, not 'oh Simon',' I call after him. The words come out of my mouth harsher than I intended.

He spins around to face me at once. 'Let me guess. She's pretty hot and wonderfully off-limits.'

'You're wrong. There's no danger there.' That's exactly how it is. I try to make the words sound casual, but they only leave my lips reluctantly. Better if I turn back to the bike now too. I take one last deep drag on my cigarette and crouch down. Carefully, I check the exhaust system for signs of rust.

'You can't fool me,' I hear Paul say. Nothing more, because he knows perfectly well I can figure out the rest on my own.

Still, he's exaggerating. Wildly. 'Don't be ridiculous, there's nothing going on.' Before Paul can start digging again, I park my motorbike next to his in the shelter and wipe my hands on my jeans. 'I really have to go. I'll see you tomorrow.'

'Yeah, sure.' He's disappointed, I can hear it clearly.

Immediately I feel bad. 'Have a beer for me,' I say and give him a pat on his slumped shoulders. 'Next time I'll be there again, I promise.'

After we say goodbye to each other, I head off right away. Still, I can't block out Paul's words, and after only a few yards a terrible suspicion hits me.

I'd never admit it, but ever since our meeting at the climbing park three weeks ago, Mira has been in my head way too often. That's not where she should be, and she definitely shouldn't be smiling at me the way she is up there right now.

I scurry home and then into the shower, but she catches up with me there too. She's always with me, follows me everywhere, and when I set off toward Jessengasse 35, she's there more than ever. The night that's descending is cool; I shiver in my thin jacket.

As I turn onto Mira's street, my phone rings. It's Sandy. Strange, but her call feels like salvation today.

'Hey, little sis,' I say in greeting.

'The two little ladies and I are going to whip the garden into shape on Friday. We've got a ton of work and we all agreed we won't manage it without your help.' She sounds so cheerful that I feel as if the sun is shining straight through the phone into my ear. 'No excuses.'

I hesitate.

'Come on, you'll be gone soon, let's spend some time together before that. Mom's going to cook for us.' Sandy doesn't give me a chance to answer. It's as if, even from a distance, she can sense how torn I am. However she manages to do that.

Soon we won't be able to see each other for many months, maybe even years. I know what that means for Sandy and our mother. For me, on the other hand, every meeting has the potential to become a horror-filled dive back into the past. Because far too often things come up that we shouldn't talk about, because it just doesn't make any sense. It only hurts. Still, I can't help it this time either. I give in, for the two of them. 'Sure, I'm in.'

'Perfect,' I hear her say happily now. 'See you Friday, then.'

I say goodbye to Sandy, hang up, and take a deep breath. By now I've almost reached Mira's place. Barely a hundred meters away I see dimmed light falling through the windows into the front garden, not a sound to be heard. Only my footsteps echo through the stillness of the night.

Still, I sense something else.

It's my heart, beating more vividly than usual in my chest. Just like at our previous meetings, it can't be controlled. In a moment I'll be at Mira's; up ahead I can already make out the handle of the garden gate.

My common sense urgently advises me to ignore the fluttering of my heart. Because there are millions of reasons why this is a damn bad thing. And not a single explanation for why it could be good.

I should turn back. I should skip doing this good deed for Peters, focus on my lifelong dream, and stop thinking about Mira. I should rave about the big wide world, party with Paul, and take it easy during the last few weeks at my job.

I should do all that. But I do none of it.

Chapter Fourteen

Sometimes seconds can feel like hours. And right now is one of those moments. Ever since I pressed the doorbell, time has stood still. Tense, I let my gaze wander over the ornaments on the dark green front door of Mira's house.

Finally I hear a click, the door handle moves down. At first I only see the yellowish light from inside the house. It paints a narrow strip on the floor next to my sneakers, which grows wider and wider until it covers me completely.

Now Mira is standing right in front of me. Barefoot, in a floor-length, bright orange dress and with a smile that almost makes me forget who I am.

No. I'm Simon. And I'm only here to help the professor. That's all. I quickly run through my program. I swallow, breathe, and bite my lip. It works. The situation is under control, I'm not crazy. Thank God.

'Hey. Good to see you.' She takes a step back and pulls the door open even wider. 'Come on in.'

I step into the house.

It's completely different from how I imagined it.

Modern, but also with pieces of furniture that look like they're centuries old. Framed by stucco, a lamp hangs from the ceiling that must have cost a fortune. It looks like something out of the catalog of one of those furniture stores for cigar-smoking upper-class types.

'Surprised?' There's a smirk on Mira's face. I can't read it. I don't know what she's thinking.

I clear my throat quickly so that the last bit of tension inside me dissolves. 'A little,' I admit, 'it's really beautiful.' Much more beautiful and much bigger than anywhere I've ever lived in my life. This place is a damn palace.

Curious, I follow her into a spacious living room with an elegant dark parquet floor and high ceilings. In the corner stands an antique tiled stove. Right next to it, a stately-looking dark green wingback chair sits in front of a bookcase as big as an entire library. On the little table beside the cream-colored couch, crystal-stemmed glasses and one of those fancy decanters are waiting.

'Would you like some wine?' I hear Mira ask. Her voice is trembling, or am I just imagining it?

I, on the other hand, am completely in control of myself. Whatever that was just now, it's gone again, and that's a good thing. 'Please,' I answer, and head over to the sofa. 'Are your kids upstairs?'

'They're spending the night at a friend's.' Her smile looks almost embarrassed. 'Wait, I just have to quickly…' With a swift motion, Mira snatches a few flyers from the coffee table. 'How could I have missed those?' she murmurs, shaking her head as she spins around. All at once, a small, gleaming white envelope slips out of the stack and sails silently to the floor.

I recognize it immediately. A few days ago, I held this letter in my hands. Excitement spreads through me. This is the moment; now I can keep my promise to the professor. My eyes dart over to look at Mira.

She looks like an icicle. Rigid, cold, and hard. On top of that, her hands are clenched into fists. A vein stands out beneath the flawless skin of her neck. I can see the throbbing movement all too clearly; her pulse is racing.

I should say something. But what?

While I'm just standing there like an idiot, Mira suddenly snaps out of her paralysis and bends down to pick up the envelope. The way she touches it, you'd think it was a dead spider. Without saying a single word, she marches over to the chest-high cabinet on the other side of the room. I can only see her back, but that's enough to sense how upset she is. She takes several deep breaths in and out, then opens the bottom drawer with trembling fingers. A moment later I see what's hidden inside.

The letters.

Every last one of them is in that drawer, crammed together with their envelopes firmly sealed. Mira hasn't read a single one.

What does that mean?

A thousand thoughts are swirling inside my head like a swarm of bumblebees gone mad. But I don't have time to catch them. Far too quickly, Mira slams the drawer shut and comes back to me, her expression turned to stone. She won't let me see her eyes, sits down, reaches silently for her wineglass, and drains it in one go.

Carefully, I sink down onto the sofa beside her. 'A-are you okay?' I ask, like a complete idiot. Of course she's not okay, anyone can see that.

After what feels like half an eternity, she lifts her lids and our eyes meet. Fear, despair, and mistrust pass through her dark eyes one after the other.

I can clearly feel my curse overwhelming me. I immediately want to comfort her, and suddenly nothing else matters anymore. So I do exactly what I absolutely didn't want to do. I move closer to her and wrap my arm protectively around her shoulders. With gentle pressure, I stroke her upper arm. 'How can I help you?'

Mira shakes her head mechanically. 'Everything's fine,' she forces out and presses a smile onto her face.

I've never felt so helpless and useless. Why else would I suddenly be asking myself what my sister would do in this moment? Maybe she would say something like, *The past doesn't fade just because you ignore it.* Or maybe not. I don't know, and it's driving me insane.

To shake off this awful feeling of powerlessness, I force myself to think about my mission. I wanted to help Peters, that's why I looked for Mira in the first place. But there's definitely a reason she's reacting to the unopened letters in this way. What if the professor deceived me? What if he noticed how soft I get when other people are suffering and only wanted to exploit my weakness for his own purposes? Does he even deserve my help?

Lost in thought, I don't notice it at first, but then I feel it very clearly. Minute by minute, Mira's tension slowly fades, her shoulders loosen. With a sigh, she finally lets her head fall against my chest.

She turns her face toward me and looks so deeply into my eyes, it's as if she were searching for something in them, some lost artefact. All at once it's like she is pulling me into her melancholic world.

'I'm here for you, Mira,' I hear myself say, because I can't stand the sadness and doubt in her gaze any longer. I want to comfort her and make her laugh again.

She clears her throat and looks at me questioningly. She shakes her head almost imperceptibly.

'I understand.' It's probably a pained smile I'm giving her now. Because there's far more in those two words than she can imagine. She must have gone through terrible things, and I know all too well what that feels like. What it's like when, all of a sudden, the ground is pulled out from underneath you. When you're falling and even stop asking yourself how far you still are from the ground. I can't let thoughts like that surface. Not now and not ever.

'Do you want to be alone?' I ask.

Mira doesn't answer. Is there really nothing I can do for her? Do I have to leave her here with her sadness?

'I have to tell you something. About me. And about my life,' she suddenly whispers into the silence. 'So you'll understand…' Her voice breaks, and I realize what that means.

The time has come, the truth is very close. But now, in this moment, I'm no longer sure I even want to hear it.

Chapter Fifteen

I search for words but can't find any. All I can find are beginnings with no endings. I open and close my mouth like a fish out of water and still don't make a single sound. As if he could sense my distress, Simon waits and just looks at me with that special expression. A mixture of warmth and concern. Can I really trust him?

'So…' I start again, and this time I even manage to get the first word out before my courage fails me once more.

Suddenly Simon is very close to me, his hand resting warm on my skin. He doesn't say anything, just gives me an encouraging nod.

'I…' I try again, '...I can't. I just can't, I'm sorry.' It's impossible to keep looking at him. It was wrong to drag him down. But letting him go wouldn't have been right either. Or would it?

'Hey.' With his index finger, he lifts my chin until I'm once more sinking into the blue-green world of his eyes. They're like the tranquil waters of a sheltered lagoon; they look like a place where I could be free. 'It's not that bad.' His voice is gentle.

I'd love to run my fingers along the contours of his jaw and feel the tickle of his three-day stubble.

I can barely manage to ignore the pull in my belly when I look at him. Even though I know it's wrong. Only an idiot would trust a man in my situation. Still, he draws me in like a spider weaving a web. My mind screams no. But my heart whispers a soft, longing yes. It wants to make me believe that nothing I do could ever be wrong when it comes to Simon. That I'm allowed to laugh and dream with him. And that when I do, I'll finally feel good again.

A smile flashes across his face. 'We should walk around a bit. It's easier to talk when you're moving.'

Is he right about that? 'Okay,' I say hesitantly, because a part of me so badly wants this not to end.

Together we get up from the sofa, stroll down the hallway, and slip into our shoes. Even as I open the front door, I can feel the relief. And I know a part of my tension will stay behind here. In this house, so crammed full of memories that it feels like a cage ready to burst open.

We step out into the starry night and cross the front yard. In the distance, the faint engine noise of a car can be heard; otherwise, it's quiet.

There are lights on in my neighbors' houses. Through the windows I see happy families at dinner, couples watching TV, and beaming teenagers on the phone. Unconsciously, I turn around and look back. My own house lies in darkness, as if it wanted to say to the whole world that no one here is really alive anymore.

Simon reaches for my hand and laces his fingers through mine as if we were lovers. 'Don't worry, it's not going anywhere,' he says, gently tugging me with him onto the sidewalk.

We stroll off, slowly and in silence. Over and over again, his thumb strokes tenderly over the back of my hand. With every step I grow calmer and stronger, not least thanks to Simon, whose proximity makes me feel as if I were surrounded by a protective shield. I want to do it. I want to muster my courage and tell him everything. So I count down to myself. Three—take a deep breath again. Two—loosen my shoulders. One—clear my throat.

A pause.

'I'm married.' The words shoot out of me, yet his thumb keeps stroking my skin, undeterred; I can't detect even the briefest hesitation. 'Heinrich. My husband. He…' No, I can't. My shoulders slump forward, my legs turn as heavy as blocks of granite.

Abruptly, Simon stops. Then he lifts his arm, his fingers touch my cheek, hold it, and turn my head toward him. There's so much warmth in his eyes, and I know that only if I tell him can I finally get rid of this burden.

'He's in prison.' I sound hard and emotionless, as if I weren't a human being but a machine. 'My husband… the father of my children… is a murderer.'

Even if I tried to blink the tears away, I'd be powerless against the pressure they carry within them. So here I am, not even five hundred meters from my house, and suddenly I feel naked. The dark asphalt beneath my eyes blurs, I press my hands to my face and give in. I'm completely quiet, I don't sob and I don't sniffle. Because the damp traces on my skin are already screaming the truth out into the world loudly enough.

Now I notice Simon's arms wrapping around my body. He doesn't do anything but hold me, and it feels as if he knows exactly how right that is. My head sinks against his chest, I breathe in the fresh scent of his skin, and I let my emotions run wild. I don't care whether it's smart or appropriate. Because now, in this very moment, it's everything I need.

For quite a while we stand entwined like lovers in the moonlight. His hand gently strokes my back, his cheek rests on the crown of my head. He doesn't say a word, doesn't try to talk me into anything, and doesn't think he knows everything. That's probably exactly what gives me enough trust to go on talking.

'I should've seen it coming, the signs were there.' Individual scenes flicker in my mind's eye. As charming and courteous as Heinrich was, there were moments when I barely recognized him. 'Once, Michael tore a hole in his new jacket while playing. And that was right before we were supposed to leave for some awards ceremony we'd dressed up for. Heinrich was beside himself with rage.'

I clench my fists because, looking at it with fresh eyes, the picture is so clear.

'Everything always had to be perfect. If not on the inside, then at least on the outside. With his jaw clenched, he was about to go for Michael.'

Simon still doesn't say anything. As if he knew he just has to let me talk. The fact alone that he understands that feels as if he's taking part of my burden and wants to carry it for me, if only for a moment.

'I immediately stepped between the two of them and let him grab my forearm instead of Michael's. For days I had bruises right where he had clutched me so aggressively, as if he wanted to strangle me. Back then it was nothing more to me than a dark moment in an otherwise bright life. He apologized and swore he'd never do it again. But there's more inside Heinrich than just one single person. I was stupid enough to always want to see only his charming side.' And at the same time so naive as to hope I could spare my own children what happened to me. A divorce that could have ended just as ugly as my parents'.'

I take a breath, because what I'm about to say will send a single bolt of pain shooting through my body.

'Then he killed Chris. An innocent child, just five years old. Can you imagine that?' All at once I can hardly breathe. The memory catches up with me like a storm front you can't escape.

He clears his throat and pulls me tighter against his warm body. 'Who is Chris?' His voice wavers.

The little boy's face appears before my eyes. I see him playing with Michael, shrieking with joy, his cheeks flushed red. A broad smile is on his lips, the autumn wind whirls through his dark hair.

'He didn't do anything, why did he have to die?' I whisper, because I still can't believe it. 'How can a person do something like that? How could Heinrich…' My voice breaks again.

'Who is Chris?' Simon repeats his question, as if he sensed how important this is.

I dive back into my memory and widen the scope. Chris and Michael are swinging in the park, as high as they can. Late summer has begun to color the leaves on the trees. Dark red, brown, and yellow, they sail from the branches and land on the weathered slats of the wooden bench I'm sitting on. The still-strong rays of the sun warm my face, the park is filled with children's laughter and dogs barking.

I'm not alone. Right next to me, arm to arm, sits Kathi. Wrapped in a colorful knitted vest, her reddish hair cut into a chin-length bob and tucked behind her ears. She smiles at me. If only I could see her like that just one more time. Full of warmth.

And full of joy.

I'd give anything for that.

Pleadingly, I look up at Simon, as if his face might hold answers to questions I can't begin to articulate. 'We could have been happy. Together we would have been one big family.' I still can't grasp that all of that no longer exists. Heinrich destroyed it. A very familiar feeling of disappointment crawls up inside me and bursts through my fists.

Simon clears his throat, shifts his weight from one leg to the other and then back again. His chest rises and falls heavily, as if my words were touching him right there. As if he could feel the pain together with me.

'Chris is—no, he was—Kathi's son. The boy next door.'

I've done it, now he knows. My husband killed my friend's child and in doing so bulldozed everything we had, right down to the ground.

'I understand,' Simon whispers and gently rests his chin on the crown of my head again.

I pull away from the hug and look him straight in the eyes. 'No, you don't,' I say in a choked voice. 'No one does.'

Pity and despair are carved into his face. His eyes shine alarmingly bright in the diffuse light of the streetlamp. 'Explain it to me. Please!' he says, and he sounds as if his own life depended on my answer too.

Not for a single moment do I wonder anymore whether I can trust him. Because in truth I already see it in his eyes. I gather every bit of strength I have left, take his hand, and start to run.

After only a few yards I start to talk. 'No one had as many dolls as a child as Kathi did. And no one cared for them as lovingly as she did. My friend always carried them with her, watched over them, and did everything she could to make sure they were all right. Having a big family of her own, that was what she always dreamed of.'

At once I see the eight-year-old version of my friend in front of me, explaining to me that her doll has a sore throat and therefore can't come outside to play. Only for a brief moment does her worried gaze wander from the doll in her arms to me, while her body sways gently back and forth.

'After Chris was born, Kathi fell ill. And even though every doctor told her she couldn't have any more children, she refused to accept it. Month after month I watched her disappointment and stood by her as best I could. We were a team, closely intertwined and always there for each other.'

Through my tear-filled eyes I look at Simon. He nods and looks as if he knows there are no words in this world that could bring me any comfort.

'Over the years Kathi began to accept that Chris would remain an only child. From then on, all her love belonged even more to that little boy.' My throat tightens. 'He was the light of her life,' I whisper hoarsely.

Just thinking about it drains the last of my strength. Simon moves closer, his arm once again wrapping protectively around my shoulders, and I hook my arm through his as we continue to wander through the night. Surrounded by silence, accompanied by the light of the stars above us.

'It was a cold, wet November day when Chris didn't come home from school. Kathi was frantic with worry and of course I was with her. I wanted to calm her down, I kept talking to her and calling around to find out what might have happened. No one knew anything, no one had seen Chris. With every passing minute my friend grew more panicked, and although it should have been my job to give her courage, I couldn't do it. I have children myself, after all! If one of my two treasures were missing, I don't know how my heart could go on beating. Simon understands that, he just has to. His hand moves up and down my spine, comforting and warm. We searched the area, over and over again. In vain. It was as if the city had swallowed him up.'

I stop walking.

'Until we found him,' I finally add.

Simon pulls me tightly against him, but even that can't make the terrible memories fade. Back then I thought this was the darkest day of my life. Because I had no idea what was about to happen next.

'He wasn't alone. Heinrich was with him.'

Even today I can still hear my friend's shrill scream in my ears, so piercingly loud that for a moment the whole world seemed to flinch. It shoots through each and every one of my bones and bores deep into my soul.

'That was the beginning of the end.' Even I can hear the emotionless sound of my voice. It's the only way I can keep what happened at a distance.

Simon clears his throat, as if he can't find any words and yet urgently wants to speak. 'I don't know…' he says in a hoarse voice, then breaks off and exhales loudly.

He's awkward, but that's exactly what does me good. So many people have pretended over the past few months that they knew exactly what was right. Everyone was smart and strong; no one else seemed to feel as powerless and weak as I did.

I try to give him a grateful smile. I can't manage it; the corners of my mouth are too heavy. 'Kathi hates me. My children keep asking about Chris and on top of that they want their father back. It's grotesque, but they love him despite everything. And I...'

'...you're stuck in the middle,' Simon finishes my sentence, because I can't do it myself.

'I trusted Heinrich, loved him, shared a bed with him. Just the thought that I left him alone with our children makes my stomach turn inside out, so violently that I know the feeling will stay with me forever. If he had done something to Moritz or Michael...' I clap my hand over my mouth. Numbing panic races through my body.

How could I not have seen it sooner? The signs were there. His obvious distance from the children, and the way he never allowed anything but his own opinion. Why was I so blind?

The questions echoed through my head and left little room for anything else. I gasped for air, yet I was suffocating. On the memory.

Even though it was hardly possible, Simon pulled me even closer to him. 'It's over,' he murmured into my hair.

'Is it?' I asked, feeling a spark of hope flare up inside me. I wanted so much to believe it, but could I really?

'Of course.' He looked at me with a loving expression in his eyes and stroked his fingertips over my forehead, as if he wanted to drive the worries from my thoughts.

'But how am I ever supposed to forget?' Inevitably I saw Michael's face before me, which reminded me of Heinrich day after day. And then Kathi's hate-filled eyes in the courtroom, her silence which spoke a thousand words of accusation, and the mute tears.

'Let me help you.' He sounded so tender and full of melancholy. Carefully he took my face in both his hands and dried my tear-stained cheeks with his thumbs.

Where everything had just been damp and cold, my skin

suddenly grew warm. Could what he was saying really be true? There was nothing I wanted more than to believe him. Desperately I searched his eyes for a sign. In the darkness they looked like the sea at night. They captured me and wouldn't let me go.

'But how?' I asked tonelessly.

In slow motion, a smile appeared on his face. Its light and warmth reached me, and I wanted only one thing.

Letting myself fall while he holds me. Forgetting everything around me for a moment, as long as he's watching over me.

As if the sky wanted to do away with me, it suddenly starts raining out of nowhere. Fine drops of water hit our heads, cold and wet, but I barely register it. Because Simon's face is suddenly so close that I can feel his breath brushing over my skin. Right where my worries usually sit, just behind my forehead, everything is now empty. There's only a profound sense of longing flooding my body.

I've been fighting it for weeks, but today I just have to do it.

Bit by bit I close the distance between us. The tips of our noses touch. His scent surrounds me like a fog that silences my thoughts, while the drizzle, growing heavier and heavier, beads over our cheeks and soaks our clothes.

The world around us disappears; nothing exists anymore except the two of us. All I can hear is the pounding of my heart.

Then, finally, my lips touch his.

I fall. But in the very next moment it feels as if I'm flying.

Chapter Sixteen

No matter how low the clouds hang over the city today, when I look through the dirty windows of my apartment, it's as if the sun were shining.

Because I can still feel her kiss on my mouth.

I shake my head quickly, because I shouldn't keep thinking about it. I clearly went too far. It was a moment of weakness, nothing more. It definitely doesn't mean anything and it's not going to happen again. Besides, that was yesterday; today I've got myself back under control. I have to, after all, because in just under five hours I'll be starting my late shift at the prison.

The buzzing of my phone grabs my attention. A message from Mira! 'Good morning' is all it says, and still I immediately feel as if I'm high. On the most damn dangerous drug of all.

I can't help it; I wish her a good morning too and casually ask what she's up to today. This is just a normal conversation. Nothing I should have to worry about.

'Kids' birthday party,' she writes. 'And you?'

Good question. 'Thinking about you,' I type automatically. Horrified, I stare at the words.

What the hell is suddenly wrong with me?

I delete the text at once. 'Nothing special. Chilling, tidying up. The usual stuff.' That's innocuous enough to send.

Her reply comes less than a minute later. 'Well then, have fun with that.'

That sounds like an ending. And I don't want an ending. Even if we spent hours talking about the best choice of cleaning rags, that would be totally fine with me.

Of all moments, the shrill sound of the doorbell suddenly interrupts my confused thoughts. I jump, as if I'd been caught me doing something forbidden, and hurry to the door. Through the peephole I see Paul's hungover face. I shove the phone into my pocket and let him in.

'Good morning.' Grinning, I hold my fist out to him.

Paul twists his mouth as if he'd just knocked back a shot with way too much alcohol in it. 'Don't yell like that, man,' he says accusingly. Then he trudges into my apartment and drops onto the sofa. The springs squeak in protest, and he flinches, his face contorted with pain.

'Repair beer?' Just in case, I head for the fridge. His strained grumble is answer enough. As I set the bottle down for him on the worn little wooden table in front of the sofa, he suddenly looks at me as if I were a stranger. 'Are you sick?'

I laugh. 'No, I just don't feel like beer.'

Suspiciously, he narrows his eyes and stares at me with his glassy gaze. 'What the hell happened to you?'

'I think the more pressing question is what happened to you. You look like you came straight from Ballermann.' And that's putting it politely. His *Final Destination* shirt is stained, he smells like a keg of beer, and the tips of his hair look as if someone had dipped them in oil.

Keeping a respectful distance, I join him and take a big swig of mineral water, which keeps fizzing away in my stomach.

Now his mouth twists into a grin. 'You missed the most awesome party ever,' he says, letting his head fall back against the sofa. 'There were women... every single one a perfect ten.'

Smirking, I watch him close his eyes for a moment. 'Got it. So what's her name?'

He immediately lets his head droop again. 'Women,' he says with a contemptuous undertone, making a dismissive gesture. 'They're dangerous beasts. You've got to stay away from them.' He sounds more than a little sad. As if, deep under his skin, something else is hurting besides his hangover.

'Could be.' Thoughtfully, I pull my phone out of my pocket. No new message. Too bad.

It shouldn't be happening, but Mira's face just pushes its way into my thoughts. That mix of suspicion and hope in her almost black eyes won't let me go. My whole life I was never shy around women, but when we said goodbye last night, I suddenly got as insecure as a schoolboy facing his first crush. For minutes we stood in the middle of the street in front of her house. In the diffuse light of a streetlamp, feeling miles away from Vienna, Europe, and even our planet. It was as if her mere proximity was enough to make me forget what I need in life. And that's definitely not her. No way.

'Should I leave again?' Paul leans over to me and nudges my upper arm.

His breath streams straight into my nose. He reeks of

alcohol and unbrushed teeth. 'For now I'd be grateful if you'd spare me your fumes.' I push him away from me. 'What makes you think that?'

Shrugging, he looks at me. 'You were totally gone for minutes, man. I thought I was interrupting something.'

'Everything's fine, I just had to think a bit.' I lean back, relaxed, and lace my hands behind my head.

'I might be hungover, but I'm not stupid. Thinking looks different. Completely different.' He nods vigorously, but quickly reins himself in and grabs the back of the sofa. 'Phew,' is all he says, and waits a moment. Then he studies me with furrowed brows, as if that would help him see me better. 'So how did your evening go yesterday? With that old Peters chick.'

'She's not old,' slips out of me. I immediately bite my tongue. I shouldn't have said that. Especially not in a tone like I wanted to defend her.

'Aha. So that's how it is.'

I quickly wave it off. 'Rubbish.'

'You don't seriously think you can hide something like that from me. How long have we known each other? Twenty years?' He shakes his head in disbelief. 'Forget it, I can see perfectly well what's going on here.'

'You're imagining things, there's nothing. I just want to find out what was going on with the family of the supposedly murderous professor.' It's hard for me to look at him. He's studying me far too closely. I'm sure he'd notice any hesitation, any suspicious twitch at the corners of my mouth and even the slightest wobble in my voice. Hangover or not. So I try not to think about the fact that I already know the secret. Peters manipulated me and lied to me. He killed the boy, I'm sure of that by now.

In silence, Paul reaches for the bottle and takes a swig

without taking his eyes off me. Then he slams the beer down on the low table in front of us and turns to me. 'Did you just say family? The old hag has kids?' he asks in a tone that doesn't bode well. 'You haven't forgotten what that means, have you?'

I feel anger rising in me. Can he just stop calling Mira an old hag?

'A family costs you everything. There are no parties and no sleeping in, just responsibility, financial obligations, and constantly putting your own wishes on the back burner.' His intense glare locks in on me. 'If you decide on a life like that, you'll end up just like your father,' he adds on top of everything else.

His words hang between us like smog on the streets of a big city. Does he really have to drag my father into this now? He's not allowed to do that. Not even when we're alone, and he knows that perfectly well. Like a robot, I run through my routine. I swallow, breathe, and bite my lip.

'Stop poking around in my life and go get one of your own,' I spit out at last.

'Just don't let that woman fool you into anything,' he counters seriously, raising his index finger in warning. 'That will only end badly for you.'

'There's no danger of that anyway,' I say, because that's exactly how it is. Everything's cool, my mission is over, I never have to see Mira again. In a week I'll have forgotten her. It's that simple.

'Please, I only have to look at you. That idiotic grin when you stare off into nowhere. That disappointed look when your phone shows neither new calls nor messages. You pull that stupid thing out every two minutes. With the expression of a child waiting to see the Easter Bunny hop past.' He snorts contemptuously. 'Watching you is like 4K television. The picture is razor sharp.'

Anger was bubbling up inside me. He should stop it; what I did or didn't do was absolutely none of his business. 'Just. Drop. It.'

He raised his hands defensively. 'I'm just saying you should be careful, that's all. If only because you'll be taking off from here soon.'

Right. My trip. That was what I should be focusing on. Relieved that we were finally changing the subject, I unclenched my jaw. 'Oh yeah, I've been counting down the days for ages.' I jerked my head toward the calendar on the small round kitchen table. I'd apparently forgotten to tear off a page this morning; it should have been showing sixty days until my departure. Or was it fifty?

'Have you already got everything? What else do you need? You're not going to forget the motorbike. But what about the tent? Sleeping bag, camping stove, all that stuff?'

All at once, life returned to Paul's previously fatigued body. Smirking, I watched him fish an unopened bill from my windowsill and scribble things all over the envelope in wild disorder.

'Thanks, Mommy, that's so sweet of you,' I remarked, amused.

'If little Simon won't do it himself, Mommy has to help.' He wrote something else on the list that could have been condoms. Then he drew an exclamation mark after it, and that was how I knew for sure. I hadn't misread it.

While Paul chewed thoughtfully on the end of the ballpoint pen, apparently searching for clues somewhere outside the window between the façades of the gray-brown prefab buildings, my thoughts got stuck on the condoms. The idea of using them on the road overwhelmed me.

On top of that, everything inside me suddenly started to rebel when I imagined how I'd say goodbye to Mira.

That must not happen.

My body is lying.

'Man, a little more interest wouldn't go amiss.' Paul looks up from his scribbling, accusingly.

'Excuse me?' I try in vain to get rid of my physical symptoms. Maybe I should go get myself a beer after all.

Like a diva, Paul rolls his eyes. 'I asked how much cash you've already saved. With all those weekend shifts last month, you must've raked in quite a bit.'

With his pen, he taps hard on the wooden tabletop next to the envelope, which is now alarmingly filled with writing.

'Ooh, no idea. I'd have to check.' I've clearly neglected my finances a bit.

'You can't be serious. Have you done anything at all? Canceled the lease for this place here, for example? Or asked about the insurance?'

I deserve his reproachful look; I really have let things slide. 'Sorry. But I'll catch up on it today, no problem.'

'Sure, then go ahead and call the office right now and find out what happens,' he says dryly. 'Today is Sunday, and I know that even though I've just had the party of my life.' He is shooting daggers at me with his glare. 'You're even more dazed by this woman than I thought.'

I laugh as if he'd made a joke, even though I don't feel like laughing at all. 'It's just been a lot, that's all. I'll take care of my trip.'

He isn't impressed. 'This is your lifelong dream,' he says urgently, waving the envelope demonstratively in front of my nose. 'The thing you've been working toward for years, the most important thing in your life.'

'Of course it is,' I cut off his lecture and yank the paper

out of his hand. 'See? I'm stuffing all your notes into my pocket and I'll work through them one by one. For you, I'll even put a check mark after every item once it's done.'

He doesn't laugh; on the contrary, his expression grows more serious. 'I'll be checking.'

'But of course, Mommy.' I punch him in the side and, for a moment, I even tolerate the reek of alcohol surrounding him. 'Don't worry, I've got this under control.' It's a simple as that.

'That's all right then.' I can see he doesn't believe me, but at least he lets the subject drop for now.

I'd love nothing more than to breathe a sigh of relief. Still, there's this nasty thought in my head. Up there it strolls back and forth as if it were looking for a place to permanently settle.

What if Paul is right? What if I really am in danger of getting lost, losing my head, and doing things that aren't good for me?

Chapter Seventeen

Another night settles over the city while I stand at Michael's bedroom window and look at the street in front of our house. His steady breathing fills the room. It sounds as if he were breathing through an oxygen tank underwater, like a diver. Even so, it can't drown out the rushing of blood in my ears.

Over there, at the spot I can almost no longer see from here, is where we stood. So close together that I could feel him everywhere.

Kissing Simon was wrong. So how did it feel so right in that moment?

The memory gnaws at me. It eats me up from the inside out and devours the most important promise I ever made to myself. Yesterday, when I let Simon get way too close to me, I betrayed myself. I let myself fall and trusted him, even though I never wanted to do that again, with anyone.

I shouldn't keep staring at that spot out there. That won't get me anywhere. On the contrary, it's driving me crazy. So I turn around, tiptoe out of the nursery, and go down the stairs into the living room. My legs carry me of their own accord to the chest of drawers next to the fireplace and fold themselves right in front of it, cross-legged on the hard, cold floor.

For minutes I just stare at the dark-stained wooden drawer with its elegantly curved stainless-steel handle. In the middle, its silver base gleams through, but on the outside it's still exactly the way it used to be. Dark gray and matte, cultivated and restrained. Just like Heinrich.

My hand rises and falls, wanting to close around the handle and then not. In my distress I clench my fists.

Where is this supposed to lead? And how long do I want to keep trying to push the past away when it so relentlessly insists on travelling with me.

I have to get it over with once and for all. Now.

I try in vain to control the trembling of my fingers as they slide over the cold metal of the drawer handle. Holding my breath, I close my hand around it and pull the drawer open. As if they had been waiting for this very moment, the envelopes spill out toward me. Every one of them as white as innocence itself.

Love or hate. Forgiveness or anger. What's right?

It's time to decide. So I take the letters and sort them by the date on the postmark. Then I push myself up and do something I've never done before. I let myself sink into Heinrich's expansive reading chair. The dark green leather is as soft as silk. And just as cold. A shiver runs over my forearms, but that can't stop me.

I'm going to do it. No matter how much strength it costs me.

In the light of the floor lamp, I carefully unfold the paper. Heinrich's sweeping handwriting threatens to blur before my eyes. There's this part inside me that fights back like a defiant, wounded child. Filled with the fear of having to endure even more pain.

I had given in to that impulse for so long, and still it didn't change anything. For months I've felt as if my new reality had been immortalized on that one November day; a still image frozen in time.

But now it's supposed to start turning again, life has to go on, and the letters will help me decide how.

With my heart pounding, I start to read and sink deeper and deeper into the version of reality that Heinrich created for me, and for me alone.

Chapter Eighteen

So this is what it feels like to live in a cell. The floor gives off the smell of disinfectant. The mattress is hard and narrow, the pillow flat. When you lie here, all you see are cream-colored walls, the bare neon light on the ceiling and, through the glass of the minimalist window, a small patch of sky. Behind the bars, rain clouds are drifting over the prison today; it's been drizzling all morning. Nonstop. It's as if we were in London and not in Vienna.

Apart from the barely audible sound of water droplets pattering onto the asphalt in front of the cell block, everything is quiet. This isn't a pleasant place, but it's still better than sitting up front in the office. So I brought my work in here. But instead of finally starting on the mail check, I take my phone out of my pocket. I'm actually not allowed to have it on me at all, but I just couldn't leave it in my locker.

I haven't heard from Mira in four days. Should I write to her? Even if I wanted to, my mind is blank. No matter how hard I search, I can't find any words. Because I don't know what I want to say to her. Because there's only one truth.

That I must never see her again.

Not just because I'll be gone in a little over a month anyway. But also because it's way too dangerous. If word gets out here in the prison about what I've done over the past few weeks, I'll lose my job. On the spot. Two whole months' salary including bonuses would be missing from my travel fund.

Why on earth did I befriend a prisoner's wife to help him? I should never have taken that risk. On top of that, I enjoyed the time with Mira and waited for the right moment to come clean about the real reason we met. At the same time, I constantly had to be careful at work not to run into the professor. What was I even supposed to say to him? That Mira is simply stunning? And that by now I'm convinced he doesn't deserve my help?

Damn it. This has gone really wrong, and on top of that, it feels like there's nothing I can possibly do about it.

Sandy could probably show me how to get out of this mess. If she were here now, what would she tell me?

I remember our get-together last Friday at her place. Even at lunch, Sandy was one thing and one thing only that day. Happy. Her radiance was even stronger than usual and her movements freer. Mom apparently didn't notice. Chatty as ever, she served vegetable lasagna and tiramisu while, like always, I had to fight with myself to seem just as cheerful as she did. For their sake, after all, they're the last people to blame for what happened.

When Mom then said goodbye, I couldn't hold it back any longer. While we were working in the garden, I just had to ask Sandy about that glow of hers. In the depth of memory I clip off a shoot of the mulberry tree with the big garden shears. Then I look at her expectantly.

'What's going on with you?' I ask curiously.

She smiles. 'You noticed?' Thoughtfully, she stuffs the garden cuttings into the organic waste bin. 'Interesting, don't you think?'

Instead of answering, I just shrug. Because I don't even want to know what she's getting at with her question.

'Something really amazing happened.' I knew that expression. And the way she now kept dropping her gaze and then looking back up at me made me absolutely sure.

'Wow.' I know she'd like a different reaction from me, but I can't give her that.

Now her hand wanders upward and, floral gardening glove and all, comes to rest on her lower belly. 'One day you'll understand,' she says with a certainty that makes me wonder where she gets it from.

What am I supposed to understand? That she enjoys having children. I'm perfectly aware of that. I just don't know when she'll finally get that her dreams aren't mine.

Instead of going deeper into the subject, I turn back to the mulberry tree. 'Is this okay for you like this, or should I cut off this branch too?'

For a moment she studies me. She considers saying something more, but apparently decides against it. 'No, that looks good. Will you help me with the weeds back there in the corner by the pond?'

Relieved that she doesn't keep probing, I set the pruning shears aside and let my eyes wander. Sandy's garden isn't a normal garden. She herself calls it an enchanted garden, and even though I'd never admit it, every time I'm here something changes. As if there was magic at work, I feel different among the wild roses, the soothing babbling garden pond, and the many cozy places to perch.

'I can stay a little longer,' I say, and I even feel really good about it.

For a while we work side by side in silence, yanking out nettles and relocating earthworms. Little by little, a guilty conscience creeps over me because I struggle to truly be happy for my sister.

'Listen, Simon,' Sandy suddenly says into the silence, and just from her tone I can tell something is coming that I don't want to hear. 'About your trip…'

Immediately, pressure spreads across my forehead. I raise a hand defensively. 'Not today.' I look her straight in the eyes so she knows how serious I am. 'Please.'

Still, my sister seems unimpressed. 'Your wounds will never heal if you ignore them.'

So here we are, in the middle of her enchanted garden, and as we do so often, we're standing at a boundary I refuse to cross. So I do what I always do. I swallow, breathe, and bite my lip. So hard that a second later the metallic taste of blood spreads all through my mouth.

'You don't have to say anything. I just want one thing,' she continues now, her voice intense. 'At least allow for the thought that beyond your pain there's something else that would make it worth overcoming. Imagine what your life could be like if you left the past behind you.'

I shake my head; I can't do anything else. 'I don't have to. As soon as I've left Vienna, the past will no longer exist.'

Without being asked, Sandy pulls me into her arms. 'Your shadows will always follow you, no matter where you are. Only when you stop clinging to this escape can you see what you really need,' she whispers in my ear.

That was Sandy's answer last weekend, and it still

echoes in my thoughts today. But it doesn't help me while I'm still lying here in the cell, as if I were a prisoner myself. I lace my fingers behind my neck and fix my gaze on the outside world. Now that all I can see is the gray beyond the bars, it suddenly feels as if several voices are crowding my head alll at once.

Freedom, one of them cries triumphantly, projecting an image of me on the motorcycle right in front of my eyes.

I'm racing under the shimmering hot sun straight through the desert of Dubai, leaving a massive cloud of churned-up sand behind me. Vienna is behind me. The memory of what happened has faded.

Safety, another one murmurs, quiet and yet so piercing that I can feel it everywhere.

'What is this supposed to be?' I protest loudly, to drown out the babble of voices in my head. As if I've startled them, my talkative companions fall silent for a moment. 'Shut up, got it?' I snap with all the fervour I can muster, clenching my teeth.

Silence, there's silence in my thoughts. I exhale, relax my muscles, and let my eyelids fall shut.

At once, it's all back again.

The scent of vanilla, the hum of engines, dark eyes, the rush of air while driving. Faster and faster the impressions race past me. They close in on me in ever smaller circles, everything blurs together. I feel dizzy.

'Stop!' I tear my eyes open and jump up. I'm back. In the cell that isn't mine, even though deep down I feel as if I were a prisoner too.

Next to me the mail is waiting to be checked. The work will distract me, and I badly need that. Impatiently I flip open the lid, but I leave the stack of outgoing letters untouched. Anything but something from the professor right now. It's bad enough having to see him from a distance in the yard and knowing what's hiding behind his façade. I much prefer the boring stories about the world out there. So I immerse myself in accounts of which repairs need to be done on various faucets, which woman has once again hit on whom, and how god-awful the kids' grades at school are.

I'm almost through the stack now, and by this point I can breathe freely again. I reach for the last envelope.

'Heinrich Peters,' it says on the envelope.

I hastily turn it over. As if an ice age had broken out in a matter of seconds, my body freezes. And with it the cell around me. My whole surroundings change, only the sender stays the same.

Mira Peters.

Chapter Nineteen

The white paper has me in its grip. I could be lying on the Golden Beach, a cocktail beside me and my toes buried in the sand. Or eating a burger on the viewing deck of a ski lodge in Montana, surrounded by the babbling of other merry guests. It wouldn't matter, because this letter makes everything else meaningless.

Once more I look at the sender, but it still says Mira Peters. In handwriting that reminds me a little of a model pupil in elementary school. I have to smirk, but only for a moment, so brief it barely lasts the course of one inhalation of breath.

Hesitantly, my fingers move to the flap and pull out the paper. They do it on their own, as if not under my bodily control. As if they had their very own opinion about what should happen next. Unlike my head, which is firing off question after question at supersonic speed.

Did she read the professor's letters? How did it feel for her? And why is she answering him?

No, this is none of my business anymore.

All the same, my fingers carry on, unimpressed, unfolding the paper and raising the text up to my eyes. There's black ink on a white background. Like grief and innocence, tightly bound together.

Heinrich,

I'm writing to you even though I don't know what to say. I'm at a loss for words, in my head and even more so in my heart. You took my voice from me, on that fateful day you left our house in handcuffs.

Maybe I couldn't open your letters because I didn't understand how you could still find words even after everything. For weeks I didn't read a single one, but today I did. And now I see, blurred but still discernible, that I can do it too. Right in this moment I'm stringing letters together, forming words, building sentences.

For you, even though I don't know if you deserve it at all.

Who are you, Heinrich, who are you really? Who am I, that I could trust you so blindly? And who are we, you and I, Michael and Moritz?

Are we a family? Were we ever, really? In not one of your letters did you mention the two of them. Like you didn't care about them, as if they didn't exist for you.

Even though you absolutely don't deserve it, Michael asks about you every day. Just like he asks about Chris. I look at him, see you in his face, and hear my heart break; nothing more than the snapping of a dry branch.

Moritz wakes up at night drenched in sweat, screaming at the top of his lungs. I wipe the sweat from his forehead, smooth his hair back, and hold him tight. Then I rock him back and forth until he can sleep again.

This is my new life. You destroyed everything. Even what was never whole to begin with.

She wrote to him. Why the hell would she do that?

I jerk up from the bed so fast that the cell around me blurs. Still, I barely notice it. Because now an image is forming in my mind's eye.

The professor is holding Mira in his arms. Far too tightly, so she has no chance to fight back. He pulls her against him, she gasps for air, and where his hand lies on her skin, a dark blue bruise appears.

I fight it with everything I've got, but the damn image just gets clearer and clearer. It glows like a billboard in the night; I can even make out the fear in Mira's eyes. I feel like throwing up, but there's nothing in my stomach except a gigantic block of ice.

Right now, one thing becomes clear to me. Paul was right.

Mira matters to me. Far too much.

All my life I've fought to be free. But now, in this moment, I suddenly feel with absolute clarity that I'm not anymore.

A deep despair rushes through me. I swallow, breathe, and bite my lip. Once, and then again. But what served me so well for so many years suddenly doesn't help at all anymore.

I want to get away from here, away from the letter and away from this terrible fear that's threatening to break through every wall inside me.

So I start running, as if I had one chance, if only I were fast enough. But before I even leave the cell block, it not only catches up with me, but it pulls ahead and plants itself in front of me. Mighty and strong, like a rock on a sheer cliff that stands firm against the thunderous waves. Just as determined, my own fear now stands in front of me and forces me to stare into its ugly face.

Chapter Twenty

The memory is everywhere, weighing heavily on my soul and making my head feel like it's about to explode. Very slowly I drag myself down the corridor. The dull sound of my shoes in the hallway makes it seem like they weighed a thousand kilograms more than usual.

They do. Because my strength is needed elsewhere. Right next to my heart, where behind this door I've hidden what I never wanted to feel again. With a thunderclap, two worlds collide inside me and leave clear marks. Even so, I have to keep this door closed; I can't allow the memory to defeat me.

I'm sick. At least that's exactly what I'm about to tell my colleagues. Because there's one thing I know for sure: I have to get out of here as fast as possible. With slumped shoulders I enter the admissions office and announce to my colleagues that for the rest of the day I'd be better off in bed than in the workshop.

Petra looks at me doubtfully, while Horst immediately

takes a step back. 'Just stay away from me. If I bring your germs home, I'll never hear the end of it.'

Feeling wiped out, I touch my forehead. 'I really should lie down.'

'Absolutely, you look like you just crawled out of a coffin. And your eyes...' From a distance he examines me. 'You definitely have a fever. Go get yourself into bed, I'll let the boss know.'

I say goodbye and drag myself straight to the locker room. I have to regain my bearings again as quickly as possible. And there's only one person in this world who can help me do that.

Sandy.

No one knows me the way she does. And no one else can understand how suddenly tight this damned cage I've been sitting in for years has become.

I drive straight to her, even though I don't know if she's at home. Barely an hour later I'm standing in front of her front door, staring at the dreamcatcher she's mounted there while I press the doorbell. The red beads and orange feathers move together with the door. Sandy appears in the doorway; she doesn't say anything, just looks at me with that knowing expression and waves me inside.

I follow her through the short hallway into the kitchen. She has clearly just been working in here; the wooden countertop is covered with small jars, and the smell of freshly chopped chives hangs in the air.

'Sit down,' she says, pouring water into a glass for me.

I sink onto a chair covered with colorful fabric, my gaze landing on the Buddha picture on the wall. With folded hands and bowed head, he sits cross-legged on the floor and looks as if nothing could disturb his calm. As if he knew exactly where he belonged.

Why can't I be like him? Then I could get rid of my baggage too and finally find peace.

Sandy says nothing, she just comes over to the kitchen table with the cutting board and keeps chopping her chives.

For a while I watch her, then I brace myself and say what drove me here. 'I don't know what to do anymore, Sandy.'

She nods. 'I can see that. How can I help you?'

If only I knew. Basically I have no idea what I need, not in life and certainly not from her. But how am I supposed to explain that to her? 'There's this woman,' I begin. 'She's…' Yeah, what is she?

'Like a drug you always want more of?' Now she lifts her gaze and looks straight at me.

I prop my head up; it's just too heavy to keep carrying it any longer. 'I can't do it, Sandy,' I say, and even I can hear the desperation in my voice.

For a moment, lines form on her forehead. Then she gets that profound expression on her face. 'As long as you cling to your pain, it won't leave you.' She sets the knife aside and dries her hands on a dish towel. 'The wise man over there in the picture claims that letting go is the key to happiness. And you know what? He's absolutely right.'

As if it were that easy. As if I could ever forget what happened. I look at my sister, see her calm and her confidence. We went through the exact same thing, so how did she manage to put it behind her? 'What do you think I've been trying to do for years? I can't.'

Her hands move across the table and rest warmly on mine. 'You're afraid.'

Right on target. That's it. For years this one feeling has ruled me. And today it hit me with full force, spread through me, and painted a whole tapestry of ugly images in my mind. Even though I already know it won't help, I run through my calming routine.

'You alone decide how you deal with your fear,' I hear Sandy say, as if from far away.

Do I even have a choice? My fear is there, it tears me apart and doesn't go away. As if it enjoyed tormenting me and giving me that gnawing feeling that it would stay with me forever.

'What does the fear do to you? And what do you do with it?' she asks, undeterred. 'Look at it, Simon, look it straight in the eye. What do you see?'

No. It had cost me far too much strength to suppress these images. If I let them surface now, then it would have all been for nothing. I would have to start all over again, I would live through everything all over again. 'Please don't,' I whisper hoarsely.

There's no trace of pity in her face, no torment and no worry. 'It's time to take a step forward,' she says quietly and strokes my hand with her thumb. 'I'm here, no matter what happens, I'll catch you.'

I don't have to look at her to know that this is the truth. Maybe that's exactly it. Or my despair. The hopelessness or the secret knowledge that things can't go on like this. Whatever it is, I want to do it. For the very first time, I give in. I let go. The door inside me, locked tight for so long and constantly guarded, swings open.

In my mind, a whole world builds itself at breakneck speed. Suddenly I'm fourteen again, hanging out with my buddies behind the soccer stadium. We're drinking beer and puffing on cigarettes, acting like we're already grown up and talking like we know absolutely everything. When it's my turn to take a drag from the cig, my mother appears at the end of the street.

She sees what I'm doing and accelerates towards us. I have to cough and pass the butt on. It's better if I go to meet her. My buddies shouldn't see my mother telling me off. That would be uncool, and I'm definitely not uncool. So I saunter toward her, making a point of looking relaxed, but with every step I lose more of my feigned self-confidence.

It's the expression on her otherwise so even, regular face that makes me pause. She isn't angry, even though that's exactly what she should be.

Instead, there's pain.

Her lips are just a thin line, the color of her skin is pale, her cheeks are sunken. But worst of all, the very worst, is what I see in her eyes. They're bloodshot, swollen all around, and full of sadness.

There are only a few meters left between us when I notice the crumpled tissues in both her hands and, on top of that, how tightly she's clutching them. The veins on the backs of her hands are standing out sharply.

'What's wrong, Mom?' I dare to ask when we're finally standing in front of each other.

I can't yet know that this is a mistake, the biggest one of my life, even.

That moment was eleven years ago now. Still, I experience it today just as intensely as I did back then. I gasp for air, my stomach and every single muscle in my body clench. So many years ago it was my mother who then took me in her arms. Today it's Sandy. I don't know when she came over to my side of the table, but now she's here. And she's holding me tight.

Overwhelmed by the memory, I say what's weighing on my heart. 'If I live our father's life, I'll end up just like he did.'

That's it. That's my greatest fear of all.

And that's the reason why I'm not allowed to be with Mira. I wouldn't be able to do it, I'd have to leave her one day just as cruelly as my father left my mother, Sandy, and me. No one should ever go through what the three of us had to endure. Least of all Mira and her children. I'd plunge her into misery, and I don't want to do that to her.

'Our father was ill,' Sandy says quietly now, as if that explained everything.

'He killed himself. Because he couldn't stand being trapped by our family anymore,' I counter. 'He couldn't bear the responsibility. Or the obligation.' Grief and disappointment. Love and despair. All of it is now pushing its way out through the door inside me, and my defenses are no longer enough to hold it back.

My muscles are shaking, I can't breathe anymore.

It's as if the feelings had been growing for years behind that damned door. Now they're surging out like a tidal wave, an unstoppable force, dragging me along with them.

Sandy strokes my back. She waits, stays silent, and holds me tight. As long as it takes for the storm to pass. Then she lets go of me and looks deep into my eyes. 'Every person lives their own life.'

'Look at me. I am him. He is me,' I protest. Sandy knows that's true. Even better than I do myself. 'There's no reason why it should be any different for me.'

'I can think of thousands,' she says softly. 'Give life a chance to show you what it has in store for you. I know you can do it. And I know that deep down you even want it.' Her hand touches my chest, right where my heart is, which starts pounding louder, right on cue.

'I can't just forget everything and pretend I'm not what I am.' It would be like suddenly taking a step that was ten, a hundred, or a thousand times greater than any before.

Sandy hands me a tissue. 'And what are you?'

Broken. I don't say it, I only think it, and still my sister can see the answer in my eyes. Behind my laid-back, cool façade I'm above all one thing. A fucking coward. Someone who thinks he can run away from his own shadow if he just tries hard enough. At least that much I understand now.

'And what do you really want to be?' Sandy asks.

Free. That's the only word that comes to mind. This burden shouldn't weigh on my soul any longer; it has to disappear. Once and for all.

'Whoever always walks the same paths will always end up in the same place.'

I've heard this sentence from Sandy so many times. But I never understood what she was trying to tell me with it. Today is different. Everything is different, right now, as her index finger wanders across my forehead. Because suddenly, all at once, I understand what she means.

I clear my throat. 'It's never too late to leave the past behind. Every day is a new chance, and it's up to me alone what I make of it.' Saying it out loud feels strange. I sound like my sister and yet I don't recoil.

Sandy nods. She smiles at me, a watery sheen lying over her eyes.

'What if I choose the wrong path?' I ask carefully. Wouldn't that be disastrous? Couldn't that end even worse than if I just carried on as before?

A smirk emerges on her face. 'What do you think?' she asks, but I don't know what she means by that. 'Think about what you just said.'

I immediately think back, and I don't have to search for long. 'Every day is a new chance, and it's up to me alone what I make of it.' It isn't a question but a fact. I feel it with a certainty that leaves absolutely no room for doubt.

And right now I make a decision.

Chapter Twenty-One

'In the summer play, I'm playing a scientist.' Michael looks incredibly proud as he beams at me from the low bench in the kindergarten cloakroom. 'I have to wear glasses, and Ms. Stephanie said my hair is going to be sprayed with gray paint!'

'Wow, that's great.' I try to sound excited, even though I'm not. Couldn't he be a flower, or a butterfly, instead of becoming even more like his father?

Quickly I turn my gaze to the buggy where Moritz is sitting, watching the surroundings decorated with drawings and crafts. I follow his eyes, well aware that I absolutely must not do that.

It's a compulsion. I know exactly what's about to happen, but I still can't stop myself.

On the wall, directly above Michael's seat, Chris's photo is still hanging. With his unique mischievous grin and his spiky haircut, he hardly looks like Kathi. But in his eyes I recognize my friend just as she used to be. Warm and lively, loving and radiant.

I'd give so much for her to look at me like that again.

Just once, then I'd know that everything would still turn out all right.

'What are you doing?' Michael's words reach my ears as if through cotton. He tugs at my skirt. 'Mommy!'

My eyes automatically return to him. Only now do I notice that my hands are clenched into fists. 'Put your shoes on, sweetheart,' I murmur and stretch out my fingers.

While I try to calm myself with a deep breath, my big boy closes the Velcro on his sandals without a word and puts his kindergarten shoes back in their place so neatly you'd think he was an adult.

Then we weave our way past the other children and go outside. We used to wave goodbye to the kindergarten teacher together. Now it's only Michael who can still catch a warm smile from the guardian. For months, I have been sneaking myself away, as if I'd done something terrible.

'What should we do this afternoon?' I ask my two sons as we leave the kindergarten. The rain has stopped. The air is warm, maybe too warm for mid-June, but at least there's that tingling feeling the sun's rays leave on my skin.

Michael looks up at me hopefully. 'Visit Dad,' he suggests, and I instantly regret my question. His light-blue eyes fixed on me, he pushes his lower lip forward, hooks his fingers together, and rocks his upper body back and forth. 'Please, Mom. Please, please, please!'

With my lips pressed together, I crouch down in front of him. 'I thought we'd have a picnic in the park. Doesn't that sound great too?' I ask, forcing a smile.

Michael furrows his brow. 'Picnics are stupid. I want to see Dad.' As if the situation weren't already awkward enough, he now stomps his foot hard on the ground and folds his arms. Luckily there aren't any other parents nearby right now. They'd definitely look at me with contempt. Because they can't even begin to imagine what it's like to live my life.

'I understand that. But it's not possible today.' I reach my hand out to him, wanting to pull him close and hug him tight.

But he shrugs me off like an annoying fly. Out of the corner of my eye I see Moritz, who is sticking his fingers through the chain-link fence of the single-family house next to the sidewalk from his buggy. If he touches the stem of the seductively fragrant rose behind it, I'll have a crying child on my hands in seconds. On top of the other one who's glaring at me, offended.

'When then? When can I see Dad?' Michael sounds defiant, but just a few seconds later tears begin to gather in his eyes.

A feeling of guilt as massive as an entire mountain range grows in my stomach. But how could I possibly allow Heinrich to have contact with our little ones? They mean nothing to him. To me, on the other hand, they're absolutely everything. No one is allowed to hurt them, and he already has. That's not going to happen again.

'I can't promise you anything.' That's the truth, and maybe Michael can even sense it. At least he lets me rest my hand against his soft child's cheek. 'I'm so, so sorry. Please believe me.' I whisper so he won't hear the trembling in my voice as clearly.

Over and over again I run my thumbs over his face. Even though I'm blinking as hard as I can, tears gather in the corners of my eyes. I close my lids one more time in the hope of delaying them, then I can't hold them back any longer.

It's just a single salty tear running down my cheek, and yet it carries everything inside it.

Now Michael raises his hand with a confused expression, his finger following the damp trail on my skin. That doesn't make it any easier. On the contrary, my body tightens as if a powerful electric shock were shooting through it.

Can't anyone help me? Who will hold me up when I can't go on anymore? Who will speak for me when I have no words?

I would collapse, right here on the spot, here in the middle of the asphalt sidewalk on our street, if it weren't for those two pairs of children's eyes. They look at me questioningly, and I know I have to be there for them. No matter what happens. I press my fingernails firmly into my palms and exhale in short bursts. Then, with all my strength, I pull the corners of my mouth up.

'So, you two, are you ready for the picnic?' I can hear myself how unnaturally shrill I sound.

'But only if we go to the big playground. The one with the kids' zip line and the steep slide.' Michael is still grumpy.

Even so, I breathe a sigh of relief. The discussion about his father is over. I know it will come back, but for this moment I've made it.

'Of course,' I say lovingly, even though that playground is on the other side of town.

I try again, and now my big boy does let me hug him. Relieved, I bury my nose in his hair and stroke his back. Moritz reaches out a curious hand toward us. I draw him into our embrace. The three of us are a family, as imperfect as I never wanted one to be. And yet I'm glad to at least still have this.

'I can't breathe, Mom.' Michael braces his fists against my chest.

His expression inevitably makes me grin. 'Sorry, I guess I just love you both too much.'

'I know that.' Michael rolls his eyes theatrically toward the sky. 'Love you too.'

'Love Mama,' Moritz babbles and stretches his short arms up into the air.

My tears threaten to come back, but this time I smile them away. 'You're the greatest kids in the world.'

Michael starts bouncing up and down like a rubber ball. He seems to have had enough of my emotional outburst. 'Whoever gets home first,' he yells, and takes off at a sprint.

Moritz squirms back and forth in the stroller too. He wants out just as badly, so I undo the buckle and give him a signal to start running. Only I stay behind and watch as the two of them race off through the adjoining park, hair flying and arms swinging.

The bright sound of their sneakers on the gravel path grows fainter, when suddenly my phone rings.

It's Simon. Five days after our kiss and four days after our last brief messages, he calls me.

Stop it, my mind protests. Finally, my heart screams. My finger hovers indecisively over the screen, then I answer the call.

'Hey.' My attempt to sound relaxed fails miserably.

For a moment the line is silent. There's a soft clearing of a throat, then he finally says something. 'Hello, water girl.' His tone goes straight to the center of my chest. Deep and melodious, with a hint of uncertainty. 'Do you miss me already?'

I quickly glance at my kids, who by now are nothing but splashes of color on the park's green horizon, and start walking. 'Not at all.' I have to grin, even though there's no reason to.

Now he laughs freely too. 'I don't miss you either. Not one bit. I actually didn't even want to call. My phone just did it all by itself.'

He sounds so innocent, like a harmless kitten, when in truth he's as dangerous as a full-grown tiger.

'Fascinating, the advances in technology these days.' My pulse is racing as if I were running, but in reality I'm just strolling leisurely along the short rose alley. Tense with anticipation, I press the phone closer to my ear. Simon doesn't say anything. It takes too long.

'I need to see you, preferably right now,' he suddenly blurts out. He sounds as if the hurdle of getting those words out had been impossibly high for him.

Right now that longing overwhelms me again. For the feeling of closeness, the scent of his skin, and the way he looks at me. It's as if my mind is leaving me. It drifts away from me, far, far out into another galaxy. All that's left are the feelings, even warmer than the rays of the sun shining directly above me.

'That would be great,' I say without thinking.

'Mooooom.' That's Michael's voice. I look ahead and see him impatiently rattling the garden gate of our house. 'Come on, we want to go in!'

Reality slams into me in a split second and leaves nothing but devastation. Where everything was still rosy just a moment ago, the gray of the sidewalk and the blackness of the trash cans now dominate the scene. 'We can't see each other today,' I say quickly to Simon.

'I won't survive this.' He sounds so determined that I almost believe him.

Involuntarily, I flinch. I want to be with him, so I run

through the options in my head. It's not the first time I regret having come to Vienna for Heinrich and leaving my own family behind in Berlin. If my mother were here, a lot of things would be easier. As it is, only Eva can take the kids. She's working today, but Friday should work. 'The day after tomorrow?'

'By then I'll have dropped dead.' It's probably meant to sound like a joke, but it still comes across terribly serious.

'I just can't make it today.' I put a contrite emphasis on my words so he knows how hard this is for me.

He exhales loudly. 'Why not?'

Because of the two little faces now watching closely as I pull the key out of my handbag and unlock the garden gate. Should I tell him that? Better not. 'I already have plans,' I answer evasively. 'I can't change them at such short notice.' Hopefully it only sounds that horribly harsh to my own ears. Nervously, I shift my weight from one foot to the other while Michael and Moritz are already waiting impatiently for me at the next door. The children come first; they're more important. 'I'm terribly sorry, please believe me.'

'What if I just come with you? No matter what you're doing, I'm in,' comes from the other end of the line. By now I can clearly hear his desperation. He hadn't been in touch for four days. And now all of a sudden there doesn't seem to be anything more important to him than seeing me. Why?

I let the little ones into the house and sit down on the top step in front of the front door. Propping my head in my hand, I try to form a clear thought.

Would that be an option? Simon, the kids, and me together in the park. As if we were a family?

No, that's completely out of the question. We've only known each other a few weeks; there's no way I'm going to introduce him to my children. I have to protect them, just as I have to protect myself.

'Are you still there?' I hear Simon ask, much too softly and tenderly.

Longing and reason are locked in a bitter battle inside me. It's a war that can't possibly have a winner. I'm torn, unable to get what I need and at the same time protect what I love. 'I can't.' Nothing but a toneless vibration has just left my mouth and now hangs between us like a glass wall that nothing can penetrate.

'Why? Tell me, Mira, please!' He begs me as if my answer meant everything to him. Why?

For a moment I hesitate, the edge of the stair landing digging hard into my sit bones. 'My kids. I'm spending the afternoon with the boys,' I say at last.

I've said it. And still, my chest doesn't feel the slightest bit lighter.

Does he understand what my words mean?

Chapter Twenty-Two

Her kids? So that's what I just heard in the background. Of course they're with her, why would they not be.

All of a sudden I get nervous. I fidget on the kitchen chair, my foot won't stop tapping on the floor. When I left Sandy a little over an hour ago, I was sure. But now, just thinking about spending time with Mira's little ones makes my stomach churn.

I've never understood children; they're strange little people who do weird things.

First I wanted to get to know Mira better before I dared to approach her boys. Meeting the two of them already would be like sprinting down my new path.

I can't do that. Not yet.

'The things we're most afraid of are often the ones we need the most,' I suddenly hear my sister's voice say. What if that's true? Damn, I wanted to stop being such a coward. Now I have the chance.

'I'd like to meet your kids,' I say before I can change my mind, trying to control the wobble in my voice.

She doesn't answer. The seconds crawl by, thick as honey, until she finally says something. 'You'll get to know them. But not today.'

'Isn't today just as good a day as next Thursday, the Sunday after that, or the Tuesday in five weeks?' I want to sound casual, even though it feels like I've put a noose around my own neck and am tightening it bit by bit.

'Don't make it so hard for me, Simon. Please.'

I can't say anything. Because I don't even know myself whether this is a good idea at all. My head grows heavy, I prop it on my arm and do the one thing I never wanted to do.

I ask fate to help me. To give me a sign. Something to show me which path is the right one.

Mira is silent too; I hear only birdsong in the background and children's laughter far away. Nothing else.

Can something that's so hard for both of us ever really be right?

'Mira,' I whisper on impulse, 'are you still there?'

At last she gives me a sign of life, even if it's only a shaky exhale. 'I'd really like to see you,' she whispers so quietly I can barely hear her, 'but you have to understand…'

Is that the sign? She doesn't want me to meet her kids. It's not meant to be; this path is wrong for me.

'I do. I'm sorry I pushed myself on you like that,' I say quickly, not least because that's the easier way out for me. 'Then have a nice afternoon.'

'Yeah… I… thanks, we will,' Mira stammers, and she sounds as if this is even harder for her than it is for me.

Now I should take the phone away from my ear and press the little red button. But I can't. My body refuses. It just sits at the kitchen table and probably looks just as dried out as the nameless green plant in the corner.

Mira breathes and says nothing. Then she draws a deep breath again. 'Simon?'

When she speaks in that hair-raising voice, it's as if everything around me blurs. The cramped apartment with its slightly stale smell, the ticking clock, and even the chair I'm sitting on. Involuntarily I close my eyes. 'Yeah?'

'We're on the Jesuitenwiese, around three.'

Did she really say that? 'You mean…?'

'Yes.'

It's only a single word, but in my ears it echoes like an entire symphony. In a matter of seconds my mood lifts, everything becomes light and cheerfully colorful. Even the leaves of the green plant in the corner perk up again, or do they?

The love chooses you, not you the love. That would probably be Sandy's explanation for what's happening to me now. Basically there are only two possibilities. Either she's right, or I'm crazy.

When I get to the park shortly after three, I spot Mira from a distance despite all the other visitors. Her loose hair is wildly tousled. Individual strands fall into her face as she helps a little boy out of the stroller. He shares Mira's dark hair; otherwise I can't make out much about him. That could be the younger one, right? How tall is a two-year-old, anyway?

Now a slightly older boy charges across the wide lawn toward her. If he weren't as lively as a puppy, he'd be a perfect miniature version of Peters. Light blond hair, skinny body. The long chin and narrow face fit the picture too.

All at once Mira lifts her head. Our eyes meet so quickly

it's as if we'd both been looking out for each other. There stands my water girl, in the middle of the lush green under an ancient birch tree, pushing her hair behind her ear in slow motion and smiling at me. The golden bangles on her wrists glitter in the sunlight, and suddenly it feels like all the other people around us have vanished.

Maybe it's true. I, Simon Herbst, free spirit and globe-trotter, joker and party clown, might actually have spent years suppressing who I really am and what I really need.

As I walk I wave to Mira; she sets the younger one down on the brightly patterned picnic blanket and looks at me expectantly. Even in the simple jeans and the bright yellow T-shirt she looks completely stunning. The closer I get, the less I can resist her pull. And I don't want to anymore. When I reach her, I carefully place my hand on her upper arm and kiss her cheek.

'Who's that, Mom?' The miniature Peters peeks out from behind Mira. You'd think he was afraid of me, and from his voice I can clearly hear that he doesn't want me here.

The little guy scares me, even though he doesn't even reach my hip. I try to push the feeling away and give him a crooked grin. 'Hey, buddy, I'm Simon,' I say with exaggerated casualness and hold my fist out to him. Is that even the right thing to do? God, I have no idea about kids.

The boy glances up at his mother. 'What's he doing here?'

With an understanding smile, Mira crouches down in front of him. 'He came to play with you. That's great, isn't it?'

'I don't want to play with him.' He folds his arms across his chest and ducks his chin.

Well, this is going great. 'No problem, maybe later.'

'Definitely not.' He sounds so snotty it's like he spits out a spoonful of mush with every word.

'Michael, behave, please.' Mira's voice has taken on a sharp undertone. 'If you don't want to play with Simon, that's fine. But there's no reason to be rude.'

So the boy's name is Michael. While I store the name away, I watch, fascinated, as the little guy nods guiltily and then immediately disappears behind Mira's legs again. Only the sleeve of his blue-and-white striped T-shirt is visible. Not that I'd know anything about it, but to me Mira is already the best mother in the world. How does she do it?

'Do you want to go on the swings?' Mira gently strokes the little guy's head.

He steps to the side, his child's eyes lighting up. A second later he nods so hard that his fine light-blond hair bobs up and down in time. Then he spins around on the spot and runs off. Across the strip of grass crowded with teenagers, along the gravel footpath, toward the play area laid out with rubber mats. There's something in the way he moves that fascinates me. Lightness and joy. Even though he was just grumpy, now he's carefree again. And happy. I watch him go, maybe for too long.

'You like him,' Mira observes, a mischievous tone in her voice.

I wave it off; now that's going too far. 'Oh, come on, we don't even know each other.'

'Is that so? Then what's with that silly grin on your face?' She looks at me with raised eyebrows, a bright giggle escaping her mouth.

'That's just for you.' I take a step toward her, but I don't get the chance to touch her.

Mira's full attention is on the smaller boy sitting next to us on the picnic blanket, awkwardly playing with plastic cutlery. 'Hey, sweetheart.' She kneels down in front of him and pulls him toward her. Only when he's in her arms does she look back up at me. 'This is Moritz,' she says and kisses the little fella's forehead; he studies me even more reservedly than the older one did before. 'Go on, sit down. He doesn't bite, I promise.'

'And if he does?' I try to grin at her. Playing the laid-back Simon would be a lot easier if this didn't feel like opening a door for the first time when everything behind it is in the dark. There could be an abyss just beyond the threshold. Or a swamp that swallows me so slowly I suffocate in agony, bit by bit.

Tiny lines form at the corners of Mira's eyes. 'Don't worry, I'll protect you.' With her free hand, she pats the spot beside her.

'Promise?' I try not to let anything show, because right now I remember Sandy's words.

'You alone decide how you deal with your fear.'

I repeat that in my head, clinging to it. Is that really true? Is Sandy right?

'Who wants watermelon?' I suddenly hear Mira ask. Then I see her pull a plastic container out of the basket as if it were a treasure chest full of gold.

The little munchkin squeals so piercingly that the chugging train of my thoughts comes to a halt for a moment. What was his name again? Oh right, Moritz. Like Max and Moritz. Now he grabs a piece of the sliced fruit and awkwardly stuffs it into his mouth.

I want to try. From now on I'm going to show my fear who's in charge here. I take one last deep breath.

Nothing bad is going to happen, absolutely nothing. 'Your kids are really great,' I say, and it doesn't feel that terrible at all.

With a dreamy expression on her face, Mira leans back on the blanket. 'They are.'

I should dare to do it. Just say it out loud and see what it does to me. 'You know, I could never imagine having kids myself, but when I look at yours…' My pulse speeds up. Is that good or bad?

'After two minutes?' Mira studies me skeptically. The barely visible line above the bridge of her nose is suddenly very deep.

God, it would be so much easier if she'd just show me that this is right for me. Instead, she makes me doubt. I clear my throat to keep the fear in check. Instinctively, I reach into the pocket of my jeans. There are cigarettes in there, and having one would calm me down. A lot, actually. Still, they have to stay where they are. Because I know it would bother Mira. And the toddler, who's now pulling a seed out of the watermelon with a look of amazement, anyway. He looks at it as if it had some magical quality about it.

His behavior fascinates me, whether I like it or not. It's quite possible that the little one and I have exactly the same expression on our faces right now.

'I always notice very quickly when I like something. Or someone,' I murmur absentmindedly. I have no idea what I look like right now. Probably like an idiot, because that's exactly how I feel. Like I'd lost all ability to think rationally.

Mira's laugh sounds tense. 'Got it.'

My eyes drifts over to her. She beams at me, and I can't help but reach my arm out to her. Now I reach her hand and let my index finger glide over her knuckles. Surprised, I notice a shaky vibration on her skin. 'Are you okay?' I whisper to her.

Out of nowhere she pulls her hand away, wraps both

arms around her knees, and draws them closer to herself. She sits next to me like an impregnable fortress. Nestled in the manicured park landscape, yet surrounded by jagged cliffs no one can climb. 'Stop that.'

Why is she suddenly shutting me out?

She doesn't want me to touch her. This is wrong, for her and for me. There's no other explanation.

Waking up in a warzone couldn't be worse than the situation I'm stuck in here. Sweat pools in my palms. 'I-I…' I stammer now too, on top of everything.

Helpless, I have to watch as she tilts her head to the side and scrutinizes me. The sparkle in her eyes is gone, no suspicious smirk plays around her lips anymore. 'Is something wrong?' She furrows her brows. 'You're acting so weird.'

I'm acting weird? Definitely not. She's the one acting like I'm just some random acquaintance.

By now her forehead looks like the Grand Canyon. 'Do you really think I don't notice? How you keep wiping your hands on your pants and squirming around on the blanket like it's a bed of nails? What's making you so nervous?'

'Everything's great.' I force a grin onto my lips; what else am I supposed to do? Tell her that this scares me to death? That I don't know if I'm on the right path and I'm waiting for a sign like I'm one of those crazies who believe in that kind of thing? No way.

She shakes her head, as if to suggest she's no longer sure herself what to think. Then she pushes herself up from the picnic blanket. 'I'll go check on Michael. Can you keep an eye on the little man in the meantime?'

A completely different kind of panic rises up in me at once. I'm supposed to look after this vulnerable little bundle of humanity on my own? For heaven's sake, what am I even supposed to do with the little guy?

'You've got this, don't worry.' With an amused smirk, Mira heads off toward the swings. She weaves her way skillfully through the crowd and waves to her older one, who is delighted by her attention.

So here we are, the little one and me. We look at each other. In a split second, he pulls the corners of his mouth down and starts screaming at the top of his lungs.

That's exactly what I'd most like to do right now too.

'No, please don't cry,' I say hastily and try to cheer him up with funny faces, like a clown. Kids like clowns, right?

Apparently this particular little human in front of me doesn't. I see his dark round eyes fill with tears. I quickly grab a tissue and dab his cheeks dry. 'E-everything's okay, you don't have to cry. I'm here,' I try to calm him down. My breathing is fast, just like my pulse.

I'd definitely be a terrible father. That elderly couple on the wooden bench over there can already see it too; I can tell from their disapproving glances.

Despair and fear spread through me. This isn't for me. Sandy just tried once again to talk me into something. And like an idiot, I believed her.

'Mommy!' the little one yells now, twisting his upper body to the side and stretching out his index finger in her direction.

I look around, searching for help. Next to me, a student looks up from her books and rolls her eyes in annoyance. There has to be something I can use to calm the child down. At least until his mother is back and can take over. In the picnic basket I discover a ball, a pack of those weird eco cookies, and something that looks like a white, fluffy dish towel. If he's eating, he can't scream. So I grab the pack of cookies.

'Mommy will be right back. Look, there's something sweet. I'm sure you like that.' I break off a piece of a cookie and hold it out to him. 'Mmmm,' I say, and feel even more stupid than I did before.

'Mommy,' the little one repeats, as if that were the only word he knew. Still, his tone changes now, growing softer and pleading. There's still a watery sheen on his eyes, his tiny fingers make grabbing motions. I can't help but smile. Because all of a sudden he just looks plain adorable.

'Yes, Mommy is great, isn't she? I think so too.' I wink at him. 'And you know what? I also can't wait for her to come back."'On reflex I raise my hand and stroke his black hair. It's as soft as down feathers. 'Shall we play a game until she gets back?'

As if he were my mirror image, he copies my vigorous nodding and even displays the same conspiratorial grin. 'Play ball.' He pushes himself up from the ground and staggers over to the picnic basket. There he pulls out the ball and throws it to me clumsily.

'Give life a chance to show you what it has in store for you,' I hear Sandy say.

I could try. If not for my own sake, then at least for the little man who's now looking at me so expectantly. It might work; after all, I managed to stop him from crying.

We start to play, and with every time the ball goes back and forth, it feels as if the layer of ice between us is melting, bit by bit.

And the one inside me just the same.

The little guy has a blast throwing the ball so that I have to sprint after it, and before long I'm showing him how to kick the thing properly with his foot. More than once the ball lands near other people in the park. We're so absorbed in our game that I don't even notice how long Mira has been gone. Only when the little soccer star and I flop down on the blanket, exhausted but content, do I realize that we're still alone. And that it doesn't bother me one bit.

'A cookie, big guy?' I ask, holding out the whole pack to him as if he were my buddy and not the two-year-old rascal of the woman who could transform my life from the inside out.

'Cookie. Hmmmm.' He bites into the snack with gusto and chews on it so thoroughly that the crumbs that were just stuck to his cheek gradually come loose. They land right on the symbolic S of his Superman T-shirt.

It's actually impossible to fathom, but this little person has won me over more than I ever could've imagined.

All at once, this whole thing here is damn real. It could be my future. And I actually like it.

Contemplatively, I let my gaze wander across the park, past the rosebushes, the fountain, and the group of teenagers chilling together. Then I spot Mira, all the way back at the playground.

Surrounded by children, she's standing at the end of a zip line that, at this very moment, starts moving with an excited Michael on it. But I'm the only one who can see that, because Mira isn't paying any attention to her son.

Her eyes are on me. With a satisfied little smile, she looks at me, and suddenly I realize what's happening here.

She's watching me. And what she sees makes her happy.

My fear loosens its grasp just a little more. 'Letting go is the key to happiness,' Sandy said, and right now I can feel what she meant by that.

Chapter Twenty-Three

I'd long since stopped trying.

Even from a distance, I'm powerless against his presence. I only have to look at him and my pulse speeds up, as if my heart were breaking into a sprint.

While Michael is having fun on the kids' zipline, I watch, far too moved, what's happening over there on the picnic blanket. Seemingly at ease, Simon and Moritz are playing and chatting with each other.

Seeing the two of them like this doesn't make anything better. On the contrary, it makes my protective shell melt away, as if I were a block of ice and this weren't the Jesuitenwiese but the Australian outback.

Out of nowhere, Michael is suddenly standing next to me, tugging at my hand. 'Why is that man playing with Moritz?' he wants to know, looking at me with a skeptical expression.

'Simon is a friend. And friends play together.' I have to smile because it feels fantastic to say that.

His eyes dart back and forth between Simon and me, as

if he first had to understand what my words mean. 'But he's not my friend.' He wrinkles his nose. 'Is he?'

'That's entirely up to you.' I stroke his shoulder lovingly. His small body is hot, his T-shirt damp. 'I'm thirsty. You too?'

Michael nods, and hand in hand we stroll back to the picnic blanket. The whole time my eyes stay fixed on Simon, because they don't want to be anywhere else. He, too, doesn't stop looking at me, as if there were only the two of us here. No trees, no meadows. No people, no birds. Neither the hot air nor the scent of roses it carries. Only him and me, drawn to each other like two magnetic poles.

More than anything, I want to start running, right now, so I can be with him as fast as possible. I need to hug him, stroke his back, and finally kiss him again.

But that's impossible.

No matter how adorably he plays with Moritz or whether Michael likes him. The two of them have been through too much in the past few months for them to be able to understand now why their mother is suddenly kissing someone who isn't their father.

Only a few yards separate us, and already I can see the expectant glow in Simon's blue-green eyes. I quickly lower my gaze; I can't let myself get any softer than I already am.

'Hey, you two?' I focus on Moritz, who looks as if he were the Cookie Monster himself. 'Looks like someone found the dessert.'

Simon bursts out laughing. 'We treated ourselves. Didn't we, buddy?' Now he holds out his fist to Moritz. In disbelief I watch my son curl his little fingers and touch Simon's hand with them. The two of them giggle like they shared a secret language.

All at once Michael dares to step out from behind me. 'I

want a cookie too.' He still sounds reserved, but he takes a step toward Simon, who holds the package out to him.

'I saw how high you can swing. Totally awesome.' Simon grins at my elder boy without judging him for shoving him away like that earlier.

The warmth in my chest keeps growing, my shoulders suddenly feel free and my thoughts light. Now I even see a broad smile spread across Michael's face. Then he stuffs the whole cookie into his mouth at once. Chewing hard, he nods and thrusts his chest forward proudly.

'Almost as high as the sky.' Simon's eyes glimmer as if he were still a child himself.

All at once I'm glad he's focusing on Michael. Because that way he can't see what, right now, this very moment, is happening to me.

I melt. Just like that.

'Not almost,' Michael protests vehemently. 'I can swing all the way up to the sky.' With his arms stretched high, he jumps up, loses his balance when he lands, and stumbles straight into Simon's upper arm.

'Whoops.' Simon catches him in a friendly way. But Michael jerks back like Simon was some strange creature that sends a shiver down his spine.

Quickly, I pick Moritz up and watch what happens next. While my elder son stares at Simon with wide eyes, Simon gets more and more agitated. His hands move restlessly over his jeans. The whole time, his gaze keeps flicking questioningly between me and the boy, but I'm definitely not going to interfere here. This is his own trial by fire, and in truth I'm the last person to know what outcome I should even be hoping for.

'Hey, want to kick the ball around a bit?' Even as he

asks, Simon grabs the same ball he was playing with Moritz with before.

Of course he thinks that what worked with one child has to work with the other too. I can't help but smirk. After all, I know what's going to happen now.

'Soccer is stupid.' Michael rolls his eyes in annoyance.

Helplessly, Simon lifts his shoulders, and again his gaze wanders to me. Of course he can't know that in some ways Michael is anything but an ordinary boy. But he'll notice soon enough.

'Alright, then not,' Simon says with a sigh and lets himself fall back onto the blanket.

Is he really giving up already?

I can feel my protective layer growing back immediately. He isn't the right one, not for my kids and therefore not for me either. I ignore the stab in my heart. For that reason alone, I have to.

Michael turns away, goes over to the stroller, and grabs his backpack from it. I watch as he pulls out his dolls and looks at me questioningly. He wants to give it a try, and I'm not going to stop him, so I nod at him encouragingly.

Just a moment later he's standing in front of Simon with his playmates. 'This is Barbie,' he says, holding the doll with the long blond hair up to his face. 'And this is Ken.'

Visibly confused, Simon only manages to get out a drawn-out 'Mhm.' Then he straightens up and runs a hand through his hair.

'Those two are married, you know?' Michael presses the two dolls together like a couple in love.

'Really?' Simon swallows, his mouth opens, but it seems as if he's completely lost for words.

What happens next is so important that every one of my

muscles tenses. Because right now, everything is being decided.

'And what are the two of them up to today?' Simon suddenly asks with an open smile.

I can practically see Michael's face start to shine. Like a waterfall, my little darling starts chattering away and tells the still slightly flabbergasted Simon absolutely everything the dolls have already experienced today. For a while I watch the two of them and see how, bit by bit, a role-play develops. Michael assigns Simon the Barbie doll, and he plays the female role almost perfectly. He even gives his voice a high, bright tone, and again and again he makes hand movements as if he himself were a woman.

Heinrich would never have done anything like that.

Inevitably, my memories paint pictures from the past in my mind's eye. I see my husband sitting in his reading chair, absorbed in the newspaper. And Michael, walking up to him with the Barbie, demanding his attention.

With a sullen expression, Heinrich looks sternly at Michael over the rim of his glasses. 'Put the dolls away,' he says firmly, then turns back to the news.

My smile freezes instantly. A punch straight to my gut couldn't have hit me harder than Michael's disappointed look. Head hanging, his Barbie pressed tightly to his chest, he shuffles out of the living room. On the way I hear him whispering to the doll. He's reassuring her, as if he were desperately afraid that Heinrich had hurt her with his behavior.

I quickly chase that horrible image out of my mind and shake the tension from my hands. Then it suddenly occurs to me that this isn't even necessary. My fingernails are only just barely scratching over my palms.

For the first time in months I've thought about Heinrich without clenching my fists.

That can only mean one thing: he really is the past. And what's happening right in front of my eyes now could be the future. Simon is different. Could he be a father to my little ones in a way they've never had before?

A shiver runs through my body, and I don't know if it feels good or frightening. At the same time I notice how Moritz is using my back as a climbing frame. With his little shoes he drums against my side, his fingers stick sugary-sweet to my upper arm. He needs attention, and that's definitely a good thing. Because the longer I watch Simon and Michael, the softer everything inside me becomes. Even my heart, which had been transformed into a massive boulder for months, suddenly seems able to beat freely again.

Hours later we set off. Gallantly, Simon helps pack the picnic basket and folds up the blanket. We grin at each other, but neither of us says a word. Probably because there's no need.

'Mama carry.' Moritz yawns and peers up at me from eyes that now look suspiciously tired. We've clearly lost track of time; he urgently needs to go to bed.

Before I can bend down to him, Simon reaches under his arms and pulls the little one toward him. His hand glides gently over Moritz's back. I wish I could resist the warm feeling that spreads through my whole body when I see how affectionate this man is with my children.

So many things would be easier. But definitely a lot less beautiful, too.

While Simon tries to keep Moritz entertained at least until we get home, I walk behind the two of them along the park's gravel path, holding Michael's hand. My elder son is unusually quiet. Maybe he's just tired, but my mother's instinct tells me there's more to it.

'Mom?' he starts a conversation.

I immediately say a quick prayer. Please don't let him ask about his father. Not now. Just one single evening without arguments, that's all I want. 'What is it, sweetheart?' I try to sound cheerful and give his hand an encouraging squeeze.

'Can Simon read me my bedtime story tonight?' He looks up at me, his gaze rivaling that of a puppy. 'Because he's my friend, you know?'

Even though it's not surprising after their puppet play together, his words set everything inside me alight. 'I see. Of course he can read you something. But ask him first if he feels like it.'

As if on cue, Michael tears himself away from me and sprints ahead. 'Simon, Simon,' he calls, wonderfully excited and full of joy.

I'm left behind on my own and watch as Simon puts his free arm around Michael's shoulders. The three of them march together along the gravel path, looking as if they'd always belonged together. A delicate feeling of happiness tingles down my back, travels to my toes and back up the front of my legs straight into the middle of my chest. I don't want this, yet every part of me starts to vibrate. Almost as if the ground beneath me were trembling just a little.

Chapter Twenty-Four

With a long, luxurious yawn, I settle into the soft cushions of the seating on the terrace of Mira's house, right next to her. The sun had long since said goodbye, but its warmth was still there. The garden in front of us lay in darkness. Maybe it looked quite nice in daylight, but that didn't really matter. Even if we were surrounded by a garbage dump, this would still be the most beautiful place in the world.

'Who would've thought that looking after kids is so exhausting?' I ask while Mira opens the bottle of red wine.

She grins at me. 'Oh, come on, just a bit of playing?' With a wink, she hands me a glass of wine.

'You're forgetting the bedtime story I read to them as well. Five times, actually!'

All at once her expression turns serious. 'You were fantastic today.' There it is again, that velvety soft undertone I'd been missing all day. With a suspicious sparkle in her otherwise so tired eyes, she raises her glass. 'To you.'

'To us.' I look deep into her eyes as we clink our glasses together.

I'd love to be able to see what she's thinking, but the cozy seating area is lit only by the hip-high candle in the corner. A shadow lies across Mira's face.

She, on the other hand, can probably read every feeling on my face. But right now I don't care at all. I want her to see everything. Even my nascent sense that being with her really could be my future.

Suddenly something becomes clear to me. I have to finally tell her the truth. She has to know why we met. Who and what I am. This secret shouldn't stand between us any longer.

'Mira, I…'

Before I can say anything, she puts her finger on my mouth. 'Shhh,' she whispers, looking so mysteriously beautiful that I can't think straight anymore. 'Don't say anything.'

For a moment we look at each other, then I dare to do it. Carefully I kiss her fingertips, glide over her palm and feel my way to her wrist. The whole time I keep my eyes fixed on her.

Then I see it. An almost imperceptible nod.

So I go on and work my way up along her arm. I even kiss the almost healed wounds on her forearm. When I reach her collarbone, I stop and deliberately inhale the scent of her skin.

I allow myself to feel what she's doing to me. I'm allowed to, because I alone decide that this is a chance.

Now she takes my face in her hands and lifts it just enough that our lips almost touch. Her breath brushes over my skin, as warm as the desert wind.

Seconds, minutes or hours later I feel her kiss. And I do something I thought would never happen.

I let go.

Immediately it feels as if I'm floating. Somewhere far

away, out in the universe. In a place where there can be no doubt.

Sandy had been right. Mira could be my future. And right now it seems easy to conquer every last dreg of fear inside me.

Chapter Twenty-Five

'That's it, ladies and gentlemen. Get to work.' The boss's voice booms in my ears, but I still have no idea what he's saying. Only the sudden commotion in the meeting room gets through to me. The morning briefing seems to be over. And I didn't hear a single word.

I glance around in a flash.

Who can I ask?

'Horst! Wait a second.' I already see the big guy disappearing through the door, but luckily he turns around again. I quickly jog over to him. 'Thanks.'

'What's up, Cheshire Cat?' he asks, giving me a thorough once-over. 'Looks like someone had a very special night.'

I hesitate for a moment. Should I admit it? As a brand-new father himself, he would understand me. 'That's entirely possible.'

'You don't have to say another word, I can see everything in your face anyway. Just watch out or she'll swallow you whole. That's what women are like.' Laughing, he thumps me on the chest and turns to go.

'Wait! One more thing.'

'What?' His eyes glance back and forth between his wristwatch and my eyes. 'You want to grab a smoke?'

I quickly shake my head. 'Not today.'

'Oh, so that's how it is.' Horst's deep laugh filled the now empty room for a moment. Then he suddenly grew serious again. 'You do realize you're going to get the hell out of here in a little over a month, right?'

I'd rather ignore that; the thought had been tormenting me far too much anyway. Instead, I leaned over to him, shaking my head, while the last colleagues squeezed past us, chatting. 'I didn't really listen earlier. Do you happen to remember where I'm assigned?'

I didn't like his amused expression at all. I jabbed him impatiently in the side, as if to knock the information out of him. Then I saw him slowly give in. 'Yard duty.'

No. God no. These past few weeks I had barely been able to escape Peters' questioning looks. And the day before yesterday he had almost caught me alone. Of course he wanted to know what I'd managed to achieve with Mira. Because he had no idea what had really happened. I'd have to lie to him or endure his disappointment, but I couldn't manage either. There was only one solution to my dilemma: Horst had to swap shifts with me. 'What did you get stuck with?' I asked carefully.

Horst's face took on a pitiful expression. 'Mail,' he said with an annoyed undertone.

That wasn't much better, but so what. I shoved my hands into the deep pockets of my dark blue work pants. 'Wow, you sound thrilled.'

'I can hardly wait,' he said with an exaggerated sigh and turned to go.

I quickly stopped him. 'Hey, I owe you. Without you I wouldn't even know what I'm supposed to be doing right now. And the only reason the boss doesn't know I overslept today is because you covered for me. So if you want, I can take the mail for you.' I tried not to sound too stressed. No idea if I actually managed it.

Horst eyed me skeptically. 'Who are you? And what have you done with Simon?'

Couldn't he just be happy about my offer? 'It was just a suggestion,' I said, deliberately casual. I would've liked to shrug indifferently, but my muscles were far too tense.

'Which I'm obviously happy to accept.' Horst grins in amusement and holds out his fist to me. 'Petra was going to pick up the mail for me, the crate's probably already in the office. Have fun with the letters!' He turns away and walks off toward the yard. 'Thanks, Simon, you're the best,' he calls to me from a distance.

Done. I let out a sigh of relief, then march down the old-fashioned tiled corridor to the offices where the prisoners' letters have to be checked according to regulations. That's exactly what I'm going to do today, because I'm definitely not going to cross the boss. Never again anyway, because this job is the only available foundation for my new life. From now on I'm going to be a model guard, even if I'm one whose thoughts drift off way too fast.

I've already kissed Mira a thousand times in my imagination since beginning work; and about as many times it has felt like I didn't have to touch the ground of my path to walk it. Thinking of the sparkle in her eyes, I enter the office and rummage through the mail crate. I find a gleaming white envelope among the other covers and quickly put it back.

I don't want to read Peters' letters any longer.

I'm sure he's guilty. And that he was neither a real father nor a good husband. Mira told me absolutely everything last night. For hours I held her in my arms and learned how the professor kept managing to show her his best side whenever she started to doubt her marriage. How he took his anger out on her and then, right afterward, gallantly opened the door for her. And how she tried to keep this marriage going for the children's sake.

Now he's history. For Mira and for me. So I devote myself to the boring drivel of the remaining messages. Only at the very end do I pull out Peters' letter and drop into the swivel chair in front of the desk.

The letter opener is ready in my hand, I slide it under the glued edge of the paper. It at least has to look as if I'd done my job. Even though I don't intend to read the letter at all, I feel like a burglar who slips in through the patio door at night while the family is asleep upstairs. Silent and hidden in the darkness, I rummage through their most personal belongings.

If Mira knew about this, she'd hate me forever. Guaranteed. I immediately feel a pressure on my shoulders. It settles into my neck too and from there spreads all over my head.

I should have told her, right from the start.

'Herbst!' The boss's voice slams into me with full force and catapults me back into reality. 'What are you doing here?'

'K-Kaufmann and I switched today, he preferred to do yard duty,' I answer quickly.

His stare remains frosty. 'Then stop standing there

daydreaming like some pony-club girl and do your job.' Now he leans against my desk and doesn't look like he's planning to leave anytime soon. 'Go on!'

'I'm on it already.' Hastily, I push the letter opener deeper into the envelope and slice it open with a single movement of my hand. Although the sound of the tearing paper is quiet, it echoes in my ears.

The break-in begins, the patio door is open.

Still under strict observation, I clumsily fumble the written sheet out of the envelope.

Now I enter the house.

I unfold it and turn it so I can read it.

The Peters family's safe is open, the beam of my flashlight aimed directly at it.

'There you go, that's better.' With a grunt, the boss pushes himself away from the desk and heads for the door. He's almost outside when he turns around one last time. 'What are you waiting for?'

Silently, I lower my gaze. My robbery of the Peters family begins, and my guilty conscience immediately starts gnawing away at my stomach.

My dearest Mira,

My hands are still trembling, my heart is still pounding with such force that it starves me of breath. Your letter is lying beside me. I have carefully smoothed it out, because to me it is a treasure of immeasurable value. Even if I were to lose all my possessions, as long as I carry it with me, I will be a rich man.

Thank you, Mira. Thank you for writing to me. Thank you for letting me be part of your world again. You ask a few questions, and I want to try to answer them as best I can.

Who are you, Heinrich, who are you really?

It may not look like it, but the answer is simple. I am your husband, Mira! The man who loves you like nothing else in this world. And the man who is in prison unjustly, for an act he could never have committed.

Who am I, that I could trust you blindly?

You trusted me because it was the right thing to do. And it still is. Not once did I lie to you, because I'm not capable of that. Not when I look at you. Not even when I only hear your breath on the phone. Not when I'm writing to you now, and not when I lie awake at night with my eyes open, dreaming of you.

And who are we, you and I, Michael and Moritz? Are we still a family?

What I have in abundance here in prison is time. I use it to think about us, Mira. About everything that happened. Today I know that I could have done better. For me, what we had was always enough, but for you, we were never the family you had wished for.

I admit that I made mistakes. I can't change the past, but I'm ready to do things differently in the future.

Still, I can't help but remind you of something crucial. My way of loving was always to take good care of you. You never lacked for anything financially or materially. I made possible for you and the children exactly the life you always wanted. Don't forget that, Mira!

Come visit me, I'm begging you! You and the boys, I want to see all of you, even if it's only for a few minutes. Give me the chance to make it up to you, even just a little bit. Let's be who we used to be. Just a little better.

With deep love,

Heinrich

The letter slips from my fingers. Countless thoughts swarm my head, loud and wild, overlaid with feelings, suspicions, and memories. But there's one thing that pushes so far to the forefront that I can't ignore it any longer.

Of course the professor took good care of the three of

them. Mira and the kids live in a palace. In the nineteenth district!

'A family costs you everything. Your freedom, your autonomy. There are no parties and no sleeping in, only responsibility, financial obligation, and constantly putting your own wishes last,' I suddenly hear Paul say in my head.

It becomes clear to me at breakneck speed what that means. How could I ever support this family on my salary? What do kids even cost, and how much does it take to maintain that luxury pad?

There's no way I can manage that. I can barely afford my tiny apartment. What I eat and a bit of extra money for parties and my trip. That's all I have.

I have to make sure that at least I get promoted to team leader here in the prison. Maybe I could put in overtime, take on more weekend shifts and night shifts. But will that be enough? My father's death threw my life into such turmoil that I dropped out of my training program and took a temp job. There was no other way; I had to be there for Mama. And for Sandy too. Where else were we supposed to get enough money to live?

What if I went back and finished school? Maybe then I'd have a chance at a better-paid job. Or I'll look for a second job. Mira and the kids should have a good life, they shouldn't want for anything.

And what if I'm not able to give them that?

All at once a nasty premonition hits me. It's happening. I think like my father. Act like him. I am him, I'm following his path and making his same mistakes. Work instead of freedom. Money worries instead of joy in life.

I can't think straight anymore, the fear hits me like a freight train.

Panicking, I march into the locker room and open my

locker. My eyes wanders to the inside of the locker door. It's plastered with pictures of hip places, cool motorbikes, and lonely landscapes. A collage of my dream life. Discovering the world unbound and free, with no responsibility, just doing whatever I feel like and being wherever I happen to be. For so long I thought that was all I really needed.

Today I don't know anything anymore, right and wrong blur together. I'm dizzy. And nauseous.

As I sink down onto the narrow bench in front of the locker, my phone rings. It's Paul.

'Tell me, are you not interested in our friendship anymore?' he asks instead of a greeting. Right after that I hear a contemptuous snort on the other end of the line.

'Nonsense.' I lean my head against the metal locker because I'm suddenly very tired. 'You're my best friend, you know that.'

'Then prove it to me. Tonight you're making time for me, and this time for real.' His words sound serious.

It's true. We've barely seen each other these past few weeks. I was distracted by something that in the end might not even be right for me. 'Fine,' I say anyway, even though I'm really not in the mood to celebrate.

We agree on a place and time. I feel better—at least that's what I want to believe. Exhausted, I put my phone back in the locker and take another look at the pictures that might actually be my future after all.

'Give life a chance to show you what it has in store for you.' My sister's words carve deep burrows in my mind. Couldn't that also mean traveling? What was Sandy trying to tell me? In the end I don't know anything anymore. Because of her I feel as if I were trapped in a room full of chairs with still nowhere to sit.

'Thanks, Sandy,' I murmur. Then I do what I always do. I swallow, breathe, and bite my lip.

Chapter Twenty-Six

'You introduced him to your kids?' Eva stares at me in disbelief. Her fine curls bounce up and down nervously. 'Well, that was quick.'

With a sigh, I let a saucepan slide into the warm dishwater. So far the evening had been relaxed. But after we tucked the kids into bed, Eva wore me down until I told her about yesterday afternoon in the park. Now I'm tracing little circles on the surface of the water with my index finger, just like Simon and I did at the Old Danube. 'What else was I supposed to do? He was so…'

'Irresistibly sweet? Terribly attractive? Damn hot?' Eva asks, moving closer to me. Excited, she twists her dish towel between her hands. 'Come on, tell me everything.'

As if I were afraid someone might hear me talking in my own house, I lean toward her. 'I don't know, he's just good for me. The way he's there for me. The way he is with the kids. The way he…'

Should I really say it?

'... kisses me,' I whisper shakily. Just saying it out loud feels like I'm doing something forbidden.

I quickly lower my gaze and start scrubbing the bottom of the pot like mad.

Out of the corner of my eye I see Eva, a satisfied look on her face as she reaches for the colander. 'So that's how it is,' is all she says as she dries it with the dish towel. 'And what happens now?'

If only I knew. I'd better not tell her about my letter to Heinrich. She'd tear my head and every single limb off if she knew I'd written to him. Instead of answering, I just give an exaggerated shrug.

'And what's that supposed to mean?' She mimics my movement.

I rinse the pot with clear water and set it upside down on the drying rack. 'No idea. I'm all stirred up and I just don't know what to make of any of this,' I say, because that's the truth.

'What, come on, that's easy.' She pushes up the sleeves of her thin knit sweater as if she's ready to really tackle the matter. 'Do you like him?'

Lost in thought, I scan the kitchen with my eyes, over the matte light surfaces, the glass inserts in the wall cabinets, and the brightly colored curtains I had to lobby Heinrich for for so long. Then on to the terrace.

We sat out there, in exactly the spot on the seating area that I can see from here.

And we kissed, as if neither a yesterday nor a tomorrow existed.

'Yes,' I admit, but only very quietly. Still, it feels as if a voice inside me is practically shouting the answer out loud. I know she's right, I feel it all over my body.

Eva's warm hands suddenly rest on mine. 'And does he like you?'

I don't miss the suggestive undertone in her voice, but I still don't react to it. 'I think so. Maybe. How am I supposed to know?' As discreetly as possible, I peek at my phone, which is lying on the glossy varnished solid-wood table next to the kitchenette.

Still no message, for almost twenty-four hours now. Why isn't he getting in touch?

'So yes,' Eva concludes firmly and gives me a loving poke in the side. 'Do the kids like him?'

I don't have to think about that for a second. 'Michael calls him his new best friend, and he managed to calm Moritz down right away when I left the two of them alone.' Even I notice the blissful smile spreading across my face.

I wish Simon were less perfect. Just a tiny bit, so I'd have something to cling to. A lifeline to help me protect myself. From him. And from everything that could happen if I trust him too much.

'Three out of four.' Eva nods excitedly and raises her index finger. 'There's only one question left. Does he like your kids too?'

I search my memory for clues. Words or gestures, actions and facial expressions. Less than a second later I find them. There's Simon's beaming face as he enthusiastically praises Moritz for a well-aimed kick at the ball. And the image of the three of them running ahead of me together between lush green trees and delicate blossoms. In one arm Simon is carrying Moritz, the other rests familiarly on Michael's shoulder, and Michael is looking up at him with delight. I hear them talking to each other. They seem as though they've always belonged together. 'Yes, Simon likes the two of them.'

Eva's gaze wanders for a moment to my hands, lying completely relaxed on the countertop, then on to my forearms with their almost healed wounds. She chuckles, but still doesn't say anything. Instead, she carefully folds the dish towel.

'What?' Instinctively, I fold my arms across my chest.

Obviously she can't stop herself from rolling her eyes, and I can understand why, at least a little. From her point of view, everything is simple. 'Four out of four,' is all she says, as if that settled every possible, open-ended question.

But for me they're not settled. On the contrary, the closer Simon gets to me, the more questions pop up in my head.

Is he really what I need? Why should I trust him? And if I managed to let go, would I crash again or finally begin to fly?

'Sometimes you just have to jump.' Eva says quietly, but with such urgency that I can feel her words all around me.

Jump. Let go. With no safety net, no second line of defense? 'I can't do that.' How could I, when not even the fractures from my last crash have healed? Helplessly, I look at her, and at the same moment I notice my fingers curling. While they close into a fist, Eva is already right next to me.

Comfortingly, she wraps her arms around me. 'It's hard, I know. But if you ever want to be happy again, you have to leave that behind you,' she whispers in my ear.

My throat tightens. So much that I can't speak anymore and can barely breathe. So I just shake my head, over and over. My shoulders slump forward; I feel helpless and small.

'Think about it, Mira. You still have your whole life ahead of you, and in the end, isn't it about having as many happy days as possible?'

Of course, that's exactly what we always told ourselves.

Back when the world was still in one piece. 'How could it ever be like that again?' I force out.

'Look at me, Mira.' Carefully, she loosens her embrace and holds me by the shoulders. So much affection and warmth radiate from her that I'm just glad to have her as a friend. 'Times are changing, and we're changing with them.'

Despite my despair, I have to smile. 'Was that on your quote-a-day calendar this morning?'

'Maybe,' is all she says as she gently helps me unclench my fist. 'But is that really important? It's true, and that's all that matters.'

'You think so?' I ask, sounding like an insecure toddler.

Part of me wants to believe her, desperately and without reservation. But that doesn't change the creature of fear that has its arms wrapped around me from behind and whispers in my ear with its rotten breath, this will never work out.

'A thousand percent.' She seems absolutely convinced.

Again I have to smile, and she joins in. 'I'll try,' I say at last, and I instantly feel a little lighter. 'Promise.'

'Very good, I couldn't have stood around here much longer anyway.' With a pained grimace, she shakes out her legs and drops onto one of the kitchen chairs. 'So, what happens now?'

Automatically, I look at the phone. 'He's not getting in touch,' I say, not even trying to hide my disappointment.

'So what?' The puzzled look on her face tells me everything I need to know. 'We live in the 21st century. There's no shame in you texting him first.'

'Maybe,' I mumble meekly and take a step toward the phone. Uncertain, I push it back and forth on the tabletop with my index finger. I'm still hoping that a message from Simon will arrive any moment.

I must have lost my mind. There's no other explanation.

'If you want something, you're going to have to ask for it. Every kid knows that.' She so skillfully glosses over the fact that I'm still not sure what I even want. 'So, now turn that thing on and text him.'

Maybe I should do that. Or maybe not? Moving in slow motion, I unlock the screen and search through my messages longer than necessary before I dial Simon's number.

'Today,' Eva chimes in, like an insistent voice-over.

She won't back down, and that's probably a good thing. What if it really is time to show the fear monster who's in charge of my life?

That's me. Just me. And I don't want to keep treading water. The hesitation has to stop.

'Today is the first day of the rest of your life.' I'm sure that's a quote Eva is whispering urgently to me right now. But that doesn't matter at all.

Because right now I want to believe that everything can still turn out okay.

With my heart pounding and my stomach in knots, I start to write.

Chapter Twenty-Seven

The bass thumps in my chest, right where my heart sits. I can't feel it beating anymore, only my muscles trembling in time with the beat. There's a pitcher of beer in front of me, and I have no idea which one it is. Next to it is a shot glass with a clear liquid in it. Did I order that?

'Cool party.' Completely out of breath, Paul weaves his way through the partying crowd. His forehead shines like the gel from his hair had run down onto his skin. His Simpsons T-shirt has suspiciously large dark patches under the arms.

I force a smile and take a sip of the beer so I don't have to say anything. It's too loud in here for a conversation anyway.

With his eyebrows drawn together and his head tilted to the side, Paul sizes me up longer than necessary. Then he grabs his glass too and downs it in one go. 'Come on,' he yells and waves me over. 'The dance floor is full of ten-out-of-ten ladies.'

Watching him push his hips forward in an unmistakable move, grinning cheekily, makes me laugh.

Still, I'm not in the mood to dance right now. And I'm not in the mood for ten-out-of-ten ladies either. 'I'd rather have another one of these.' I point at my glass with my index finger.

'Fine, then.' Paul isn't happy, but at least he shrugs and heads off again.

I watch as he's swallowed up by the crowd, which now, as if on cue, jerks its arms into the air. In the wildly flickering light of the spotlights, it looks like they're moving in slow motion.

With a sigh, I knock back the shot, because I don't feel like doing anything else either. I don't really know what I'm doing here anyway.

Suddenly, arms slip around my shoulders from behind and glide smoothly, like two snakes, down to my chest. My T-shirt gets tangled in neon pink bangles.

'Hello, stranger,' a female voice whispers in my ear.

In a flash, I tear myself free, whirl around, and in the hazy disco light I see a pair of doll-like eyes in an unnatural shade of blue. 'What the hell are you doing?'

Unimpressed, she nibbles on her slightly too full lower lip. 'I just wanted to keep you company. You look pretty lost, sitting here all by yourself.'

This game isn't for me. Not anymore. 'Thanks, but that's not necessary.' I pull an apologetic face and turn back around. Still, out of the corner of my eye I can see that she doesn't move even an inch away from me.

On the contrary. As if she hadn't heard me, she leans down to me again. 'You sure?' Her fake fingernails scratch lightly at my neck. 'A hot guy like you shouldn't be all alone.'

'Absolutely.' I grab her wrist, push her away from me, and put on a stern expression. 'Cut it out. Please.'

She gives me a sugary grin as she sweeps her honey-blond hair out of her face with a single flick of her hand. 'You're missing the night of your life.'

A few weeks ago I wouldn't have hesitated. I would've stormed the dance floor with her, and we would've rubbed up against each other to the beat of the music until neither one of us could stand it anymore. Today, everything is different.

'I already told you. No, thanks.' I push myself up from the chair in one abrupt motion, but I regret it immediately. The whole club tilts, just like the disappointed face of my admirer.

I leave both behind; only the wave-like motion that runs through my body with every step stays with me as, not even a minute later, I stumble out into the night. The oxygen-rich air hits me like a slap in the face, I reel against the house wall and stay there for the time being. My hand goes to my phone by itself, as if, despite all my efforts, I were addicted to staring at the display until the end of time.

There's a message. From Mira. 'I can't stop thinking about you,' I decipher. 'All the time.' I read the text again. And then once more. She's thinking about me. That's fantastic. Or is it more of a disaster?

Confused, I tap a cigarette out of the pack and pat my pants pockets for a lighter. Where the hell did I put the damn thing?

Suddenly a small flame appears right in front of my face. Not again, please. Can't this woman just leave me alone? My eyes raise to the owner of the lighter. Relieved, I realize it's Paul.

'You okay, man?' he asks, his expression worried.

I hold my cigarette to the flame and take a drag. It tastes disgusting; I stub it out again immediately. 'Too much beer.'

'And that nine you had at your table earlier?' He lights a smoke for himself and fixes me with an expectant look.

'Too much plastic,' I answer, trying to give a crooked grin. No idea if I manage it, but I feel like my muscles are doing whatever they want anyway.

'Bullshit.' Paul comes closer and leans against the wall next to me. He stands at my side as if he wants to support me. 'I can see something's off with you. What's going on, Simon?'

'No idea what—'

'No,' Paul cuts me off sharply. 'No more lies.' He raises his index finger in warning. 'We're friends, aren't we?'

Anyway, we are. My head automatically sinks onto his shoulder, my gaze losing itself somewhere between the dark house walls and the faint light of the streetlamps. Then I just do it.

I say out loud what I myself would never have thought possible.

'It happened.' As if to prove it, I feel a stab in my chest.

'The wife of that inmate.' It isn't a question but a statement. 'I knew it.'

'You'd have to see her.' My shoulders slump forward, my head suddenly feels heavy. 'She's my water girl,' I murmur, thinking of the moment when we kissed for the first time. In the pouring rain, on the street in front of her house.

'And now what?' Paul drags on his cigarette and releases the cloud of smoke straight into the sky above us.

Thoughtfully, I watch it disappear into the darkness of the night. 'I should stop this. But I…'

Paul lifts my head off his shoulder and grabs my arms.

'Look at me,' he demands, and I find myself staring into a pair of sensible eyes. 'This can't go on. For weeks I've been watching what this woman is doing to you.'

Every muscle in my body tenses. 'What do you know.'

'I've got eyes in my head. And that's all I need to see that you're not yourself anymore.' He draws out the last words, emphasizing each one as if he wanted to hammer them into my skull one after the other.

'Nonsense.' I wave him off, even though I know he's right. I've lost myself, no longer knowing who I am or what I really need.

'Oh yeah?' he asks in a sharp tone. His eyes narrow to slits. 'All of a sudden you hardly have time to meet up with me. And when it does happen, your mind is somewhere else entirely. Parties don't interest you anymore. Just like that. From one moment to the next. And the worst thing, Simon, the very worst thing is that you've obviously forgotten what matters to you in life.'

I can only stare at him, having no idea what I'm supposed to say to that.

Paul, on the other hand, seems to have all the words bottled up inside him, and I wonder for how long they have been sitting there, under the surface. Bit by bit they tumble out of him like kernels from an overflowing popcorn machine. 'There was only ever one thing you wanted. To be free. To live your life by your own rules. And now, without even thinking about it, you're chaining yourself to a wife and kids? You know what it means to have a family!'

Right. Everything he says is true.

I'm too drunk to fight off the image of my father that now appears in my mind. It pushes itself in front of Mira's face, powerful and oversized.

With his head resting on his hands, he sits at the kitchen table talking to my mother. They're so absorbed in their conversation that they don't even notice how my fourteen-year-old self, protected by the darkness of the hallway, is leaning against the doorframe in a night shirt.

'I can't do this anymore,' he whispers, shrinking a little more with every word. 'It's too much. All of this is crushing me.'

Mum wipes the tears from her cheeks with a tissue, then crumples it tightly in her fist. 'So we're a burden to you? Your kids and me too, we're making your life hard?' There isn't the slightest hint of reproach in her voice, only disappointment and helplessness.

'Life is making my life hell,' my father answers weakly. Maybe I should get it, but I have no idea what he means by that.

My mother's hand wanders across the kitchen table and comes to rest on his. 'It's hard, I know. But it'll get better, someday. The kids will be independent soon enough. Then we'll only have to take care of ourselves.'

'I won't make it till then.' His lips tremble, and now I see a single tear running down his stubbly cheek.

If only I had known back then that this would be the last moment when I could be close to my father. I would've run to him, hugged him, and whispered in his ear how much we need him.

But that's not how things were. And the fact that Paul is bringing up the memory of my father of all times right now, right here, isn't fair. He knows what that does to me. The words from Peters' letter boil up in me again. I can never give Mira as good a life as he did. I can't do it.

'Fuck.' I slam my fist into my own thigh with full force so that, for once, my body will hurt somewhere else.

'It's not too late.' Paul puts his hands on my shoulders and shakes me so hard it's like he thinks he can shake Mira out of me.

But that's not how this works. If it were that easy, I would've done it myself a long time ago. 'Oh please, as if you'd understand,' I snap at him.

'Now listen up, really listen. That woman is poison. Forget her. You don't need her. Focus on your dream. You only have to hold out for a bit more than six weeks. Then you just drive off and leave her behind.' He sounds like he's trying to cast a spell on me. All that's missing is him swinging a pocketwatch back and forth in front of my eyes.

'You have no idea. How could you? I can't remember you ever managing to keep a woman for more than a night.' Yeah, that's unfair, but he can't talk to me like that.

Not when it comes to Mira.

And especially not when this topic is tearing me up inside already.

'Seriously, Simon? That's what you're coming at me with now?' Angry, he lets go of me and gives me a shove. I stagger backward and slam hard against the wall. 'For fuck's sake, I'm only trying to do what's best for you. Forget that old bitch and pull yourself together!'

'Right, you're only trying to do what's best for me? You're jealous, that's all! Because you'd like to have someone yourself.' I yell at him at full volume, so loud that the other people out here in front of the club turn to look at us. But I ignore them. My gaze is fixed on Paul, who's staring at me just as coldly as I'm staring at him.

'That's bullshit, and we both know it.' He sounds like a sulky little kid. 'I'm leaving now before I lose it. And you'—he jabs his index finger into my chest—'you make sure you get a hold of yourself, got it?'

Without waiting for my answer, he turns around and marches off. Maybe that's for the best anyway, because I can't think of a single thing I still want to say to him.

Chapter Twenty-Eight

Of all days, today the stupid June sun is blazing down from the sky with the full radiance of a thousand suns. Every single ray drills through my eyes and shoots into the back of my head, where it already hurts anyway.

I push myself up from my desk chair and drag myself over to the window of the admissions office. The blinds have to go down or I really am going to lose it in here.

'Rough night?' Horst looks over at me. He's holding a letter in his hand as if it were a newspaper. With the gray-rimmed reading glasses perched so far down his nose they're about to slip off, he looks a bit like a school principal.

Sighing, I shake my head and sink back down onto one of the chairs. Today I just want everyone to leave me alone. Even if I'd never admit it, my fight with Paul is getting to me at least as much as all the shots that went down the hatch last night.

Unimpressed by my dismissive hand gesture, Horst now rolls his swivel chair over to me. 'Come on, out with it,' he says, patting my upper arm like I'm a sick little kitten.

'Just way too much partying yesterday.' As fond as I am of Horst, we don't share any secrets; we just do the same job and try to have as much fun as possible while we're at it.

Understandingly, he hands me a can of drink. 'How about a little energy?'

'Oh yes.' The anticipation even makes me smile a little. I grab the energy drink, open it, and immediately take a sip. The liquid runs down my throat sticky-sweet and fizzy.

After that I still don't feel ready to finally deal with the discharge forms for today's release, but I reach for the folder anyway and start leafing through it. Probably just to get rid of Horst. I don't want him to keep asking questions, and he mustn't uncover what I'd most like to forget.

I'm stuck, in a dead end with no way to turn around. Over the past few weeks I've been heading straight for a wall. Nothing is right anymore.

'Give life a chance to show you what it has in store for you.' That's what Sandy advised me. And now?

Paul is furious. He didn't get in touch this morning. That says it all. He thinks I'm making the mistake of my life.

At the same time, the dream of my motorbike trip suddenly feels as if someone has dipped it in different colors. I was going to set off in six weeks, and until now that day in my imagination had been sky blue, grass green, and bright orange. Now it's running through my mind like an old black-and-white movie, pale and pixelated. And Mira? Imagining a life with my water girl feels like a particularly brutal contrast. And yet I can't stop.

Mira's message from yesterday had thrown everything into turmoil. I had to answer her. Or did I? What else could I have done but arrange to meet her on Friday evening?

When I think about seeing her again so soon, my

stomach tingles like crazy. And I know perfectly well it's not because of the energy drink I've finished by now. I crush the can and toss it into the trash. What if I'm really walking straight into my own disaster? What if I end up like my father, with three jobs and the constant feeling that I'm still not getting enough done?

My eyes wander over to the window, but all I can see is the blind I just pulled down myself. The world and its answers are hidden from me. Very fitting.

'Now that's interesting.' Horst jolts me out of my thoughts. Once again he steers his office chair toward me. 'Take a look at this.'

Oh God, can't he just leave me alone? 'Sorry, I really don't have time for that. All of this has to be finished by three.' I grab the thousand or so loose sheets on my desk and hold them up pointedly.

'Don't tell me the Professor doesn't interest you anymore.' Horst studies me over the rim of his reading glasses with his piercing green eyes.

My gaze jerks to the letter between his fingers. That's Mira's handwriting. Her reply is here. Do I want to know what she has to say to her criminal husband? No.

Horst eyes me suspiciously. 'What's wrong with you? Have you forgotten rule number one or what?'

'I haven't,' I snap at him more sharply than I'd like.

Horst's expression remains skeptical. 'Don't you let the inmates get to you. Especially not the ones who seem harmless. That can only end badly for you.'

I nod. 'I know that.'

All of a sudden Horst clears his throat at length. 'Heinrich, you want to be my husband?' In a pitch higher than usual, the letter stretched out far in front of him and with a theatrical expression on his face, he has begun to read the text out loud.

The hairs on my forearms stand on end.

'You want to be the father of my children? Biologically and financially, maybe, but you were never a real father. Raising the children, taking care of them and putting a smile on their faces, that was my job alone. You only wanted them nicely dressed, polite, and not too loud. And now that you don't have them with you anymore, you suddenly want to be their father?'

Horst throws me a questioning look. 'Wow, what's going on there? First-class marital crisis, huh?'

'Sounds like it.' I don't want to, but I keep listening to him anyway.

'For years that's exactly what I wished for. There was nothing I wanted more than for us to be a real family. If that were truly possible, I'd dance for joy. With tears in my eyes, my arms raised high and a smile as radiant as back then when you asked me if I wanted to marry you. You know why. Because back then you were still a different man. Even if I still believed in your innocence, that wouldn't change the situation. The three of us are here, you're not with us. And I haven't wished for it to be any different in a long time. Why do you think you could be a better father to Michael and Moritz with a few ridiculous visiting hours than you were all those years before?'

Horst pays no attention to me. He doesn't see how I furrow my brow and sink deeper and deeper into the armchair. Instead he turns the sheet in his hand and keeps reading.

'I don't know if I can do that, Heinrich. All I can promise you is that I'll think about it. For the sake of your few good qualities. And for our children's sake, because you're still their father and they miss you. Not for you. And even less for me.'

For a moment everything is quiet, even my head falls silent. I understand that she wants to make this sacrifice for the children, but I'm against it anyway. Because it makes no sense. On the contrary, it puts her happiness at risk.

I hear Paul in my head now, saying, *She's poison.* Is it true? Did Mira poison me?

I stare at the letter, watching in slow motion as Horst's fleshy fingers fold the delicate piece of paper and slip it back into the envelope. Mira's message goes into the mail crate. Horst says something, I don't hear it. I nod mechanically. No idea if that's the right thing to do. Then the mail crate disappears from my field of vision, probably along with Horst.

With my head resting in my hands, I try to form a coherent thought. It takes a long time, how long, I don't know. Seconds could be minutes, or even hours. But then at least I know one thing for sure.

There's nothing I want more than to be there for Mira, but at the same time I can't manage it. That's the truth.

I feel as if I'd survived a meteor strike. And now there's nothing left but an oversized crater right in the middle of my chest. Every one of my muscles hurts, but I still push myself up and head for the locker room. Barely awake enough to grasp what's going on around me, I walk down the corridor. One of the neon lights flickers. Somewhere someone shouts something. It sounds like a cry for help. Are they calling me?

I look up. There's Horst, with two inmates at once. One in each hand. 'Come on, Simon!' he yells, and suddenly I realize what's going on here.

The two inmates are fighting, the situation is on the verge of escalating.

Quick-thinking, I grab the baton at my belt and race toward the three of them. With every step I take in more of the unfolding situation. One of the inmates is Peters, the other is our corridor boss, Joe. Horst stands between them like a rock, pushing them apart with all his strength.

I grab hold of Peters and pull him out of the danger zone. Out of the corner of my eye I see Horst slam the drug lord against the wall. 'You okay?' I call to him and push the professor a bit farther down the corridor.

'Now I am. Why did that take so long?' Horst grumbles grouchily and snaps handcuffs onto Joe. The bright click of the lock is a signal that the danger is over. The situation is secure, but I still keep a firm grip on Peters' arm. 'Please take him back to his cell,' Horst says with a nod in the professor's direction.

Only now do I really look at Peters. A storm is raging in his watery blue eyes. His whole body is trembling, even the tips of his dark-blond hair are quivering.

I ignore his crazed expression. 'Come on,' I say, turning to go. The adrenaline drains from my body and far too quickly I crash back down to where I was a few minutes ago. Maybe even lower, because at my side now is exactly the man with whom all of this started.

Any second now he's going to ask me about Mira, I'm sure of it.

And it hits me that, in truth, the two of us are both locked up. Each in our own way.

For a while we walk to his cell in silence, then he clears his throat. 'Mira writes that we'll find our way back to each other,' he says in his pleasantly warm voice. 'I have you to thank for that.'

That's what he thinks? That he and Mira have a future together? I have no idea what I'm supposed to say to that.

Peters stops dead and looks at me just the way my father used to when I was sad. 'You look like you're carrying a heavy burden. Would you like to tell me about it?'

How considerate and careful he suddenly is. His eyes are warm, with no trace of the hate-filled guy from earlier. He's trying to wrap me around his finger. Again. 'No.'

'I understand.' He pats me on the upper arm, then leaves his hand there. 'If you need me, I'm here. The way you were there for me. Because often it's better to talk about what's weighing on you.'

As if my inner conflict weren't already big enough, he keeps throwing me off even more. Somewhere between my feelings for Mira and the fear of taking responsibility for a family, there is, despite everything, still a sympathy for the professor sitting right in the middle of my chest. I don't want that, because it was exactly this feeling that got me into this mess in the first place. Besides, I shouldn't trust him. Not after everything I know by now. I glance over at him.

How does he always manage to make me feel aligned with him, over and over again?

He smiles gently. And then I suddenly know.

It's the way he looks at me. The gestures of his hands and the timbre of his words. Too many things about him remind me of my father. I'm sure it's wrong, but I can't fight this one basic desire inside me. I want him to comfort me and put his arm around my shoulders. For a moment I want to feel as if I still had a father.

No, I mustn't go soft. I quickly walk on and pull him along with me. We're almost at his cell; I can make it until then.

Swallow, breathe, bite my lips. This has to work.

I repeat my ritual until we're standing in front of the cell door. Mechanically I unlock it, let him step inside, and immediately turn to go.

'You can do this,' I hear Peters whisper just before I close the door and lock it from the outside.

Then I'm alone with myself again. Only my despair is still there with me. And also the love and the fear. The two of them are fighting each other, and I no longer know myself which one is supposed to win.

'The things we do out of love give us freedom. But if you do something out of fear, it'll follow you forever like a shadow. You get to decide.' That's what Sandy once claimed, and back then I didn't understand a word of it. Now I'm starting to sense what it's supposed to mean.

I decide where my life takes me and who's by my side. In three days I'm going to see Mira again. And no one but me gets to decide whether I give in to love or to fear. Whether I run toward something that might just be a slice of heaven, or run away from the monster I might not be able to escape in the end.

Chapter Twenty-Nine

Now we're sitting across from each other. And I feel like I'm thirteen again and this is my very first date. My palms are damp, no matter how often I try to dry them on my clothes. Once more I run my hands over the flowing fabric of the turquoise dress. Hard to believe I'm wearing it. My keepsake from better times. Maybe I'm only doing it because it lets me hope my days will grow brighter again.

With Simon, or at least because of him.

If he keeps smiling at me from the other side of the table the way he is now, I'm going to get dizzy any minute. Even though he's only wearing a polo shirt, he looks ridiculously good. He almost makes me forget that we're in a restaurant. Surrounded by the murmur of voices, the clatter of cutlery on porcelain, and the smell of curry. In the background Indian music is playing, the waitresses are wearing saris in bright colors.

'So this is your favorite restaurant.' With an approving nod, Simon looks around. 'Want me to let you in on a secret?'

Faced with his conspiratorial expression, I have to chuckle. 'You find women in saris exceptionally attractive?' I tease.

'That too. But there's something else…' He leans across the table toward me, and I automatically mirror him.

Being this close to him feels like edging my way to the end of a cliff and looking down.

'This is my first time,' he says, and his blue-green eyes sparkle in the candlelight.

I stay serious. 'You're pretty late to the party, don't you think?'

'Maybe I was just waiting for you.' Suddenly the cheeky grin disappears from his face. Instead, he looks at me so intensely that a glow spreads through me at lightning speed.

'Mhm,' I say. I should say something. But what?

Now he moves his hand closer to mine. We almost touch, and even though I can't feel him, countless tiny sparks hit my skin. 'It's nice to be here. With you.'

Something's wrong. Where is the fun, easygoing Simon? Instinctively, my eyebrows draw together. 'I think so too.'

For a moment no one says anything, and I think I can see in his eyes that he doesn't understand what's happening either. He seems unsettled. A little bit as if he doesn't even know what he's doing here.

'Have you decided yet?'

I flinch. The waitress is standing at our table like she had appeared out of nowhere. Her deep purple sari is embroidered with golden ornaments, her hair is braided in the traditional style. Her gaze wanders back and forth between Simon and me. She's like a pivot point from the normal world that I can hold on to. I exhale in relief and order everything from the menu that I want Simon to try.

After the waitress leaves the table, Simon grins again. 'Masala? Sounds delicious!'

Thank God. Everything is normal. And I can finally do what I'd planned for today. Find out more about him.

'Tell me about yourself,' I urge him and run my hand over the smooth, cream-colored tablecloth to relieve my tension. 'Tell me something I don't know yet. Something special that matters to you.'

He takes a deep breath and lets it out again before he answers. His features are tense. 'You matter to me,' he forces out, as if admitting it is hard for him.

My pulse immediately speeds up, my hands sweat a little more. I slide back in the armchair as far as I can. What am I supposed to say to that? I have no idea, so there's only one thing left for me to do: ruthlessly ignore Simon's words. 'I meant before you met me. What do you dream of, what kind of life do you want to live?'

That's the question that will decide so much. Could Simon actually be there for me and my children? Would he stand by my side the way I've always wished a man would, but which I've never truly experienced?

Simon lowers his gaze, his fingers close around the glass in front of him and push it back and forth. Only a strained clearing of his throat can be heard, his right leg taps a staccato into the tiled floor. 'I dream of you,' he suddenly says quietly, without looking at me. It sounds like a wistful plea for something he believes he can't have.

Absentmindedly, I study him. Should I dig deeper? Better not, I mustn't let myself get distracted, I have to keep asking the questions that are so important to me. 'That's not what I meant and you know it. Regardless of me, or us. What does your life plan look like?'

With a sigh, he runs his hands through his short, brown

hair. 'I…' Now he lowers his gaze. He squirms like a small child who's afraid to admit the truth.

There's something there, a secret he's hiding from me.

'So that's how it is.' My voice is steady and firm, but inside me whole dams are bursting.

I fold my arms across my chest, but it still doesn't give me any protection. Maybe I'm exaggerating, but the fear that Eva took from me only last night comes flooding right back to me as fast as a boomerang.

Simon isn't what I need. Getting involved with him would be my downfall.

Chapter Thirty

This feels like she's slamming the door to her heart in my face. She sits opposite me, her expression turned to stone. In the middle of the busy Indian restaurant, accompanied by exotic sounds. The air between us is completely still, yet the candle on our table flickers so violently it looks as if it might go out.

'Listen to your heart,' Sandy's voice now whispers in my head. At the same time, I feel doubt gnawing away at me. But a little higher up there's this longing, and it's stronger than anything else. It even beats the fear.

My heart isn't speaking.

It's roaring with all its strength.

For Mira.

I can't just sit here and watch her withdraw on the other side of the table as if she were a snail and the softly cushioned chair were her shell. So I do it. I'm going to tell her. She's going to know absolutely everything.

'Mira, listen to me,' I begin, even though it's unnecessary. From the way she's staring at me, all her senses are probably turned up to the max. 'Before I met you, my life was one big party. I loved freedom, didn't want to make any commitments and didn't want to take on any responsibility.'

I immediately see panic in her eyes, hear the unevenness of her breathing.

I reach for her hand. 'My lifelong dream was to travel. For years now I've wanted to explore the world on a motorbike.' It's out, but I don't feel the slightest bit lighter. Maybe because that 'was' slipped into the sentence involuntarily and made the 'is' disappear. Or because this trip is only a small part of the truth.

'When will you leave?' All at once she sounds like a robot. Her fingers are cold.

I can't look at her any longer, so I lower my eyes and clear my throat. 'Early August. It's all planned. Just a few more weeks, then…' Saying it out loud feels wrong. And quite suddenly, I know I can't do it.

Going on this trip won't make me happy. I'd just be giving in to my fear and probably still wouldn't get rid of it. Even though I know that, I can still hear Sandy's voice in my head. 'The things we do out of love give us freedom,' she says, sounding so caring it's as if she's hugging me right now.

The fact that at the same moment I can also see how disappointed Mira is about my trip makes my last doubts disappear. She's trembling, so I hold her tight. And that's what I want to keep doing. 'I'm not going to leave, Mira,' I say with complete conviction and feel strangely liberated. 'Because I want to be with you. And with your children.'

She doesn't say a word. Instead, she slowly stretches her hand out to me across the table. I lean toward her, her fingers wander along my hairline, feeling their way to my temple and stroke my cheek.

In a strange way, that gives me courage. Maybe I'm crazy, but in this moment I'm sure we can make it. 'I tried to fight it. I mean the feelings. For you.' Of all times, now I'm in danger of stuttering. I can feel it clearly, my sentences are getting short and choppy.

All at once I can feel her pulse at her wrist. It's irregular and so hard it's like she's just finished a hurdles race.

One last breath, then I'll say it. Now. 'I-I've fallen in love with you. Completely. In love.'

It's out, so she knows. At once my muscles give way, my head feels heavy. I feel as if, for a moment, I had single-handedly kept the whole world turning through one great, big, tremendous effort. Still, I don't take my eyes off her face. Her lips move as if she wanted to say something she then doesn't say after all. She doesn't have to. I can feel what's going on, so I dare to speak for her. 'You fell in love with me too?'

With a desperate expression on her face, Mira lowers her head. Just a little. Then she lifts it again.

That's a nod. She's nodding!

Suddenly even the last trace of my fear is gone, and I know exactly that we're going to make it. Now there's only one thing I want.

I have to kiss her.

Impulsively, I push myself up from my chair and lean across the table. But before I reach her, she raises her hand defensively. 'Wait,' she whispers hoarsely.

I don't back away. 'Wait for what?'

'There's something I have to do.' Her expression turns serious, the flurry of energy between us discharges in a flash.

I stay exactly where I am and look at her expectantly. I don't dare ask anything more. Especially not now, when she's also pushing me away from her. Confused, I sit back down on my chair. The waitress brings our food, but I don't pay any attention to her. All my attention is on Mira.

Nervously, she picks at her fingernails. 'Give me a few more days.'

What's happening here? Just a moment ago everything was fine. 'What for?'

'I have to take care of something.'

The pain in her face is almost unbearable. I want to help her, I just have to be there for her. 'You can tell me.'

A tortured smile appears on her lips. 'I know that. Let's do something together the day after tomorrow. I'll be free then.'

'Free?' I ask tonelessly. What's that supposed to mean? A bad premonition gathers in my thoughts like thunderclouds in a sky that was still bright blue just a moment ago.

She hesitates. Studies me. Pushes her hair behind her ear. 'I have to see Heinrich one last time. Even if a lot went wrong, I owe him that. And our children.' There's fear in her eyes, I can see it clearly. 'Tomorrow I'm going to visit him in prison.'

Her words hit me without warning. All at once I feel so sick, like I'd eaten a plate of rotten fish.

Chapter Thirty-One

It's decided. I've said it out loud, so I'm going to do it. I have to see Heinrich one last time to finally put the past behind me.

I study Simon. The skin of his cheeks is suddenly as pale as the porcelain of his plate. He looks a bit as if he's seeing a ghost. Or as if he were one himself.

'Y-you…' he stutters blankly to himself. Then he clears his throat, shifts his chair, and smooths the already crease-free tablecloth.

His behavior scares me. My gaze jumps back and forth between his tormented eyes and his plate. Is the food not agreeing with him? Has he even tried the curry soup yet? 'Is everything okay?'

Just a nod, that's all I get.

'What's wrong all of a sudden?'

'I-I don't think you should visit him,' Simon says, fixing me with an intent look, and it feels as if thunderclouds were gathering right here in this chic Indian restaurant, between the colorful table decorations and the muted music. 'Because…'

No, I don't even want to hear the reason. 'That shouldn't be your concern.' The words leave my mouth harsher than I intended. My body shifts into a defensive posture. With my legs entwined and my arms crossed, I lean back in my chair.

Simon's posture changes immediately; he leans far across the table, reaches his hand out to me, and strokes a bit roughly along my forearm. 'Of course, it's your decision.' He squirms nervously on his chair. 'I just don't want you to be unhappy. Seeing him could hurt you.' His voice is nothing but a whisper, and with his thumb he traces a circle on my skin. Round and round again.

Heinrich and I, that has to end. A final closure. Only then can I give myself fully to Simon. 'I just have to do it, no matter if it hurts,' I say firmly.

Each of my words makes him flinch. 'You should let the past rest. Why rip open old wounds?' He looks at me with his shoulders raised. 'Besides, there's something…'

All at once, distrust rises up in me. 'They're my wounds. And I'll rip them open whenever I want.' Even though I mean to give my words a gentle tone, the exact opposite occurs.

Why is he clinging so desperately to his request? He's too passionate, putting far too much into convincing me. Is it really only his concern for my happiness?

Or is there more to it than that? Something he doesn't want to tell me?

I scan every inch of his face. The muscles beneath his three-day stubble are tense, his jaw hard.

'It's decided.' The sound of my voice leaves no room for doubt. This has to stop.

As if he's finally accepting it, Simon lifts his arms in a calming gesture. 'Okay,' he says, so utterly drained of strength that my heart suddenly turns heavy.

While I try to bring my body back under control, I watch Simon press his lips together, like there are words in his throat he doesn't want to let out.

So here we are. In my favorite restaurant. We've confessed our love to each other, and yet there are still unspoken words on our tongues. This is going wrong, and I can't begin to understand why. All I wanted was to kiss him, free at last, very soon. To lie in his arms, learn more about him, and drift away with him into a world full of lightness and warmth.

'Let's eat,' Simon suddenly says into the silence between us. 'This evening is too beautiful not to enjoy it.'

It's as if we're thinking the same thing. As if we're one, even though we've only known each other for a few weeks.

I push my doubts aside, move my chair close to the table and lean over toward Simon as far as I can. Relieved, I watch him do the same.

His face is now so close that I can touch it. With my index finger I trace the fine scar above his eyebrow, wander over his nose and on to his mouth. At first he keeps still, but then he starts kissing the tip of my finger. A thousand tiny electric shocks pierce my skin and find their way straight into my chest. Once there, they make my longing grow at a speed that incomparable with anything else in this world. It outgrows the fear, overtakes my doubts, and pushes the mistrust to a place where it no longer has any power over me.

Very soon nothing in the world will be able to hold me back. I'm going to kiss him. And it will feel as if I were leaving my old life behind forever to begin a new one.

Chapter Thirty-Two

'It's really urgent, sir.' A pleading look in my eyes, I stare deep into the boss's eyes across his metallic gray desk.

With a sigh he props his head on his arms. 'Herbst, I already told you, today is not possible. Two colleagues are already on vacation, Schwarz is still sick, and Weininger has to go to a funeral. I'm already down four people; I can't afford to lose another one.'

'It's a family matter,' I say without thinking and pray that he won't ask for more details.

His right eyebrow climbs toward his hairline. 'Oh yeah?'

I just nod vigorously while I desperately search for a really good reason for the last-minute vacation request. But my mind is blank. I only know one thing: if I stay, Mira will see me here. And she'll find out that I know Peters. That I know more than she thought so far and that she trusted me even though I'd been deceiving her from the very beginning. So many times I wanted to tell her the truth about how we met. But I never managed it. And now…

Damn it, how could I let this happen? How could I keep

putting it off and silently hope it would never be necessary to tell her at all?

'Anyway,' the boss says now with a shrug, snapping me out of my thoughts, 'I can't approve the request. Next time just stick to the deadlines and then it'll work out.'

No. Please don't. My mind is racing while he turns back to his work. Damn it, I went about this the wrong way. I shouldn't have asked for time off; I should've faked a stomach bug right away. Then he wouldn't have had a choice, he would've been forced to let me go.

With narrowed eyes, he focuses on the screen and starts pecking at the keyboard at a snail's pace with both index fingers. 'Anything else?' he asks absently, his gaze fixed on the monitor.

Of course there is. I can't stay here today.

Absolutely not!

'Herbst!' he barks at me. 'What on earth are you waiting for? Get to work. Go on.'

Mechanically, I spring up from the tiny visitor's chair in his office. When he looks like that, you'd better make sure you get yourself to safety. Still, I can't leave any stone unturned. 'And if I just...'

'That's enough!' he cuts me off and stares at me, a dangerous flash in his eyes. 'From now on, apart from the careful closing of the door from the outside and your footsteps fading into the distance, I don't want to hear another thing, understood?'

'Yes, sir.' I'd better skip the saluting gesture, or his carotid artery will start throbbing too. Instead, I drag myself to the door with slumped shoulders and close it behind me with the delicate care he requested.

Leaning against the wall next to the boss's office, I let the back of my head thud again and again against the cream-painted wall. It hurts, but so what. Anything that gets my thoughts flowing is welcome. Even if it's pain.

How am I supposed to avoid running into Mira when I don't even know exactly when she's coming? On top of that, I have paperwork to do today. In the admissions office right by the entrance. I can't just hide under a desk when she walks through the door. I don't have any choice but to keep an eye on the parking lot. And as soon as Mira appears out there, I'll disappear. But where to? And when can I come back to the office? After an hour? Or two?

With great effort, I push myself away from the wall. If the boss comes out and sees me standing here, all hell will really break loose. I march down the corridor, my gaze wandering to the plain clock above the double doors to the waiting room. It's just after eight. What if she heads straight over here after dropping the kids off at kindergarten?

I slip through the door to the admissions office; no one is there. If she comes now, I'll have to fill out the visitor's pass with her as well. Please no. Just the thought of it speeds up my heartbeat, my palms feel like a frog's skin. Damp and cold. I try to breathe in and out deeply, but over and over the air gets stuck somewhere between my throat and my lungs.

Out of nowhere, Horst is suddenly standing behind me. 'You should lay off the hard drugs,' he says, amused, and claps me on the shoulder. 'Or this is really going to end badly.'

What did he say? There's no room in my head for his words today; they bounce off my eardrums and vanish into the nowhere of the dusty office air. Confused, I stare at him.

'A drowned corpse would look more attractive than you do right now,' he adds, as if that explained anything. He strolls past me and drops into one of the desk chairs with a flourish. It creaks under the sudden weight, but I barely hear it. My stare is fixed so firmly on the window at the front of the building that it's as if someone had lined it up precisely and glued it there.

Is she here already?

No one is in sight. I try to relax, slide soundlessly onto a chair, and pull it up to the desk with the best view of the parking lot. Horst might still be muttering away as usual. I don't hear him. It's like only one of my senses is working. Sight. I register every car and every tiny movement of the leaves in the courtyard. I can even see the flies taking off from and landing on the windowpane one by one. Suddenly a dark shadow flits past. Black hair whirls. Then I recognize a face.

Mira. She's here. My eyes follows her strides. For far too long I watch one breath of air after another ripple through her loosely fluttering white summer dress. I can even hear the countless golden bangles on her wrist clinking as she reaches for the door handle.

'Bam,' Horst murmurs, somewhere very far away.

I jump up, the swivel chair crashing loudly against the filing cabinet behind me.

What are my legs doing? Why are they just standing there? They should be moving, but they're stuck to the dark gray laminate floor.

'What's wrong, buddy? Don't tell me you're leaving that hot babe to me?' Horst's voice cracks and he looks at me in astonishment. 'Are you sick?'

I don't answer, just stare back at the entrance door, which is almost halfway open. It's like I'm trapped in a horror movie. The seductive monster, that actually isn't one a monster all, is almost here, and I still can't run.

'Since when do you let a chance like this slip by?' I don't

know if Horst sounds surprised or worried. I'm not listening carefully enough to make it out. My attention is on Mira alone.

She steps into the hallway and, even though it's impossible, I can already smell her vanilla scent. It's everywhere. Around me and inside me.

I have to get out of here. Now.

Chapter Thirty-Three

I still don't move, individual beads of sweat slowly running down my temples.

If Mira sees me, in the uniform, in the middle of the office and with the inmates' files in my hand, it's all over. My head understands that, and still it can't do anything about it. Not as long as my damn body won't do what it's supposed to.

The door slams shut loudly behind Mira while she seems to pause for a moment. Then she straightens up and marches off. Fast and full of energy, with her chin raised and her gaze fixed on her goal.

'Come on over here to me, you hot thing,' I hear Horst murmur, and I'd pretty well like to pounce on him like a lion on its prey.

How dare he talk about her like that?

Now Mira steps up to the reception counter and lays her decorated forearms, clinking with jewelry, on the ledge in front of the glass window. My heartbeat is suddenly everywhere. In my chest, behind my forehead, and even in the tips of my toes.

In slow motion she turns her head in my direction.

Any second now she'll see me. I have to do something. Right now.

Far too loud, I hear the scraping sound of the glass window insert whose doors Horst is opening now. Really it's so quiet I hardly ever notice it, but today it shoots straight into my bones.

That's good. My legs are still alive. And they finally get what they're supposed to do.

In a flash they pivot on the spot and hurry toward the office door. Is it her penetrative stare that I feel on my back, or am I just imagining it? Does she see me? Is she looking at me, right now, and does she know who I am?

'I'd like to see my husband. Heinrich Peters.' She sounds sober and clear. As if she had left her emotions at home. As if only her beautiful outer shell had come here.

I no longer hear what Horst answers. I slip through the door and close it behind me with trembling fingers.

It's done. At least I want to believe it.

From the cloakroom you can see the doors to the visiting rooms. That's where I have to wait until Mira leaves the prison again. For a moment I hesitate. My personnel file already has too many entries, and the boss has warned me too many times. If he finds me in my hiding place, he'll definitely throw me out. That must not happen under any circumstances, and yet I have no choice. No matter what I do, with every option I risk absolutely everything.

Even though my rubbery bones can hardly carry me, I start walking. Accompanied by an army of guilty feelings. They stay with me until I reach the changing room. That's where the waiting begins, and there's nothing I can do but sit pressed into the corner of the room and stare at the metal door behind which Mira and Heinrich Peters are now facing each other for the first time in a long while.

Just the two of them. No partition. And no handcuffs.

As if knowing that weren't bad enough, images now appear in my head like fragmented film scenes.

Peters gently stroking his wife's hair. Mira giving him a fearful smile and telling him that she wants to put an end to it. All at once Peters gets that crazy look. He grabs her by the wrists and presses her bangles so hard into her skin that she screams.

I feel sick, and if I weren't surrounded on two sides by thick walls, I'd collapse on the spot. Still, my mind keeps going and shows me everything I don't want to see.

Now the professor presses his lips together. He stares at Mira, cold and full of hatred. Then he squeezes even harder, his muscles trembling.

Oh God, I can't take this! Still it doesn't stop.

He looms over her, she's frozen solid with fear. Then it happens. I want to scream, step in, stop it. But I'm paralyzed. In disbelief I stare and have to watch as he draws back his hand.

He does it. He hits her. With full force.

Then he bends over her and whispers something I can't understand. It sounds like vicious threats.

Let her go! Even though I'm screaming it in my head, he doesn't hear me. He keeps going.

My legs give way; pressed into the corner of the cloakroom, I slide down. The rough plaster scrapes across my back. If what's happening in there, behind that opaque door, is really happening right now, then… No, there is no then, because I have no idea what I'm supposed to do.

Suddenly something moves at the edge of my vision.

Instinctively I spring up, my eyes fixed in panic on the corridor behind the glass panel in the cloakroom door.

Mira comes out with her head lowered. Her posture doesn't tell me anything, no matter how closely I study her. Are her fingers trembling? Is her breathing steady? I don't know, I just can't see it. And on top of that, she disappears from my field of vision far too quickly.

At that moment the door of the visiting room opens once more. The professor comes out, accompanied by my colleague Petra. I have to know that Mira is alright, right now. So I rush out into the corridor. I really shouldn't be doing that, but there's no other way. I can't stand it for a second longer.

'Petra, you're a first aider, right? Could you go and help Horst at reception? I think he's got stomach problems or something.' I sound frantic.

'Of course,' she says quickly. 'Will you take Mr. Peters back for me? Cell H-33.'

'Sure, no problem.' I grab the professor by the upper arm, maybe a bit too tightly. But that really doesn't matter right now. We set off at once and I don't let a single second go to waste. The way to his cell is far too short anyway. 'Was that your wife?' I ask bluntly.

Peters lifts his gaze and looks straight at me. 'Yes,' he says, not even trying to hide his tears. Quietly they glide down his cheeks. The skin beneath is flushed red.

Is that a sign that his anger has ebbed away?

'What did she want?' I sound as if I'd swallowed a wasp. But I ignore that; it's not important. All that matters now is his answer.

Chapter Thirty-Four

If I could, I would scream. Loud and furious, without rhyme or reason. Yet I stay very quiet, politely say goodbye to the overweight guard, and push the door open to the outside.

I step over the threshold and I'm free. Exactly where Heinrich won't be for a very long time to come.

With every step I take, I notice how the pent-up emotions churn more violently inside me. They want to break out, but I won't allow that. Not now. I keep walking, on and on, all the way to my car. Impulsively I yank open the driver's door and drop onto the seat. Even the cold leather of the backrest can't stop the impending volcanic eruption. No more than the silence of the car and the distance that now lies between Heinrich and me.

Tears well up in me under pressure, like magma in the throat of a volcano. A violent tremor seizes my whole body, the earth quakes and with it everything around me. Even the pale blue time display on the dashboard blurs before my eyes.

I fall apart.

There's nothing left, only the salty droplets that now relentlessly force their way out.

Did I really just do that?

Chapter Thirty-Five

If the professor keeps staring at me in silence any longer, I'll have to shake the truth out of him. I'll just grab his shoulders and rattle him until the words tumble out of his mouth on their own.

'S-so, what did your wife want?' I ask, even more insistently than before, as we move inexorably toward his cell.

Shaking his head, he puts one foot in front of the other; nothing can be heard but the dull sound of our soles on the softly gleaming plastic floor.

I probably shouldn't even be asking. And I should be more patient, too. But I don't have time for that. 'Come on, just tell me. After everything I've found out, I just have to know how your story together continues.' As I say the word 'together,' my stomach twists itself into one big knot.

'Mira, my wife…' He finally speaks. 'She…' He clears his throat, then falls silent again.

What the hell is this? No torturer in the world could torment me the way he's doing it right now with his silence. Questioningly, I raise my eyebrows. 'She…'

'She wants a divorce.' Even more tears well up at the corners of his eyes. They look like raging rivers. And although I know he's only playing the sad man for me here, it still doesn't leave me untouched, just like always. Despair, helplessness, and grief. All that is what I think I can see in his face now. 'You helped me, Herbst. How could this happen?' A trembling whisper, that's all it is that just left Peters' mouth.

'Shit, man, I don't know.' I squeeze the words out from somewhere. I watch him out of the corner of my eye. Again and again he touches his cheek. Only when he takes his hand away can I see why.

There are fingerprints on his skin.

I realize immediately what happened. He tried, he wanted to force her to stay with him. With violence. And she fought back. There's no other possibility, that's what must have happened.

More than anything I'd like to slam him against the wall right now for what he just tried to do to Mira. Press my forearm against his throat and force him to finally show me his true face. But if I've learned one thing by now, it's that I'm just me.

Just as little as I contain of my father, I'm like him. So I press my lips together and try to let go of my anger. Even though it's only a few more steps to his cell, they seem terribly long to me. Then at last I can shove him through the door.

All at once he grabs my arm, his eyes are cold. 'She'll regret this.' Even his tone makes me shiver.

I try to tear myself free, but I don't stand a chance. My body freezes because now I finally have the very last proof. Peters is an insane psychopath.

The whole time he put on an act for me, and even though I already knew it, I, the idiot, felt sorry for him.

'You're going to go to her and give her a message from me,' he hisses now, squeezing even harder. 'Tell her I'll find her. As soon as I'm out of here...' I see how hard he's pressing his teeth together, a vein stands out at his temple. 'And now get out. I want to be alone.'

Abruptly he lets go of me. I stagger against the cell wall, dizzy from the thoughts that keep spiralling in my head.

I should have known from the start that it would end like this. But I didn't want to see the signs. Mira must have felt the same way all those years. I can all too easily understand why she stood by him until he was convicted. After all, he managed it with me too. He wrapped me around his finger with his feigned despair and his masterful way with words. He put on his act for both of us, and he was able to deceive us both with it.

I spin around quickly and leave the cell. Then I lock it from the outside. Because I'm the one holding the key. I walk to the locker room and take my phone out of my locker. With trembling fingers I type a message to Mira. 'Hey, water girl. Can we see each other today?'

Not a minute later I get the answer. 'Absolutely,' it says. Just this one word, and yet it tells me everything I need to know.

Nothing is holding us back anymore. Peters is the past, and even my own fear has disappeared. We can finally be together, or, as Sandy would put it, give life a chance to show us what it has in store for us.

Chapter Thirty-Six

'Thanks, Kathi.' I take a deep breath, and it's as if, for the first time in months, I can really breathe again.

Feeling liberated, I press the little red button on my phone's display. I did it. Kathi listened to me. She hardly said a word herself, but the mere fact that she picked up my call feels like a miracle. Inevitably I smile as I walk down the dimly lit hallway. I feel light. And free. As if my feet no longer touched the marbled tile floor.

So this is it, my fresh start. Not just with my friend, but also with Simon.

When I reach his apartment door, I ring the bell. He'll open up for me any second, and I can feel in every fiber of my body how ready I am. Once more I tuck my hair behind my ear and wipe my palms on my jeans. In vain. Even though it isn't particularly warm today, I'm sweating so hard you'd think it was a tropical night.

Now I hear Simon running toward me behind the door. I breathe out as best I can and straighten my top. There's no reason to be nervous, and yet my heart is pounding so heavily in my chest it's as if it can't believe it's actually about to get what it so desperately needs.

The handle moves down, and in slow motion the door opens.

There he is. He smiles at me. With radiant eyes, blue-green like the Indian Ocean. His brown hair sticks up in wild disarray, as if he'd just been lying in bed. That three-day stubble makes him terribly attractive; I have to look away to keep my legs from giving out.

'Hey.' He comes toward me and wraps his arms around me. Strong and gentle at the same time, he holds me tight and buries his nose in my hair. 'My water girl,' he whispers. His voice trembles, just like the fingertips that stroke down my back.

All at once I can feel it. His heart is galloping. In the same rhythm as mine. And I'm sure that's a sign.

I can't wait any longer. So I push him a little away from me. Just enough so I can lift my head and look into his eyes. Then I rise up onto my tiptoes.

He smirks. Waiting patiently, he stays exactly where he is. It's my decision. That's what he wants to tell me.

I do it. Here and now I press my lips to his. Very gently, as if it were a promise.

He tastes like summer on the Italian coast, of rosemary and lemon. My eyes fall shut and at once I feel like I'm diving into his world. I sink deeper, and yet I don't drown.

On the contrary. I'm far more alive than I have been in a long time.

It's possible my knees give out. My fingers might be trembling. But I don't notice any of that. I only want to feel his kiss and what it's doing to me. With every second I feel it more clearly. Being with him is all I need. I lose my sense of time and space, only registering that at some point he pulls away from me again.

'Come in,' he murmurs, brushing my hair out of my face with both hands and kissing my forehead. 'Are the boys at your friend's place?'

I nod absentmindedly, because only now do I notice that we're still standing in front of his apartment. In a stairwell tiled in beige that suddenly seems utterly romantic. I must be crazy. My senses don't work anymore, but nothing could be more beautiful than this.

Hand in hand, we enter Simon's apartment. It's tiny and furnished like a typical bachelor pad. I don't even have to take three steps before I'm standing right in the middle of his life.

Between the sofa bed, the TV, and a little kitchenette, there's room for only a small round table with two chairs. In the corner, a terribly sad plant ekes out a shadowy existence. The yellowish light of a solitary candle on the worn coffee table flickers.

'What do you think?' Simon sounds hopeful, maybe a little excited too.

It's not particularly big. And anything but childproof.

Before I can answer, I see panic in his face. 'Yes, it's smaller than your house. And much less nice. But…'

'And you think that matters to me?' I give him a wide smile.

Nervously, he shrugs his shoulders. 'Well, I just thought, the way you're living now, so…'

I press myself against him. 'The house is nothing but a gilded cage,' I whisper in his ear and run my hand along his arm, right where the fine hairs are now standing up. 'Pretty on the outside, but no real home on the inside.'

He wraps his arms around me, and I think I hear him exhale with relief. 'I don't earn that much, you know.'

So that's what he's afraid of. He thinks he has to give me a life of luxury. I quickly shake my head. 'Simon, I want to be with you. The where doesn't matter, as long as we have each other.' I let my hands glide over his back and look into his eyes so intensely that he has to know how serious I am.

He takes a breath, so deep it's as if he'd been underwater for minutes. Then he lets the air out again, shaky and hot. Suddenly he seems like he'd just gotten rid of a burden that was hard for him to carry. 'You do realize where this is going to end, don't you?' he says in an urgent voice. Then he kisses me, as full of promise and passion as never before.

'Absolutely.' My head is spinning. Up there it's wonderfully dim, pleasantly warm, and gloriously free.

I let myself fall, straight into his arms and down onto the sofa with him. His hand glides over my collarbone and then farther down. There he stops his movement and looks at me questioningly. It's like he's afraid to touch me, as if he's worried I might feel uncomfortable.

Nothing could prove to me more in this moment how important I am to him.

Smiling, I lay my hand on his and guide it downward. His fingertips flutter over my stomach and carefully slip under my top. That's exactly where they need to be, and everywhere else on my body.

Now Simon bends over me and covers my face with kisses. His breath brushes my ear. 'Mira, I…'

Suddenly the longing I've carried inside me for as long as I can remember falls silent. There's no doubt, nothing that could hold me back.

'I love you too,' I whisper, and it has never felt so right to say those words.

Chapter Thirty-Seven

'Kaufmann, Steininger. Yard duty.' In his usual strict tone, the boss rattles off the work assignments. At a volume that makes it seem like he thinks we're all hard of hearing.

'What are you grinning about?' Horst leans over to me; I can clearly see on his face how hungry he is for some exciting news.

Keeping my eyes fixed on the boss, who is standing up front at the board like a bear on two legs, I grin broadly. Today is June 26; in four days I had planned to hand in my resignation. But by the looks of it, I'll be doing this job longer than planned. 'No idea what you're talking about.' I whisper, since the duty roster is being announced right now.

'Oh, come on, I'm not your mommy.' Horst jabs his elbow into my side. 'I can see perfectly well what's going on.'

Shaking my head, I shift my weight onto the other leg. 'If that's the case, then you don't need to ask. Do you?'

Even though I don't look at him, I know how Horst's face twists into one big question mark. 'Hot night, huh?'

Before I can answer, the boss sternly locks eyes with me. 'Is there a problem, Herbst?' he asks.

I straighten up at once. 'Of course not,' I say with the precision of a Swiss watch, because one thing is absolutely clear. This job is the foundation of my new life. I won't risk a single thing anymore.

'Good, then. You're on office duty.'

His devious grin doesn't get to me. Not today. I smile. 'With pleasure. I'm already looking forward to it.'

For a moment he inspects me intently. Then he abruptly turns back to the board. 'Weininger, bakery. Together with Schwarz.'

Horst fidgets nervously beside me. He stays quiet, but only until the boss finished his speech and the meeting in the conference room slowly breaks up. Even when I head from reception toward the open-plan office, he practically sticks to me. 'Come on, out with it,' he urged me again.

I remembered every single second of last night, down to the smallest detail. I could still feel Mira's hair, silky as it slid over my stomach, I could taste the salty film on her skin and hear her breath at my ear. Just thinking of how she smiled at me, lit only by candlelight, catapulted me into another world.

'So that's how it is.' Horst started nodding vigorously. 'I get it. Congratulations.' In a matey way he clapped me on the back and, blow by blow, hauled me back into reality.

All right, whatever. There was no reason to hold it back anymore. 'Thanks,' I said, 'but I've got to go now. You heard how much there is to do today.'

He didn't buy my apologetic look; I could see it clearly in his face. 'You don't need to say anything anyway, I already know everything,' he said proudly and turned off toward the bakery. Then he looked back again. 'I'm happy for you.'

Instead of an answer he got nothing from me but a dismissive wave of the hand. That was going a bit too far; after all, we were in prison here, not in some soap opera. Still, I couldn't help whistling a tune to myself on the way to the admissions office. Nobody could spoil my mood, not today and not on any other day. Mira and I were a couple and we had a future I was absolutely ready for. The world could have ended today and I still would have been as happy as I had ever been in my entire life.

On the way I typed a message to Sandy into my phone. 'Thanks,' was all I wrote, because she definitely knew how many other things I wanted to say to her with it.

Just a few seconds later her reply came in. 'Sometimes we're afraid of falling. We don't see what's coming. So we cling to what we know, no matter whether it's good for us or not. In doing so we far too often forget that after we jump we might not only fall, but also fly.'

I couldn't help shaking my head. At myself. I used to call sentences like that Sandy's 'esoteric nonsense.' I had been blind, mute, and deaf on top of it.

Today, that's not the only thing that's different. So much has changed, and nothing could ever be better than this.

'Shall we do something together tomorrow? Mom, the girls and you, you're all invited,' I type on impulse.

'As I live and breathe…,' my sister replies immediately. For a change, there's a winking emoji shining following her words.

We arrange the details, and for the first time in my life I feel a sense of anticipation at the thought of spending time with my family. There are no shadows and no fears. Only cheerfulness and this long-awaited sense of freedom.

When I get to the office, I simply smile away the stack of papers on my desk, even though it's terribly high. I should probably get straight to work, but my thoughts drift off again. To the moment when I woke up next to Mira this morning.

The world around me wakes only slowly; I begin to hear, to smell, and to feel. Warm, soft, and breathing quietly, Mira nestles against me.

Naked.

Her hand rests on mine while I wrap my arm around her from behind and hold her like a treasured prize. My fingers wander over the barely visible crescent-moon-shaped scars on her forearm. I bury my nose in her hair, and then it happens all of a sudden.

A tiny tear squeezes itself out of the corner of my eye, just like that. Without warning, as if my senses were overloaded. As if they wanted to show me what I already knew to brue. Waking up next to my water girl is what I want to do for the rest of my life. And nothing else.

It's the tears that show us the right way, my sister claims. How often I didn't take her seriously and just shrugged it off. But not anymore. Because there's one thing I know for sure. What we truly feel is what defines us. Not what we think we want to feel.

A loud stomping in the hallway jolts me abruptly out of my thoughts.

Where am I? What's going on here?

I look around. Work, of course. The stack of folders lies untouched in front of me. Instinctively I grab the top file. If that out there in the corridor is the boss, he definitely needs to see me working. So I open the documents and pretend to read them intently. At that exact moment, the door right next to me is flung open. There's a boom, a cold draft pushes past me. But to me, it all feels like it's happening far away. Because what my eyes are processing right now catapults me to a completely different place.

I'm not here.

Not with Mira either. And not in my bed.

No, I'm in hell.

I read again what's written on the cover sheet of the documents, but the letters don't change. The words stay as they are and stare back at me.

Heinrich Peters. Release.

A feeling as if I were falling from way up high, down into the deepest trench, seizes me. I can't breathe. And I can't think. All I can do is fall.

Peters is free. Impossible. That can't be true.

He is guilty, after all!

Or was he never really to begin with?

Chapter Thirty-Eight

My fingers raced frantically over the paper, but they couldn't erase the writing. Instead, the letters started to dance before my very eyes. It was true. The Professor was being released. Today.

'Are you going to get on with it sometime?' I heard an exasperated female voice ask in the middle of the roller coaster ride of my thoughts and emotions.

Was someone actually standing next to me? I looked up and saw the annoyed face of my colleague Petra. Oh right, that bang earlier. That must have been the door.

With narrowed eyes she examined me. 'Everything okay?'

For whatever reason, I could only stare at her. Not because the feminine sound of her voice didn't fit her boyish short haircut. No, my head was spinning, I couldn't find any words, and before long I was going to run out of air.

'Then step on it, the one from cell H-33 has been waiting an eternity in the release room for his papers.' Her head jerked toward the door.

Neither her contemptuous snort nor the affected eye-roll hit home. Less than a minute ago my nightmare had become reality. Over there, behind that wall where an office chair had beaten countless deep black streaks into the plaster, the Professor was sitting. Without handcuffs. Free to go wherever he wanted. And to do whatever he had planned.

'Simon, get a move on. If the boss notices you're sitting around doing nothing again, you're in for it.' Petra doesn't even turn around to look at me, she just throws her warning into the room while she marches over to the filing cabinets. 'And you really don't have many more lives.'

Damn. She's right, of course. But…

'Do you hear that?' She taps her index finger against her ear.

What does she mean? I try to make it out, but the blood is pounding so hard in my veins that it drowns everything else out. 'What?' I at least manage to ask.

Now she does turn to face me. 'He's coming,' she says, and she sounds like she's announcing the zombie apocalypse in a horror movie.

I spring to my feet, grab the documents, and start running. My mind is completely blank. Only my legs are working. They put one foot in front of the other.

This just can't be happening. Maybe I'm actually not on my way to the Professor right now. I'm probably not pressing down the door handle this very moment, and who can say whether I really enter the room?

Am I smiling at him? Am I breathing? I don't know.

'Herr Herbst! How nice to run into you one more time,' he says, adopting his falsely paternal tone. 'I truly want to thank you. You've done so much for me.'

On the table in front of him lies a transparent plastic

bag with the personal belongings that were taken from him when he was taken in. I've seen bags like that a thousand times, and still this one is different. Everything is different anyway. The temperature. The light. Even the colors in here.

I sit down at the table opposite Peters. Mechanically, I open his file and lay the papers out in front of him. 'Y-you still need to sign here. And on pages three, nine, and ten as well.'

For a brief moment, his eyebrows draw together. Then he turns to the documents and leafs through them page by page with his well-groomed, long-fingered hands.

That's when I see it.

He's wearing his wedding ring. It gleams golden and slender on his ring finger and looks as if it didn't belong anywhere else.

I swallow, but it doesn't help. The panic rises in me unstoppably. It floods through my body and reaches all the way to the ends of my fingertips, which drum on the tabletop like crazy.

As if he didn't notice at all, he suddenly starts talking. 'I was innocent, and it was finally proven.' With a sweeping movement of his hand, he puts his name in the empty field on page three. 'Now everything can be the way it used to be again.' Abruptly, he looks up at me, his light-blue eyes like a frozen-over lake. 'What almost tore my marriage apart was nothing but a harmless little puff of smoke.'

'Mira broke up with you,' I remind him, because I simply can't help it. My fingertips are still drumming on the tabletop, making a sound like raindrops pelting frantically against a skylight.

'Because she thought I was guilty.' He nods instinctively,

with a terrifying calm. 'But I'm not, it was even proven. I'm free and can be with her again.' The certainty in his expression and the dangerous, cold glint in his eyes hit me harder than Muhammad Ali's fist ever could.

'N-n…' I want to scream no, but only helpless stammering comes out of my mouth.

He can act as cultivated as he likes; I know exactly what's going on in his head. Still, I have to stand by and watch as he puts his final signature on the paper, closes the folder, and pushes it across the table to me. 'All the best, Mr. Herbst,' he says now with his faux friendliness and gets up from the chair.

He must not leave this room. Because once he's outside and goes to Mira. Then he'll…

I have to stop him!

While I rack my brain as to how I could possibly do that, the professor picks up his personal belongings with a self-satisfied smile and strolls off. He pauses briefly beside me, then puts his hand on my shoulder. 'I hope your problem was able to dissolve into thin air as well?' he asks now too, on top of everything else.

I'm definitely not going to answer that. My head is occupied with far more important things. He must not go to Mira. But how can I hold him back? What can I do? I bite my lip.

'I understand,' he murmurs and strokes my upper arm. 'Don't worry, you'll find your way.'

He doesn't understand a thing, that damn liar.

'Goodbye.' He's already at the door, puts his hand on the handle and pushes it down. It opens a small crack. The scent of freedom drifts in, surrounds me, and brings me to my knees.

All at once I feel so powerless, as if I had lost a war I hadn't even known I was fighting when I woke up this morning. I'm left alone on the battlefield.

Full of panic. And without a plan.

Chapter Thirty-Nine

'Sleep well.' I kiss Moritz's forehead and stroke the soft skin of his cheek while his eyes fall shut. However it's possible, today just seems perfect. Nothing is difficult. On the contrary, it feels as if the world is turning for me, and me alone.

Only a soft groan can be heard from my little one, then he slips into his afternoon nap. Grinning broadly, I slip out of the nursery and float downstairs to the ground floor. There I put on my headphones and do what I've been wanting to do all morning.

I dance.

The living room spins in circles before my eyes, together with the orange summer dress. It flutters excitedly around my legs and looks exactly the way I feel. Light. It's almost as if my bare feet are about to lift off the floor.

I'm floating, like a soap bubble on its way to a new horizon.

I stretch my arms higher and higher and spin faster and faster. Until I'm out of breath and let myself fall, exhausted, into the soft cushions of the sofa. That's where I sit now, with only a single thought in my head. Life is beautiful. Finally.

Just as it has been all morning, my mind is on Simon. I caress his strong upper arm, taste his lips, and hear the contented sigh that leaves his mouth whenever I snuggle up to him.

I have to write to him. 'Can't wait to see you again today,' I type into my phone, but before I can send the message, the sound of the doorbell distracts me.

A glance at the clock tells me it can only be the mailman. Despite my good mood, a queasy feeling immediately stirs in my stomach. It's this grotesque fear of getting more letters from Heinrich. The worry that he won't stop, even though I made it perfectly clear during my visit that he must never write to me again.

No, he'll stick to our agreement.

I quickly shake the doubts from my mind and set off. With Simon's face right after waking up in my mind's eye, I dance down the hallway. How adorably rumpled he looked this morning, with his hair sticking out wildly and the imprint of the cushion folds on his unshaven cheek.

Maybe I'm grinning like a girl in love after her very first kiss, but I'm happy, and as far as I'm concerned the whole world can see it. So I don't even try to hide it as I open the front door.

Chapter Forty

I'm still crouched on the hard wooden chair in the room where the professor from cell H-33, sentenced to life in prison, has just become a free man. All I can hear is the ticking of the clock above the door. From time to time, a long hand jerks forward with a dull vibration. I, on the other hand, don't move; I just stare at the wall and try to understand what has happened.

Heinrich Peters is innocent. I don't know anything more, and I don't need to. Because in my head, completely different thoughts are pushing to the front, glaring like neon signs and accompanied by dramatic music.

I see him on the street in front of Mira's house. With a devious smile, he steps through the garden gate. Nothing about him trembles, not even his perfectly groomed fingertips as he reaches for the doorbell. Its shrill sound shoots into my bones. It sounds like a warning signal.

Something is about to happen.

Damn it, why can't I turn off this mental movie; stop the tapes rolling completely? Desperately, I press my fist against my forehead. Over there in the corner of the pale-painted room, there's a crack in the wall. I stare at it, but that doesn't help. Because even it won't stay still. It gapes wider and wider, just like the chasm that's opening up inside me now. And it feels as if I'm standing on one side. On the other is the woman I love, together with her violent husband.

I can't let that happen. I have to get to her to prevent the worst.

I spring up from the chair, but already on the way to the door a terrible thought seeps into my head. It pools at the very bottom, like a dirty puddle on a rainy day.

If I go to her now, everything will come out.

Mira will find out who I really am and what I knew right from the start. About Peters, and about her too. She'll hate me. With every fiber of her being. Forever.

'Anyone who fights can lose. Anyone who doesn't has already lost.' That's exactly what Sandy would say now if she were here. But I don't need that advice. Because by now I know myself what really matters.

Mira. That she's okay is the most important thing.

She can hate me all she wants. But I'll protect her from Peters, even if it costs me our love. I don't know what I'm going to say to her. Only that I have to go to her. So I start running. Past the reception desk and the front door.

'Everything okay?' I hear a man's voice call, so far away that I can't place it with anyone. Probably because it doesn't matter. It doesn't matter at all. Because the only thing that counts now is being fast.

At a run, I raise my arm. 'Sorry, I have to rush off,' I gasp, not even knowing if anyone hears me. Breathless, I reach the lockers and yank on my jeans and T-shirt with frantic movements. I drop my phone several times in a row, the laces of my sneakers refuse to be tied.

This has to go faster. Much faster.

On the third try I finally manage it. With a heavy bang I slam the locker door shut, the key goes into my pocket. At least it should. But I can't register it anymore. In a trance, I leave the prison and feel far less free doing it than the Professor would have earlier today.

Sixty-five agonizing minutes later I'm standing in front of Mira's garden gate, just as Peters had before in my thoughts. Everything is quiet; even the heads of the daisies beside the paved path to the house don't move.

Are the two of them in there? Is he trying to lull her with his pretty words? Or has he put on that crazy look? Is he threatening her? Is he hurting her?

The thought makes me feel sick. I immediately march on, push open the unlocked gate and head straight for the front door. Then I see it out of the corner of my eye. Something moves behind the mid-length curtain of the kitchen window.

Like some deranged stalker, I step closer and peer in through the delicate foliage of a tall plant.

I see Peters. He's holding Mira by the forearm. Tears are running down her cheeks. With a helpless expression she opens her mouth and then closes it again. The sight hits me as if a bomb exploded right in the middle of my chest.

There are only a few centimeters between them. If he grabs her other arm now as well and…

No. That must not happen.

Blindly, I rush to the front door, push the handle down and storm inside. I don't hear what the two of them are saying. Instead, I'm all the more aware of the blood coursing through my veins.

The kitchen is my goal. Just a few more meters and I'll be there. But it's exactly these last few steps that feel as if I'm wearing concrete shoes. I can't let up now, so I force myself on. My heart is pounding so hard against my chest that I can feel my pulse all the way in my temples.

Hesitation is not an option. It hasn't been and it never will be. I'm going all in. My new life, my future, and my love. In this very moment, as I step into the kitchen doorway where the two of them can see me.

Two pairs of eyes fix on me at once, as unerringly as spotlights on a stage actor. Everything around me goes dark.

This is my cue. And now, of all times, I forget my lines.

Chapter Forty-One

Abruptly, Heinrich lets go of my arm. I feel the blood suddenly flowing back into my hand, breathe a sigh of relief, and give Simon a grateful smile.

Now everything will be all right.

Heinrich's gaze rests on Simon, his brow furrows. 'Herbst?'

How does he know his name? And why do Simon's features look as if he were a statue? Not a sound comes from him, only his right hand lifts.

'What are you doing here?' Heinrich wants to know, turning further toward him.

I feel a bit as if I were sitting in a movie theater. And I don't like the film that's flickering across the screen right before my eyes. Something's wrong here, I can see that very clearly.

Heinrich takes a step toward Simon. 'Did I forget something?' he asks, with an undertone I can't place.

What does he mean? Forget what?

Still mute as a fish, Simon shakes his head. His gaze

jerks to me, he's panicked and full of fear. A feeling of dread rises up in me, even though I don't even know why.

'Then why did you come?' Heinrich seems to be the only one of us who isn't in shock. Because he doesn't know who Simon is. Or does he?

No, it's obvious. Heinrich knows Simon. But from where?

'B-because of Mira.' Simon exhales so forcefully it's as if he'd been holding his breath until now. Then he looks straight at me, with an expression on his face I can hardly read.

Wait a second. Does he also know who Heinrich is? Probably. And he knew Heinrich would be here.

It's as if I had a thousand puzzle pieces in front of me that refuse to fit together. 'What's going on here?' I dare to ask, even though I sense that the answer could drive me to the edge of an abyss I never wanted to stand at again.

Gallant as an old-school gentleman, Heinrich gestures toward Simon. 'Please forgive me, my love, I neglected to introduce you to each other. This is Mr. Herbst. One of my prison guards,' a mild smile plays around his lips, 'and a friend. Without him I wouldn't have survived the last few weeks.'

'Prison guard?' Like a parrot I croak back what Heinrich has just said. Still my mind refuses to grasp it.

Simon lowers his gaze and buries his hands in the pockets of his jeans. Despite the three-day stubble, I can see how all the muscles around his lower jaw tense even more.

Guilty.

As if someone had spun time back at a furious speed, I hear the judge's voice again.

But this time it's directed at Simon.

Guilty. Guilty. Guilty.

'Is something wrong, my love?' Heinrich's caring gaze bounces off me because my shell suddenly turns so hard it might as well be made of steel. 'Sit down, you look pale.' Helpfully, he pulls a chair out for me.

I let him push me down onto the seat, I don't resist. But when he also runs his hand soothingly over my hair, I flinch. I quickly knock it away while I fix my stare intently on Simon. 'Who are you?' There's a coldness in my words that, even on this warm summer's day, easily freezes the air between us.

Simon raises his head, our eyes meet. There is pain in his. How dare he look at me, as if he were the victim here. He is a liar. A fraud.

Guilty.

'I-I…' he begins a helpless explanation, but breaks off his pathetic attempt at once.

'One moment, please,' Heinrich cuts in now, 'you two know each other.'

It isn't a question, more a statement. As unshakably certain as the fact that Heinrich is standing in front of me, even though he should be in prison. No matter how little I can understand that and how much I fight against trying to.

I just nod. What else could I say? That Simon is the new man by my side?

He isn't. Not anymore.

But even without anyone spelling it out, Heinrich seems to understand more and more. 'You knew what this woman means to me. And you still had the shameless nerve to come on to her? To my Mira?' His words grow sharper and sharper as he turns away from me and plants himself right in front of Simon. 'This is outrageous, I'm going to file a complaint against you today.'

You talked about me?

It's too much. If there were ever a good moment to lose consciousness, it would be right now.

I reel.

The chair under me wobbles. The kitchen shakes. Still, I stay conscious and stare at the two men, eyes wide. Simon seems to shrink with every passing second; with slumped shoulders and a sad look, he stands in the middle of my kitchen like a complete wreck.

'How could you? I trusted you, while you only pretended you wanted to help. In truth, you betrayed me more brazenly than anyone has ever dared before.' Hatred and unbridled rage—that's what vibrates in Heinrich's voice. His index finger raised in the air and the corners of his mouth curled down in contempt, he pierces Simon with his gaze. 'You're not getting away with this unpunished.'

Suddenly my feet brace against the floor and push me up from the chair. 'Enough.' Startled by myself, I flinch. 'Heinrich, you haven't been here for months. And in reality you left me and the kids on our own long before that. Don't you dare think you can just come back and forcefully take what doesn't belong to you.'

My gaze shifts to Simon. 'And you?' I begin, but all at once I don't know how to go on. I clench my fists and stare at him.

How could I have been so stupid as to trust him? How could I have broken my own rules?

'Out,' I hear myself bellow. So loud it sounds like I've lost my mind. 'Both of you.'

I don't know which of them looks more surprised at me, but that doesn't matter. I don't want to see either of them right now, and yet they're still here. As if strength were gathering in my legs that I'd never known existed, I take a step toward them.

'I said I want you gone.' It's strange how calm I suddenly sound. As if some foreign power had taken control of me, one that knows exactly what to do in this situation. 'Fortunately, you both know where the door is.'

But the two of them don't move an inch. Only their eyes are still alive.

Heinrich is furious. But what did he think? That he could come back and pick up where we left off more than half a year ago? As if our marriage hadn't already been in pieces back then?

Simon's gaze, on the other hand, is practically begging me. He's asking me to forgive him for something I will never be able to forgive.

Never.

In the distance I hear Moritz screaming. My shouting must have woken him. 'When I get back, I don't want to see either of you still here!'

I turn on my heel and run to the stairs. I don't look back once as I hurry to my son, taking the steps two at a time. I storm into the nursery, gently pull the crying Moritz against my chest, and stroke his back.

'Shhhh,' I whisper, rocking him back and forth, my nose buried deep in the fold of his neck. 'It was just a nightmare, my darling. Just a nightmare.'

In a choked voice I repeat that one sentence. Over and over again. While Moritz slowly calms down, I start to tremble more with every repetition. Only when his tears have long since dried can I no longer hold back my own.

His nightmare is over. But mine has just begun again.

Chapter Forty-Two

There's nowhere I can hide, Mira is everywhere. On the wall next to the coat rack, in the shower, under my duvet. No matter where I look and no matter where I am, she's with me. As if every crease in the couch cover and every little scratch on the floor had a story of her to tell. She clouds my thoughts; inside my head it's November. Gray and cold.

Nothing can change that.

Not even the sunlight that falls like a spotlight through the window onto the small dining table where we were still not even one week ago. Our feet tangled together, we told each other the stories of our lives. Now I trace with my finger exactly the gap in the tabletop that she touched too. As if that way I could at least be a tiny bit closer to her.

Yes, I've lost my mind. But I don't even care about that.

I have to try again. Because I can't give up before I've had the chance to explain everything to her.

So I pick up the phone. Bravely I dial her number and send up a quick prayer to a heaven whose very existence I've only ever laughed at out loud. Now I need it. Or at least that's what I tell myself.

The phone is ringing.

Dial tone, that's what the steady beeping is called. That suddenly comes to me while I'm waiting. And I ask myself, what is freedom, anyway?

Is she free? Am I?

Probably not, yet the signal keeps reaching my ear. I count every ring, keeping track of exactly how many chances I have.

Ten. Eleven. Twelve.

'Pick up, Mira,' I beg into the phone, but nothing happens at the other end of the line. It's ringing. Still.

Fifteen. Sixteen. Seventeen.

I start pacing up and down the apartment, stamping imprints into the carpet, carving a furrow into the floor. It's been like this ever since Mira found out the truth about the professor and me, and every time it plays out the same way.

Twenty.

In a second it will click.

Now it's time. I stop at once and press the phone more tightly to my ear.

'This is the voicemail of…,' says an electronic female voice, mechanical and cold. I ignore it, because I know what comes after the brief pause.

'Mira,' I hear the best voice in the world say. That single word shoots through my body like an electric shock.

That's it. That's all I have of her.

'Please leave a message after the tone,' the electronic voice explains to me, its tone now etched into my head. How many times have I heard it in the past few days? A hundred times? A thousand times?

I don't know, but I know something else. That the

moment is about to come when I have to say something. And for the hundredth, thousandth, or hundred-thousandth time, a feeling of helplessness overwhelms me.

What could I say that would get through to her? Are there even any words left that I haven't already tried?

The tone sounds. Then everything is silent.

All at once, it's as if I've fallen into a pit of quicksand in the middle of my apartment. It pulls me down and squeezes the air from my lungs. I clear my throat, want to speak, but I can't. This chance doesn't last long. Still, I sink deeper and deeper. The sand is already up to my neck. Three more seconds, then the recording will stop.

Three. I bite my lips until they bleed.

Two. Cool sand collects tightly around my neck.

One. I stopped breathing.

'Please, Mira.' The words left my mouth hoarsely; they sounded as if someone else were speaking. That wasn't me, just a remnant of what was left of me. 'I...'

Before I could say whatever it was I didn't even know, the line clicked.

Chance missed.

Exhausted, I let myself fall onto the couch, curled up like a cat, and rest my head on my hands. It was heavy and overfull. I glance over at the half-burned, cream-colored candle on the coffee table. There it stood, the one candle from our night together, like a symbol of everything I had lost.

'It smells like you,' I had whispered into Mira's ear back then. Then I had pulled her so close that nothing could have fit between us. I was happy. We both were.

I should throw that stupid candle away. Still, I stared at it. Behind it, the sun's rays came through the pane of glass and illuminated the otherwise invisible dance of the dust mites. Some things never change, I thought as I followed their movements. No matter how much you wish they would. Mira and I, the two of us mustn't be like that too. But how am I supposed to make her understand that if she won't talk to me? She doesn't answer any of my messages; she ignores all my calls. She doesn't even open the garden gate for me. All I have is her voice on the answering machine saying 'Mira,' and the fluttering movement of the curtains behind her kitchen window whenever I stand on the sidewalk in front of her house, hoping she'll still let me in.

She was disappearing from my life, a little more every day. Still, I couldn't let her go. And as if that weren't devastating enough, I had also been fired. Without notice. The Professor had kept his threat and told the boss everything that very same day. I had to pack my things immediately; I wasn't even allowed to say goodbye to my colleagues.

This had to be the end. What did I even have left?

A dream that isn't one after all. A love that's no longer reciprocated. And a wallet that'll soon be as empty as I am.

I only have Sandy to thank for all this crap. It's my damn sister's fault that it even got this far.

I dial her number; she picks up right away.

'Why did I ever listen to you?' I ask instead of saying hello.

'You didn't.' Her voice is completely calm, as if she doesn't hear my accusation at all.

I snort wearily. 'You're the one who talked me into this nonsense. All that crap about letting wounds heal and so on. Everything in my life was fine. Until I stopped sticking to my plans.'

'Is that really what you believe?' my sister asks, and I can practically see her sinking down onto one of her brightly patterned cushions. She's sitting there now with her legs crossed and her back straight, pretending to see things that don't exist at all.

'What do you mean, believe? I know it for sure!'

I should've stayed away from Mira and kept the past in the dark. Like those damn specks of dust, I wouldn't have had to see it if Sandy hadn't forced me to shine a light on it. What's the point of facing one kind of pain only to go through another one afterward?

'When was the last time you were truly happy?' Sandy suddenly asks, as if that mattered right now.

I bite my lip.'That so doesn't matter.'

'Yes, it does.' She sounds unwavering, and like so often she makes me feel as if she knew more than I do. 'So come on, when?'

When I was sure I could start a new life. When I could clearly feel that I was free. But I'm definitely not going to rub that in Sandy's face. Because it doesn't make any sense.

'Fine, you don't have to say it out loud. It's enough if you think about it,' I hear my sister's melodic voice from the other end of the line. It's crazy, but she sounds like she's smiling. 'Do you remember why you were so happy in that moment? What happened?'

I know immediately what Sandy means. The moment is right in front of me. And it won't go away anymore, it's like a freeze-frame in my head.

I see Mira and me standing here in the middle of my apartment. 'I want to be with you. Where we are doesn't matter as long as we have each other,' she says. Her words relieve my chest of the very last bit of pressure.

That was the moment when I thought I could see a path right in front of me. The possibility of having a family, closeness and security. Without fear. And without having to go through the same thing my father did.

'Shit, this is pointless,' I force out. What is Sandy trying to achieve with this? To make me feel even worse?

'Mhm.' For a moment, all I can hear is her calm breathing. 'There's no life that's only light. We all carry our shadows with us. We can't stop stones from lying in our paths or thick clouds from drifting in front of our suns."

No, I can't listen to this right now. 'Drop it, Sandy.'

As if I hadn't said anything at all, she just keeps talking. 'But it's the light from the bright times that can carry us through the dark ones. If only we let it.'

Of course I could hang up, but there's something that forces me not to.

'Everything in life happens for a reason. And even if you can't see it now, meeting Mira was exactly the right thing.'

Why on earth was that supposed to be right? 'Nonsense.' I sound harsh, and that's a good thing.

'Think about it, Simon…'

That's enough. I can't stand her babbling any longer. I hang up and bury myself in the sofa cushions, suddenly even more tired than before.

So this is it, my new life. Among specks of dust that only dance in the light and dial tones that, in truth, are anything but free.

How could this even happen?

My eyelids are heavy, but I still don't let them close. Because I know what would happen then, and that torture is far worse than sleep deprivation could ever be. So I just lie there and stare into nothing with an empty mind. Until I hear it, thudding as if from far away.

'Simon!' A man's voice, muffled but urgent. Where is it coming from? 'Open up, man. I know you're in there.'

Paul. He's at the door.

With my hands pressed over my ears, I pull my knees closer to my chest. He should go away, I don't want to see him. But the pounding doesn't stop. On the contrary, it keeps getting louder, as if someone were slowly removing the wad of cotton from my ears. Paul's voice also becomes clearer, comes closer, and begs me more and more urgently to finally give in. 'I don't care how long it takes. I'm not leaving.'

If I could laugh, I would. I'd at least smile, but the corners of my mouth refuse to lift.

'Come on, we're friends. Let me help you.' As if he were capable of that. The only person who can make me whole again is Mira. 'Trust me,' he suddenly says, as if he could read my thoughts through the thin apartment door.

Maybe it's that, or something else. I only know that his last words have an effect. My legs slide off the couch, and I drag myself to the door. Once there, I hesitate, my head leaning against the cool wall, my eyes fixed on the metallic gleam of the door handle.

'That's good.' Has Paul pressed his ear to the door? Or can he see me through the peephole? 'Now just open up, I'll take care of the rest.'

Tired, I lift my arm; I don't want to fight anymore and I don't want to think any longer. My hand falls on the door handle, the lock clicks open.

Paul storms into the hallway. 'Damn, what the…?' He doesn't get any further, because he immediately claps his hand over his mouth and nose. With his eyebrows drawn together, he looks first at me, then accusingly at my studio apartment. My eyes follow him as he walks over to the window and yanks it open.

Okay, it is a bit chaotic. The empty beer bottles on the

floor probably don't need to be there, and the corners of the pizza box on the stove are covered with a suspiciously fuzzy green film.

Sighing, I let my hand wander from the top of my head down to my neck. 'Sorry.'

'How long have you been in here?' There isn't the slightest hint of reproach in his voice, only concern and maybe even a bit of fear. 'And when did you last shower?'

I look down at myself. The T-shirt used to be white, at least I think so. And the pants? No idea. With a shrug, I shuffle over to the fridge. It's cold and empty. How fitting.

'We're out of beer,' I say, as if that were the answer to his question, lean against the kitchen counter, and let my head fall back against the wall cabinet.

Paul comes to stand shoulder to shoulder next to me. 'That bad?' is all he asks, shoving his hands into his pockets.

Can't he just be funny or say something stupid? It would be easier and hurt a lot less. I try to make a dismissive gesture, but even that doesn't work. Before I can even lift my arm properly, it drops back down, heavy as if it were carrying a ton of weight.

'That's not how this works, man.' He nudges me, very gently. 'You can't just hole up in here, that's not going to help.'

'Who knows.' I sigh, staring at the plain lamp above the dining table. One of the bulbs is broken. Since when, actually?

'I do,' he replies dryly. 'That thing up there isn't going to help you anyway, trust me.'

He seems sure of that, for whatever reason. 'What else then?'

'First, a shower. You stink like a train full of soldiers after a week in the field.' He grabs me by the shoulders and steers me into the bathroom.

When I come back into the living room a few minutes later, I strangely feel better. Paul has used the time to bring some order into the chaos. How cool would it be if it were just as easy with the mess inside me? Then I could just leave my body for a moment while Paul calmly picked up the broken shards that are lying around everywhere inside me and jabbing sharply against my insides.

Right now he's in the middle of changing the bed. He tosses the old covers carelessly onto the floor. As if they didn't mean anything at all.

'Hey, be careful.' I'm at his side in an instant and take the pillowcase from him.

'Believe me, this is easier,' is all he says, like he knew exactly what that little bit of fabric means to me. 'And now you're going to take these things into the bathroom and put them in the washing machine.'

I stare at him in disbelief. 'No way.' He can't be serious. What will I have left of my water girl if the covers just smell like spring freshness, like in every other bed in this world?

Paul presses the used sheet into my hand. 'Do it.' His tone is urgent and firm, his expression leaves no room for doubt. 'I know what I'm talking about.'

He once had a girlfriend? When was that supposed to have been? This is my best buddy standing in front of me, and yet all of a sudden it hits me how little I know about him. Our friendship has been just as superficial as the rest of my damn life. We were cool, nothing more.

'That's not important right now.' He answers without me having asked him anything. 'Go now, come on.'

Confused, I trudge into the bathroom and put the sheet

and duvet cover into the washing machine. Only the pillowcase is still in my hand.

Carefully, I fold the fabric and smooth it out. A long black hair comes loose from the material and slowly sails to the floor. As if I were no longer in my right mind, I bend down, pick it up, and gently place it between two layers of the pillowcase.

This is crazy. I'm crazy. I know that, but I still can't do anything about it.

'What's taking so long?' Paul's footsteps are coming closer way too fast.

Hurriedly, I stuff the cover all the way in the back of the cupboard and turn to the detergent. In the very next moment Paul shoots around the corner.

'All done.' Almost proudly, I shovel the detergent into the washing machine drawer and press one of the many buttons.

Paul nods appreciatively. 'Very good. The first step is done.' He comes closer and pats me on the shoulder. It's weird, but it feels good when at least someone thinks I've done something right. 'Now comes the next one. Grab your stuff, we're going.'

Everything in me rebels, even my body suddenly goes stiff as a board. 'Where to?'

Paul laughs as if I'd made a joke. 'To where there's still beer.'

'Don't feel like it.' That came out fast, but it's the truth. What am I supposed to do out there when I can't even handle being in here?

Unimpressed, Paul grabs me by the shoulders and pushes me out of the bathroom. 'Wallet, keys,' he says in a commanding tone. 'Your phone stays here. You don't need it.'

He's lost it. What if Mira gets in touch? Then I have to pick up, absolutely, before she changes her mind again. I shake my head vehemently and shove the phone into my pants pocket. 'Forget it.'

'I'm telling you this one last time: trust me.' Very slowly, syllable by syllable, he pronounces the words, as if that would somehow make them sink in more easily. Then, without asking, he snatches the keys and wallet from the kitchen table and pushes me further toward the hallway. At least he leaves me my phone.

I don't know why I let him do this to me. Maybe because part of me so badly hopes he's right that it wants to give in. Whatever he has in mind—if it lets me forget, even just a little bit—wouldn't that already be a step forward?

'Put these on.' Paul sets the black sneakers down in front of me like I'm a kindergartner, and I slip into them without interest. 'Very good. Then let's get going.'

Mechanically, I open the door. Even before my foot touches the ground of the world out there, I suddenly want only one thing.

To run away.

And that's exactly what I do. Because that way it's easier. Because it would always have been easier that way.

I hear the door click shut behind me and imagine how it keeps my misery from coming with me. For all I care, it can wait for me in the apartment. It can ambush me when I come back. But right now I want to be my old self again, just for a few hours.

All at once I hear Sandy's voice in my head. 'Whoever always walks the same paths will always end up in the same place,' she says.

'Shut up,' I hiss tensely. I swallow, breathe, and bite my lip.

Then I start to run.

Chapter Forty-Three

It's dark. Only the numbers on my clock radio light up the room with their reddish glow. They show me what I already know anyway. Still, I stare at them as if I could somehow find answers to questions I don't dare to ask. Shivering, I pull the thin blanket up to the tip of my nose, even though now, at the beginning of July, one tropical night follows the next. I should sleep for at least a few hours before the kids wake up. But every time I close my eyes, it starts all over again.

Like on an endless loop, Simon's face appears before me. He looks at me with that pleading expression in his blue-green eyes. And then there's Heinrich, full of hate and rage. It doesn't stop. The horror movie of my life can't be switched off.

I pull my bent legs close to me, right up against my body. I wrap my arms around myself and still feel as if there's nothing left holding me together. I am and remain broken, while the minute display in front of my eyes keeps ticking on as if the world were still intact.

Simon lied to me and abused my trust.

It was a mistake to get involved with him. My mistake. I betrayed my own principles. That's the truth, and I don't allow myself to think otherwise. Even though I never wanted to do it again, I dig my fingernails into my forearm. Not a little, but with full force. So I can't feel any pain but this one.

How could I have been so blind? Again.

My phone lights up in the darkness, and my hand reaches for it instinctively. It's this insatiable craving inside me, even now, that makes me unlock the screen.

This addiction. To him.

I'm sick. Just as Simon predicted when we first met. With only one single difference. He can't save me.

Of course it's a message from Simon. 'Please, let me explain. That's all I want.'

I read the text so often that every word burns itself into my brain. That's how it is: my head is full of memories of our time together, his messages, and his voice, which can be heard on the voicemail day after day.

I'm torn, drifting helplessly between love and hate. But there's one thing I'm sure of. I won't give in.

Like everything in life, Simon will fade with time too. Maybe it's a matter of months, maybe it'll take years. But the day will come when I can forget him. I cling to that thought like a castaway to a piece of driftwood, desperately hoping it will carry me to the salvation of the shore.

Chapter Forty-Four

The beer glass in my hand is almost empty, but it's still cold. I knock back the last gulp, push myself out of the dark corner at the end of the bar, and ask the waiter for a refill. Then I lean back again and let my head fall against the wall. The bass thumps through my body, a babble of voices reaches my ears. The stool I'm sitting on presses hard into my thighs.

But I don't notice any of that. Because all my attention is on my phone. I feel a bit like a snake charmer who's lost his flute. No matter what melody I try, the lid stays shut. The damn thing is so silent it's as if I'd sent all my messages into the void. Mira isn't answering.

'Siiimoon.' Sweating, Paul squeezes in next to me. 'Dance that crap out of your head, come on.' He tries to pull me off the stool.

I shake my head in refusal. 'I just ordered another beer,' I mutter, pushing his slippery fingers off me.

Paul snorts. 'You can drink that later. Come on, the party's really going off over there.'

A party? That's not what I need anymore. 'I'll catch up,' I say, just to get rid of Paul. There's no point in arguing with him anyway.

Nothing makes sense.

For a moment he studies me, then a grin spreads across his face. 'If you're not there in ten minutes, I'll come and get you. Okay?'

I nod; I just want him gone. Just as he turns away, the waiter sets a fresh glass of beer on the sticky bar in front of me. Since he's already here, I might as well order something else too, so I ask for a shot. I want to forget, and beer alone won't do the trick.

A second later I'm alone again, and I immediately grab my phone.

Nothing. Mira stays silent.

Will that ever change? And if so, how?

There has to be something I can do. Something that will get through to her. She has to know the truth. But how?

I empty my beer glass in a rush. Little by little, the alcohol starts to keep me from thinking fully. My head grows dull, just like I hoped. A few more drinks and I might have a chance, for a few hours, to be the way I used to be.

Unburdened, impulsive, and full of life. At least on the outside.

I sneak a look at the dance floor, where Paul is going wild like he's popped some kind of special pill. Together with our party buddies and a horde of women, he's got his arms in the air and is jumping up and down to the beat.

He looks happy. So happy that suddenly there's only one thing I want. To feel the same way he does. But how is that supposed to work? With a sigh, I empty my glass and set it down on the bar, right next to my phone, which is just lying there in silence.

Damn, I hate this thing. Why didn't I just leave it at home?

It rules my life, dictates my mood, and can catapult me anywhere just by flashing a tiny white light. Or not for that matter.

Lost in thought, I don't even notice Paul coming back to me. It's only when he hooks his arm through mine that I realize what's happening. 'You're coming with me now,' he says in a commanding tone. Unbelievable, but some of our friends are standing behind him, obviously ready to help. 'If you won't walk on your own, we'll carry you. Your choice.'

His stupid grin doesn't work on me today. 'Don't feel like it.' A bit awkwardly, I try to wriggle out of his grip, but he's stronger than I thought.

'I couldn't care less.' He pulls me to my feet. Now the others come over as well, grab me by the arms, and together they push me toward the dance floor.

I should probably just give in. Let go. Have fun. If you always walk the same paths, you'll always end up in the same place. That's what Sandy says. So if I at least want to feel halfway okay, I just have to do what I used to do. It's that simple.

I look around and see bodies dancing as if hypnotized, shining eyes, and ecstatic faces. In the middle of the party-hungry crowd, I force myself to move to the pounding beat. Slowly at first, then more and more intensely.

It's a miracle, but it happens. The dance floor swallows me up, the music overtakes my worries the way freshly fallen snow makes dirty ground disappear. Airy and light, innocent and pure. Whatever is dragging me down suddenly feels muffled and, at least from the outside, no longer visible. I close my eyes and let myself drift, floating far away, all the way to the other end of our galaxy. That's where I want to stay, preferably forever.

When I come to again a few minutes later, I'm staring straight into a pair of magically green eyes. They're so mesmerizing I can't look away. With every flash of the disco lights, more laugh lines appear around this pair of eyes. As if my body switches to autopilot, I scan the owner of the eyes from head to toe.

Long dark hair, pale skin, hot curves, a stunning smile.

'Good choice,' someone murmurs in my ear. A moment later an elbow jabs far too fast into my side.

I whirl around. Of course it's Paul, who presses up against me with a highly delighted expression on his face. Shaking my head, I wave him off.

'Are you crazy? That is exactly what you need. Have some fun, take your mind off things.' A huge grin appears across his face.

My gaze drifts to the green-eyed beauty. Could Paul be right? No, definitely not. 'This isn't happening, man.'

'You said the same thing about dancing, and just look at you now.' He moves a bit closer, as if it's important to him that I hear every single one of his words. 'Do it. You won't regret it. Just trust me, one last time.'

Right then the woman in front of me smiles at me so seductively, it's as if the two of them have conspired together. Against me or for me, I can't really say. Still, it does something to me. My head wants to believe Paul. He claims I could be my old self again. And that Mira was a dead end.

That's the truth. The only one.

'Forget her. You're free, and that's how you want it,' Paul adds now, as though he can read my thoughts.

If he's so sure, how could I not be?

Chapter Forty-Five

'I'm Bianca.' The woman with the magically green eyes smiles and holds out her hand to me. Dimples form in her cheeks, which I definitely would've found cute in the past.

Paul notices my hesitation and shoves me in her direction. My blood alcohol level does the rest; I end up so close to her that I almost hug her. She smells sticky-sweet, but at least not like vanilla.

'Simon,' I introduce myself, while I try to find my balance again.

She laughs, lifts her arms, and moves to the beat of the music. Supple like a cat and seductive like a belly dancer. That's exactly what she looks like. Still, it doesn't tempt me; the woman is like a pill with no active agent at all. Now she comes closer and lays her hands on my chest.

I just have to try. What else do I have left?

Nothing.

So I do it. I let her pull me along; we dive into the music together, let ourselves drift, and try to forget what's happening around us.

Forget. That could feel simply fantastic. Light and free.

It takes a long time, but eventually we're dancing so tightly wrapped up in each other that I can even feel the absence of her underwear through the thin fabric of her skirt. That's what I focus on; everything else has to stay outside.

With all my strength, I push my feelings back behind that one door inside me that has already served me well in the past. Then I slam it shut. I swallow, breathe, and bite my lip.

Now Bianca turns to me and looks at me with a seductive gaze. 'Your place or mine?' She moistens her lower lip, her hands wandering over her hips.

My heart is roaring loudly for Mira. But my mind says this has to stop. The expression on the attractive woman's face in front of me, my blood alcohol level, and the charged atmosphere all take its side.

Life has to go on. It can become a good life; I just have to really want it. And believe that I can make it.

'One night. No strings attached.' Can she hear the desperation in my words? Can she see how everything inside me is rebelling?

My innermost self protests, but I ignore it. Because I have to.

Bianca's smile grows wider. 'Sounds just like my kind of thing.' She dances closer to me, wraps her arms around my back, and lets them slide lower.

'Your place,' I whisper in her ear, and then I bite my lip so hard that I can't feel anything else.

She could barely keep her hands off me in the taxi, and ever since we got to her apartment, everything has been moving at breakneck speed. Somewhere a door slams shut, she tugs at my T-shirt. Her hands are everywhere, her tongue pushes into my mouth. Hot air and salty dampness, that's all there is between us as she keeps driving me through the darkness toward her bedroom.

'You're so...' she murmurs into my mouth, but then leaves it at a deep sigh and starts fumbling with my pants.

I don't say anything, I mechanically fumble with her skirt until it slides to the floor. This feels like I'm a robot running a preinstalled program.

Her top finds its way to the floor and she's already standing naked in front of me. I force myself to step out of my pants, which are now only hanging around my ankles. She turns around and walks to the bed with a seductive sway of her hips. Her hand glides through her black hair.

In the very same moment I freeze. Because my senses fail me. I know it isn't true, but they still trick me into thinking it's Mira standing in front of me. A second later I feel a wave of longing that crashes over me like a full-on tsunami.

What the hell am I doing here?

It's my heart that suddenly takes command so completely that I can't fight it anymore. Not my head and not my virile instincts. Not the green-eyed beauty and not the passionate movements with which she slides onto the bed. All of that loses its meaning because of this feeling that's now spreading through my body so intensely that I can feel it everywhere.

'What's wrong?' the naked woman in front of me breathes seductively and comes toward me on all fours along the mattress. The diffuse city light falling through the window beside us traces the perfectly shaped lines of her body.

'I-I…'

She straightens up in front of me and blinks at me with her glowing cat eyes. 'Come on,' she whispers, tugging at my boxer shorts.

Instinctively I grab her wrists, stop her, and immediately see a questioning look on her face. 'I-I'm sorry,' I manage to force out. Then I spin around on the spot, grab my pants and T-shirt, and just run.

Out. Away. Gone.

Faster and faster I race down the stairs of the apartment building. I stumble, grab the railing, pick up my pace again. Then I finally reach the front door, shove it open, and flee out into the darkness.

I slip into my clothes, breathe in the air that's supposed to calm me down, and look up at the sky in the hope that it might help. But the night is warm and stuffy, the world above me full of clouds. Exhausted, I lean against the wall of the building, reach for my pack of cigarettes, and let it wander back and forth between my hands.

'Everything in life happens for a reason. And even if you can't see it now, meeting Mira was exactly the right thing.' Sandy's voice is suddenly omnipresent in my head. And like nothing else in my life, one thing becomes clear to me.

She's right.

Our time together changed me. I stopped wanting to be someone I had never been. And I stopped forcing myself to wear a mask so no one would see how broken I really am.

With a wistful smile, I toss the half-full pack of cigarettes into the nearest trash can. Mira turned me into a new person. And at least that's a good thing.

Chapter Forty-Six

'Do you ever sleep anymore?' Eva's worried look pierces me, and I know she can see everything.

'No,' I admit openly, slowing my pace. I'd love nothing more than to enjoy the pleasantly cool forest air, listen to the excited chirping of the birds, and let the scent of fir needles and earth distract me. But these beautiful things don't reach me. It's as if I were trapped in a bubble where there are only dark clouds and drizzle.

Amazingly, I still feel Eva put her arm around me, and I let my head drop onto her shoulder. She catches me, and that's exactly what I need right now. 'No one could have known it would turn out like this.'

'No.' I shake my head vehemently. 'It was my fault alone. I was stupid. So endlessly stupid.' If I still had tears, I'd be crying them now. But my eyes stay dry, only my nose swells up. I clench my fists because I just can't help it.

'Don't be so hard on yourself, Mira. You're not responsible for everything that happened. On the contrary, you're the victim here, you understand?' Eva stops and forces me to look at her.

Still, her intense gaze bounces right off me, her words vanish into nowhere. 'I made myself the victim, I trusted Simon and got involved with him.' I swallow, but the tightness in my throat doesn't ease. 'I should never have done that.'

She brushes a strand of hair out of my face. 'The river carries away everything that happened yesterday.'

Eva and her calendar sayings. I wish I could smile about them today too. 'I could never forget it,' I say, my gaze wandering up to the sky. Even though it should be impossible, it's shining bright blue above us. 'Just a year ago, my world was at least partially okay. And now…'

I see Michael in front of me, how he asks about Simon with the expression of an innocent child while he eats his breakfast cereal. Instantly my heart breaks all over again, and again I don't know how much longer I can bear it.

'You still have me. And Kathi,' my friend reminds me.

Right. Eva is my anchor. Kathi and I are slowly growing close again, and even though the bond between us is still as delicate as a single strand of a spider's web, it's there.

'You know what?' Smiling, Eva links her arm through mine and pulls me along with a spring in her step. It's as if she wants to give me a little bit of her energy. 'Forget the men. Both of them.'

'I already filed for divorce ages ago,' I say, while my thoughts wander into the past.

Heinrich gave me the family I'd always wanted. But, in truth, it was only the boys and me who were a team; Heinrich never wanted to play along. He was only the one who set the rules of the game. And made sure they were followed. That's over, I can feel it clearly.

'You should let go of Simon too and start over again.' Encouragingly, she strokes my arm. 'I'm here for you, you're not alone.'

Let go of Simon. Could that be the solution?

His face appears before my eyes. I see the disappointment and feel his affection. Even so, I have to push him away from me. I place my hands firmly on his chest to put some distance between us, but my arms feel as if they're made of cotton wool. Yielding and soft, powerless and weak.

Instead of moving away from me, he comes closer. A little more, and a little more. He keeps looking at me the whole time, murmuring apologies and professing his love. The way he lays his fingers on mine and strokes my skin with his thumb makes me defenseless.

Everything goes quiet inside me. I want to give in, let myself fall, and be with him.

If only I could turn back time and undo everything.

'I wish I'd never met Simon,' I hear myself say, and now it happens after all.

Wherever these tears come from, they force their way out unstoppably. As hot as thermal water and as salty as the Black Sea. As if only they had been holding me upright until now, I collapse.

Eva catches me, wraps her arms around me, and rocks me back and forth like a child who has just woken from a nightmare. 'I know,' she whispers over and over, running her hand reassuringly over my head.

'What if I can't forget him?' I ask in despair, because that's exactly what I'm most afraid of. I can't forgive him for what he did, and yet he haunts me whenever my strength leaves me.

With his blue-green eyes, that infectious smile, and the

lips that kiss me so passionately, the whole world around me disappears.

'Time heals every wound.' A little awkwardly, Eva trots out the most worn-out of all clichés. She surely knows herself how ridiculous it sounds. 'Let's get away. You, the kids, and me. We'll spend a few days by the sea. Vienna, and everything that happened here, will stay in Vienna.' Her smile is warm and heartfelt. 'What do you think?'

Nothing would please me more than that, and yet I hesitate. Because right now I hear Simon's voice. 'My water girl,' he whispers longingly in my ear. He, the water, and I—we used to belong together.

'Forgetting sounds great,' I say thoughtfully. Could a vacation by the sea really do that? Maybe. Simon and I never swam in the sea together, never dug our feet into the sand, and never watched a single sun disappear over the water on the horizon.

He, the sea, and I—we don't belong together.

'Perfect, I'll organize everything. We'll leave next week.' Eva beams at me.

She's so happy that I can't help but nod. Suddenly it feels as if the bubble that shuts me off from the sunny side of my life is starting to crack. It's tiny, almost invisible. But I can feel individual sunbeams piercing the damaged spot, crossing the gray threshold, and arriving exactly where I need their warmth most. Something like hope suddenly appears inside me, and I cling to it for dear life.

Maybe it's possible to forget Simon like this. At least for a brief moment. That would be enough for now.

Chapter Forty-Seven

Every step is exhausting, yet I wander aimlessly through the streets of Vienna. Everything around me is quiet, somewhere behind the houses the sun will probably rise soon, but I'm not really interested in that. Ever since Mira hasn't been with me anymore, my life has been like an old black-and-white film. Colorless and blurry. The hours melt into one another, consisting only of waiting and sleeping. A new way of counting time has begun. For months I counted the days until my departure, now it's the days without Mira that dominate my thoughts so overwhelmingly that I don't even have to write them on a calendar.

Today is July 22, Day 26.

At least by now I know one thing. Even if Mira can't forgive me, I won't lock her away behind my door. She'll stay in my thoughts. Because she'll forever be the one person who helped me see what I really need in life.

With a deep breath, my eyes wander over the houses of the housing estate. I've never noticed before how loveless this environment is. The gray-brown façades look as if they could swallow all the rays of sunshine in the world. Each of my steps echoes dully through the deserted street; it smells of organic waste and exhaust fumes.

Only a few yards separate me from my old workplace. The light blue gates of the Simmering Correctional Facility are closed; wistfully, I look up at the barbed wire at the top of the wall. It was a good job, it gave me a future that no longer exists now.

I count the barred windows on the second floor of Cell Block H. There it is, the fourth from the left. Behind that pane of glass I promised Peters I'd stand up for him. If I had had even the slightest idea what was waiting for me behind the doors of the elegant, white-painted house with the green shutters in the nineteenth district, would I ever have gone there?

Yes.

Incredible, but despite everything that's the right answer. That suddenly becomes clear to me. So clearly that, without thinking any further, I pull my phone from my pocket and dial Sandy's number. She should know that I see it too now.

'Simon?' She sounds sleepy.

'Sorry, Sandy, I didn't mean to wake you. But I really have to tell you something.'

In the background I hear a rustling; she's pulling the blanket up to her chin. 'What's going on, bro?'

My fingers glide over the rough plaster of the prison wall. For a moment I even smile. Because what I'm about to say comes easily to my lips. 'Sometimes we think we're dreaming about something,' I begin, sounding exactly like her, 'we think we know what we need, what makes us happy and where our life is supposed to take us.'

'Some pictures are only beautiful from a distance.' Sandy's voice is very soft.

I stroll on. 'Thanks for everything, Sandy,' I say, and we both know what I mean by that.

'Life's too short not to make the best of every single day. I know you'll do exactly that.' For a moment the line is silent. 'Good night, Simon.'

'Sweet dreams.' I end the call and take one last look at the window of cell H-33. Inevitably, I imagine Peters sitting at the desk there, bent far forward as he wrote his letters. With his glasses on the bridge of his nose, he swept the pen across the paper. Only a faint scratching could be heard.

How beautiful the words were that he found for Mira. So loving and gallant, and yet they were nothing but an illusion.

I should write to her too. No ridiculous short messages and no shallow phrases. Mira deserves the truth. She has to know who I am, on the outside and on the inside. I want to show her everything about me, because there's nothing left I want to hide from her.

Yes, I'm going to write her a letter, and I already know where.

I arrive less than an hour later. The park lies deserted before me in the light of the morning sun. Armed with pen and paper, I sit down by our lake. I let my gaze wander to the exact spot where Mira and I first met.

Water is our element. We searched for our reflections in the Old Danube and bathed in fountain spray. We went water-skiing and walked in the rain. It all started with this lake here. Will it end here too?

No, I can't let that happen.

I turn to the blank sheet of paper. But when I want to start writing, I suddenly feel thrown back into my school days. Back then, when we had to write a short story in German class. For a whole hour I did nothing but stare at the paper. White and untouched, it lay before me like a memorial that drove me out of my mind. Without a single written word, the paper ended up on the stack of finished assignments.

I can't write. Not the way I should be able to.

Still, I set the pen on the paper and take a deep breath. Uncertain, I draw the first lines.

The beginning is easy.

'Dear Mira' is written a few seconds later in my angular handwriting at the top edge of the page. How am I supposed to go on?

A thousand thoughts shoot through my head, and even more feelings boil up inside me. I feel hot and at the same time my fingers suddenly turn cold and stiff. This is a decisive moment, I can feel it clearly. So I do something I never would've thought myself capable of. I think about what Sandy would advise me to do now.

'Turn off your brain so you can listen to your heart better,' she'd probably say.

I follow her advice. My breathing is calm, my fingers aren't trembling. Then I close my eyes. And wait.

At first there's only silence. Until, barely perceptible, the first words rise to the surface. I don't ask where they come from or what they mean. All I do is write them down.

Chapter Forty-Eight

'How many more sleeps?' With the same thoughtful gesture as his father, Michael presses his index finger to his temple and studies me intently. His blond hair is tousled, and a big orange juice stain blazes on his light blue T-shirt. Air holes and juice don't go together particularly well on a plane, especially not with children.

If we'd been traveling with Heinrich, we would've had to change the T-shirt right away.

I quickly push the memory of him aside and pull the suitcase out of the car. 'Five more.'

His eyes widen. 'That many?' he wants to know, and he starts fidgeting on the spot. 'That's forever.'

'All the more reason your party will be that much nicer.' Smiling, I set off to free Moritz from the child seat.

Michael doesn't look as if he believes me. 'Why can't it be my birthday already?'

With Moritz in my arms I come back and reach for the suitcase. My elder boy watches me with his lower lip stuck out. 'Because you were only born on the thirtieth of July. Now go on and run ahead to the front door.'

I hand him the keys, then he races off. I breathe a sigh of relief and turn to Moritz, who is looking at me through half-open eyes. I kiss his forehead, and his lids fall shut again.

Then the moment has come; I can't put it off any longer.

We're back home, whether I like it or not. The past week on the North German coast was simply fantastic. Being there with Eva and the kids, where my memories don't belong. Walking along the beach, with the wind in my hair and grains of sand between my toes. Breathing and actually getting air. Smiling and actually feeling a bit of happiness. All of that was so wonderful that now I feel only one thing: fear.

My eyes pan across the garden, which is no longer quite so meticulously kept, and on over the white plastered wall of the house with its green-painted shutters.

The memories are lurking in there. They're just waiting to ambush me as soon as I set foot across the threshold.

Everything in me resisted it and I did it anyway. Mechanically, I marched toward the front door, my lips pressed together and my jaw as hard as stone.

'Mommy, look what I can do.' Triumphantly, Michael holds the contents of the mailbox up in the air. He needs both hands, the stack is so thick.

'Great job, big guy,' I praise him and quicken my pace.

With his little fingers he takes one flyer after another, glances at it briefly, and lets it sail to the ground. 'Boring,' he mutters over and over, and suddenly he's no longer like his father, who used to study the ads with intense concentration, always on the lookout for bargains.

I immediately shake the thoughts of Heinrich from my head, open the front door, and step inside. The stale air hits me; it's hot and stuffy. But there's no real reason for the knot in my stomach. And even less for the pressure that suddenly settles on my chest. I peer around the corner into the kitchen.

That's where it happened.

With tense muscles and my back straight, I stand there, flooded with memories I'd rather erase from my mind.

'There are letters, Mommy.' Michael sounds muffled, as if he were very far away.

My gaze lands on him and then on to the pile of mail in his hand. I recognize my mother's handwriting. Those must be the birthday cards for Michael. 'I'll take those,' I say quickly.

With a shrug, he hands me the envelopes and runs toward the living room. 'I want to play dolls,' he calls as he runs, then disappears around the corner.

That was definitely too loud. I don't need to look to know that Moritz is waking up now.

'Mommy?' With his short fingers he rubs his eyes clumsily and lets out a long yawn.

'I'm here, sweetheart. We're back home.'

The words echo in my head.

Home.

Is that even the right word for this place?

Right here, where I'm standing now, Heinrich had handcuffs put on him. He was led away through the dark green painted wooden front door. Even now I can still feel the icy cold draft of that November day on my skin; just like back then, I flinch. With a dull click the door closed behind him, and I was left alone. Broken and disappointed. In him, but in truth, even more in myself.

Just looking at this door, with its carved recesses and the paint that's already chipping a little at the bottom edge, weighs me down.

Because Simon was waiting behind this entrance too. Through the peephole I watched his hand constantly wandering through his hair. With my heart pounding and my breath catching, I stood right there, at the spot where the striking marbling in the parquet floor can be seen. And even back then I knew it. Against all reason, and against my will, it had happened.

I clench my fists, but I still can't do anything about it. Once again I'm powerless. When I think about how loving he was with the children and how much he made me laugh, that warm feeling still wants to rise up in my chest. When will it finally stop? There's only one solution:

To leave this house behind me, and with it everything that happened here. I'm going to move and make a completely fresh start somewhere else.

That way my life can become good again.

Searching for support, I pull Moritz closer to me. I stroke his velvety soft hair and kiss his cheek. Just as I've pulled myself together a little, I suddenly hear the doorbell ring.

My gaze darts back to the entrance. What if Simon is standing out there?

There it is again, this longing that won't let me go. It floods me, sweeping everything else away in its wake.

This can't be allowed to happen anymore.

I shake my head vehemently, but it doesn't help me. All the suppressed feelings keep rising up inside me, and with them a single wish. He, and no one else, should be standing on the other side of the entrance now.

I walk up to the door and push the handle down. A

crack opens. It grows wider and wider. I send a quick prayer up to heaven, fully aware that I'm asking for something a part of me doesn't even want.

Then the moment comes.

Within a fraction of a second I recognize who is standing in front of the door. I stop moving. A wave of disappointment washes over me. My throat tightens.

'Heinrich,' I hear myself say. As matter-of-fact as if this were a meeting between businesspeople who have to negotiate a deal.

'We should talk, don't you think?' He sounds completely calm and courteous. Through the gap in the door I see the clear expression in his eyes. He looks as if everything could be all right again simply because he has set his mind to it.

No matter how convinced he is of that, I'm not. How much I'd like to just slam the door and shut him out of my life. But he's still the father of our children. And in fact, that's exactly why we have quite a bit to discuss. So I press my lips together, nod, and pull the door open wider.

The gap becomes a path. And the path becomes a way in. The door stands open.

Chapter Forty-Nine

The sun had long since disappeared behind the horizon, but I still stayed here. Like a complete idiot, I stared at the narrow gravel path that led from the other end of the park to this spot. No one was here, just me and the fish that surfaced on the lake now and then to snap at insects. And millions of mosquitoes that latched onto me faster than I could shoo them away from my bare skin.

I barely felt them, because in my mind I went over the lines I had written here, in this place, a week ago.

Dear Mira,

Right now I'm sitting at our lake. I'm writing to you in the spot where we first met. Maybe it's wrong. Maybe I'm crazy. But whenever I'm by the water, I feel closer to you.

But that's not the reason for this letter.

I lied to you, and you already know how sorry I am. What you can't possibly suspect is what's hidden behind our messed-up story. That's exactly what I want to tell you.

At first all I wanted was to help your husband. I wanted his despair to end, that was my wish. So I went to see a woman who I thought was someone else. Instead I met you, and you turned my whole world upside down. I want you to know why.

I was fourteen when my father hanged himself because he couldn't bear the pressure of being responsible for a family anymore. Seeing what that did to my mother was at least as bad for me as losing him. So I made a decision. I never wanted to do to anyone what he had done. There were to be no serious relationships for me, and certainly no family. I was sure that if I followed his path, I'd end up just like him.

In truth I was afraid. No, I was in a panic. And I thought freedom was the only thing I needed in life. That was the only reason I wanted to travel the world on a motorbike.

Then I met you.

Without even realizing it, you forced me to look in the mirror. I had to face the past, and today I know for how long I'd been fooling myself.

My sister Sandy says that everything that happens in life has a meaning. And that the fact we met was exactly how it was supposed to be.

You know what? She was damn right. Because you were the person who showed me what I really need in life!

I accept it if you can't forgive me. I don't want to hold on to you if you don't want to be held by me. I won't force my love on you if you don't want it.

Twenty-six days ago I lost everything. You, the dream of a future with you, and my job. So I have no choice but to go through with the motorbike trip after all. But at least it's no longer about running away from something. It's about finding something. A life that will hopefully be just as beautiful as the one we could have had together.

But until I leave, I still want to hope that you'll find a way to forgive me. Starting tomorrow, and every evening after that until

August 5, I'll be waiting for you. Every time the sun sets. At the spot by the lake, right where we met for the first time.

If you come, we can be happy together. If you don't, I'll let you go. Not because it's easy for me, and not because I don't love you anymore. But because I want to respect your wish.

Yours, Simon

Today is July 29, half the countdown is over. With my hands shoved into my pockets, I look up at the dark night sky. There are stars, all of them shining, and yet their light doesn't reach me.

All at once I hear a crunch in the stillness of the night. I prick up my ears. Someone is walking through the park.

Mira! She's come.

My pulse suddenly races. In the darkness I search for the source of the sound, scanning the surroundings for people.

Over there, where the cone of light from the streetlamp just barely illuminates the path, someone is there. Any moment now I'll see her. I try to breathe calmly, but I can't. Can it be true? Can we find our happiness together?

There she is. She's really here. Her dark hair gleams in the lamplight.

Relief, joy, and excitement make it hard for me to think. I don't know anything anymore, only that now, after all, everything is going to be all right.

Full of anticipation, I watch her, when suddenly I realize she's not alone.

The Professor is with her. They're strolling side by side like an old married couple.

Now I see her lift her head. She brushes her hair behind her ear and looks at him with a closed-off expression.

What the hell is going on over there right now?

Chapter Fifty

Michael's eyes were barely visible behind his eyelids. 'Tomorrow is my birthday,' he said proudly and slipped into his Superman pajama pants.

'Exactly.' I handed him the top and then got his toothbrush ready. A glance at the clock next to the white-tiled washbasin told me that we were already far too late with our evening routine today. If everything was going to go smoothly, he urgently needed to be where Moritz already was. In bed.

As soon as he pushed his head through the neckline of his pajama shirt, Michael gave me a tired grin. 'Then Simon can play dolls with me again. That'll be fun.'

My hands immediately balled into fists. But my voice stayed soft, for Michael's sake. 'I already told you, Simon can't come.'

'Why? All my friends are coming, and Simon is my best friend.' Despite his protest, he willingly took the toothbrush from me and put it in his mouth.

'He's gone on a trip.' Wow, I couldn't come up with anything better than that? In my mind I crossed my fingers, hoping my boy wouldn't keep asking questions. Then I quickly bent over the tub to let out the bathwater. For a moment, the smooth surface showed me my reflection. The woman looking back at me was so different from the one who had beamed at me from the Old Danube only a few weeks ago. She had been so wonderfully happy, so endlessly in love.

That was the past, I reminded myself sternly. Just as the water was disappearing down the drain now, she would be gone one day too.

I straightened up quickly and spun around. Michael's eyebrows drew together and he tilted his head. When he looked at me like that, there was more to come. Definitely.

'Are you excited about your party? And about the presents?' Maybe it was a pathetic attempt to distract him, but I still had to try. I gave him an exaggeratedly cheerful smile as I pulled the grass-green towel off the hook.

At first I heard only the sound of the toothbrush gliding over Michael's baby teeth. But then he abruptly took it out of his mouth. 'Why is Simon going away when it's my birthday? He'll miss my party!' The foam ran down his chin and dripped freely onto the fabric of his dark blue top.

'I'm not exactly sure. He just said it was urgent.' I quickly point to the stool in front of the sink. 'Rinse and wash your face, please, then it's straight to bed.'

He obediently does what I tell him and then rubs his face dry. A few strands of his light blond hair stick damply to his forehead as he looks at me again with the same doubtful expression as before. 'But—'

'No buts,' I cut him off a little too harshly. 'He's terribly sorry, but Simon can't come. End of discussion.' I steer him out of the bathroom toward the kids' room.

With his head hanging, he stumbles along beside me, his bare feet making a smacking sound on the parquet floor of the hallway. Seeing him like this gives my already broken heart a fresh stab of pain.

First Heinrich, then Simon. Two men disappeared from his life in quick succession, and at least one of them is on me. How could I have been so naive? I should've kept Simon away from my children. Then I'd be the only one suffering now.

I lay my hand comfortingly on Michael's back, we enter his room and I dim the light. 'What should I read to you tonight?'

Without a word he climbs into bed, then stares at with his sad eyes. 'I don't want some stupid book,' he says defiantly, folding his arms across his chest.

'What do you want then?' I sit down on the edge of the mattress and force a smile onto my face.

'I want to see Simon.' Tiny tears roll down his cheeks. He sits in bed like a little bundle of misery, lips trembling, shoulders slumped.

'So do I,' slips out of me, and with that I say for the first time what, deep down inside, I still wish for. 'It's just not possible.'

I try to reach my hand out to him, but my body no longer obeys me. As if all my energy were needed just to keep me upright at all. As if I were running on an emergency reserve that could be completely used up at any moment.

'Then I'm going to call him tomorrow.' Michael pushes his lower lip forward.

How could I tell him that that's out of the question too? 'We'll see about that.' I take a deep breath and desperately hope that his idea will fizzle out overnight. 'But right now you need to go to sleep.'

He still looks at me skeptically, but he loosens his arms from their defensive position, slides farther under the blanket, and snuggles into his pillow. 'I still want to hear the story about the farmer Peter,' he then murmurs.

I breathe a little easier, at least a bit, and pick up the book.

Before I've even finished reading the story, Michael's eyes close. Very gently I kiss his forehead and turn out the light.

Another day is done. Again, I don't know how that was even possible. And even less can I imagine how I'm supposed to survive tomorrow.

Michael's birthday party.

Heinrich will be there. How could I have refused him that? No matter what happened between us, he's still the father of my children. He has a right to see them.

On tiptoe I sneak out of the children's room and make my way to the kitchen. There I pour myself some wine and sit down at the kitchen table. So this is what it's come to. I sit here completely alone and feel as if I've failed across the board.

Absentmindedly, I turn the wineglass in a circle on the table in front of me. The light from the kitchen lamp reflects off the rim of the glass and makes the red liquid glow almost magically.

My thoughts wander back to last night. Heinrich had talked me into going for a walk with him in the park at sunset. He probably thought it would be romantic, and with any other man it would have been.

Once again I stroll silently beside him through the mild summer evening, accompanied by the chirping of crickets and the rustling of leaves in the wind.

'You've changed,' he says, a sad undertone to his voice.

With a shrug, I shove my hands into the pockets of my overly wide, light linen pants. 'Maybe. What about you?'

For a moment he hesitates, as if he isn't sure which answer is the right one. 'I had plenty of time to think. About us. Our marriage and the children. About how we lived our lives and about all the things that went unspoken between us for far too long.'

I prick up my ears. That's what he wants to talk about? How often had I longed for this moment, and yet right now I'd rather run away. I've drawn a line under this marriage. Everything that happened between Heinrich and me in the past no longer matters.

'I made mistakes, and I regret them deeply. Every day in prison I wished for another chance to do the right thing. Now I have it. Today I'm a different man, a better husband and a fantastic father.'

Forcing yourself to love someone isn't enough. That was what I once told him, before our life finally went down the drain. Has he actually understood that now? 'You want to take care of the children? Bathe them and put them to bed? Cool their foreheads when they have a fever and play dolls with them for hours?' I look him straight in the eye. 'And you're willing to accept that each of us is an individual person and that not everything can follow your rules?'

Heinrich stops. The light of the streetlamp flickers across his face, but I still see how he presses his lips together for a moment. 'I will.'

'Oh yeah?' is all I say, and I turn to leave again. 'Why didn't you start with that right away earlier? The kids were beside themselves with joy to see you. But when Michael wanted to show you all his new drawings, you brushed him off as if he were an annoying fly.'

An exaggerated, strained sigh leaves Heinrich's mouth. 'Step by step, my love. Give me time, please.'

'You're never going to change.' Shaking my head, I gazed over the avenue of linden trees in front of us, behind which the sky has now turned a deep orange.

The sun disappears on the horizon. This image couldn't be more fitting for what is happening right now between Heinrich and me.

'I can do it, trust me. Have I ever lied to you?' There's a plea in his words; he seems shaken and weak.

He can't fool me with that anymore. 'No, you haven't,' I admit, 'but that alone doesn't make for a happy family.'

'What does, then? Tell me so I can be everything you want me to be.' He comes closer and puts his arm around my shoulders. 'I love you. More than ever before,' he whispers shakily.

His closeness feels wrong; I sense it very clearly. I quickly take a step to the side. 'Don't say that, Heinrich.' I falter, a noose tightening around my neck. 'Those are just empty words. Hollow shells with nothing inside.' It had always been like that.

'You're mistaken.' His voice is as thin as rice paper, almost breaking with every further word.

How can he not see it? 'You've always claimed you were a family man. But you never wanted to come with me to Berlin to visit my parents. My friends think you consider yourself too smart to bother with them.' I look at him intently. 'You fly into a rage when the kids don't sit quietly on their chairs like dolls and look pretty. And I…'

I can't go any further; the memory hits me far too hard, the scenes from our time together rise up far too painfully, right in front of my eyes, as if I were living through them all over again.

Heinrich falls silent, embarrassed. He knows that I'm right. About everything.

'You only love me because you see me the way you'd like me to be. The dutiful housewife, the self-sacrificing mother, and the beautiful lover.'

Now it's out, and it feels desperately good. All at once I become completely calm and even manage to look him straight in the eyes. Because what comes next is important.

'You're a wallet man,' I say insistently, and immediately find myself looking into a confused face. 'Someone who wants to flip open his wallet and present his perfect life in photos. My house, my wife, my children, my car, my garden fence.'

Now I'm the one who touches him. My hand moves to his upper arm and squeezes it as tightly, as if, that way, I could wake him up. He really ought to get angry. But he just shakes his head and is as speechless as I've ever seen him.

'I don't want that anymore,' I say firmly. 'You had thousands of chances. Every new day for years brought one with it, and yet you let them all pass. I'm going to move out and start over in a little house on the edge of town. It's over. Sign the divorce papers, please.'

His eyes widen. 'Who are you?' he suddenly asks me, and he sounds as if something inside him were breaking. 'What's happened to you?'

I let my eyes glance him up and down as if it were for the very first time. By now, only the darkness of the night surrounds us both; we're alone. Each on our own. 'I had time to think too,' I say in a voice as sober as a Monday morning.

That's exactly how it happened in the park last night. And the memory of it still makes me shudder as I sit at the kitchen table, absentmindedly spinning my glass of red wine. Even if my words weren't a real answer, everything had been said.

So that was it. The second end of my marriage.

With a sigh, I drink the last sip of wine and then head into the living room. There's still a lot to prepare for tomorrow's party. Balloons need to be blown up and game stations set up. The teddy bear–shaped ice cubes are already in the freezer, the cake is waiting to be glazed and decorated. And then there are the greeting cards I wanted to hang up over Michael's seat as decoration.

I'll start with those. I reach for the impressively tall stack of letters and spread them out on the kitchen table in front of me.

I wish Kathi were here. Will she come to the party tomorrow? So far she hasn't been able to give me an answer, and of course I understand why. Still, I reach for my phone.

She answers my call right away. 'Hey.' Her voice sounds very tentative, almost questioning.

'I miss how things used to be,' I say bluntly. 'Don't you?'

I hear only her breathing, at first very shallow, then it falters. 'Mira, I—'

'No. You don't have to say anything.' I lift my hand defensively, even though I know she can't see it. 'I know it's not like it used to be and it never will be again.'

On the other end of the line there is complete silence. As if she were holding her breath because she's in danger of drowning in my words.

There's nothing I want more than to save her from that.

So I start to tell her. 'Heinrich was released. He was innocent the whole time.' I sound so matter-of-fact, as if none of this had anything to do with me. 'It was a serial killer who finally made an obvious mistake with his next victim. The police were able to make the connection, and...'

I can't go on.

'I've known that for a long time,' Kathi snaps at me. 'Do you think the police didn't inform me?'

I have to tell her, that much is clear to me. 'Our marriage is over, but he's still the father of my children. He'll be at the party tomorrow.'

I listen intently to what she'll say next. 'I understand.' She sounds like a computer voice.

'You're not going to come, are you?' I ask tonelessly and close my eyes. That's what you do when you desperately need help, isn't it? You wait and pray, hope and fear.

Not a single word comes from Kathi while I clench my fists so tightly that I can hardly feel anything else. 'I can't do it,' she finally breathes into the phone. 'Whether Heinrich is there or not. Seeing happy children...'

'If there's any way I can help you, with anything at all, let me know, okay?' I don't need to say more. Kathi knows I'd do absolutely anything to see her laugh again.

'Sometime. Maybe. I don't know.'

I repeat my offer once more, then we say goodbye to each other. Only now do I notice how much air has built up in my lungs. I let it escape, and bit by bit I shrink down into my armchair.

No, I mustn't let myself go now.

Eagerly, I fix my gaze on the envelopes with the birthday cards that are still lying on the table in front of me. Then I get to work. One after another I open them, punch holes in the corners of the cards, and fasten them to a rainbow-colored string. In between I add balloons in different colors and a 'Happy Birthday' banner. All together it will look cheerfully colorful and might even distract me for a few hours. Even now, while I'm working on it, my mood is improving. When I pick up the last letter, I can even manage a small smile.

I quickly notice that what's inside is too thin to be a card. I open the envelope. Sure enough, there's only a single sheet of paper inside. Someone has written Michael a birthday letter, my father maybe, or his great-aunt Devi. A really nice idea. Carefully, I unfold the sheet.

'Dear Mira,' I read. The handwriting looks angular and scrawly, like that of an eight-year-old.

Instinctively, I turn the paper over. My eyes fly to the end of the text.

'Simon.'

Seconds pass. Maybe minutes.

Only then do I understand.

My heart wants to leap, but I forbid it. Only my mind is allowed to decide what happens next.

And it knows one thing for sure. The letter has to go. Immediately.

With trembling fingers, I shove the paper back into the envelope. The corners bend, the edges crumple. It doesn't matter. I whirl around. What now? What am I supposed to do?

'Straight in the trash! Best would be the dumpster out on the street,' my head demands.

'Read it,' my longing orders.

I'm stuck in between, overwhelmed by the war raging inside me, and even clenching my fists can't help me now.

I don't want to agree with either my head or my longing. I can't make a decision like that. Not now and not here. I need time. So I slide the envelope into a kitchen drawer and push it shut in a rush. The scraping sound burns in my ears, the dull bang makes me flinch. I quickly take a step back, not letting the drawer out of my sight.

That's where it's lying now. Simon's letter. And I have no idea what I'm supposed to do next.

Chapter Fifty-One

'Damn it, didn't you see that?' Paul sounds upset.

Confused, I look up. 'Excuse me?'

'I know, in your head you're already in Honolulu.' With theatrical flair, he throws his hands in the air. 'But if you knock over the oil canister, you can't just ignore it, okay?'

I knocked something over? Really? Distracted, I looked around our motorcycle shelter. Sure enough, I spot a large black stain on the gravel floor beside me.

'Sorry,' I mumble absentmindedly, wiping the grease off my fingers with a rag, and leaning back against the half-height tool cabinet behind me.

With a sigh, Paul joins me. 'Listen, Simon, this won't do. I know what's going on with you, but you still need to finally get your head clear again.'

I nod, but my thoughts are already somewhere else again. Far away, beyond the allotment garden, halfway across the city, behind the green front door.

Paul's elbow digs into my side and yanks me out of my thoughts. 'Tell me, when's the party happening, anyway?'

'What party?' Whatever he's talking about, I haven't heard anything about it so far.

He eyes me with a smirk. 'Your farewell party, of course.'

'There isn't one,' I say truthfully.

His grin instantly gives way to a grim, questioning expression. 'That's even worse than I thought. Man, oh man.'

I want to answer, Maybe, but I let it go. 'It's all good. I just have a lot to do. Packing and stuff.' I shrug, not even trying to hide how little I care.

As if I'd just said a magic word, Paul's eyes start to shine. 'Aren't you excited at all? I sure as hell would be. I'd be going crazy with anticipation. Only six days left!'

'It's pretty cool, yeah,' I reply as my thoughts wander to the day of my departure.

I see myself, alone with the fully loaded motorbike. Thanks to the darkly tinted visor of my helmet, no one can see my expression. And I don't even want to know what it looks like. With a jerky movement I swing myself onto the bike, start the engine, and ride off, even though I'd much rather stay.

'Don't overdo it with excitement,' Paul mutters beside me, not understanding. 'Other people would be glad to have this opportunity,' he adds so quietly that I can barely make it out.

'I am excited, but that doesn't mean I have to jump around here like a little girl in the schoolyard.'

I rest my forehead against the cool metal of the tool cabinet. If only I could breathe without feeling the tightness in my chest. And sleep without dreaming of her. And how much I wish I could be genuinely happy. About what comes next. For weeks I've been tinkering with my motorbike, replacing worn parts and polishing the bodywork. Now it's ready for the big trip. This exact moment was what I pictured whenever I most wanted to quit my job. Running my hand over the cold leather of the seat, the smell of gasoline in my nose, and the deep rumble of the engine vibrating through my whole body.

That was my life raft. Still, now it feels as if I'm drifting alone on the open sea.

Chapter Fifty-Two

I jolt awake.

Where am I?

Who's with me?

Not even the moonlight comes through the windows; it's pitch-dark. Only a distant rushing sound can be heard. No one is breathing except me. Carefully, my hand wanders to the other half of the bed, but there's no one there. I'm alone, Simon isn't here, even though he just was. In my dreams.

Like every damned night. And especially today I shouldn't be surprised about it.

All on their own, my thoughts drifted back to the afternoon. Michael's birthday party was already in full swing when the doorbell rang. There were no parents or children outside. Instead, two packages lay on the doormat. A big one for my son and a small one for me.

Full of excitement, Michael opened the box with his name on it in my memory.

'Mommy, look!' he squeals and lifts the present into the

air. A Barbie doll in a bright pink glitter ball gown. 'It's from Simon,' he adds with utter conviction.

I glance over at Heinrich; his expression looks petrified. With the corners of his mouth pulled down, he's breathing in and out far too quickly, then he looks away.

Of course, he's ashamed of his son. Because he likes dolls that also like to wear pink. Nothing has changed, and this is the proof.

Shaking my head, I turn back to Michael, who is brushing his new Barbie's hair back. 'You can sit with me today. Here, this is our seat. Do you want a bit of cake too?' he asks the doll tenderly.

Simon would never be ashamed of my children. On the contrary, he'd get up to every bit of mischief with them. I shouldn't think about that, and yet I do. My feelings threaten to overwhelm me, so I excuse myself and march out of the living room. Still holding the smaller of the two packages in my hand, I walk up the stairs, burst into the bedroom, and sink onto the bed. Awkwardly, I scrape the tape off the box, then open the flaps.

It takes only fractions of a second for me to realize what's in the package. With difficulty, I hold back the tears rising inside me.

Just like this afternoon when I opened Simon's gift, my chest tightened again now, in the darkness of the night.

I grope for the switch of the night-light, the bright glare blinds me, but as soon as I've gotten used to it, I see it. That one special candle. There it stands, right next to me on the nightstand. It's still there. Like a memorial. I should have thrown it out right away. And yet I couldn't do it.

On our first and only night together, this candle burned for us. There isn't much left of it, even the vanilla scent is barely noticeable. I let my fingers glide over the curved rim and at once I'm flooded with memories.

'It smells like you,' Simon whispers in my ear. He is so close that we're touching everywhere. His skin nestles soft and warm against mine; there's no space left between us.

I bury my nose in the hollow of his collarbone. 'Like the two of us,' I say with a smile.

His hand feels its way down my back, vertebra by vertebra. We lie next to each other like that and savor what we have. I watch the flame, gently stroke Simon's chest, and wish for only one thing: to be with him forever.

No, that memory has to go. I mustn't think about it. I make the candle disappear in the nightstand drawer, exhale in short bursts, and switch off the light.

Forget, I have to forget. Him and everything that happened.

Over and over I recite the same phrase to myself, as if it were my own personal rosary. And in fact, I feel better. So much better that I dare to relax my muscles. My eyes close.

In an instant Simon is back. His blue-green eyes sparkle. A longing smile plays on his irresistible lips. No matter how strong I'd like to be, everything inside me goes so soft it feels like I'm melting.

One thing's for sure, I won't be sleeping anymore tonight. Not again.

I throw back the covers and slip out of bed. In my dressing gown I creep downstairs and put some water on. Leaning against the kitchen counter, I watch as first small, then larger and larger bubbles rise in the kettle. They break the surface, churn up the water and throw everything into chaos. Just like Simon's gift.

A few minutes later, with the steaming mug in my hand, I wander over to the dining table and sink down onto one of the chairs. My gaze drifts to the kitchen counter, exactly where Simon's letter is hidden.

I stare at the drawer. It stares back. Should I do it?

I shake my head vehemently. 'This won't help, Mira,' I scold myself in a stern tone. And yet I can't take my eyes off the drawer.

Like in a film I see myself walking towards it. I open it, reach for the envelope, pull out the sheet of paper and start to read. Then the film in my head tears and starts again. As if my thoughts were trapped in an endless loop. As if I could never escape.

The letter has to go.

As long as it's here with me, I'll think about him. I hurry over to the kitchen counter, yank the drawer open and grab the envelope. The urge to read Simon's words grows stronger. And I know I have to move fast now, because I won't be able to resist it much longer. I march out the front door, cross the garden and open the gate. Back there, at the other end of the street, stand the garbage containers. That's my destination.

The way there feels as if I had to climb a mountain. With every step it becomes more arduous, with every meter the envelope in my hand seems to gain weight. As if something suddenly began to seethe inside me, I grow restless. That restlessness hasn't reached the surface yet, but it's a warning to hurry.

Now I'm there; with trembling fingers I push back the lid of the garbage container. My breath catches. Heat rises in me. Scalding hot.

'Come on, Mira,' I tell myself. Then I press my lips together.

I do it.

Now.

As if the letter were a volleyball, I slam it into the recycling bin and instantly close the lid of the container.

From now on everything will be fine. That's what I keep telling myself, over and over again. And yet it takes less than a second for my feelings to boil over. Unstoppable and powerful, they force their way to the surface. Everything is a mess, I don't know what's right anymore. Who am I? And what do I need?

As if by remote control, I yank the lid of the trash container open again. There it is, lying among newspapers, pizza boxes, and delivery packaging. I grab it and tear the letter out of the envelope.

There's nothing I can do to stop it. Without being asked, my fingers unfold the paper.

Here, in the middle of the street, under the starless sky and in the cone of light from a streetlamp, it happens. Wearing only my dressing gown, with bare feet and not breathing at all, I find out what Simon wants to tell me.

Chapter Fifty-Three

If I had superpowers, I would stop time. The reeds at the pond would stop swaying in the wind. The birds would fall silent. And the clouds on the horizon would remain forever dipped in that bright orange.

Still, I watch the sun sink lower and lower. Only a small arc of it is still visible; in a moment it will disappear completely.

'Love always finds a way,' Sandy whispered in my ear yesterday, full of conviction. I wanted to believe her, because I know she's so often right.

But this was the one time she was wrong.

Today is the last day of waiting. And right now, the darkness is catching up with me one last time. There isn't the slightest glimmer, not a trace of confidence left.

This is the final moment of our last chance. There is no more tomorrow, only today.

And there is still no sign of Mira.

Chapter Fifty-Four

From my hiding place behind the rosebushes, I stare over at Simon. Hypnotically drawn to him and paralyzed in my whole body at the same time. I don't know why I came. And even less what I'm supposed to do next.

Even from a distance I can see the pain in his face, and I see the disappointment in the way he holds himself. But more than anything else, I'm aware of how my heart is pounding. As if it wanted to leap out of my chest. As if it wanted to flee, to gallop away and not stop until it reaches the edge of the pond over there. Right against Simon's chest.

But my legs don't move. It's like they were caught in a noose that keeps tightening, they become less and less able to move with every passing minute.

Now he turns around. His hands move over his head to his neck and claw into it. For a moment, in the light of the streetlamp, I can see the worries in his eyes before his lids close. Right where his lashes touch, I spot a shimmer. It travels down his cheeks to his jaw and then disappears into the darkness.

I can't help it. Wrapped in the still darkness of the night, I cry along with him.

I could end all of this. I could go to him, wrap my arms around his shoulders and press my lips to his. I could kiss him until he can't breathe anymore and whisper to him how much he means to me.

And yet it's impossible.

My mind and my heart drift apart. I'm torn, no one can save me.

While the battle inside me rages like a ferocious typhoon, it suddenly happens. Simon starts to move. With slumped shoulders, his hands buried in his pants pockets and his gaze fixed firmly on the ground, he walks away.

If I want to stop him, it has to happen now. In this very moment.

I have to decide.

Now.

My storm doesn't calm down. On the contrary, it grows fiercer and sweeps everything along with it while Simon becomes smaller and smaller right before my eyes. Just a few more meters and he'll be gone completely.

Out of my sight and out of my life.

My fists clench with all their strength. 'No!' my heart roars loudly. And yet it's nothing compared to my ears, which trick me into thinking they hear an electronic beeping. It sounds like an ECG machine. The intervals between the signals grow longer, while I myself remain paralyzed. I can't even reach out my hand to him, my lips don't move.

I can't call after him, and even less am I able to run after him.

Frozen, I watch him turn onto the avenue of linden trees and, in the very next moment, I can no longer see him.

The ECG in my ears sends me a continuous ringing tone.

Flatline.

Chapter Fifty-Five

I'm awake. All night long. Now I hear the traffic noise outside growing louder and louder, the sun's rays find their way through the narrow gaps in the blinds. They bathe my apartment in a diffuse light, just bright enough for me to make out the tear-off calendar on the kitchen table.

A big number one can be seen on it.

It's from yesterday, its time is long past. I know that for sure, and yet I don't want to accept it.

I clench my teeth, throw back the covers, get up, and head out. When I reach the kitchen table, I hesitate for a moment.

I know I have to do it. No matter how much it hurts, time doesn't wait for me. Any more than Mira does.

So, with a nervous movement, I take the top sheet of the calendar between my thumb and index finger.

Then I tear it off.

A single, oval-shaped circle appears on the paper underneath.

Day Zero is here. Today everything comes to an end.

Chapter Fifty-Six

I love you.

A tender whisper, a warm embrace.

I love, love, love you.

Morning sun, birdsong.

My water girl.

Fingertips brush featherlight over my cheeks, wander to my neck, and trace my collarbone. I let myself sink, feel safe and sheltered. I don't want it to stop. For a little while I just want to lie here, be kissed and caressed. Breathe in the scent of his hair and feel the tickle of his stubble on my skin. The moment is too beautiful. I'm happy, with no wishes and no worries. And all at once I know it for sure.

'I love you too,' I whisper with a smile, because it's the truth. Then I lift my arms, wanting to wrap them around his broad shoulders, to feel him, taste him, and breathe him in.

But my hands close on nothing.

Abruptly I tear my eyes open, my eyes land on the other side of the bed. It's empty. I blink hard, but the image in front of my eyes doesn't change. I feel over every inch of the mattress; no one is there.

I'm alone.

Of course I am. Tired, I let my head fall back onto the pillow, and immediately I feel tears crawling up inside me.

'No, please don't. Not again.' I say it out loud and clear.

Since last night everything has been decided. Still, I feel as if I'd spent my whole life dreaming of a parachute jump. But when I was finally sitting on the floor of the plane at the pivotal moment, my feet dangling over the vast nothingness, I was paralyzed.

Ever since I read that letter, I've wanted to jump, and yet I couldn't. I was blocked. And I still am, even though the countdown is already at zero.

The constant beeping of my ECG is also still unchanged in my head. My heart hasn't been beating properly. For hours now.

It has already happened, my chance to jump is over. Watching him leave was supposed to set me free. But in fact, it only made everything worse.

I've read Simon's letter a thousand times; now I'm doing it again. And, as always, I get stuck at one point.

'My sister Sandy insists that everything that happens in life has a purpose. And that the two of us met was exactly the way it was supposed to be.'

Can that be the truth for me too?

By now my longing no longer whispers; it screams, rages, and rebels.

It won't let me sleep, forbids me to eat. And when I let Simon go yesterday, my heart stopped beating.

Dead hearts can be resuscitated, it suddenly flashes through my mind. If you act quickly. Chest compressions. Breathing. And then again from the beginning. You just have to keep going stubbornly until it starts beating again. There's no room for doubt and no time for fear. There's only one goal.

Life. Because it's the only thing that matters.

As if my longing were finally winning the fight, the fear inside me retreats. Second by second, it grows smaller. It loses its strength, its power fades, and it becomes clear to me what I have to do.

I have to stop Simon.

Chapter Fifty-Seven

The motorbike looks like a pitch-black pack mule. There's barely any room left on the seat, but I still wedge myself in between the bags and push the bike off its stand.

Sandy comes over to me and pulls me into a tight hug. 'We're all searching for happiness and sometimes we think we can't find it,' she says weightily, without taking her eyes off me. 'When it suddenly appears, we forget that happiness is really like a butterfly. You can't catch it, and the harder you try, the faster it flutters away. But if you stop trying to hold on to it, if you stay completely calm and do nothing but be glad that it's there, if you forget what happened yesterday and stop thinking about what tomorrow might bring, then, and only then, you have a chance that it'll stay with you for a little while.'

I can only hope she's right about that. But by now I know that everything Sandy says makes sense.

'That's exactly what I'm going to do, sis,' I whisper in her ear and hug her again as tightly as I can. Then my eyes wander down to her belly. 'Take good care of the little one in there.'

She smiles at me with her incomparable contentment and lifts her hand in farewell.

Hardly has my sister taken a step back and Paul is already standing next to me. 'I envy you, man.' There's a strange melancholy in his eyes.

I hug him as tightly as I can and try to smile. 'Take care.'

'Do it better.' Grinning, he holds out his fist to me.

Behind him my mother is still waiting. She has tears in her eyes, even though there's absolutely no need for that. I look at her, and for the first time in years I can do it without being afraid that the memory will overwhelm me.

Nothing happens without a reason. And as hard as the breakup with Mira was for me, without her, I never would have been able to make peace with the past.

'Bye, Mom.' I pull her in too, even closer than everyone else. 'We'll talk, okay?'

Her body is shaking; I stroke her back soothingly. She doesn't say anything, but she doesn't have to.

A minute later it's time. There's no reason to wait any longer. Taking a deep breath, I put the helmet on my head and take one last look at what I'm leaving behind here.

The apartment building that has been my home for the past three years.

Paul, who had already been the best friend I could have imagined when we were only six years old.

And my family, whom I had kept at a distance for far too long.

In my thoughts they stay with me, together with my water girl.

I'll never forget Mira, but right now I don't have a choice. So I start the engine.

Chapter Fifty-Eight

I feel a bit like I'm taking part in an illegal street race across Vienna. Ever since I dropped the kids off at Eva's, my body has been running at full speed. It's only a few more meters and then I'll have made it. Up ahead I can already see the dirty gray-brown façade of Simon's apartment building. I park, jump out of the car, and rush to the front door.

My eyes race over the doorbells. Which one is the right one?

Walter, Kachelbauer, Platzer. All sorts of names are written next to the little silver buttons, but nowhere do I find what I'm looking for. Instead, right in the middle, I spot a blank label.

He's gone.

No, I can't think like that. Maybe he's still packing and just took the label off already.

I ring. A steady buzzing sounds. At first with every fifth of my heartbeats, then with every tenth. Nothing else happens.

My world threatens to collapse, but I don't let it.

Hurriedly I press the other doorbells until someone finally buzzes me in. Then I rush into the cool stairwell and squeeze past the woman with the stroller. I take the steps two at a time, and still it takes far too long before I'm finally standing in front of his door.

I ring the bell again.

Nothing.

I knock. At first very cautiously, then harder and harder.

Nothing.

'Simon?' I call and keep pounding on the door. 'Simon!'

Nothing.

As if pitch-black shadows suddenly descended over me, I start to shiver. The beads of sweat on my forehead turn into tiny pellets of ice. I pull the phone from my pocket and dial his number.

Nothing.

Not even his voicemail picks up; it just rings until the call cuts off on its own. I try to breathe calmly, but I can't manage it.

'Am I too late?' With trembling fingers I type the message and send it off in a hurry. Then I focus on my breathing. I wait for twenty breaths; every single one is torture.

Nothing.

Does he even still have his phone?

I hardly dare think about it. Still, in this very moment, a terrible truth takes hold of me.

My chance has disappeared.

Simon is no longer here.

I could collapse. I could let my knees give way right here and now. I could let myself fall helplessly and slide down to the floor with my back against the apartment door. But that's not going to happen. Because I'm going to find another solution.

Someone has to know where he is. Or where he was planning to go.

The prison!

No place in this world fills me with greater horror, and yet that's exactly where I have to go. It's my only chance, the last option I have left. How else could I find Simon among billions of people spread across millions of miles?

I rush off. I run to my car like a madwoman. I get in. I speed away.

When I reach the prison, I squeeze the car into a parking space. Then I stumble out of the car. I keep walking faster and faster, even though my summer dress is already clinging, soaked with sweat, to my back. Impetuously, I yank open the prison's front door and hurry to the reception desk.

A woman with a boyish short haircut and delicate features is sitting there and looks up at me. 'Yes?' she asks, bored, while I gasp desperately for air so I can utter any words at all.

'Simon,' I force out. 'Where is he?'

Her eyebrows draw together. 'Simon Herbst? He hasn't worked here for a long time.'

'Listen, I really need to find him. So if you know anything…' I'm aware of how impatient I sound, but I don't have time for long explanations.

'I'm sorry.' She gives an apologetic shrug, but her face makes it clear how little she cares.

That can't be true, someone has to be able to help me! 'Maybe a colleague? Someone who was in close contact with Simon?'

Absentmindedly, she reaches for the breast pocket of her

uniform. 'Horst,' she says, pulling out an old-fashioned cell phone. 'I'll give him a call.'

She gets up from her chair and marches to the back of the room, where I can't hear her. All I can do is stare at her, transfixed. And hope.

I brace myself against the reception desk and shift nervously from one foot to the other until she comes back.

'From what people are saying, he wanted to go through with this motorbike trip. Apparently the first destination is Paris.' She twists her mouth into a grimace. 'But we're talking about Simon here…' she adds, as if that explained everything.

Maybe she says something else. Maybe I answer. All of it happens on its own while the thoughts in my head are riding a roller coaster of their own.

Paris, then. Which route would he take?

I walk back to the car. Then I zoom off and take the A1 towards Salzburg. At such a speed as if I was escaping my very own apocalypse.

Chapter Fifty-Nine

First it was a pond in a park in Vienna. Then the Old Danube. Now it's a lake next to a rest stop in the middle of Upper Austria that reminds me of Mira. Sitting cross-legged on the grass, I keep my eyes fixed on the water. The waves lap, full of life, against the shore, the sun's rays break on their edges and dazzle me. It feels cheerful and free.

How wonderful it would be if a bit of that mood rubbed off on me. But I can't feel a trace of it. There's still a pull in my chest. And Mira's face before my eyes, from a thousand different angles, in a million different colors. It follows me wherever I go and catches up with me no matter how fast I drive.

Thoughtfully, I pluck at the blades of grass on the lawn where I'm sitting, pull them out and peel them apart layer by layer until nothing is left.

What good does it do me if I know the key to happiness but can't use it for myself? If I want to let go but just can't manage it?

With every question my head pounds a little more. Still,

I don't push them away. Because if I've learned one thing, it's that you have to face your feelings. It's the only way they can lose their power.

I pick up a pebble and throw it into the water. Just like Mira did when we first met, I watch the little waves spreading out in wider and wider circles. It takes a long time, but I want to wait until the surface of the lake lies before me again as if nothing had ever happened.

Now it happens. The water grows calm. It has found peace.

'There's no life that's made of light alone. We all carry our shadows with us. We can't stop stones from lying in our path and thick clouds from gathering in front of our suns. But it's the light of the bright times that can carry us through the dark ones, if we only let it.' That's how Sandy put into words what I can feel deep inside me now.

Yes, times are dark. But I can remember the beautiful moments with Mira, and that's exactly what I'm going to do.

It's probably a wistful smile that spreads across my face now. But it's a smile.

I get up, brush the grass off my motorcycle pants, and take a long, deep breath. Then I put on my backpack and walk back along the narrow path through the overgrown bushes to the parking lot.

A few minutes later I emerge from the thicket. I straighten the helmet in my hands as I walk toward my bike. Then I look up.

I freeze on the spot.

Only my eyes blink rapidly. Still, it's the same image over and over again that forms on my retina.

Mira.

Mira is standing next to my motorbike. And she's smiling at me.

Shouldn't I be doing something? Go over to her? Talk to her? Or at least smile back?

My body is missing the commands because my head can't make sense of it. Not even now, as she slowly walks toward me. Her golden bangles gleam in the sunlight, I can make out a henna tattoo on her shoulder. Then I look into her eyes and finally get the answers to all my questions.

I know where I am, who I am, and why I am.

Only a few meters still separate us. She stops, lowers her gaze, and brushes her hair behind her ear, almost shyly. 'I knew you'd stop here. You, me, and the water. We just belong together.'

My paralysis evaporates as if it had never existed. I start walking, on and on, until there isn't a millimeter left between us. Gently I put my arms around her and in the very same moment she does the same. It's like we're following our very own choreography. As if no one had to say anything for us to know what comes next.

It happens. Just like that.

The two of us let go. And we start over.

A feeling as fierce as a summer thunderstorm seizes me. A thought as clear as a mountain lake takes shape in my head.

It's time. I have everything I need.

Epilogue

I pull the cream-colored paper closer and let my fingertips glide over the smooth surface. Then I reach for the pen lying next to me on the wooden kitchen table.

It can begin. With a smile on my face, I start to write.

Simon,

There is one thing I believe in with all my heart. Meeting you is the best thing that has ever happened to me in my life.

When you look at me, just the way you are right now, and I feel our love all through my body. How it tingles across my skin, passes through my chest, and even wanders all the way to the tips of my earlobes.

When you play with the children in our little house on the edge of town as if you were their best friend. When you romp around with them and cook up mischief. Carve funny faces into their apple slices and chase away the monsters under their beds so they can sleep.

When you take me in your arms and kiss me with a passion like there is nothing more important in this world than the two of us.

Then I know for sure. You mean everything to me, and so much more.

Standing here in front of you today, surrounded by our families, in a white dress and with flowers in my hair, makes me so incredibly happy that I can't even begin to describe it.

'I love you. That's all I can say.'

The pen slips from my hand, and it's only right. Because there are no more words, no letters and no sentences that can still express what I feel for Simon.

That's how it is with true love, I suppose. Even the most brilliant language can't do it justice. You have to experience it with all your senses to really know it in your bones.

A feeling of happiness with a never-before-seen intensity sweeps over me. Because there's one thing I know for sure: for the rest of our lives we will belong to each other. We will laugh and cry together, grow old together and forever gaze up together at a sky that belongs only to the two of us.

More by Belinda Benna

vinci-books.com/thedreams

I was hired to care for his daughter... not his heart.

Single dad and world-famous pianist Josh Friedberg is focused, distant, and impossible to resist. Spending time with his daughter Sophia brings us closer, and the slow-burning spark between us is undeniable—but risking love could cost me my heart all over again.

Turn the page for a free preview...

The Dreams We Share: Chapter One

MAYA

A heart-wrenching whimper reaches my ears. Though barely audible amid the lively sounds of the kindergarten group, I am immediately alarmed.

It's Frida.

I look up from the cardboard butterflies I'm cutting out for the summer festival, blowing a strand of my long black hair away from my face. The bright June sunlight streams through the windows, casting a colorful glow over the whimsically decorated room. The glass beads of the mobile above the entrance sparkle with a rainbow of colors, and the vibrant red of the play kitchen glows even more intensely.

My gaze continues to wander until I find the crying girl, who shows up at the kindergarten day after day, only wearing tights and a T-shirt. Over in the corner with the building blocks, she buries her head between her tightly drawn-up knees.

"There she goes again." My boss, Nadine, shakes her head with an exasperated snort and reaches for the hot glue gun. "Can't this child go a single day without creating drama?"

I look into her icy-blue eyes. "Why did you become a preschool teacher, anyway?"

Of course, she's the boss, and if I've learned one thing during my internship here, direct criticism is unwelcome. Nevertheless, I can't help but ask her the question.

"That's none of your business." Nadine shrugs indifferently and crumples the red tissue paper in her hand into something that was supposed to be a lovingly shaped flower for the wall decoration.

If it were just about me, I wouldn't say a word. But her cold demeanor is directed at the little innocent beings we have the privilege of caring for.

"Not mine, but it is the children's business." I reply so quietly that she probably can't hear it, pushing the tiny wooden chair behind me as I stand.

I walk past the dollhouse, the construction workshop, and the painting corner. I almost stumble over a miniature train that one of the wild rascals left in the middle of the room.

A few seconds later, I sink onto the soft carpeted floor of the building corner and pull three-year-old Frida into my arms. Her red curls reek of cold cigarette smoke.

"What happened?" I ask the little one, stroking her back reassuringly.

She doesn't answer. I only notice how she plays with my oversized earrings, sparkling in all colors. Frida sure loves that.

"Together, we can solve any problem, you know," I whisper while gently rocking her back and forth. "You remember, don't you? We're both..."

"Superheroes." Frida's voice is so faint that I can hardly hear it.

I smile. Because suddenly, I feel strong too. "Exactly. And what do superheroes do?"

She pushes herself away from me slightly and looks up at me with her green eyes. "They can do anything." A conspiratorial grin appears on her freckle-covered face.

"So if a superhero can handle anything, nothing can happen to them that they can't fix, right?" I lovingly wipe the tears from her cheeks. In the corner of my eye, I see Nadine throwing her arms up in the air. Due to her sour expression, she looks completely out of place in the group room, which appears so cheerful with its yellow curtains and children's drawings on the wall.

"Do I have to do everything alone?" She rants in a volume she knows I can hear. Then she turns with a grim expression to the rainbow-colored stack of construction paper sheets on the craft table.

"Nadine is mad at you." Frida wrinkles her button nose.

Though I flinch inwardly, I mimic the little one's grimace. "So what?" I whisper back. Then I turn my face away so Nadine can't see it and contort my features until the little one giggles.

Experiencing her laughter is worth any sacrifice. No matter how difficult it can be having Nadine as my boss, time with the children makes up for it. With them, I am in a different world. A place where there's no pressure. They don't pretend; they don't lie. And they see the world just the way I love it. Like through a magical kaleidoscope that casts a rainbow hue over everything.

I nod encouragingly to Frida. "Do you want to tell me now why you were crying?"

She lowers her eyelids in shame. I can barely understand

what she murmurs, but as I also let my gaze fall, I don't need to understand anymore. She tries to hide the dark stain on her beige tights with her hands, but I can still see it clearly.

"Please, don't tell on me," she whispers with a voice choked with tears.

Instantly, I empathize with her. I feel her shame and guilt as if they were my own. Still, I smile at her reassuringly.

"You can rely on me. And you know what? Coincidentally, I brought a magic cloak with me today." I pretend to pull a cloth from my bright blue flowing skirt. "Anything this covers becomes invisible."

The girl's eyes widen. "Really?"

"Yeah, of course. What do you think?" I hold the nonexistent piece of fabric in front of her face. "My goodness, Frida, where's your head?"

She leans to the side as if peering out from behind a curtain. "I'm here!"

"Thank goodness. I thought..." I pretend to be relieved, wiping away imaginary sweat from my forehead. The numerous plastic bangles around my wrist make a dull clacking sound while I wrap Frida in the imaginary cloak. One last time, I hug her tightly. "Now you can follow me unnoticed to the restroom. On the count of three, okay?"

"Okay," she whispers almost inaudibly. She nods against my shoulder.

Hand in hand, we make our way through the group room. Fortunately, none of the other children take notice. Melinda and her best friend David are drawing ships, and the preschoolers are having a tea party with the dolls.

Only Nadine notices that we're sneaking outside. She scrutinizes me, the color of her eyes resembling an iceberg.

Without reacting to her, I turn toward the exit. Only Frida matters now.

After tending to the girl, I reluctantly take a seat next to Nadine at the craft table. I can feel her eyes on me as I reach for the scissors. Immediately, I'm filled with tension, which threatens to overwhelm me.

"Did she wet herself again?" Her thin eyebrows rise. The hot glue gun in her hand oozes, and the adhesive smell fills my nostrils.

I shouldn't lie to her; that has gone wrong several times already, leading to reprimands. "No, she just wanted to show me something," I say anyway. For Frida's sake. After all, I made her a promise. Hastily, I take the pine-green cardboard and place the leaf-shaped stencil on it. My brightly painted fingernails add a cheerful mood to the plain surface.

"Don't get too attached to the little ones, Maya. You supervise them, teach them something, and when they're old enough, you release them into their future lives." She lazily sticks a tissue paper flower onto the wire stem. "That's it. They're not your children."

Is it supposed to be that simple? Even though my intuition tells me otherwise? "I understand that, but..."

She raises her hand. "I don't want to hear it."

"Something may be wrong at Frida's home." I shouldn't speak that thought out loud, but I can't help it. "Her shoes are too small, and her clothes are frayed and rarely washed. Shouldn't we do something?"

Heat rises within me as I think about what could be happening in her life.

"Enough of that," Nadine warns me emphatically. "Maybe her parents don't have much money, but they're doing their best. And it's not uncommon for a three-year-old to forget to use the toilet while playing. I can recognize children with problems, and Frida isn't one of them."

Surprised, I let the paper and scissors drop. So she has been observing the little girl too. Has she been to her home or talked to her parents? Perhaps Frida's family isn't as bad as I imagined?

It's possible, yet I search Nadine's face for signs that she might be lying to me.

"You're just an intern." She suddenly sounds as if she pities me. She puts her hand on my forearm. "Why do you think that after a few weeks, you can assess a situation better than a seasoned educator?"

Ashamed, I lower my gaze. Because the facts can't be denied. She's the professional, and I'm the intern.

For now.

This internship is the foundation for my special education studies. Only if I accumulate the required practical hours, submit a written assignment, and pass the four partial exams for study eligibility will I be allowed to attend university. If I had completed school until graduation, it wouldn't be necessary. But that's just not how it turned out. At twenty-six years old, I haven't accomplished much in general.

That's about to change.

I want to help children with problems. Children like Frida. This dream has accompanied me my whole life, and a few months ago, I finally found the courage to pursue it.

I'd love to tell Nadine about it. But I don't dare. She wouldn't believe that I could follow through anyway.

Her strained cough doesn't bode well. "And one more thing: I would strongly advise you to dress like an adult. Just a tip." With a disdainful sniff, she scans my rainbow-colored T-shirt.

The children love my cheerful style. And so do I. "A little color brightens up anyone's life," I reply defiantly, but I can't even look her in the eye while saying it.

With a loud creak, Nadine pushes her chair back. "Did I ask you a question?"

No.

"Exactly." She stands up and tugs at her mouse-gray T-shirt as if trying to conceal her rounded hips beneath the fabric. Then she tilts her chin up and calls the children to the gymnasium at a deafening volume.

After all the children have been picked up in the late afternoon, I enter the group room. Completely alone, Nadine sits at the craft table, struggling to handle the decorations for the summer festival. She cuts the leaves so carelessly that I almost want to take the scissors out of her hand. I straighten my back and cross the room, which feels eerily quiet without the children.

"Where should I continue?" I ask as cheerfully as possible, taking a seat on one of the small wooden chairs next to my boss.

She doesn't respond.

Better to start working right away. But as I reach for the box with the pre-cut tissue paper flowers to assemble them on the wires, Nadine stops me.

"We need to talk," she says wearily.

I follow her into her office, which is more of a storage closet than an actual workspace. There, she gestures for me to sit on the chair in front of her desk, piled high with folders and books. I feel uneasy. She maneuvers past the table and rests her head on her hands.

Heaven, when she looks at me like that, I feel like I'm four years old again.

"Maya," she begins, letting out a heavy sigh. "This is an educational institution for children aged three to six."

Yes, I'm aware of that. I might be scrunching my face because I have no idea where she's going with this.

"For two months, you've been working here, and I've done my best to make this fact clear to you," she continues, leaning back in her chair. The squeaking of the backrest pains my ears. "I don't like to admit a mistake, but if you have made one, you have to own up to it."

What? Nadine wants to admit a mistake? Something stirs within me. A spark of hope that perhaps my future holds more for me than financial worries and temporary jobs that no one could endure for long.

Positive thoughts are the beginning of all good things, I hear my father's voice echoing within me. For years, I've carried his voice inside me, and whenever he whispers something in his warm bass, I feel a little stronger than before. Even today.

What if behind Nadine's rough exterior, there's a soft core? What if she's been testing me all this time? And what if I've passed the test?

With anticipation, I gaze at Nadine, barely able to contain myself and eager to finally hear what she has to say. She grabs a piece of paper on her desk with the blank side up.

This could be my evaluation.

My legs refuse to stay still any longer. With a fantastic internship certificate, the first step toward admission to university is taken. In just three days, I'll take the second step by completing the required biology exam. A warm tingling sensation runs through my arms, while my palms become damp and simultaneously colder.

Everything seems to be happening in slow motion. Nadine turns the paper over and places it directly in front of me. Curiously, I lean forward.

Termination.

Does it say termination?

No, that's impossible. I read the word again, but *termination* stubbornly refuses to turn into *evaluation letter*.

"Dammit, what's going on here?" Did I say that out loud?

"Your behavior has been unacceptable in this institution from the beginning. Today, you lied to me again. Frida did wet herself," Nadine says.

Dammit. How did she know...?

"The replacement tights had a different color." Nadine raises her eyebrows. "Did you really think I wouldn't notice?"

Dammit. She must have noticed during the changing for the gym class. I shouldn't have lied to her. But abusing the trust of the little ones would have been just as wrong. "I wanted to—"

"Enough," she interrupts me. Suddenly, she looks exhausted. "I've never witnessed such unprofessional behavior. Denying it only makes it worse."

But that wasn't my intention. "Let me explain," I stammer.

Nadine shakes her head. "That's not all. You can't handle criticism and consistently execute my instructions incorrectly." She looks at me, full of disappointment. "You know we've discussed this before. You're not suited to be an educator. In fact, you should be thankful that I'm telling you this early."

"But..." Nadine's words circle in my head, but I can hardly comprehend them.

None of our little charges has ever complained. I'm there for them, so it can't be wrong. Or can it?

What if my dream is bigger than I am? What if I'm not meant to help children?

Disappointed in myself, I lower my gaze. "I—"

Once again, she doesn't let me finish. "My decision is final. Today was your last day of work."

What? I can't even stay until the end of the kindergarten year?

What will happen to the summer festival? I had planned game stations and rehearsed songs with the children. And what about Frida? Who will remind her she's a superhero when I'm no longer around?

"How can I make it right?" The pleading in my voice is unmistakable. I slide forward on the chair, almost landing on my knees. "Give me another chance."

Nadine's body tenses up. "You've had too many already."

"I've learned my lesson, honestly. This internship means everything to me. Don't take it away from me." I look at her desperately. She has to understand that my entire future is at stake.

Nadine bites her lip. "Don't make it harder on yourself. Just sign it." She nods toward the termination paper.

Defiantly, I cross my arms in front of my body. "And if I don't?"

"You see, that's part of the problem. You're behaving like a child. Grow up already."

Grow up? Why should I? So that I can become as cold-hearted as she is? I shrink on the chair, feeling hardly taller than a Lego figure.

She stands in front of me and thrusts the pen into my hand. "Just sign it." Her index finger impatiently taps on the paper. "Working with children is not for you. You need a job that suits you."

I swallow hard. Even if my heart refuses to understand, at least my head has to. My goal is unattainable. It always has been; I was just foolish enough to hope it would be different.

"Go ahead." Nadine's tone leaves no room for argument. So I do it. Resignedly, I let the pen glide across the paper. My jagged signature seals in blue on white the end of my dreams.

It's over. I have failed. Once again.

The Dreams We Share: Chapter Two

JOSH

Warm air builds up under my jacket, and the headlights blind me. I turn my head so that I can still see the host of the television show. Maybe it would have been better not to because looking at her is anything but calming.

Her forced smile and the hair tightly tied up in a bun make her appear like a wax figure. Only one thing seems alive, and that's her eyes. They are alert like those of a tiger, and my gut feeling tells me that this predator in the little black dress will soon bare her teeth.

"We are live in three, two, one..." a voice calls out from the darkness behind the four cameras, all focused on the two of us. The lively murmur of the audience in the hall fades away.

This is the moment to check my posture once again. I run my hands through my short-cropped hair and straighten my shirt collar while the host greets the viewers at home and in the studio with her melodic voice.

"Tonight, I have the pleasure of introducing a special guest to you." She pauses, presumably to build suspense. "As a composer and pianist, this thirty-year-old fills even the largest concert halls, and many female fans have already tried to win his heart." Another insincere smile, but this time, I see her teeth. "Good evening and welcome Joshua Friedberg."

The camera pans to me, and the audience applauds.

"Thank you for the invitation. I'm delighted to be here." I smile back. Not for her, but for the people who have come to see me.

She nods politely, then turns her attention to the cards in her hand. "Joshua, your rise in the past years could certainly be described as meteoric. What makes your success?"

Answering this question is routine, yet it always takes my breath away to utter these words. Because they are as important to me as nothing else in the world. "Playing the piano is my great passion. I owe being able to live it solely to my fans. Without the fantastic people who allow themselves to be touched by my music, I wouldn't be sitting here today."

The host's eyes suddenly glisten with tears. She quickly clears her throat. "Critics say your music cannot be categorized. It is neither classical nor modern. They call it nothing more than the naive background melody of an intermediate world that shouldn't exist. What do you say to these accusations?"

I hold her intense gaze. "My compositions are new and unlike anything that has come before. They don't require extravagant stage shows, nor do they belong in dusty opera houses. They belong solely to my listeners, whom I want to carry away from their everyday lives for a few minutes. If I can achieve that, I'm happy."

Unimpressed, she scrutinizes me. "As a child from an

affluent background, it was easy for you to establish yourself with your new concept, wasn't it?"

Of course. Because talent and hard work can be easily bought. Actually, my wealthy dad just invested a few million, and that's how I became a successful pianist. Even if my father had ever believed in me, his money alone wouldn't have been able to do anything.

I suppress the rising memories of the dark sides of my childhood and smile at the host as composedly as possible. "My parents have always supported me, and I'm very grateful to them for that."

Although I have delivered an answer, the camera remains focused on me. I feel the pressure to keep speaking, but I stand my ground. These seconds of silence are a popular way to get the interview guest to reveal more than they want to. The woman sitting across from me also searches for a vulnerable spot. She needs an opening through which she can intrude and delve deep into my soul, in pursuit of scandal or sensational news. Anything that boosts ratings is welcome.

I endure the silence because I am just as professional as she is.

Now she wrinkles her nose. It's clear to her that she won't get as close to me as she would like. Internally, I relax. Interviews are always challenging. Words get twisted too quickly, opinions are formed, and wrong conclusions are drawn.

Her mouth curves into a triumphant grin. "Rumor has it that your first piano teacher was certain that you lacked talent," she says, raising her eyebrows and fixing her gaze on me, causing a murmur to ripple through the audience.

Dammit, where did she get this information?

I didn't see this blow coming. I have to respond. And

appropriately. "I had my first piano teacher when I was four years old. You'll understand that I can't remember everything he said."

That was meager. We both know it. Now it's entirely up to her. Will she pounce on me once and for all? Or can she hold back? Beads of sweat form on my forehead. It's difficult for me to maintain a casual smile.

She straightens up in her cream-colored leather chair and leans slightly toward me. "Are you implying that false information has been fed to us?"

Actually, I mean to convey that there's nothing I desire more than to end this conversation immediately. She must not poke around in this wound, as it has yet to heal.

Feeling somewhat helpless, I raise my shoulders, my gaze flickering to the wristwatch. The interview will be over soon; I just have to preserve a bit more composure. "Do you have every detail of what you did or experienced as a child at the forefront of your mind?"

A crease forms between her eyebrows. "One never forgets impactful experiences," she says with a dangerous undertone.

I must refrain from nervously tapping my fingers on my thighs. In any case, I cannot show any reaction. I regulate my breathing, endure the silence once again, and focus.

Twenty-one, twenty-two, twenty-three.

Disappointed, she leans back in her chair, and the audience begins to buzz with excitement.

Twenty-four, twenty-five, twenty-six.

"Your divorce last year must have been an equally impactful experience for you," she continues mercilessly. "How did it come to this?"

Not that I enjoy discussing it, but at least my manager prepared me for this topic. "We grew apart, and I'm glad we were able to separate amicably, remaining the best of friends."

"For Sophia?"

"For everyone involved." I smile again, although I've had more than enough of it by now. When will this charade finally be over?

"Of course, our female viewers are particularly interested in your love life. An attractive, successful man like you..." Her gaze sweeps over my body as if I were every woman's dream even though I'm just an ordinary human.

The press has tried so many times in the past months to uncover something about my love life. But the truth is, it doesn't exist.

"My love belongs to music, and it will always stay that way," I respond.

A resigned sigh escapes her lips. "If that's the case, of course we want to hear you play now." She gestures toward the concert grand piano located on the side stage next to us. Its half-open lid glistens under the spotlight, the stool covered in blue velvet, and the keys magnetically drawing my fingers.

This is what I've been waiting for. Interviews are not my favorite pastime, but everything else becomes unimportant when I sit at the piano.

Relieved, I rise and approach the piano. I let my fingers rest on the pleasantly cool keys for a moment, close my eyes, and release all the tension from the interview through my breath.

Let's begin.

I cautiously play the first notes. My fingers dance across the keys, finding their place and creating a melody that carries me away.

Every movement is perfect—no mistakes and not even

the slightest hesitation. The sequence of tones becomes more and more intense, and everything within me begins to resonate.

I smile, no, I radiate, as I pour all my passion and emotions into this one piece. As I approach the grand finale, even my heart beats faster. The music permeates me, and I become one with it, forgetting the world around me. This is happiness in its purest form.

Another triplet.

The crescendo.

Then the final chord.

With my eyes still closed, I wait until the last notes have faded away in the room. This moment belongs to me and my listeners. We are all connected, experiencing the power of music and letting it affect us.

Only when absolute silence sets in does the audience begin to applaud. I hear enthusiastic cheers and open my eyelids. The lights in the hall turn on, allowing me to see the people in the audience. There's a little girl with thick glasses clapping devotedly. And an old lady, sticking her fingers in her mouth like a teenager and whistling so loudly that I can hear it from here.

I know I'm beaming. My eyes are moist, and my cheeks are glowing. Because at this moment, above all else, I am grateful.

After so many years of rigorous practice, of striving to be seen and never giving up despite countless setbacks, I am finally able to live my dream of playing the piano.

Shortly after, I leave the studio through the back exit, get into the car, and drive to the nearest shopping center. Once

I arrive, I put on the dark baseball cap for safety and slip into the subtle gray sports jacket. That, along with my inconspicuous jeans, should be enough to stroll through the center unnoticed.

Walking along the wide corridor with glossy tiles, I focus on my mission today. My daughter, Sophia, will be spending the summer with me. I want to give her a warm welcome and provide her with everything she needs. That's why I make a stop at a toy store. My gaze searches the display. The horses and the horse stable might appeal to Sophia. Every little girl likes that sort of thing, right? Or does she prefer one of those wooden train sets?

Feeling more uncertain than I'd like, I enter the shop. The dusty smell of the carpet hits me, and a faint children's laughter can be heard amid soft background music.

"Please, Daddy, the pirate ship is so beautiful," says the little boy by the side shelf, unable to keep his legs still.

A man who is undoubtedly his father lovingly strokes his blond hair. Then he crouches down in front of his son. "We can build it together and go on an adventure. What do you think?"

"Oh, yes!" The little one's face lights up, and with a cry of joy, he throws himself into his father's arms. "You're the best dad in the whole world."

Hearing those words pierces my heart.

Because as much as I look forward to having Sophia with me soon, I mainly feel fear. Her mother always took care of everything, freeing me up to focus on my career. My daughter and I hardly know each other. Moreover, since the divorce, she has oscillated between two extreme emotional states: silent and quick-tempered.

Will she look at me the way the little boy looks at his father? Will she ever reach for my hand and hop alongside me like that little guy who now disappears with the man toward the cash register?

Longing and doubt simultaneously creep up within me. The fear of not being a good father threatens to overwhelm me.

To stop that, I hastily look around for a salesperson. The man at the cash register, who looks exactly like I imagined Santa Claus as a child, is busy. The lady with the knitted vest and oversized glasses is already assisting a customer.

In the back, I spot a young woman with long black hair, her top sparkling as conspicuously as the doll she holds in her hand. Indecisively, she looks back and forth between the doll and the shelf. The miniature Christmas tree ornaments on her extra-long earrings sway in rhythm. She appears nervous, almost desperate.

Helplessly, she looks around and places the doll on a shelf. It immediately falls out.

"No, no, no," I hear the woman murmuring in the distance, her voice growing increasingly panicked. She nervously brushes her hands against her expansive blue skirt.

She appears anything but competent. I doubt she can help me find the right welcome gift for Sophia. As I skeptically observe her, one of my pieces plays through the speakers. "Freedom."

The delicate notes begin to sound. Soon, the orchestra will join in. The music will swell, and the intensity will increase.

But it's not there yet. Only the piano can be heard, and although the melody is soft, the stressed woman's face suddenly relaxes. With the doll in her hand, she closes her eyes and sways to the rhythm.

A smile spreads across her lips. The clearer it becomes, the more the cute dimples flash on her cheeks.

Spellbound, I watch her. I see the peace that suddenly dominates her expression. And I realize how her chest rises before she exhales with a deep sigh.

Then she starts to dance. Right in the midst of the bustling shopping mall. Holding the doll tightly against her chest, she twirls around. She stumbles over her skirt, regains her balance, and laughs for a moment.

All of a sudden, I'm overwhelmed with emotion. Because I know it's my music giving this woman a carefree moment. It makes her radiate with such warmth that it reaches me despite our distance.

Her facial expression carries a special kind of bliss that I have never seen before. I feel connected to her.

Perhaps I shouldn't stare at her, but I can't look away. Not even as the last notes of the piece slowly fade away. And certainly not when she opens her eyelids and looks directly at me with a dreamy gaze.

Without any effort on my part, my mouth corners lift.

A fraction of a second later, her expression changes. It's as if she just woke up and realizes where she is. With a startled look on her face, she turns her back to me and tries once again to place the doll on the shelf. Her hands tremble, and her upper body shudders.

Strange.

Something like this has never happened to me before. Has she mistaken me for someone she fears?

Confused, I return my attention to the toy shelf where I still stand.

Grab your copy…

vinci-books.com/thedreams

Afterword

All I Need is a story about letting go. It shows that sometimes we only think we know what we really need. But the novel is also about love. About what it can set off inside us, and how defenceless we are against it when it finds us, even though we weren't even looking for it. That's exactly why I want to dedicate this book to someone very special. Lukas, this is for you! Let's never stop looking up together at that one sky that belongs only to the two of us.

He wasn't the only one who accompanied me while I was writing *All I Need.* A huge thank you for all the help and support also goes to my family, as well as to the book professionals Anne, Serena and Steffi. And also to my tireless beta readers, book bloggers and release helpers, who by now are so numerous that I can't even name you all anymore. A thousand thank yous, my dears—without you, *All I Need* wouldn't be what it is today!

A very special thank you also goes to you, dear readers, for buying and reading this book. You alone are the ones who can breathe life into this story. Because without you, this book would be nothing more than a colorful cover filled with white pages and black letters. I hope you enjoyed reading *All I Need* as much as I enjoyed writing it.

Lots of love,

Belinda.

About the Author

Belinda Benna is an award-winning author whose moving romance novels are filled with emotion, allowing you to lose yourself between the lines and find yourself at the same time.

Experience stories that will make you cry, laugh, and fall in love—each with a message that will stay with you for a long time.

www.ingramcontent.com/pod-product-compliance
Ingram Content Group UK Ltd.
Pitfield, Milton Keynes, MK11 3LW, UK
UKHW010130110826
474298UK00003B/133

9 781036 734114